CAROUSEL

CAROUSEL

J. Robert Janes

First published in Great Britain by Constable & Company, Ltd.

Copyright © 1993 by J. Robert Janes

First U.S. paperback edition published by

Soho Press, Inc.
853 Broadway
New York, NY 10003

Library of Congress Cataloging-in-Publication Data

Janes, J. Robert (Joseph Robert), 1935–
Carousel / J. Robert Janes.
p.   cm.
ISBN 1-56947-175-4 (alk. paper)
1. World War, 1939–1945—France—Paris Fiction.
2. Police—France—Paris Fiction.   I. Title.
PR9199.3.J3777C36   1999
813'.54—dc21   99-26934
                                           CIP

10 9 8 7 6 5 4 3 2 1

To R. M. Heney who has been my friend
for more years than either of us would care to count

Life doesn't just go round and round, it goes up and down.

.

AUTHOR'S NOTE

Carousel is a work of fiction. Though I have used actual places and times, I have treated these as I have seen fit, changing some as appropriate. Occasionally the name of a real person is also used for historical authenticity, but all are deceased and I have made of them what the story demands. I do not condone what happened during these times. Indeed, I abhor it. But during the Occupation of France the everyday crimes of murder and arson continued to be committed, and I merely ask, by whom and how were they solved?

1

The coins were Roman and the girl was naked. That there was blood spattered about the room would be an understatement. Hermann was none too quietly rejecting his dinner into the girl's wash-basin.

The coins had been thrown at the corpse. One had been dipped in blood and placed squarely in the middle of the forehead. The wire, twisted from the right, hadn't just strangled her. At the last there'd been a sudden, savage twist cutting the jugular and then the windpipe.

She'd drowned in blood and had pressed futile hands against the carpet, arching her body up against the killer.

He'd raped her. The blood had been flung from his hands to speckle the pistachio-coloured walls and mingle with the smears of terror.

'A pretty mess,' said St-Cyr. 'You okay now?'

'No!'

Kohler shot back to the wash-basin. His 'Bastard! Bastard!' could be heard on the floor below and on the one below that. Even on the street perhaps.

Yet no one will have heard a thing, said St-Cyr ruefully to himself. It was always so in situations like this, more so under the German presence, the Occupation.

Paris in the winter of 1942-43 had become a city of the silent. It was Thursday, 10 December, and just before curfew, just before midnight. Not a happy hour. Grief, too, in the all-too-recent loss of wife and little son, no matter how estranged. He'd have to conquer the loss, would have to force himself to concentrate.

The room was a mess but not so much as to indicate the most fearsome of struggles. The girl lay about two metres from the right foot of the bed. She had avoided it like the plague after she'd tossed her clothes there. Had run to the left, had been caught, had struggled, had gripped the wire ...

9

A bookshelf had toppled over. A small table beside it had been smashed. A glass tumbler had rolled about.

Yes . . . yes, the struggle had been to the left.

St-Cyr gave Hermann another glance. Had the corpse reminded the Bavarian of someone? The drive into Paris had been even more memorable than most of Hermann's drives. The rain teeming and murder, murder in the dank and frigid air.

The Parc des Buttes-Chaumont first, a carousel looming out of the darkness at a wooded turning on a steep hillside, the thing mothballed with sideboards for the winter. A lantern . . . A voice, the voice of urgency calling into the rain, 'The rue Polonceau, Inspectors. Hurry. Hurry! A courtyard. The Hotel of the Silent Life.'

'But . . . but . . .'

No buts. The lantern smoking as it was held aloft so as to see them better.

'The Préfet has given me the message, Inspectors. You are to go there immediately.'

Four storeys of jaded retirement behind whose flaking, cracked walls and Louis XIV iron balusters hid the downcast retainers of the Third Republic with their deflated pensions and the piety of their medals. Not for them the Defeat of France. Ah no. Simply the frayed cuffs of the suit jacket and shirt, the shine of the knees and the button hanging loosely by its single thread.

But why a girl like this in a place like this? There were hundreds of these little hotels in Paris. The girl was far too young, a pigeon among the buzzards. Had one of them hired her?

It was doubtful.

Again he asked, 'Are you okay, eh?'

When no answer came, St-Cyr began that most patient and intimate of studies. Left to himself, Kohler fingered the long, stitched gash that lay across the whole of his left cheek. Gingerly he touched the swollen volcano that had risen over his half-shut right eye. He ached like hell. The storm trooper's chin was still okay, the broad, firm lips hadn't suffered. He'd lost no teeth, but his hands . . . *Gott im Himmel*, the poor mitts were all but broken. His chest was still on fire.

They had made a stop on the run to Paris from Vouvray. The sudden end to another murder investigation and news, news like no one should get. Poor Louis.

Jesus must they go through the same thing again without even a rest? Sleep!

He'd had the sirloin and the potatoes, then the Pear Genoise, a place for generals, a flashing of his Gestapo shield, but had lost it all at the sight of that poor kid lying on her back, her head farthest from the door. Her eyes . . .

Louis would have noticed them too.

The girl's earrings were on the washstand. Gold and emeralds – were they really emeralds?

There was a butterfly pin, a chatoyant, enamelled thing in silver. It was leaning against the back of the washstand, next to her handkerchief. There was a strand of pearls, a choker of them too – had she been about to put them on? Had she been deciding what to wear?

How could she have left things like these in a room like this? Where the hell was her purse?

The pearls, the pin and the earrings were swept into a pocket.

Forcing himself to turn away from the mirror, Kohler went over to the girl.

She was not pretty, she was not plain. The pubic hairs were jet-black, glossy, curly and well flanged in their thick triangle, neat against the pure white of her lovely gams. Clouded with semen. Webbed by it, the hairs clinging to one another up the centre of the mat, caught in the glue.

He let his gaze run swiftly over her. The body was good, the breasts round and full and normally uptilted to rosy, sweet nipples, but sagging sideways now, the nipples collapsed. Blood . . . blood everywhere.

The waist and hips were slim, the legs slender, the height perhaps 158 centimetres, the weight fifty kilograms.

Nice feet, nice toes. Clean, too, and a size four maybe. No bunions yet. No broken toenails either but no war paint, and that was odd, or was it?

The right leg had been thrown out and was now bent in at an awkward angle. The hair on the head was black, cut short, bobbed and curled, the lashes long and curved, the eyes . . . They were of that unforgettable shade of hyacinths in their prime, a violet like no other.

'Twenty-one, Hermann. Perhaps twenty-two. No more.'

'And well set up. So, what gives, eh, Louis?'

The bushy dark-brown eyebrows lifted. The dark brown ox-eyes were moist. 'If I knew, my old one, I'd say. Me, I want to know why Talbotte should be keeping his hands off this one too.'

Paris and its environs were the Préfet's beat. The Sûreté and the Gestapo murder squad – this one in particular – could pick the bones of the rest of France or while away their time tossing dice with the apaches, the small-time hoods in some sleazy, beat-up bar. It was all the same to Talbotte.

The violet eyes had the limpidness of cool spring water into which a man dying of thirst or wounds could drown himself.

Louis was fifty-two years of age, himself fifty-six, a sore point when age was used to settle an argument in lieu of the Gestapo shield.

A chief inspector once again.

The girl's blood had only just begun to congeal. Rigor had not yet set in. Kohler knew he'd best contribute something. 'The coins must be fake, Louis.'

'The coins . . . Ah yes, perhaps they are, Hermann, but then perhaps there were to have been more of them and she held out to the end.'

'Couldn't we cover her for a bit?'

'Really, Hermann, for a man so accustomed to death you surprise me.'

'She's not been dead two hours, Louis. If we hadn't stopped to eat . . .'

'My thoughts exactly. If only we hadn't stopped.'

'We couldn't have known. We'd not been to the carousel.'

'The carousel, ah yes. One grisly murder for us and now this, the silence of another in the Hotel of Silence. Is it that you are thinking the same as I am?'

'Hushed before we could get to her.'

Hermann was a big man, broad and stooping in the shoulders, tall and solid, with the hands of a plumber and a countenance that was normally bagged to bulldog jowls, puffy eyelids, shrapnel scars and well-rasped cheeks. The hair a tired sort of frizzy fadedness, not black, not brown, but something in between and greying fast.

They'd been through a lot, the two of them. They weren't involved in any of the rough stuff, the beating to death of suspected *enemies* of the State, the Third Reich! Not Gestapo stuff. Ah no. Not yet and never! Hermann was simply his Gestapo partner, his little helper and watcher to see that he behaved himself. Not a good Gestapo, not by any means, but always on the knife-edge.

The faded blue and often expressionless eyes were bloodshot

and wary. 'Talbotte must have known this would happen, Louis.' A whisper.

St-Cyr nodded. 'A wise owl shits only at night.'

'It is night.'

Again there was that shrug. 'That's what I meant.'

'Boemelburg did say Pharand had a small job that would suit us.'

'Pharand would not have said that if he hadn't wanted to get back at us for what happened in Vouvray. Besides, Boemelburg would have told him to say it. The mouse always squeaks when stepped on.'

'It was supposed to keep you busy, Louis, to give you a rest from . . . well, you know.'

The explosion. The snuffing out of Marianne and Philippe St-Cyr.

'Talbotte is incapable of a humanitarian thought, Hermann. Boemelburg may well have told him to leave the job to us, but the Préfet of Paris would have had his own reasons for allowing us the pleasure of his turf.'

'We're to scrape the surface and see what's beneath. My chief was definite on this.'

His *chief*! The Sturmbannführer Walter Boemelburg, Head of Section IV, the Gestapo in France!

'But of course Walter is invariably definite, but was this one really the girlfriend of the one at the carousel?'

Kohler was a little taken aback. 'Why shouldn't she have been?'

'Why, indeed? Perhaps she was, but then . . .' St-Cyr tossed a hand to indicate the room and the clothes that lay not neatly on the bed but thrown there garment by garment when ordered.

The shoes having been first placed neatly just inside the door against the wall, the thin raincoat hung up with its scarf, no gloves . . . Had she lost them?

Together, they began to take a closer look. Louis again knelt beside the body. He brought his nose close to the girl's lips. He examined the wire – thin and flexible but not braided. Simply scrap wire, a little rusty too. He ran his gaze swiftly down each of her arms to the hands, noting that, though both were very flat against the carpet, both were also close in to the seat.

There were no rings. There was no jewellery of any kind. She had been forced to strip. Why hadn't she cried out for help? Had she done so? Had no one responded?

'The bastard must have had a gun or a knife, Louis.'

'Perhaps, but then...'

Kohler began with the feet. Again he thought her clean. Bathing wasn't what the French did too often, especially not these days. Others too, for that matter. Not in a stone-cold room with the Paris skies pissing ice. Besides, the French doused themselves with cheap perfume, only this one hadn't. He'd have smelled it. Louis would have grimaced.

She'd have stood in that wash-basin sponging herself down and shivering. Goose-pimples all over her seat and those ripe rosebuds sticking out hard, straining for relief as the towel had rubbed her down.

'She'd have been getting herself ready, Louis. A client.'

St-Cyr could not ignore his total disregard of the positions of the clothing on the bed, or the fact that the towels were dry. Hermann was just not himself. Too beaten up and still on the run. 'Take another look, idiot! The girl was probably followed. She didn't know it. She came in here in a hurry. She was late and expecting someone. The shoes, Hermann.' St-Cyr tossed a hand in the general direction. 'The coat. No, my friend, she had only just arrived. The concierge has much to answer for and me, I hope he hasn't cut her throat because she was *not* peering out of her cage, Hermann. The outer door was open. *We* are the ones who are supposed to have found the body but quite obviously someone else did.'

Louis had worked his way down to the hips, the hands and the crotch. The semen troubled him.

'Hermann, what do you make of this?'

'Premature ejaculation,' snorted Kohler.

'*Nom de Jésus-Christ*, smarten up! Coitus was interrupted at its fullest by some noise in the hall or downstairs.'

'A flic's whistle?'

'Perhaps.'

'A *rafle*?' shot Kohler. A round-up...

'You must check with Section IV. That's not my job.'

'The rooftops?'

'Perhaps.'

The invective ceased. Though the stitches in his cheek would hurt, Kohler grinned. The lapse of clear thinking on his part had made Louis angry, a welcome sign.

In his heart of hearts Louis was a fisherman, a gardener, a dreamer of Provence and the little cottage to which he'd retire away from the slime. Communing with Nature and smelling the flowers, counting the honey each would produce. A reader of books in wintertime; a student of life's foibles with the distant air, at times, of a pipe-smoking muse when he could get the tobacco ration.

A widower now, but the possible lover, if he'd but get over this next little while, of an incredibly well-stacked column of woman with stupendous eyes.

Just like this one's. Ah yes. A coincidence.

The thick brown moustache bulged as the lips were blown out in exasperation. 'Talbotte, Hermann!' It was a curse.

'Boemelburg, Louis. *And* Pharand. Your boss, my little Frog. The boss of the Sûreté Nationale.'

'Let's take a look around. You do the bureau. I'll take the armoire.'

'Fingerprints? Photos? The details? Should we call in the troops?'

'We'll leave those for Talbotte. We'll *make* him take a hand in this and the other one also. We'll propose that we work together for the good of the Third Reich!'

Amen. 'Then the bed and the dressing-table, and the washstand,' muttered Kohler, suitably chastized. Louis would never *work* for the Third Reich, not in a thousand years.

'We'll leave the washstand to the last,' said the Frog.

'But turn back the carpet.'

'No one will notice that you've just palmed a couple of those coins, Hermann.'

Kohler snorted majestically. 'They *are* fake. I think I've broken a tooth.'

'You'll never learn, will you? The question is, did she try to flog them to her killer, eh?'

'Did the bastard kill her when he discovered the truth? Is that what you mean? Was she trying to buy her way out of this?' Kohler indicated the room while pulling the sheerness of a midnight négligé out of a drawer.

He began to finger the thing as a connoisseur would.

St-Cyr knew his partner would be suffering the tragic waste of those legs and arms, the lips that could so easily have kissed his own had she been a girl of the streets, which she hadn't.

'She'd not have been for you, Hermann,' he said, flinging open both doors of the armoire to sweep his eyes over the dresses. 'This one was being kept. Money had her.'

The lace-trimmed underpants were sheer and of silk. Distracted, Kohler said, 'My thoughts exactly, Louis,' and judging his moment, stuffed the things into an overcoat pocket.

A satin chemise followed. Good goods.

'Those for your wife?' taunted the Frog, not turning from the dresses.

'Be careful what you say, my friend. Besides, Wasserburg's too far, and my Gerda wouldn't know what to do with them on the farm.'

Hermann always had to have the last word. One had to let him. It was best that way. Sometimes.

They went at it in silence. The armoire, although substantial, held only five dresses, a couple of hats and one pair of shoes, but the dresses were of good quality, pre-war, as were the high-heels. The shoes were crimson to match a sleeveless sheath whose neckline was a modest concave, the wool so soft and fine it felt like a woman's skin when warm.

The girl would have looked well in that crimson dress, with a black slip to match her hair, a black lace-trimmed brassière and black underpants, ah yes, except, of course, that the hair was not naturally black at all but very light, as evidenced by the hairs on her forearms.

A blonde. These days blondes were at a premium. Blondes with blue or violet eyes – grey even.

So she'd taken great pains to hide the fact. An almost complete dye job.

'Louis, take a look at this.'

A stuffed canary.

'It was nestled in its own little box on a bed of crushed velvet. There was an elastic band around the wings and breast – this one.' Kohler expanded the elastic. 'Heavy and thick, but the wings don't seem to need holding in.'

Gingerly St-Cyr took the canary from him. The bird's skin had been tightly sewn, fitting the little body to perfection. 'Not a feather out of place, Hermann. Did the girl often take it out to caress it, I wonder?'

'Perhaps she was lonely? Is that what you mean?'

'The work of an artiste,' he said, not pausing to comment on the Gestapo's offering. 'A real taxidermist, Hermann. No ordinary stuffer of neighbourhood cats and dogs in good times when there is money for such remembrances. Ah no, not this one. The set of the beak and the eyes are too real. He has captured the bird in death as in life.'

'Then why the elastic band?'

'Why the coins, Hermann? Why any of this? Why the abandonment by Talbotte, eh, unless the higher-ups want to burn us?'

The girl's identity card, residence papers and ration tickets had been stuffed into a stocking, along with seven 100-franc bills and a clatter of sous.

'Christiane Baudelaire, a student, Louis. The École des Beaux-Arts. Twenty-two years, two months and seven days.'

The photo was passable. It was the corpse all right.

St-Cyr ran an exasperated hand through the thickness of his dark-brown hair. 'Baudelaire was a poet who lived in poverty, Hermann. The girl has chosen well.'

'It's not her name? But the photo, Louis? It's –'

Though he knew he shouldn't, St-Cyr let him have it with acid. 'A student? This room? Everything about it says she lived elsewhere, Hermann. There is no laundry, no food, no *crumbs*! Too few clothes. Ah *Mon Dieu*, if an art student, then where, please, are the sketches, where the much-guarded portfolio, eh? Where the chalks, the paints, the canvases that are so difficult to come by these days? The rags with the turpentine, Hermann? The smock?'

'Okay, okay, I get the point. Don't let grief and guilt over Marianne and Philippe get your ass in a knot. Just remember I'm your friend.'

'Of course. Forgive me. But, Hermann, there is not even a piece of gum-arabic eraser? Not even the smell of paint? No, my friend, this was but a room for one purpose.'

'Then where's the real ID?'

'Outside, in the courtyard, under a stone. In behind something, Hermann. She would not have walked the streets without it. Not this one.'

Gestapo streets. Jackbooted streets. The patrols, the curfew.

'Perhaps she left the ID with a friend,' offered Kohler lamely.

'Perhaps, but then . . .'

St-Cyr thought better of saying it. The friend, if there was one, could well be dead or in hiding.

'Louis, this thing is fast becoming too big for us.'

'Exactly, my old one. Exactly! That is why we need Talbotte's help.'

'I'd sooner have the Devil's.'

'They are one and the same, or hadn't you noticed?'

In alarm, the concierge threw her jaundiced grey eyes up at them. 'Messieurs . . .' she began, thinking to huff and fart about.

'Sit down!' roared Kohler, turning swiftly to slam the slot of her cage closed even as Louis shut the door.

Now the hall and the entrance to the hotel were hidden and she was trapped in her cage as never before.

'So . . .' began Kohler, towering over her in the cramped enclosure with its shabby divan and dusty, faded purple cushions.

Lisette Minou gripped the armrests of her chair. The big one was formidable. A fresh wound . . .

The mouse elbowed his way between her and the giant. His voice would not be like a balm but the salve of a cop!

'Oil your way, monsieur,' she shrilled with admirable tartness. 'It will do you no good. I know nothing. *Nothing*, do you hear? Absolutely nothing.'

'A tough one, eh?' breathed the Frog. The place was a rat's nest! They'd get lice if they weren't careful. 'Mademoiselle Baudelaire has been murdered, madame. Ah yes, please do not distress yourself too much. Save that for later, eh?'

'A murder in my hotel?' gasped the woman, visibly shaken.

St-Cyr nodded. Hermann glowered.

'Did you see the man who went up that staircase to kill her?' asked St-Cyr.

The furtive gaze slid away to the mange of a torn-eared cat whose one encrusted eye wept as it limped towards her.

They would discover the truth, these ones. She just knew they would. 'My aching bones, monsieur . . .'

'Fuck your bag of bones! I'm tired. I've not had any sleep for days. I've not even been home yet!'

'Hermann, *please*! Madame Minou has had a long and difficult life. There is also the shock of what we have just told her.'

The eyes rose up in doubt and deceit from the doughy pan of her face. The rounded shoulders hunched, folding the knitted grey cardigan with its holes.

'I did not see anything, Monsieur the Inspector. Arfande, my cat – I was at the moment feeding him a little titbit. These days . . . Ah what can one say, eh? Things are so hard to get. I had acquired a tin of –'

'The black market?' leapt Kohler expectantly.

Her calm was shattered. 'Hermann, *please*! For the love of Jesus, just let me deal with this one.'

'She's all yours, chum.'

The rolls of flesh about her throat rippled. 'A tin?' reminded St-Cyr.

The woman swallowed. A murder . . . She had known it would come to no good, an arrangement like that. 'A tin of sardines, Inspector. My back was turned to the wicket – for just a moment, you understand.'

St-Cyr feigned surprise. 'You heard someone come in, yet you did not turn to look?'

'My bones. My back. This world. This work. The war. The Naz . . . is.'

'All right, all right. What time?'

The cardigan rose. The tired bosom, with its twin soccer balls, was held.

'About nine?' offered St-Cyr.

Eight as in the old days, but now that Paris ran on Berlin time, nine of course. The Sûreté was plucking at straws and that was good. So, they would barge into her office, would they?

'About nine. Yes, yes, but I heard nothing more, Inspector, and no one came back down so, you see I was not sure anyone had actually come into the hotel.'

They'd never get done with her.

Hermann lit a cigarette – one of the woman's. He tapped Louis on the shoulder. The swollen eye opened a little. The lower lid of the other one was pulled well down. 'The wireless,' he breathed.

St-Cyr sought it out, noting with alarm the position of the tuning dial even as the woman noted this herself and the cat bolted off her lap and went to hide under the divan. Oh-oh.

It wasn't illegal to own a wireless set, ah no. It was simply illegal to listen to forbidden broadcasts.

Smoke billowed from the dragon's lips. The voice, when it came, was decisive. 'The slut's been listening to the BBC Free French broadcast from London, Inspector. That's an offence under article seventeen. The nine o'clock time is okay but she had her ear screwed to the set. She'd have been so wrapped up in the Russian Front, God Himself could have farted and she'd not have heard Him.'

Or seen him. 'Hermann, must I ask again that you go easy, eh? Madame Minou is in a very difficult position. The killer – the rapist, madame, a specialist with the garroting wire, a sadist! – might well come back.' He paused. 'And yet, Hermann, if she does not open the purse of her lips, she will not have the protection of those she and her kind so despise.'

19

The *flics*. Kohler's grin was huge, and it drew beads of blood from between the sutures on his cheek.

The woman rebelled at the sight of them. 'Pigs!' she boiled. 'You call yourselves cops? Is that it, my fine sweet lemons? If you'd been doing your jobs instead of fighting whores, you'd have saved that one.'

Ah yes. She tossed the frowzy grey mop of hair as she lifted her eyes to indicate the fourth floor and a certain room.

The folds of her neck revealed their creases. The acid came. 'You have not asked my permission, messieurs. *That*,' she simmered, 'is against the law. The search warrant, please? Come, come – quickly now, *mes amis*, before I take offence.'

Kohler let her have it. 'It's your job to watch and notify the cops of anything suspicious!' he shouted, richly enjoying the exchange.

The jaundiced eyes narrowed. 'No prune could have an anus mouth like yours, monsieur. Kindly telephone the Préfet of Police.'

The slut! 'There is no telephone.'

'Of course there isn't! Find one.'

Stung by her, Kohler again nudged the Frog aside and pulled out his shield, which he flung up in front of the woman. 'Gestapo,' he whispered. 'Now open that hairy twat of yours, my fine garlic loaf, and spill the lentils, eh?'

The felt carpet slippers were shabby, the toes turned in. The half-stockings were of that heavy combination of beige cotton, wool and other things. One had lost its elastic.

She saw the Frenchman's gaze travel up her. Was he weeping for her or calculating the space she'd need in one of those boxcars nobody talked about?

'I have not seen the man who has done this thing, messieurs. I . . . Oh, Mon Dieu, may Jesus forgive me. *Yes*, I was listening to the forbidden. Me, Lisette Minou, whose husband could have been one of the Broken Mugs and proud of it! readily and *gladly*, messieurs, GLADLY admit it!'

The hairy upper lip was licked in doubt.

A confession. 'Her heart's glowing like a furnace, Louis. She *wants* to become a martyr.'

One of the Broken Mugs, one of the badly disfigured from the last war, but she'd qualified this by saying 'could have been' . . . St-Cyr heaved an inward sigh.

'Such are the ways of simple folk, Hermann. The brave. Now

look, madame. The girl – who was she? We know she did not live here but came only at certain times.'

The woman filled her lungs. 'Gestapo pig!' she shouted. 'Lackey! Bootlicker! Collaborator! How can you live with yourself, eh? No one else would!'

He ignored the slurs, though struck to the quick. 'What were those times, madame? Who was it came to visit her? Why was she killed? You will have a thought or two, perhaps something the girl has said, isn't that so? Perhaps something her lover has said in passing – he could not have come and gone without your knowledge.'

She drew herself up in the chair. 'You have too many questions, monsieur.'

'They are but the first of many,' he said softly.

'My head, my memory – I am an old woman, Inspector, but I do know my rights.'

'You have none,' breathed Kohler. 'Let's take her with us, Louis. The schmuck might come back to feed her tongue to the cat.'

'There is the matter of the girl's papers, Hermann.'

'This one won't know where they're hidden. The girl would have been too smart for that. We'll take a look later on.'

'The carousel?'

'We have to, Louis. This chicken's too old for the pot. It might help her to see a little blood.'

'Then drive by the house. That might also help.'

The street was narrow, the hill steep, the car flat out. At 1.35 a.m. Berlin time, the rue Laurance Savart gave up the gun barrel of its rabbit's burrow.

As the houses flashed past, the concierge, trapped in the back of the car, broke the long-forgotten rosary she'd been telling. The beads went everywhere, and the houses . . . the houses . . . two- and three-storeys high perhaps, some too close to the road, some . . . The rain – they'd skid! Oh Mon Dieu!

Kohler slammed on the brakes! The woman screamed. St-Cyr swore. 'HERMANN, THE BRAKES WILL FAIL ONE OF THESE DAYS!'

The car swung tightly across the road. As it rocketed into the doorway of someone's house, it bumped up over the narrow sidewalk.

Lisette Minou shrilled; 'In the Name of Jesus, monsieur, you should not be allowed to drive a car!'

The headlamps began to fall, the car backing slowly away to bump down off the sidewalk. Kohler drove on a little. The front of Number 3 came into view, held by the stabbing lights. 'Louis, don't! Leave it, for Christ's sake. Marianne was no good for you. She made a cuckold out of you, damn it!'

A cuckold ... Ah now, what was this? The one from the Sûreté ...

'Just leave it, will you, Louis? *Please*.' The front of the house was a shambles – nailed-up boards and vacant windows. There might still be chunks of meat.

'I must, Hermann. If only for a moment.'

'You'll get wet.'

'That does not matter.'

The car door slammed. Lisette Minou filled her lungs. The French one flipped up the collar of his overcoat and pulled down the brim of a misshapen hat. The Gestapo one was lighting a cigarette. Suck lemons, you dog's offal, she wanted to shout. They'd get nothing more from her. Nothing!

Without a word, Kohler passed the fag back to her, then lit another for himself.

The windscreen wipers beat the rain away and the lights shone upon the Frenchman.

'That one stands like Judas before the Cross,' she said.

'The Resistance did this, madame. A mistake of course. He's far too loyal to France, but ...' Kohler hesitated. 'His wife and son, a boy of four years, got it instead. The woman was coming home to him. She hadn't wanted to leave the nest of sin but ... Ah, what the hell.' He hit the steering-wheel with both hands. 'War is war.'

'Did he beat this wife of his?' she asked. When no answer came, she added begrudgingly, 'Some men do, monsieur. Mine did, but he's gone to his reward on the end of the Kaiser's bayonet and me, I'm glad he got the spit right up the ass!'

Kohler ignored the venom. 'Louis didn't beat her. He loved her. Now shut that cavern of yours and don't try to keep the car warm with your farts. I'd better go to him.'

There'd been a small garden behind the half-wall of bricks. The cement, Louis XIV urns that had once stood atop the posts were gone. Cucumbers had been grown there in season, in defiance of ration tickets and famine. Cucumbers and pole beans.

Marianne St-Cyr had not been a gardener – she'd hated it – and the cucumbers and beans had been stolen. Or had they died from lack of watering?

All the lower windows had, at best, been crudely boarded up. By order of the SS General Karl Oberg, the Supreme Head of the SS and the Gestapo in France.

The house had been 'sealed'. Trespassers would be shot, looters . . . Even possessing one of the stray bricks would command the threat of death. It was a plague upon the house, but had the notice been deliberate on Oberg's part?

Of course it had. A worry.

Louis was reading the word TRAITOR someone had scribbled across it. There was glass everywhere, smashed cakes of the white-painted stucco that had once covered the front of the house.

'Louis, come away. We've a job to do.'

St-Cyr tried to find his voice. 'I could have stopped this, Hermann. I wanted to warn her. I knew there would be trouble. The Resistance, they . . . they had my number.'

'They probably still do.'

Louis stooped to pluck a shred of cloth from the rubble, the remains of Philippe's shirt.

'Stop punishing yourself. Come on, let's get to work, eh?'

'The house will have to be repaired, Hermann. Building materials are so hard to come by.'

'Look, I'll see what I can do. The boys down at the Todt owe me one. They should be able to pull a few things for us. We'll nail them up together.'

The Organization Todt handled all the construction for the Reich and had, of course, an insatiable appetite. Hence the shortages.

'Sons should never make their wives live in the houses of their mothers, Hermann. That was part of the trouble. It was always Mother's house, never hers.'

His mother had died more than fifteen years ago! Kohler reached out to him.

'The trouble,' muttered St-Cyr, still staring emptily at the shred of cloth. The house and the Sûreté, the murders, et cetera, et cetera that had kept him away from his first wife and had left that one so terrorized he'd never come home, she could stand it no longer.

Then Marianne, his second wife, a Breton and quite a looker.

'Marianne's eyes were sky-blue, Louis, not violet.'

'Ah yes, not like the girl who called herself Christiane Baudelaire. Not like Gabrielle Arcuri's either, eh?'

'Come on. I really will see if I can't get the boys down at the Todt to help us out.'

'You do and my neighbours will hate me, Hermann. No, my friend, I must fix it myself.'

It hadn't been Louis' fault at all, but there was little sense in trying to tell him this. They retreated to the car. Madame Minou, looking like God in hiding, was peering out at them.

'Hermann, let me tell her how it really was.'

'Don't be silly. Let her think this is what will happen to that dosshouse of hers if she doesn't co-operate.'

'She's protecting someone.'

'My thoughts exactly.'

They both threw a last glance at the house. The trip-wire that had set off the Resistance bomb had been deliberately left in place by Glotz of Gestapo Section IV, the Watchers.

These days one could be an enemy of more than one group, ah yes. 'Madame, I am not one of these people.'

In desperation the one called St-Cyr tossed his head to indicate the scarface called Kohler.

Lisette Minou exhaled. 'Beware of what you say, monsieur. The carp are always easiest to take when the pond is shallow.'

The cop on guard at the carousel had fired up the boiler to keep himself dry and warm. Seen in the near distance, the chimney pipe from which the whole apparatus of the roundabout was suspended, funnelled sparks into the darkness of the Parc des Buttes-Chaumont, in flagrant defiance of the blackout regulations.

Kohler drove on up the steep incline to the tableland, a fairground in former days, perhaps. Light was also leaking out through gaps in the sideboards.

'My friends, if it is all the same to you, I should prefer to stay in the car.'

'You don't *prefer*,' said the Gestapo, flinging an arm over the back of the front seat. 'You *have* to come in there with us, madame. We can't have you walking home. It's after curfew.'

She crossed herself, wincing as she did so, making him experience a misguided pang of sympathy.

St-Cyr opened the door for her. 'It will be warmer inside,' he said.

Her knees were not quite right. The drive perhaps. 'Is it that you know the dead one here, madame, or is it simply that you fear the worst has happened and must therefore shrink from it?'

She gave him a terrified glance. Blinded momentarily by the blazing lights, they left the night and the rain behind. The brightly painted menagerie, poised in collective silence, stood suspended in motion, caught frozen on the roundabout, waiting for the gears to mesh and the music to begin.

In this day of missing lightbulbs not a one was absent. There were mirrors of bevelled glass, barley-sugar brasses, spiralling brass poles through each of the animals, an eagle in hot pursuit, a rabbit on the run, a leaping pig, a duck, a goat, stallions with wild eyes, the great, thundering herd foaming at the mouth.

Five rows of animals, each seen against a background of others and the glitter of carvings in gold and mirrored glass, of nymphs, yes, and golden cherubs blowing golden horns among billowing white clouds. All the animals racing, racing, crowding each other. Not a one of them moving, all caught in motion. Not a sound but that of the falling rain and the hiss of escaping steam.

The *flic* on duty was calmly eating a snack not a metre from the corpse. He was sitting on the very edge of the carousel, dangling his boots just above the earthen floor.

Blood had long since ceased to drip from the slashed throat of the victim. What there was of it – a lot – had congealed on the wooden feathers and at the splayed feet of the chicken to which the victim, riding backwards, had been tightly tied.

The expression of death was unpleasant. Frozen, too, like the expressions of the animals who now seemed to rebel and brake at the sight of what had happened and yet were still forced by their momentum to race towards the corpse.

The victim was young, with jet-black hair that despite the struggle which must have occurred was still glued into place by pomade. Everything about him said gigolo or pimp, yet Madame Minou forced herself to search out the gruesome face. Again and again she muttered, 'It is not him. It is not him. May God be praised.'

St-Cyr took the *flic*'s tin cup and poured her a stiff tot of the Armagnac he'd brought from the car.

'That's the monkey's cup,' offered the flic, tossing his head but not neglecting the crusty sandwich with its mound of sausage – real sausage – and cheese. Real cheese. A point to consider.

'I have not yet had the opportunity to wash it out,' he added. 'There's no water here.'

'There is outside,' said Kohler, noting the richness of the feast and implying that the man had not only overstepped his mandate but would suffer for it.

Clément Cueillard judged he could afford to grin. He favoured the scruffy moustache that was raked out at its mottled, greying ends. He touched the chin that was narrow and round, the cheeks that formed their crinkled bowl and extended upwards to the pinched forehead and the mangled dark-brown hair which protruded carelessly from beneath the shiny visor of his dark blue kepi.

The woman tossed off the brandy, monkey spit or no.

'Talbotte is slipping,' said Kohler of the cop.

'It's the war,' offered St-Cyr. 'It has brought out the worst in us, Hermann.'

'Do you want me to run this thing for you when I'm finished?' quipped the flic.

The man was in his late forties. A father no doubt. A recipient of someone's largesse in these hungry times.

'That you can eat so well in front of us, my friend, is the shame of our nation.'

'Louis, let's leave him. Let's get to work.'

'Is the sausage to your liking, my friend?' asked the one from the Sûreté. The mouse.

'The cheese is Swiss; the sausage from Alsace.'

'And the beer?' shot Kohler.

'Alsace also,' oozed the flic, continuing to eat. 'You bastards left me out in the cold. What did you expect me to do?'

'Not bring your larder with you.'

'It wasn't mine. It was his.' Cueillard jerked a thumb towards the corpse. 'Since he's done with eating, my fine detectives, I can indulge myself. There's more in the centre if you want some. By the boiler. Behind the organ.'

'You weren't to touch a thing,' warned St-Cyr.

'The stomach doesn't touch. Its juices dissolve.'

'A scientist, eh?' snorted Kohler. 'A smart-ass.'

'You may start the machine,' said Louis. 'Give us the privilege of your expertise. Set your snack on the ground. No one will step on it.'

'Music, maestro?'

A real card. Talbotte must have given him all the rope he needed. 'Of course, why not the music? It will help us think.'

'Stand back then.'

Threading his way among the menagerie, Cueillard disappeared through a gap in the panelled mirrors that surrounded and hid the boiler and its workings. 'All set?' he cried from in there.

'Proceed,' shouted St-Cyr, feeling the fool.

And the thing began to turn – slowly at first, the stallions rising and falling, the body also. All in slow motion but as if straining to throw off the shackles that had bound them. The glitter, the vivid colours, the wicked eyes of the animals now intent, now in flames enraged, came at them. Faster . . . faster . . .

The lights above, and from the many mirrors, swirled to the music of a stupendous band organ, a grandiose thing of brass pipes and Louis XIV gilded carvings under the name of GAVIOLI, PARIS, 1889. A calliope superb!

Boom, boom.

'What's the march?' shouted St-Cyr.

'That of the Bulgarians,' came the reply. 'Punched cards that are fed by a belt of themselves into the machine.'

The man was obviously something of a mechanic and lost on the police force.

The band organ passed by them. Eventually the body came up again. The corpse no longer threatened Madame Minou but intrigued her. 'A chicken?' she asked with all the incredulity of her years. 'Why a chicken, Inspector? One of the gondolas would have been far better for a murder such as this.'

Hermann had gone off some place. 'Why indeed?' shouted St-Cyr. 'It's magnificent, isn't it?'

The carousel.

'Very fashionable in the old days. Perfectly restored by a lover of such things, monsieur, and until quite recently kept in excellent repair.'

Good for her. She'd noticed it too.

The march past was completed in four and a half minutes. Now it was the 'Sidewalks of New York', and then 'Daisy, Daisy, give me your answer do. I'm half crazy all for the love of you.'

Hermann was hanging on to one of the brass poles, going round and round. 'He's overtired, madame,' acknowledged St-Cyr. 'Things like this tend to make him forget the real world.'

'For detectives, the two of you are a puzzle.'

'We work in mysterious ways. Now please, allow me to experience the turning as it must have been seen by the grandmother who found this one and reported the murder.'

The woman hunched her shoulders. 'It turns. It goes up and down in time to the music. It is loud, brassy and bright, and for children.'

'And whores,' snorted Hermann, leaping off the thing. 'Louis, I'm going to have to invite the girls from the Lupanar des Oiseaux Blancs.* Madame Chabot will be intrigued by its possibilities.'

'The chicken, Hermann. He's tied to the chicken, remember?'

'Two men?' asked Kohler.

'Perhaps, but then the girl was killed by one, isn't that so?'

'Almost certainly, and almost a day later.'

Kohler offered a cigarette. St-Cyr struck the match and held it out for him. 'The girl this evening, Hermann, the killer quite possibly knowing we were heading home to have a look at this one.'

'Two killings, Louis, separated by at least twenty-four hours. Us to take care of things because Pharand had spoken to Boemelburg and the Sturmbannführer had said we should.'

St-Cyr nodded grimly. 'Talbotte accepting the arrangement, a thing he would never do unless he knew there'd be egg in his trousers if he meddled.'

'Egg in his trousers . . . I like that, Louis.'

'Then tell me, please, are we supposed to think the girl was this one's chicken?'

The man a pimp, a mackerel. 'It's not possible, Louis. She was too . . .'

'She was *what*, Hermann?'

'Too much the lady; too much the . . . well, the innocent.'

'Precisely! It's what I have felt myself.'

'Perhaps, then, the two murders are totally unrelated, or are bound only by the third party?'

The 'client' of the girl.

'Then why the fake gold coins?'

'They'd been tested with nitric acid, Louis.'

'Not brown? Not a trace of that discolouration?' Gold would turn brownish under the acid.

'As green as a gardener's thumb.'

Bronze – the copper.

* The rabbit hutch (the brothel) of the White Birds

28

'So why the canary?' asked Kohler.

St-Cyr took the thing out of a pocket. The music had changed to the 'Gypsy Fortune-teller'. There was now no sign of Madame Minou.

Lost in thought, Louis fingered the bird. The galloping menagerie came at them, going round and round as the music blared and the lights played their magic on the mind.

'Was it a talisman, Hermann, or merely a reminder of a lost friend?'

'Let's take a look at the corpse.'

Madame Minou had gone to sleep in one of the gondola cars. There was no need to disturb her. Indeed, it would be best not to stop the music.

'So, the jockey rides a chicken and has two chicken-catchers from the slaughterhouse to puzzle over him.'

Pacquet, the city's Chief Coroner, had come to do the job himself. Yawning at 2.30 a.m. and inclined to be touchy.

'You're looking well,' enthused St-Cyr.

'Sarcasm I don't need. Did you stick a thermometer up his rectum?'

'He's been dead for well over twenty-four hours. Rigor's set in like concrete.'

'An expert, eh? What about the girl? Did you shove one up hers?'

'We are not permitted to do such things. Besides, Hermann broke the thermometer on a prostitute and Stores have not been willing to release another to us. This war ... the shortages ...' St-Cyr gave a futile shrug. In truth, Pacquet had always made him feel out of place.

'Can't you stop this bloody thing?'

Hermann gave a shout and the music began to unwind as the carousel beat its wings to tired submission.

Cruising to the last. Up and down.

'Want the lights left on?' shouted Clément Cueillard.

'Idiot! Of course,' screamed Pacquet, his narrow cheeks jerking.

Fastidiously, the Chief Coroner took the small, round, wire-rimmed spectacles from their pocket case and carefully worked them on to the bridge of his angular nose and over his pinched ears. A frizzy mop of greying dark-black hair protruded behind and from under the speckled tweed cap Pacquet wore both when at the races and when not. In all the years St-Cyr had known him, he had never worn anything else up there.

That he was bald over the crown of his head was understood. That the rest of the hair, the tangled bush of a moustache in particular, had been grown long and thick in defiance of that baldness was silently understood.

One didn't dare cross Pacquet on that subject, or on anything else.

Gesturing, the coroner threw the agonized police photographer into battle, held the boys in blue with their canvas stretcher in reserve, and set upon the corpse, flinging his battered black bag down as if fed up.

'Twenty-six years of age.'

An eyelid was pried up. The shirt collar was teased away to better expose the wound. 'This one, having successfully avoided the patriotic defence of his country, has succeeded equally in avoiding the forced-labour requests of the glorious Third Reich. He's reaped his just reward, eh, Kohler?'

Hermann didn't get a chance to reply. 'Who's the old dear? His mother?' shouted the Chief Coroner.

Louis explained things but it was as if Pacquet had already been briefed and had forgotten her. 'Identity?' his voice leapt.

'Not yet, Chief Coroner. The papers were stolen. Records will know him.'

'You hope.'

It was a prayer freely given.

Pacquet examined the gaping wound that had cut through to the spinal cord. 'His neck's been broken. The head was pulled back like this,' he demonstrated, 'by cupping the bastard beneath the chin and pressing the knee against the centre of the back. Tied for good measure and then the throat opened. A straightforward gangland killing, Louis. Vengeance! The pinstriped suit, the broad lapels of the typical mackerel – one has only to look at him to know his nature. The candy-striped tie. One ring finger is missing – you would not have noticed that.'

The little finger of the left hand had been hacked off. The ring had been too tight. A bad job.

The finger was lying on the floor, stuck to the congealed blood. 'As a matter of fact, I did notice it.'

'Please don't swear under your breath. The Sûreté's most infamous murder squad should be more forthcoming with their lungs.'

The victim's arms had been pulled down on either side of the chicken's tail, then tied and roped to the ankles so that he straddled the thing in a most incongruous position. The rope had then been passed up and over the back a few times before being securely knotted to the brass pole upon which the chicken was mounted.

'He'd not have fallen off,' came the dry comment. 'The killer must have searched for this among the workings, after he'd dragged the body over to the chicken.'

The rope was flicked with a forefinger.

'We're working on it,' said St-Cyr.

Sufficient play had been allowed for the chicken and the corpse to rise and fall as the carousel went round. A nice touch.

Kohler let the two of them fuss. The ticket booth attracted him.

The cage was just big enough for a girl to stand in. A small seat, hinged to the back, would give momentary ease when lifted up and fixed into place. Rolls of tickets hung handily above, on either side of the brass bars of the wicket.

Looking out of the cage, he saw the boardings that had been put up to mothball the carousel: lions and tigers leaping through fiery hoops to whips, or standing on hind legs; an elephant, a monkey ... 'The monkey's cup,' the *flic* Clément Cueillard had said.

'Come to think of it, where the hell has the monkey got to?'

It was a thought.

The cash box was empty, but that would have been done as a matter of course at the close of each day. Robbery couldn't have been the motive, not the few sous this thing would take in.

The ticket booth was fixed to the carousel next to its outer edge, and went round and round with it. At the end of each ride the attendant would step out of her booth to unhook the chain and let the riders off, taking back the tickets and tearing each in half. Then she'd get behind the wicket to take the money in and hand out fresh tickets to the new batch of riders.

The system had its faults. When the boards were down there'd have been ample opportunity for the kids to jump on and off, snitching rides at will. The little nippers would have driven the attendant and the operator crazy. The success of the venture had depended on the riders being honest!

'Perhaps that's why the apache was hired to run the thing?' Or had he been hired at all?

Kohler ran his hands over the black lacquer of the tiny counter. The attendant's knees would have touched the iron door. The girl would have chafed her stockings against it and worried about them. *If* she'd had any left. These days the girls used a wash of beige, drew lines up the backs of their gams and went barelegged. Her shoes would have scuffed the floor. She'd have been like a little bird in a cage.

A bird that had called herself Christiane Baudelaire? Was that it?

When he ran his eyes up into the vaulted dome of the booth he found a gold-painted hook, and reaching up, let a finger wrap itself around the thing. A cage within a cage. Christiane Baudelaire.

Louis was waiting for a ticket. Pacquet had seen enough.

'Dead a good thirty hours, Hermann, so exactly as we'd thought.'

Nine, nine-thirty, Wednesday night.

'A vengeance killing. Pacquet's leaving us to sort out the details. He only came here at the request of your boss.'

The Sturmbannführer Walter Boemelburg.

'What's Walter really got to do with it, Louis?'

'That I wish I knew, my old one. Ah *merde*, but I do.'

'The girl had one of those coins placed squarely in the middle of her forehead, Louis.'

The Frog's eyes were moist. 'It is the custom always to pour gasoline on the fire, Hermann. He who holds the can determines the size of the blaze.'

'The avenue Foch?'

'Perhaps.'

The General Oberg, the Butcher of Poland, and his deputy, the Obersturmbannführer Helmut Knochen. The SS at Number 72 the avenue Foch!

'Louis, whoever ran this thing had plenty of coal and firewood.'

'Yes . . . yes, I am aware of that, Hermann. While virtually the whole of Paris freezes, some have all the luck.'

'The girl's client?' asked Kohler, not liking the drift.

Louis only nodded sadly, then shrugged as he walked away. The chips were down and the poor Frog knew it.

2

The shutters were drawn, the street was empty. At 5.30 a.m. Berlin time the curfew had broken, but the dawn was still some hours away.

St-Cyr stood alone on the sidewalk at the entrance of the courtyard that led to the Hotel of the Silent Life.

There was only a small wooden placard to mark the location of the hotel. They'd not been able to afford bronze when what had once been the villa of a bourgeois merchant had lost its innocence and become a *pension*.

Armed with Hermann's Gestapo flashlight, he'd been searching for the girl's papers but had come out here to experience the city's awakening.

Those that had stayed late had begun to seep homeward or to their places of work. Here in the *quartier* Goutte-d'Or, on the rue Polonceau it was no different. All over Paris there would be this same indefinable hush. It was as if guilt drove the honest to scurry or to coast one's bicycle when passing others in the dark, instinct having given warning and the gently ticking breath of the sprocket answer.

The wind in a girl's skirt in summer; the clasp of her overcoat as now.

The opening of a door directly across the street broke his thoughts. He knew a bicycle was being pushed out on to the road.

'Marianne, take care.' A whisper.

'I will, Georges. Until tomorrow, my love, I die with waiting and hunger.'

'Until tomorrow.'

Marianne . . . Could she not have had some other name? Must God do this to him?

St-Cyr held his breath. The door softly closed and the girl rode silently away, letting her bicycle gather its effortless momentum.

Quickly he crossed the street but did not shine the light over the place. It was a shop of some sort – a sign-painter, a tailor, a shoe-repair – Montmartre, like Belleville, was the earth of such things.

The window glass was cold, the surface a mirrored lake through which the bottom of what Paris had become would be certain to appear.

He chanced the light but briefly. It was a bakery and pâtisserie in which the sugared almonds were not real but made of pressed paper that had been allowed to dry in the summer sun then had been painted or dipped in glue and covered with a sprinkling of coarse salt.

The éclairs were as plastic and everyone would know this and no longer bother to ask if they were real.

The flan with its glazed fruit – fruit like something strange and forbidden – would be as hard as the glass that sheltered it from the window-shopper's betrayal.

Marianne . . .

He switched off the light. 'It's finished,' he said. 'God has them and he's had the great kindness to give me two more murders to solve and quickly.' But was God laughing at him again so soon? Was He beckoning him to climb up into Heaven to have a little look down at himself?

God had a way of doing things like that.

His steps echoed in the courtyard. The hotel was at the far end, perhaps some thirty metres from the street. There was a carpenter's shop, a printer's – the smell of ink – a man who bound old and rare books, a seamstress who specialized in wedding gowns few people would want.

They'd all have to be questioned. It was invariably difficult. One had to be so tactful and Hermann seldom was.

The girl who had called herself Christiane Baudelaire had left her real papers somewhere. She'd lived elsewhere and could not have come and gone without them. Where . . . where would a girl of that age and circumstance have chosen to hide her most valuable possessions?

Search as he did again, he could not find the papers. They weren't tucked behind the gas meters or behind the cast-iron drainpipe that plunged down the wall in its far corner beside the trash cans. They weren't beneath any of the worn lino runners on the stairs of a narrow entrance that leapt off to the right to some warren of other rooms a good ten metres from the hotel.

Marianne ... he'd have to force himself to question that one and her Georges. They might have seen or heard something. They might indeed have hidden the papers for Christiane, but if they had, and if they'd known, as they surely must by now, what had happened to her, then why the *joie de vivre* in that young girl's voice?

Always there were questions, and often there were no answers.

One had to ask because one had to.

Kohler eyed the concierge. There were twelve coins he'd allow for common viewing, and when washed of their blood, they presented a rather shiny impression to the uninitiated.

Greed glowed through the exhaustion in Madame Minou's eyes. 'It is a fortune, monsieur,' she croaked.

'Roman, madame. Solid gold aureii from the first century BC. *That* one,' he emphasized, stabbing the coin with a forefinger. 'That's Julius Caesar himself.'

'And that one?' she asked. 'It is smaller, no?'

Good for her. 'That's Nero – first century AD, between fifty-four and sixty-eight AD, to be precise. He's the guy who burned Rome for the sheer pleasure of it. He watered the money. That's why the coin is smaller.'

'Was he a Nazi?' she asked in all innocence.

He'd have to let it pass. 'This one's dated about the second century BC. That's the head of Mars, the God of War. There's an eagle on the other side.'

'There were Nazis back so far?' She couldn't believe it possible and was deeply troubled, so much so she asked, 'Is it that you people will burn Paris, monsieur, when you leave?'

'Who says we're going to leave?'

The old girl found the coins again. 'The Russians perhaps.'

'I've two sons who say the Russian Front will extend well beyond Moscow by the New Year.'

It was a hollow boast and one to be given its due. 'How is it that you know so much about such as these?'

The coins, none of which were larger than two centimetres in diameter, were lined up in a row on the tiny counter that served as her desk. A letter for Room 4-7 hadn't been picked up. The girl had been in too much of a hurry, and Madame Minou had let her go on up the stairs, thinking she'd catch her later on.

The Bavarian took the letter. She asked again about his knowledge of the coins.

'We come fully equipped, madame. All things to all situations. Gestapo, remember?'

And German, and therefore wise and all-knowing. The Gestapo seemed to fancy the head of Mars most of all and when, on picking it up to drop it into her hand, he said 'Exceedingly rare,' she knew he would not part with it.

'Those were called sestertii. They come in three denominations – a sixty like that one, a forty and a twenty. Later they made the sestertius out of brass and equal to four copper Asses, and coined the gold into aurei.'

'Why are you showing me these, monsieur?'

'Me? Ah,' he gave the Bavarian rendition of a Frog's shrug, 'information costs money, madame. Instead of there being twelve of these little beauties in my report, I'm willing to let there be ten.'

She heaved a contented sigh. She had been right about him after all. 'What is it you wish to know?'

'Choose first. Take one Caesar and one Nero. There are duplicates. No one will question their absence.'

The coins were heavy but felt hard. One had a small scratch in which there was a trace of green.

'It's nothing. Don't worry about it. Here, take this one instead.'

There was no sigh. Fear had replaced the greed in her eyes.

'The "lover", the client?' he asked, towering over her.

'A chubby, older man like your friend. A man with the greying moustache yes, but brushed outwards at the ends. The frank look, monsieur. Dark-brown eyes. Ah yes, he and I understood each other perfectly. No questions, you understand. Not even a spoken word beyond those of Mademoiselle Baudelaire. Simply the lifting of the eyelids and the very quick step for one in his late fifties, but then men ...' She gave a shrug. 'Perhaps he was fifty-six or fifty-eight, even sixty. It's hard to tell with men like that. Successful. The good suit, the stiff black bowler hat, eh? The small pin in the lapel – I have decided it must be a diamond. The necktie, the well-pressed knees and polished shoes.'

'Name?'

Her eyes grew hard. 'That I never knew, monsieur. The girl, she has called him Monsieur Antoine.'

'How charming,' breathed Kohler, taking back the Caesar.

'Me, I do not think that was his real name.'

'How many times a week did they meet up there?'

'Once, somtimes twice. The days varied. Sometimes a Monday, sometimes a Friday. It's been going on for nearly a year.'

'And you asked no questions? Come on, madame. Operating a *clandestin* is against the law.'

'This hotel is not a secret bordello, monsieur! Who am I to question what goes on behind closed doors when the rent is paid and the book signed?'

'Who paid the rent?'

'She did. Each and every week. In advance.'

'What time did they usually meet?'

'Sometimes eight, sometimes nine at night. Never later, never earlier except for one Tuesday afternoon. Then they met at four p.m. sharp. Of this I am positive.'

'When was that? Which Tuesday?'

She would stop her lungs.

He handed back the Caesar, pressing it into her palm and holding it there. 'Coins with blood on them, madame. Lying causes that, just like withholding information or letting a *clandestin* operate behind closed doors without a licence.'

He'd have her charged, she knew it. 'Last Tuesday. Now three . . . three days ago. The girl was most distressed. He did not stay long and she . . . she did not change her clothes or wash herself.'

So much for keeping things private behind closed doors.

He gathered up the coins and put them away in a vest pocket. She did not like the way he hesitated, or that he stood so closely to her.

'That your late husband?' he asked, causing her to jerk in alarm.

'Yes . . . yes, that is him. He was awarded nothing, monsieur. Nothing!'

'And this one?' he asked.

She'd not had time to hide the photograph. Ah Mon Dieu, what was to become of Roland? Of herself? 'That . . . that is my son, Roland Minou.'

A young man of twenty-six. *Gott im Himmel* but it was a popular age! 'When did your husband die?'

She sweltered under the look he gave her.

'In the summer of 1916. Me, I . . . I had not seen him for nearly two years, you understand? The father . . .'

'The father of your son wasn't him,' glowed Kohler. 'You old sinner, madame. Never mind, your secret's safe with me.'

Safe with the Gestapo!

The cement of the arrangement was pressed into her hand. Another Nero.

'We'll keep in touch. We'll ask the *flics* to keep an eye on you but just in case, be sure to lock up at night.'

'A *café au lait*, please, and a croissant.'

'*Pardon*, monsieur?'

The mistake was realized. There were no croissants, of course, and there was no milk. 'A coffee then, and two fists of bread.'

The proprietor, dwarfed by an oversized jersey, looked perplexed as he waited.

St-Cyr fished in a pocket and, dragging out the green ration tickets Marianne had left for him, shrugged and said, 'Just the coffee then. These are out of date.'

The small café was next to the bakery. From there he watched for Hermann and for the *flics* who would cart the girl's body off to the morgue. The photographer had already left. The boys were just winding things up. The crudities would be over. She'd be covered by a piece of filthy canvas. They'd not be saying dirty things about her now.

He knew there'd be fingerprints in plenty, that the girl's killer hadn't cared a damn about those. That the man had considered himself above prosecution was only too evident, a bad sign these days. Ah yes.

The roasted-barley water was bitter. There was no sugar. One didn't even ask.

Salt would not help.

When Kohler found him, Louis was sucking on his pipe and staring off into oblivion at pigeons huddled high above the rue Polonceau. An old man, a retainer of some sort, was sharing the last of his bread ration in contemplation of a winter's funeral and a pauper's grave.

Kohler indicated the man. 'How the hell could he have climbed the stairs, Louis?'

Hermann didn't care for stairs. Having been caught once between floors, hanging by a thread, the lifts of Paris were too untrustworthy for him, and in true Germanic style he considered everyone else must feel the same. Stairs had to be conquered.

'The exercise will be good for him.'

The last few crumbs were thrown into the frigid air. The birds fluttered to the street below. There was no traffic apart from a few bicycles, two vélo-taxis and an ancient *gazogène*.

Kohler filled him in, then said, 'You're hungry, Louis.'

'A little, yes. Hermann, *don't*! Please. Just this once. Be my guest and have a coffee, eh? We'll eat later. Somewhere else.'

The Gestapo shield was reluctantly put away. Highly nervous, the proprietor spilled the coffee, but took the trouble to wipe the table with a fistful of apron.

Kohler thanked him. No one had chosen to sit near them. The talk had all but ceased.

He lowered his voice. 'So, Louis, what do you make of things?'

The traffic posed no danger whatsoever to the pigeons. 'The Tuesday-afternoon rendezvous presents us with a problem. Quite obviously they had some means of communicating in emergencies. This Monsieur Antoine, whoever he is, said something that upset her.'

'He didn't stay long.'

'But did the girl?'

'Madame Minou didn't say.'

'And you didn't ask! Was it that you were preoccupied, Hermann, and thinking of using those "gold" coins for yourself?'

'No one in their right mind would buy them.'

'But obviously someone did.'

'And sent the killer to pay her back.'

'Precisely.'

Louis tapped out his pipe and debated whether to ration himself, deciding only with difficulty to tuck the furnace away.

Kohler asked, 'Was the client the one who bought?'

'Perhaps, but then why the quick visit of last Tuesday, Hermann? Why the distress, the agitation of our little angel? Was it that she knew this Monsieur Antoine could be hard with her if necessary and if so, where and how did she come by those coins?'

'Perhaps she thought they were for real. An honest mistake?'

'Perhaps, but then if she did, did she steal them from their rightful owner who, in turn, had considered that such a possibility might happen some day and had substituted the fakes?'

'And didn't think to warn her, eh?'

The urge to add 'Perhaps but then,' was all but overpowering. Instead, St-Cyr finished his coffee with a grimace. 'That was positively awful, my friend.'

'What? The coffee, or the suggestion that she wasn't warned?'

'Both, my old one. Both.'

Kohler knew he'd best tell him. 'The fakes aren't all that bad, Louis. The girl might not have known, and neither might their owner.'

'*Merde!* Why must you torment me this way? At a time like this, Hermann? Come, come, give, you Bavarian son of a bitch! Don't keep an honest French detective waiting.'

'You're scared.'

'Damn right!'

Kohler found three of the coins and thumbed them out into the middle of the table. 'So, okay, the dies were good and probably made by casting them from the real thing.'

'The letters?'

'All okay. C(aius) CAESAR CO(n)S(ul) PONT(ifex) AVG(ur), et cetera.'

There were traces of brownish discolouration that both disappointed and disheartened. 'Why didn't you tell me?' he asked. 'We're in this together, Hermann. If I fall, so too do you. Isn't that right?'

It was – a sheepish grin said so. 'Sorry, Louis. All right, there was some brown, some gold present. It . . . it just came over me.'

To lie about it! 'How many were there?'

'Twenty-seven.'

'Is that what you confided to Madame Minou?'

'I didn't tell her about them. I just hinted at it.'

St-Cyr knew there could well be thirty of the coins, or even forty. Madame Minou might even have heard them being flung at the girl's body.

Thirty aurei and sestertii. Damn Hermann for holding out on him. 'I would have thought you'd have learned your lesson by now.'

The coins were good and of billon, a mixture of gold and silver with lots of copper, but gold in colour, every gram. A gold-buyer's file had been used on each. The nitric acid had penetrated to the truth.

'A few are scratched, but that's in keeping with their supposed age.'

'Touched up?' demanded St-Cyr.

Kohler nodded. 'The counterfeiter's good, Louis.'

Given the inflation in such things and the fact that new francs were at the usurious exchange rate of twenty to the mark, they were still looking at a considerable sum. Perhaps 5,000 marks. One hundred thousand new francs.

For thirty of the coins. *If* there were only thirty. 'Don't try to sell them, Hermann. Not a one. For my sake and for your own.'

'Don't get in a huff. I would have told you anyway.'

The Sturmbannführer Walter Boemelburg was waiting for them. Gestapo HQ Paris and the Sûreté's offices were on the rue des Saussaies, just off the boulevard Malesherbes and the Place de la Madeleine.

'A full report, Kohler. Leave nothing out. Some son of a bitch of a terrorist has shot and killed a Wehrmacht corporal.'

'When?'

'Late last night or early this morning. We don't know yet. Louis, listen to his song and tell me if it's off-key.'

Boemelburg's fist hit the boards that enlarged the antique lime-wood desk Osias Pharand had once favoured. He threw the fairy nuisance of a Louis XIV inkstand into the plain galvanized milk pail he'd chosen as a waste-basket. 'Commence!' he bellowed. 'Don't piss in your trousers.'

Hermann started to take something out of a pocket but thought better of it. Boemelburg sat down heavily. A big, tall, heavy man, his bristled grey dome and broad forehead showed the creases of anger and worry. France's top cop, the Head of SIPO-SD Section IV, the Gestapo, was not happy.

Boemelburg spoke perfect French, even to argot, the slang of the *quartiers*. He was a wizard of a cop when he wanted to be, which was usually always.

St-Cyr turned away to take shelter by one of the windows. The rue des Saussaies looked lonelier than ever. The merry-go-round that Paris had become had suddenly stopped. A dead corporal . . .

'*Listen*, Louis.'

'Of course, Walter. You have my ears.'

'And your asses! Don't either of you forget it!'

He was in rare form. Hermann began again, but Walter was hardly listening. The killing of the corporal was not good. Ah no. It meant trouble, always trouble for him. There'd not been many of these killings yet. Just a scratch or two.

Before the war Boemelburg had been a much respected police-man. They'd worked together on several occasions, notably the visit of King George VI to France in July of 1938, when the government had been worried about yet another assassination and the Vienna office of the International Organization of Police, the I.K.P.K., had been all aflutter.

Now such an acquaintanceship was worth only so much. Ah *merde*, what was one to do? wondered St-Cyr.

'Coins!' shrilled Boemelburg.

'Forged,' murmured Hermann.

'I want the truth! How many coins were there? Where did they come from? Why hasn't this forger been apprehended? Who has the real coins if, Hermann, *if* they even exist?'

'We're looking into it, Herr Sturmbannführer.'

'*You're looking into it. Gott im Himmel*, is that all you have to say?'

'We've only just got back. We've not even been to sleep.'

'SLEEP? Who sleeps these days? Only the dead.'

Among Boemelburg's many duties was the task of taking hostages and choosing those who would be shot.

'Walter, perhaps we could use a little help? A few days?'

'It's time you don't have, Louis. *Gott im Himmel*, why can't you French behave?'

'The corporal . . . Where . . . where was he killed?'

'Where indeed!'

Kohler held his breath. Louis looked quite ill.

'The rue Polonceau?' asked the little Frog. It was a cry, a plea to that God of his for some sort of an understanding with fate. 'I heard no shot, Walter. I was standing at the side of the street. A girl . . .'

'What girl?'

'A girl of my imagination, Walter. My dead wife. I . . . I was merely recalling that the two of us had once had lunch in the Bistro Demi-Matin on that street.'

Kohler was impressed. Even when crushed the Frog could still think fast and not let it show. A good sign.

Boemelburg ran an irritated hand over the bristled dome. 'Hostages will have to be taken, Louis. I'm sorry, but that's the way of it.'

'Six . . . eight . . . ?'

'Thirty.'

'But . . . but it's nearly Christmas . . . ?'

'That can't matter. I have my orders.'

Kohler found his voice. 'Which end of the street, Herr Sturmbannführer?'

'The lower end, where it runs into the rue de la Goutte-d'Or. Not far from the Church of Saint Bernard. Some bastard must have dragged him into a courtyard. They've only just reported it. A priest. The cloth had the courage to telephone.'

St-Cyr threw himself into a chair and dragged out a handkerchief to blow his nose and hide his tears. Thirty hostages. Thirty deaths for one corporal!

Boemelburg was moved to a momentary compassion. 'I don't like it any more than you do, Louis.'

'But you have your orders.'

The giant thumbed a telex at him. 'Right from the Führer. He's in a rage.'

'You once lived on that street, Walter. Years ago you ate and drank with those people when you were selling and servicing central-heating systems to the wealthy.'

The Gestapo's gaze didn't waver. 'I know that, Louis. I don't need to be reminded of it.'

The meaty hands gathered in the coins. There were twenty-seven of them and that was an odd number. Kohler? he wondered. How many had he stolen?

'These are not bad imitations, Louis. Did the Italian do them?'

That dusty page had been torn from the last century, from the annals of great criminals: one Luigi Cigoi, who had worked in copper and billon alloys to produce late-Roman issues that had baffled and shattered the faith of the experts of that day.

'Some of the dies could have been his, Louis, or the originals. The Romans minted in Gaul as they did on the Danube. They left their garbage lying around for others to use.'

All of which St-Cyr would have known, but there was still no sign of interest.

Boemelburg began to sort the coins, fingering six to one side and three to the other.

Kohler thought it best to enter into the spirit of things. 'Not cast from old coins?' he offered.

A cloud descended. 'How many are missing?'

'Three, Herr Sturmbannführer.'

'Where are they?'

'With the concierge, in temporary payment for information.'

'Good. See that you get them back. Now, gentlemen, take a closer look, eh? Tell me what you think.'

He thumbed two more of the coins to join the six. 'At first the Romans used bronze dies, just as the Greeks did before them, but when struck with a ten-kilo sledge, those dies tended to give, so ...' He paused.

Kohler swallowed. 'They've all been struck from iron dies but...'

'But *they could not possibly have been.*' Boemelburg gave him a rare grin of pleasure. 'The edges of the early ones are far too sharp, those coins far too round. The relief of the figures stands out too sharply.' He paused. 'The later coins, which would have been made from the much stronger iron dies, are perfect as they should be.'

'Perhaps the forger was in too much of a hurry, Herr Sturm-bannführer? Perhaps he didn't have the bronze he needed to make two sets of dies. Maybe he simply thought to improve on the earlier ones.'

'Perhaps, but then, is that it, Hermann? Don't be a *dummkopf.*'

St-Cyr heaved a patriot's sigh. 'It's the one who bought the coins that worries me, Walter. He must have been German and if so...'

'Louis, stop wearing your allegiance on your sleeve. At least stick it in your pocket. Common sense...'

'Is that a warning, Walter?'

'Damn you, you know I can't always look the other way. They're asking questions about your loyalties over on the avenue Foch. Oberg's not happy.'

'No one is these days.'

'Then perhaps you'd best tell him that. The two of you are to cart your sestertii over there later on.'

The brass ones. Four Asses each. Was the Chief losing his memory? asked Kohler of himself. *Gott im Himmel*, no! Yet that accusation had been made more than once in higher circles, and the word was out that Walter was to be replaced.

The old lion was having none of it.

'Solve this thing, Louis, and I'll see what I can do about the hostages.'

'Take the old ones, Walter. Not the young. Let us talk to them, in case they know something we need.'

'Then come with me. Leave Louis' car behind, Hermann. Ride in front with my driver.'

It didn't take long. In the span of time since they'd left the café, the Wehrmacht had moved in to plug the street and shake everyone out into it.

The hostages were randomly chosen. Some took it with dumb

44

faces, still not realizing what was about to happen to them; others tried to get away or begged on their knees.

Some had only hatred in their expressions, not pride. One man spat at them from a distance too great to matter.

'Take that one,' said the Chief.

'*Bâtard!*' screamed the man. A rain of rifle butts bloodied his nose and lips, and broke his teeth.

'And this one.'

'She has a child, Walter, a little one.'

'Oberg will want a cross-section, Louis. So will General von Schaumburg.'

The Kommandant of Greater Paris, Old Shatter Hand himself. Rock of Bronze to those who knew and loved him best.

Screaming at them, the woman was carted off to one of the iron salad baskets, the forbidding black steel-meshed vans of the police. Would she be taken to the Santé or to the rue du Cherche-Midi?

Some still huddled in their nightdresses though they should have been up and about by now. Perhaps they'd been ill in bed. One old man still wore his stocking cap, nightshirt and slippers, as if he'd awakened on another planet and was waiting for the nightmare to clear.

The collection moved on up the rue Polonceau like a nervous wind. The bag was now almost full.

'Out of deference to you, Louis, I'll leave the hotel and its courtyard of squirrels.'

St-Cyr prayed no one had overheard. The last thing he wanted was to be seen in public with the Nazis at what could well turn into a mass execution.

Hermann must have sensed this for continually he had tried to put himself between the Sturmbannführer and his partner and to push his little Frog away.

'And that one.'

'No, Walter. Please. Not that one.' The baker was dragging off his apron. 'That one I need to question.'

Boemelburg looked the man over, nodding as he did so. 'All right, Louis, he's yours. You can have him for ten minutes.'

'Alone, Walter. No one else. Not even Hermann.'

'Louis, don't. Let me come with you.'

'Hermann, just this once do as I have asked.'

'Four men, one room. The men to cover the exits, Louis. Orders to shoot if he makes a run for it,' grunted Boemelburg.

It was his turn to nod.

They went into the shop, to a back room with a rumpled bed, a table, two chairs – nothing much. A hotplate, an empty wine bottle, two glasses and some cigarette butts. A pair of dirty socks . . .

St-Cyr offered a cigarette. 'Monsieur, I am not one of them. No, please do not interrupt me. If you do not wish your girlfriend to be arrested, you will answer what I have to ask.'

The man drew on the cigarette. 'Marianne had nothing to do with that killing. She . . .'

'She stayed here the night.'

How had the cop known?

'Your papers. *Papers*, please! Look, I hate myself for having to ask for them.'

The wounded brown eyes looked up at him from the edge of the cot. Georges Lagace was not quite fifty years of age, so had missed even the last of the call-ups in the spring of 1940 and had probably gone underground for a while. He was of medium height and build and totally nondescript.

'I lost the wife and kids on the road south during the invasion, Inspector. We . . .' He gave a futile shrug. 'I have thought I was taking them to safety, not into the cannon shells of their Messerschmitts.'

'And the girl?'

'She lives over in Montparnasse, the rue Boulard – look, is this necessary?'

Reluctantly Lagace gave up the address. 'Number 37. She has a room on the third floor. She . . . she rents out the rest of the flat to some friends so as to make ends meet. We . . . we met quite by accident in the Cemetery of Montparnasse, she to see her husband, me the wife and kids – the stones anyway. Not the bodies. They're all buried elsewhere but it's closer here, and for a small charge you can, if you know the right people, have a stone to remember.'

One was always learning. 'What's her name?'

'Marianne St-Jacques. Look, she's . . . she's only twenty-eight. An . . . an artist's model, that and part-time in a hat shop, but there's less of that work now so she has to do more of the modelling. Because there's no coal, she's got two days off. We were going to meet to –'

'Georges, there was a murder.'

'She didn't kill him and neither did I. I swear we didn't, Inspector.'

'Look, I know that. It's the other murder I'm interested in.'

'Oh, that one. Marianne won't know anything useful. You'd be wasting your time. She didn't come here all that much. I usually went to her place.'

'Then what about yourself, eh? Did you see anything that might help us?'

'Me? I'm far too busy fighting off the bitchers and the forgers to worry about what goes on across the street in that place. It's full of shits. Misers! who don't pay their bills.'

The forgers . . . the ration tickets for the bread, of course. It was happening all the time now.

'At least I was too busy. Now . . .' He tossed his hands in despair. 'Now I no longer have to care.'

'Let me see what I can do.'

St-Cyr went back to the street. Twenty-nine of the hostages had been taken. Only the tidying-up remained.

Boemelburg was sitting in the back of the Daimler, Hermann in the front with the driver.

The window was rolled down. 'Well, Louis?'

'Walter . . .'

'Herr Sturmbannführer, if you please.'

'Sorry. Herr Sturmbannführer, regardless of what the man knows, he is responsible for supplying the local barracks with their bread. It would be better not to choose him.'

'Then who do you suggest, Louis? Pick one. Any one, only hurry it up.'

Kohler found the old man with the pigeons. 'This one, Herr Sturmbannführer. Take this one.'

The car rolled away. The street held its silence, immobile as a carousel before the gears began to mesh.

Louis, poor fool, was crying. 'Come on. Let's go and get something to eat.'

The music had begun.

'Two eggs on horseback, the split-pea and ham soup, the sausage, lentils, cabbage and beer. Bread and borsch on the side.'

Poised on the balls of his tiny feet, Rudi Sturmbacher took the order with gusto. A Brown Shirt from the days of the Munich

Putsch, a man with fists – a survivor – he had received his just reward.

Chez Rudi's was on the Champs-Élysées just across the avenue from the Lido through the naked branches of the chestnut trees. Right in the shadow of the Arc de Triomphe itself – well, almost. A bustling place, now in its mid-morning quietude.

The ham-fat fingers stopped their scribbling. The small, pale-blue eyes blinked up and out from their red rims under thatches of ripened flax.

At 166 kilos Rudi wasn't losing any weight. Paris had been good. So, too, his little Julie and Yvette who took such care of their 'big' Rudi. Big in the loins.

Greed and larceny brightened his eyes. A student of the black market, Hermann could usually be 'touched' when necessary, but Hermann had cut himself. Mein Gott, the whip, it could do wonders!

'And for your "friend", my Hermann?' fluted the mountain, enjoying the sight of the stitches and the gossip they'd entail. 'I regret there is no asparagus.'

'What? No limp asparagus?' shouted Kohler. '*Gott im Himmel*, Rudi, I thought all things were possible under the Third Reich?'

The cook-proprietor let his voice fall to caution. 'Some little things are beyond us, Hermann, but the Gestapo could always oblige?'

'And change the seasons?' roared Kohler. 'Give Louis the hero food, damn it! He needs feeding up.'

Another whisper came. 'Or cutting down to size.'

'What's that supposed to mean?' asked Kohler darkly.

The grin was huge; Chez Rudi the centre of all gossip, a mine-field of it. 'That you are to enjoy your lunches, or your dinners.'

Or your breakfasts for that matter.

'Hermann, must you?' groaned St-Cyr when the man had departed. 'You know how I hate coming to this place. I cannot eat in any case.'

'You'll eat because you have to, and that's an order.'

'The Resistance . . . one of these days they'll hit it. Me, I would not like to have to scrape you off the walls.'

'Relax. Rudi's okay. Try to get on his good side, eh? Use your charm, Louis. Oberg's on top of the wave, remember?'

'He doesn't *eat* here.'

'Of course he doesn't but we need to. Besides, you're out of ration tickets. Remind me to get you some.'

Two eggs on horseback ... unheard of these days unless one ate in places such as this.

A few of the regulars sat about. An SS major was slumming with his coffee and *Berliner Tageblatt*, fresh in on the morning's Junkers JU-52. Were the papers getting thinner yet again?

A girl in a short black skirt, red silk jacket, cream blouse, gloves, chic grey-blue angora cloche and black stockings was sitting all alone over by the windows.

A girl with short, straight jet-black hair, strong, decisive brows, good hips, lips, legs and all the rest. About twenty-two or twenty-three. On her third or fourth cup of coffee and watching the street as if the window was a mirror.

'She's waiting for me, Louis. We'll let her wait.' Kohler dragged out a vial. 'Want some?' he asked.

Messerschmitt Benzedrine. 'Take a couple and we can go for a full forty-eight.'

'You'll not be of much use to her without them. No wonder you threw up your guts!'

'Quit suffering. That *rafle* had to be. It was fate, Louis, just like I couldn't avoid meeting her. Here, come on, at least take them with you.'

He shook four of the capsules on to the red-and-white chequered tablecloth. 'Two for you and two for me.'

With beer. Rudi was in the kitchen. His youngest sister, Helga, slung the suds, giving Hermann a knowing leer and tossing her round milkmaid's eyes towards the windows. Blonde braids and all. 'She's nice, my little *liebling*. Very nice and anxious.'

'Tell her to go away then. Louis and I have to talk. We're for it if we don't.'

'Then let her wait.' Helga trailed teasing fingers over the collar of his coat, then, wetting her ruby lips, touched the wound across his cheek. 'I like it, Hermann. When it heals it will look exactly like a duelling scar. You'll be able to lie about it.'

Her ample bosom rose. Everyone would know exactly how Hermann had received the gash.

She departed with a saucy flick of her chunky hips, the pale-blue workdress hugging her behind. One *did* have to get a man, a husband! And what better place than Paris? So many of the German women came.

'They certainly know you here,' sighed the Frog.

'And you too.'

A pair of sheer, dark-blue briefs with lace was dragged out of an overcoat pocket. A corner of the midnight négligé could not help but show itself.

At last Hermann found what he was looking for. Hunching forward, he lowered his voice in earnestness. 'Louis, listen to me. As God is my witness, I'm going to tell you everything this time. Everything! I took these from the girl's room. I was going to show them to you anyway.'

A pair of gold and emerald earrings – were they really emeralds?

'And these,' confessed the Gestapo. 'A choker of pearls and a single strand of the same. That kid would have looked good in them, Louis. Not a stitch on but the pearls and those.'

The earrings.

The Bavarian nodded towards the windows. 'Giselle, she's perfect for me, Louis. Just what I've been looking for.'

'Our girl wasn't dark-haired, Hermann. She was a blonde.'

'But...?'

'Never mind. For now let's just chalk it up to experience, eh? Why did you keep these from me?'

'Why else?' Kohler nodded towards the windows again. The girl had noticed the two of them, of course, but had turned quickly away when she saw them looking at her.

Wounded perhaps. Hurt in any case. 'Go and talk to her, Hermann. It's all right. I, who now have only *three* murders to contemplate and who could be as old as that one's grandfather, forgive you. It's the times. Fighting with death brings out the worst in us.'

He gave the shrug of a priest in difficulty. 'Oh by the way, my friend, did the other one have a purse too?'

The murdered girl. Kohler shook his head. 'It must be some place, Louis. Probably with her papers.'

St-Cyr heard him say to Helga, 'Hold the eggs on horseback. Give me five.'

'Rudi won't like it. You know they're a specialty of the house.'

The house ... Ah Mon Dieu, the arrogance of the Germans ...

'Then tell him to toss them out and start again. He'll understand. I want to watch my partner enjoying them.'

The pain of the *rafle* in the rue Polonceau began to ease. It would, of course, never go away – how could such a thing vanish?

Nor would the humiliation of being referred to as wet, limp asparagus by that Munich Brown Shirt.

Duty called to take him away from all such thoughts and he welcomed this with a sip of beer. The earrings were quite old. In his haste to pocket them, Hermann had failed to notice that they were far more than simply antique. Tiny gold platelets had been linked to each other to flash and dangle to single emeralds of perhaps three or four carats in weight and of a stunning depth of green. The cut was a tabled square, the ancient facets sharp if simplistic.

The gold platelets had been hammered. They were not precisely round, giving further evidence of great age.

Gold never quite lost its lustre. Inca? he wondered. Had the girl's ears been pierced? Ah now, that was a good question.

An anxious tremble passed through him. He wasn't sure about the ears. They'd have to check at the morgue. He hoped the body wouldn't be disposed of too soon. Surely they'd keep it around for a day or two unless . . .

Hermann was earnestly explaining things to his girlfriend who was trying not to cry. Rudi had come out of his kitchen . . .

The SS major had taken an interest in things.

Closing a fist about the earrings, St-Cyr slipped them away, adding the pearls too. As if the moment had been suspended, he saw the other girl lying naked on her back in that room with the coins scattered about her.

Christiane Baudelaire had been expecting someone. Madame Minou had been listening to the BBC Free French Broadcast from London.

A Wehrmacht corporal had been killed in the rue Polonceau or was then but a few brief hours from his death.

The operator of the carousel on the slopes of the Parc des Buttes-Chaumont had already been killed and Madame Minou, when forced to witness the corpse, had been worried it might have been her son but had soon got over this.

The girl had kept a stuffed canary in a bureau drawer in that room. There had been a heavy elastic band around its wings but no need for this.

The earrings . . . why had she had them? A girl like that, in a room like that?

It was a case, a puzzle, a *real* murder – he knew this now. A crime of passion? Ah no, not in the strictest sense, though hatred must have entered into the savagery of her killing and rape.

The two would have occurred almost simultaneously. A matter which must have taken some skill.

An unpleasant thought. Ah yes. Most unpleasant, as was the coin someone had placed on her forehead.

'Louis, eat your eggs on horseback.'

Rudi Sturmbacher waited for the verdict. There was a butcher knife in his right hand, a frown...

Each egg covered a layer of shaved Gruyère whose partially melted nest lay atop a thick slice of *pain miel*, of honey bread, the whole concoction toasted in a very hot oven so as to congeal and firm the white of the egg but leave the yolk loose and molten as a summer's sun.

'In the Name of Jesus, Rudi, me, I have never tasted better.'

The asparagus had meant it too. 'From now on you're one of us,' roared the mountain, grasping him by the shoulder. 'Helga, did you hear that? Louis likes them.'

Sometimes it was so easy to flatter the Nazis.

The split-pea and ham soup came – it, too, was good. *Superbe! Magnifique!* As were the sausages and all the rest, so the flattery had not been misplaced after all.

And he did not regret it. One must be honest in war, even more so than in peace.

Food brought out the sage.

The girl, Giselle, sat quietly between them at the table's side, taking morsels from Hermann's fork between sips of ice-cold Chablis. It was really quite a joy to see the slashed-up detective-grandfather with her. But the girl's magnificent violet eyes were wary, full of moisture, not joy. Guilt drove her to the Chablis; fear to the morsels.

The rosy blush young girls get in winter when excited was not there.

St-Cyr lost himself in the sausage with lentils. He'd leave the cabbage and the borsch. He'd eat a little more lightly now, but damn the girl for spoiling what would have been a decent meal. What the devil was the matter with her? Uncertainty over Hermann? That fear of love lost when the security it provided was so necessary these days?

Had her pimp warned her to seek out Hermann or else?

The Gestapo's detective showed no signs of noticing anything. Sparrow to the proffered fork, the girl pecked at another morsel – a bit of sausage dripping applesauce. Was she eating for two? Was that it? These days so many young and not so young girls ate for two.

The sparrow darted to the Chablis to refresh the lovely milk-white throat. A tiny droplet spilled away from a corner of her glass. Blinking, she touched it with a fingertip and, flushing with embarrassment, said quite shyly, 'Excuse me.'

For just an instant their eyes met and, Chief Inspector of the Sûreté that he was, he looked deeply into hers until the sparrow ducked away again. Ah yes.

'Wait for us. We won't be long.'

The anguished look the girl threw from the back seat troubled Hermann.

'Hey, it's okay, *chérie*. Come on, Giselle. Everything is all right. It's just a bit of business. There's nothing for you to worry about. Louis and I just have to stop in to say hello.'

To the Butcher of Poland, the Brigadeführer und Generalmajor der Polizei, the Höherer SS und Polizeiführer of France!

Hermann touched the pale cheek and then the white, white crowns of her front teeth through the slightly parted lips that were so red.

She knew he was thinking she had lovely lips.

'She's really something, eh, Louis? *Gott im Himmel*, am I glad to see her again.'

They left her then, and though she could not force herself to watch, in her mind's eye she saw them hurrying between the jackbooted sentries who stood under the swastika flags that hung above the entrance.

Merde! what was she to do? Press her knees together to stop from shaking? Grip her thighs and seek the other side of the avenue? Wait as Hermann had said and as she knew she must? Ah yes.

Even the traffic avoided this place. The rush of bicycles pushed a little harder as the stream of them approached the dreaded Number 72. Those who were on the far side of the avenue Foch looked the other way when passing; those less fortunate came towards her with downcast eyes. Where once there had been so many cars, there were now only those of the Germans and their friends. And she did not know which were the worst, the Nazis or their friends . . .

Occasionally the sound of a bicycle bell interrupted the agony of her thoughts, once the shout of, 'Hey, there, look where you're going!' as if she were the one in the road, she the one with the shaky handlebars.

Karl Albrecht Oberg was forty-five years of age and married, with a wife and two children in the Reich. A man from the north of that country. Tall, but not so tall as Hermann Kohler – really just a little over medium height.

A man who had worn thick spectacles with wire rims and who had leaned well back in his chair when he had examined her.

Had she been so offensive to him? Had he been near-sighted, had that been it?

A man with a small paunch. A man who had looked as if the corset he had worn had been a little too tight.

The Butcher of Poland . . . The Höherer SS.

The pale blue-grey eyes behind those glasses had been round and bulging but not with hatred for her or anything like that, though they had frightened her at first. Terribly, ah yes. Not even with interest in her body, which had been fully clothed, she left to stand as if naked in front of that desk of his, that magnificent desk!

Just the look of a middle-aged businessman wearing the field-grey of the German Army but with the flashes of the SS, a general. A man who had been impatient to get on with his work.

The policing of France and the hunting-down of traitors and terrorists.

The one who had been at his side, the one who had had her brought to this place from deep in her sleep this morning, had spoken French but with a German scholar's accent. It had been he who had translated what he had judged fit for her ears.

'Okay. It's agreed. You can go now. Please do not forget our little arrangement.'

Our little arrangement. The brothel on the rue Chabannais should she fail. The largest of the forty or so that were reserved specifically for the common soldiers of the German Army who came to Paris for a few days' leave and wanted to get it all out of their systems in a hurry. Bang, bang!

Right from the Russian Front. Ah yes, that's what he had said to her, knowing quite well she would have understood. Everyone knew those girls never lasted. They retired sore and broken unless they were big where it counted and crazy.

He had had a perpetually mocking twist to his lips, the left side. Tall and thin – a little taller than his chief, so as tall, perhaps, as Hermann. A man with spectacles, too, and very good manners.

A little arrangement . . . Oh Mon Dieu, they had her just where they wanted! She could not confess a thing to Hermann even though the Bavarian did, perhaps, care a little for her. Even though he was, ah yes, a detective from the Gestapo.

This Obersturmbannführer, the Herr Doktor Knochen was a much younger man than his chief – a man of perhaps thirty-two or so, one who had stripped her body naked with his grey-blue eyes and had laughed at her nakedness, at what she would do to her Gestapo detective, had laughed with that mocking smile of his. Sardonic, knowing, all-perceiving. A man after power, a man who knew his place in the hierarchy of the Nazis at this and other addresses.

A man who had enjoyed her little predicament. Their little arrangement...

They'd kill her if she didn't do what they wanted! Never mind the threat of the rue Chabannais, the ruin of her tender life and the end of her days in the profession. Never mind the ravaging thrusts of sixty front-line soldiers a night!

Never mind any of that. 'Me, I must be the realist. I must steel myself. Hermann must never learn of this. Never!'

Unfortunately her horoscope for the day had told her to stay indoors and keep out of trouble. A tall, thin man would come into her life if she didn't heed the warning, a man who would ask certain things of her.

There'd been no mention of his coming to get her. None, either, of Hermann's friend. Just keep an eye on Hermann Kohler and report everything he says. Ah yes. Everything.

Three hundred metres of Aubusson carpet smothered the inlaid parquet and kept it warm. Gilded eighteenth-century mirrors – tall, richly carved, ornate things – hung on the wall to the right; plush Prussian-blue drapes to the left on either side of each of the many tall windows. Number 72, the avenue Foch. Head office.

'Nice, Louis. Really nice. Not bad for a banana merchant.'

Lalique chandeliers, great ice-cakes of crystal, gave light on dreary days. A sumptuously gorgeous nude, a life-size painting of a coy and raven-haired innocent from biblical times, hung next to a marble statue of Hercules loitering naked as the hanging fruit of his loins betrayed.

Hermann couldn't resist making light of things. The effect of the painting and the statue was electric. Hercules bearded, all frightening, with flat, hard muscles, had an arm draped over something, a shrouded little friend. Death perhaps.

The girl ducked her head away from the loins and appeared as if afraid and uncertain of what that uncircumsized thing of his might mean for her.

Again St-Cyr heard Hermann saying, 'Nice, Louis. Really nice.'

The girl in the painting sat on the edge of something concrete with the toes of her left foot planted on the step below and those of the right foot peeking demurely from behind the tender calf of that supporting leg. The folds of her dressing-robe were sumptuously gold and equally crushed beneath her seat and flaring hips.

'A little Jewish princess, Louis. *Gott im Himmel*, do you suppose they hadn't noticed?'

'I'd no idea you were such a connoisseur, Hermann.'

'They liked their women ample in those days, Louis. The waist not too slim, the tummy pouting a little, the breasts perfect toys for some biblical scholar to play with.'

'He's not a biblical scholar. He has a Doctorate of Philosophy in English literature, I believe.'

'What's it matter? Doctor this, or doctor that? It's this that I'm interested in. Knochen must have taken it upon himself to be art director of this little palace of theirs, Louis. A Jewess set to be ravaged by Hercules! It's his little joke on all the others. It fits his sense of humour, if he has one. *If*.' A warning ...

Marble busts of Greeks and Romans stood solemnly sentinel, facing the windows from across the carpet. There were other paintings between the mirrors. A Correggio, a Dürer, a Frans Hals ... gorgeous things. 'Does he change them periodically?' asked the Frog, their steps hastening now towards the far end of the room and trouble ... trouble ...

'Perhaps, but then ...' offered the Gestapo's Bavarian explorer.

A life-sized bronze of Julius Caesar – a truly remarkable thing – stood in the far left corner nearest the hammering, intruding and incongruous telex. Berlin on the line at all times.

The desk was Russian – Napoleonic in anticipation of conquest. The top was of polished malachite holding scattered files and papers – huge mounds of them. Papers, papers, always it was papers with the Germans.

The malachite was superb and the Gobelin tapestry that hung huge and richly on the wall behind the man with the grey-blue pop-eyes was fantastic. Ruby reds and golds et cetera, et cetera.

The Finding of the Baby Moses among the Reeds. Interesting . . . **very** interesting. Jews again.

St-Cyr clutched his hat and heart. The pop-eyes didn't **even** bother to look up.

'Sit down. The two of you. I won't detain you a moment.'

Hermann hesitated. St-Cyr knew he must wait for his **partner's** lead.

The glasses winked with their thickness, the orbs were bulging, and the bent, domed, diligent head showed pinkly **from** beneath its close-cut cropping of fair hair.

Oberg scribbled a signature as he might have authorized **a bill** of lading in the Hamburg warehouse of the West India **Bananen-** vertriebsgesellschaft where he'd been a purchasing agent **from** 1926 until 1929.

'And this one, too, Herr Generalmajor.'

Knochen, the Doctor of Philosophy, had not yet deigned **to** notice them. All business that one. Somewhat emaciated **and** with that sick little smile. The wounded academic? wondered St-Cyr, or the one who has perpetually the tongue in cheek **for his** superiors and everyone else?

Ah yes, the latter. Most definitely. St-Cyr took in **the hastily** brushed auburn hair that was thick and badly in need of **cutting.** Was Knochen the Bohemian in the Nazi flock? The blue-grey **eyes** behind their glasses seemed to say he couldn't have **cared less** what anyone thought. The pinched face said it too.

A strange combination these two who held the threat **of life or** death over not just Paris's millions, but every living **soul in** France.

Power, this was power. Fate at its cruellest.

Kohler saw Louis glance up at the ceiling and knew **the Frog** was asking his God why He'd had to smile down upon **the Earth** in this particular fashion.

Another and then another of the papers were signed. **Were** they witnessing the signing of the hostages' death notices? **Had it** been deliberate on Knochen's part? That skinny aesthete **who** had missed out on being a professor of literature?

Of course it had been deliberate. *Gott im Himmel*, why **hadn't** that God of Louis' granted the bastard a tenured position **in some** university?

For the same reasons, perhaps, that He'd decreed young **Adolf** should not have been admitted into the Academy of Art!

Knochen had been Reinhard Heydrich's man in France; **Oberg,**

57

Himmler's. And just as that God of Louis' had shut the doors of academia to the assistant, so, too, He'd opened those of mass unemployment and dissatisfaction to the banana merchant.

Oberg had drifted into tobacco and cigars as a small shop-keeper, only to find that the Great Depression had stopped the ships from bringing in the supplies and the coins from flowing out of sailors' pockets. In June 1931 he'd joined the Party. Card Number 575205. The money troubles had ceased and the wife could get pregnant.

Knochen's turn had come a little later. In 1933 he'd joined the SA and had been given the lowly rank of obertruppenführer, a company sergeant-major, just to show the world what you can get when you've got a Ph.D.

Since then that same fate or God had been merciful. Meteoric rises to power for both of them. Heady rises.

And now all this. The Palace of Wonders, of All Things Possible. The avenue Foch, Number 72.

Hermann finally sat down. St-Cyr watched the signing of the last of the death notices.

'Sit down.'

It was Knochen who, gathering the notices, had said this. Unable to react, the Frog stood there feeling desperate. 'How many are to die?' he croaked.

Oberg didn't glance questioningly up at his assistant. So this was the Frenchman who, together with Kohler, had been responsible for the Vouvray mess, the disgracing of the SS on another murder case.

'Twenty-seven. The three others are to be spared.'

'Transported,' said Knochen.

Louis sat down heavily. He tried to find a place to put his hands and hat, and the two behind the desk watched him in silence.

Twenty-seven were to die. Had Oberg got up on the wrong side of the bed or something? Why not all thirty, or why not only a few?

Oberg didn't like the look of either of them. The Frenchman was trouble and the Bavarian dishonest and disloyal! 'Your futures are both in question. You are here, at my command, to be given a second chance.'

So much for Vouvray. The banana merchant was clearly not happy. The Führer and Himmler would both have heard of it.

'This murder . . .' began Oberg. He'd make them sweat! Betray the SS, would they? Hold the Service up to ridicule?

'There are two murders, Herr Generalmajor,' interjected Knochen.

'Yes, yes, a young gangster and his filthy prostitute. Coins –' Oberg snapped his chubby fingers. 'These coins. Gold, I understand.'

'Forgeries, Herr Generalmajor.' Knochen indicated the coins should be produced.

Hermann got up to fumble in his pockets. The coins had that certain ring on the malachite. One of them spun dizzily. The telex hammered. Oberg thought to turn, then thought better of doing so.

Impatient at the interruption, he snapped, 'These coins. Who did the woman sell them to? It's illegal to sell such things without first having declared them. By the decree of June 1940 all such valuables were to have been reported in writing!'

All, that is, above a total value of 50,000 *new* francs, no matter what!

St-Cyr got to his feet. There was no sense in sitting around. 'We don't know that yet, Herr Generalmajor. She could well have not sold them to anyone.'

Stunned, Oberg blinked. Knochen cautiously straightened in alarm.

Again the banana merchant's voice leapt. 'But it's obvious she sold them, *dummkopf*! Why else would her killer have thrown these forgeries at her?'

They both knew more than they should about the murders, and the Frenchman had forced Oberg into admitting it.

Knochen was impressed. Jean-Louis St-Cyr was defiant. That could only antagonize Oberg and make the thing go round.

'Sit down. Sit down, the two of you,' shouted Oberg.

They sat down. The Bavarian's mouth open in apology. 'My partner and I seldom agree on things. You're absolutely correct, Herr Generalmajor und Höherer SS.'

'Und Polizeiführer, Herr Kohler,' came the icy response. 'Please do not forget for a moment that it is to me you owe your livelihood.'

And your life.

Again Hermann confessed that Oberg had been absolutely correct about the girl. 'The killer must have been insane, Herr Generalmajor.'

'He *was* insane,' breathed Knochen warily.

'Perhaps, but then . . .' St-Cyr shrugged. They were all looking at him, waiting, even Hermann, poor Hermann who had debased himself before his masters. 'There was another killing. At the foot of the rue Polonceau. A corporal.' He indicated the death notices and deportation orders that were now gathered in Knochen's slender fingers. 'I ask myself is there not some connection to the other killings, General? Is it not possible that all those death notices you have signed are but a mistake?'

Mein Gott, help him! A mistake!

'Why should that be?' asked Oberg darkly. The French would never learn.

Heroically defiant, Louis drew himself up. 'In murder, General, all things are possible.'

There wasn't a sound. Even the typewriters in distant rooms had ceased their yammering.

Kohler knew he had to break the impasse. 'We always look for linkages, Herr Generalmajor. Louis didn't mean to imply that . . .'

Knochen snorted. 'We're not talking of sausages.'

'Assassination!' shrilled the banana merchant. *'This we cannot have! It must be stopped, stopped, stopped!'*

So much for trying to stop the death notices. 'The meat's all ground up. It's all the same,' offered Kohler lamely.

'Hermann, how could you equate a German corporal with the other two corpses? Please, I think I understand what the Obersturmbannführer Herr Doktor Knochen is implying.'

Sausages . . .

'Good, then that is good,' grunted Oberg, slightly mollified, and the thing came round to the coins again.

'Who made these?'

'A professional,' said St-Cyr, glancing from one to the other of them.

'The dies were of iron. The faces on all the coins are exceptionally sharp,' offered Hermann.

Oberg touched the coins. He wanted to scream at these two schmuck cops! 'The French are notorious for hoarding their gold, Herr Kohler. Greed is in their mother's milk! It has to be rooted out! *Out,* damn you! These are from someone's hoard.'

Hermann thought to please. 'They're really quite good. The owner might have been fooled . . .'

'Idiot! Don't be stupid! A collector of such as these would know exactly what to buy and what not to.'

'But you just said . . . ?' Oh Mein Gott, what were the two of them really after? 'We've no idea who made them.'

A smile flickered briefly on that chubby face. 'Come, come, Kohler. Surely you must know who would be a likely candidate? I thought you were supposed to be a good detective? Don't the two of you know the Paris underworld any better than that? They are good copies, are they not, Herr Obersturmbannführer?'

Knochen acknowledged that they were.

Oberg was vicious. 'We can't have forgers operating in our midst, Kohler. *Find* the scum who was responsible and bring him to me!'

Never mind the murderer or murderers! Just find the forger. '*Jawohl*, Herr Generalmajor.'

'Perhaps if I were to talk to the two of them alone,' began Knochen, leaning close to whisper something into Oberg's ear while still watching them.

'Yes, yes, of course. It would be best that way. Good of you to have thought of it, Helmut.'

The pudgy fingers gathered in the coins. Apparently the gold sestertius bearing the head of Mars and the eagle on its obverse side was the rarest and most valuable. And yet the forger had struck all of them with iron dies that could not possibly have been in use at such a time.

The Frenchman would know this, so, too, the Bavarian. They'd both be wondering why an able forger should think it possible to pull the wool over someone's eyes with these.

Goering ... would they think of the Reichsmarschall and Reichsführer Goering, Commander-in-Chief of the Luftwaffe?

'That is all. Now get out of here, the two of you.'

Knochen led the way. Once up the stairs to the second floor they came to the vault, a room whose barred entrance gave subdued light to the contents within.

There were paintings in richly gilded frames, old masters, young masters, stacked and leaning every which way against exquisite pieces of sculpture, antique cabinets, vases, Louis XIV and XV chairs, crates ... silver, much silver ... an Aladdin's cave.

Knochen let them look. 'All confiscated from those who refused to obey the law and failed to report their valuables. Jews, Freemasons, reactionaries – enemies of the State. Vermin, gentlemen. *Hoarders*. Find out where the girl got the coins and you will, no doubt, unmask the forger and discover the loot.'

'And if there is no loot?' hazarded St-Cyr.

Knochen took a moment to study him. 'Then the suspicions of

our friends over on the rue Lauriston are incorrect and the forgeries were not used to hide the real thing.'

The rue Lauriston . . . The infamous Monsieur Henri and his sidekick, the ex-inspector Bonny. Ah no. No!

'Old friends of yours,' said Knochen, watching him closely.

Kohler was certain then that the whole meeting had been for this one moment of revenge for what had happened at Vouvray in that last case.

'Acquaintances,' acknowledged Louis with admirable steadiness.

Kohler flicked a troubled glance at Knochen. That little smile was there, the moment of triumph slowly savoured so as to prolong the pleasure.

'You're to work with them on this, Inspector.'

'It's Chief Inspector.'

'Louis, *don't!*'

The warning was an added bonus. 'As I was saying, Inspector St-Cyr, your friends over on the rue Lauriston have much to offer. You would be wise to ask for their help.'

'Has this forger done your people in before?' asked the Frog, failing to conceal the little triumph he, himself, felt at exposing the Nazis to their gullibility.

The look the academic gave was cruel. 'But of course he's taken us in before. Why not? There are always those who are eager to buy, and the forger knows this. *Find him!* Now get out of here and don't come back until you have him.'

Giselle was no longer waiting in the car. The bird had flown and no doubt with good reason.

'Louis, let me come with you.'

'No, Hermann. Not this time.'

'Then at least let me give you a lift?'

'The exercise will do me good. It's not far in any case.'

Kohler knew that his partner wanted to be alone, that Louis, being Louis, would have to breathe the air of Paris before descending into the slime.

'Talbotte, Hermann. This is why he has left us to clean up the mess. He is afraid we are tainted and the SS do not want to breathe the same air as we do.'

'We'll meet later?'

'Yes, yes, of course. You to Records, me to the rue Lauriston.'

'The morgue at five?'

'Let's make it four. I want to get back to the house before dark.'

'But aren't you staying at Gabi's flat?'

St-Cyr's eyes betrayed only emptiness. 'Not now, Hermann. Never. Not with them taking such a fine interest in us. Me, I could not live with myself knowing harm might come to her.'

Poor Louis. They'd just wiped the street with him and he knew it.

3

There was little traffic on the Étoile as St-Cyr crossed to the Arc de Triomphe. The humiliation of what he was about to experience was almost more than he could bear. In 1936 he had put the infamous Monsieur Henri of the rue Lauriston away for ten years for armed robbery and the 'accidental' wounding of two cops, both fathers, who'd come to question things and had somehow got in the way.

In the years before that he'd crossed swords with Pierre Bonny and had seen that one into Fresnes for a term of not less than *three* years for accepting bribes while under the oath as an officer of the Sûreté.

Later it had been embezzlement, but by then the ex-inspector Bonny had been eking out a living as a private investigator.

Now, of course, it was from Knochen that the two received their orders and amnesty. *Amnesty* for hardened criminals, for murderers and thieves!

Bonny was the organizer of that little operation; Monsieur Henri the schemer, the searcher of hidden valuables, and Knochen the supplier of cars, gas, guns and Police ID cards that offered protection with impunity.

Much of the loot that filled the avenue Foch had come straight from the rue Lauriston.

The brim of his hat was crumpled, the felt stained, the sweatband rather too grimy to look at.

Pigeon droppings were at his feet and, in the background, the steady rumble of a German Army convoy broke the patient silence of bicycles.

All points radiated from the Arc de Triomphe. The rue Lauriston was a narrow, straight artery next to the avenue Victor Hugo, a street of the wealthy, the upper class. Less than a kilometre of it lay between him and Number 93.

There was a small café across the street from the unassuming three-storeyed grey house. Empire-style railings protected the tall windows of Number 93's ground floor; Nazi bars, those of its second and third floors, the third most especially. Ah yes.

'A pastis without water.'

The crook who ran the café was obviously an informer for the avenue Foch and a friend of the rue Lauriston.

'Large or small?' he asked, not grinning.

'Large. A double.'

The humiliation had begun. There were a few tables near the street, time enough to toss one's hat on the fake marble and have a smoke.

Number 93 rue Lauriston – some called it the offices of the French Gestapo and they had every right and reason to do so. The servants' quarters on the third floor had been made over into cells so as to keep the sounds of torture a little farther from the street. The bars up there were to prevent people from leaping to their deaths. The offices were on the second floor, with others on the ground floor, together with the storerooms.

Though hidden from the street, there was an inner courtyard, a small garden. How nice.

Up to now he'd managed to keep clear of them. He'd avoided that confrontation he'd always known must inevitably come to pass.

Henri Chamberlin, alias Henri Normand, now Henri Lafont, had been born in 1902, a child of the Paris slums. In the thirty-eight years leading up to the Defeat he'd been arrested for a host of crimes – burglary, assault with a deadly weapon, fraud, arson, swindling, the pistol-whipping of a young girl he'd tried to force into prostitution.

On 16 June 1940, he'd been evacuated along with the rest of the convicts from the Cépoy Prison and had escaped during the confusion of the invasion.

A tenure with the Abwehr had followed – he'd kept good company in prison. His cellmates had been Abwehr agents caught for spying. But it hadn't all been easy. The Abwehr had wanted proof of his abilities. His trapping the leader of the Belgian Resistance who'd been hiding in the South of France had suited well enough. Nearly a hundred patriots had been taken as a result of that little escapade.

Sensing that the Abwehr would fall from grace and the Sicherheitsdienst rise to far greater heights, Lafont had gone over to the other side, to the SS. He still had friends in the Abwehr, friends in very high places, a German citizenship now and a certified German Police card, Number 10474R.

Early in 1941 he'd moved into the rue Lauriston. Recruitment while with the Abwehr and here, too, had been from the jails, the cream of France's underworld. Lafont had personally chosen them and in May of 1941 Pierre Bonny had come to work for him. A nice touch. An ex-inspector of the Sûreté joining forces with a hood. Partners in crime without restriction.

The pastis was good – pre-war stuff. He took the two Benzedrine tablets Hermann had given him, telling himself they were for the morgue and not for the house across the street.

'Another,' he shouted, ignoring the, 'With pleasure,' but lifting moist, warm, doubtful eyes at the proferred, 'It's on the house, Inspector. They're expecting you.'

'Then do me the honour of announcing my arrival.'

Pastis was no joke, but its 90 proof suited him. In the early afternoon the street was all but empty, the wind unkind.

'St-Cyr to see the boss.'

'He's on the third floor. You can take the lift. It works.'

'I'll walk up. Tell him I'll wait in his office.'

'They're sweating someone's cherry. It might be fun.'

'Get lost, scum. Don't talk to me like that.'

'Swallow gasoline, my fine Inspector. Monsieur Henri will be only too glad to light the match.'

The stairs were hard. The girl gave a scream. No lonelier sound could have been heard. She cried out again and again in terror, and he didn't know if he could stand to hear much more.

Weeping when she wept, clutching his heart when she stopped in panic, he waited as she waited, then heard the blow, the cough, the gasp, the choking as vomit spilled from battered lips and nose.

'*I won't tell you. I won't!*' she shrieked.

Unable to control his hands, St-Cyr clutched the stuffed canary in one overcoat pocket and the pearls in the other.

Again he was forced to listen. Again a shrill scream ripped through the upper halls. She hit the floor above him; the boots were being applied! He knew he had to go up there to put a stop to it, that this was what the bastards wanted of him.

And yet . . . and yet, he knew he could not do so. And they had known it too, and had shown it to him.

'Louis, it's good to see you.'

'You're sweating, Henri. Is it because you have had such a hard time with that one upstairs, eh, or are you still afraid I'll put the bracelets on you?'

Once a cow, always a cow! Lafont roared with laughter. The high falsetto that was so incongruous in that tall, muscular handsomeness, shocked as it bounced off the walls, the paintings, the sculptures and *objets d'art*.

'Still the same old Louis. Well, my fine, things have changed. Sit down or stand, it's all the same. Nicole, a glass of the lime for our friend.'

Polite custom? An attempt at manners? 'I refuse. I've had sufficient. I'm not thirsty.'

'But you will drink it anyway.'

The girl, a dress designer's mannequin in off-white cashmere and gold with generous cleavage, moved quickly away to an antique cabinet.

Lafont sat down behind the desk he'd looted from one of the Rothschild villas. 'So, Louis, a small matter, eh?'

At forty, he'd gained a bit of weight – all that high living these days. The face was incredibly not what one would expect in a gangster, more that of a film idol. Good, clean-cut, clean-shaven cheeks, a wide, strong jawline and admirable chin. The wide and slightly sensuous lips were what a woman might have wanted – and many of them did. The eyes . . . only in the eyes was the lie of it given. Even the dark-brown hair, well cut and brushed towards the left, was what one would have expected in a banker or an investment dealer.

Which was what he was, in a sense, these days.

The brows were neither thick nor too thin. The nose was long and prominent but the eyes . . . the eyes: these were small, round, hard, glistening, watchful things. The eyes of a falcon just before it takes the sparrow.

Lafont examined his fingernails. He would have to gauge the wind the avenue Foch had put into St-Cyr's sails. Nicole had turned from the cabinet and remained with her back to it. The glass of lime was in her hand.

'Louis, you're going to need our help. No, my friend, don't get your ass in a knot. Just listen, eh? Sometimes it is necessary.'

At a nod the girl came forward. There was mischief in her lovely brown eyes but more than this, a feral excitement St-Cyr found disconcerting. She fairly breathed it. The fine nostrils were pinched. The pinkness of her tongue touched the crowns of her slightly parted teeth. The mop of auburn curls was short, cute, saucy, so many things. Perfume . . . What was that scent she was wearing? Mirage – could it be Mirage? Ah no. Why? Why must God do this to him?

'Your drink, m'sieur.'

St-Cyr met the look she gave with a steadiness and cruelty he hated in himself.

There was a boldness in her eyes, no shame, lust . . . was there still lust? Had she . . . ?

Nicole de Rainvelle moved away from him again. He had understood her only too well, this Chief Inspector from the Sûreté. Had it shown so much?

She went to lean back against the window-sill behind Henri. She'd fold her arms over her chest and stare at this cop.

There were droplets of blood on her dress but she'd not yet noticed these, had been too excited, too caught up in the beating of that girl upstairs.

Mirage . . . why was she wearing Gabrielle Arcuri's perfume?

St-Cyr still didn't miss much. Lafont massaged the middle finger of his left hand with the thumb and forefinger of the right. 'The coins aren't bad, Louis, but the forger's new to the game.'

'Continue.'

The lime squash, a hideously vile concoction of ersatz fruit essence and saccharin, still hadn't been touched. 'The girl who was murdered in the Hotel of the Silent Life was not the pigeon of the mackerel who operated the carousel.'

The prostitute of the pimp. 'Did they know each other?' asked the cop.

Lafont smiled inwardly. Teasing St-Cyr was like teasing a fish. 'Perhaps, but my sources think the mackerel knew of the girl but she didn't know of him.'

Then she was being watched, sized up for future working perhaps. 'And the owner of the carousel?'

The detective had taken the bait. Was it to be so easy? 'We've not been able to find him yet.'

Then they were still looking for him. 'Any ideas?' asked St-Cyr.

'A room facing on to the quai Jemmapes, above the Café du Paradis.'

The Canal Saint-Martin, in the 10th *arrondissement* not far from the Hospital of Saint-Louis.

'He hasn't been seen since early this week. The concierge says he went to visit his dying mother.' Lafont shrugged. 'Mothers do eventually die.'

'Where?'

Again there was that shrug. 'The Kommandantur has turned up nothing. The *ausweis* must have been a forgery.'

'Or he never left the city. Who was he? Surely you must have a name?' insisted St-Cyr.

'That's for you to find out. The Préfecture will give you nothing, and neither will your famous "Records". The carousel was here in the city before the Defeat but the thing was sold for a song, dumped during the invasion. The guy who bought it could be anyone.'

'And not have a proper licence? Come on, you know me better than that!'

'Find out. Try the previous owner. Maybe he can shed a little light on things.'

'Who was he?'

'Someone, obviously, but there is no record left. It was lifted. Destroyed.'

'And the girl?' They were giving him the run-around.

'Pierre has the dope on that. Ask him.'

Nicole de Rainvelle's eyes lit up with excited anticipation at this new development. She uncrossed her slender arms and, smiling, pointed to the back of the room, to a far corner and the insignificant desk behind which sat that face from the past.

The trembling couldn't be stopped – ah, *Mon Dieu*, the lime squash!

A little of it ran down over his fingers. Hastily St-Cyr fumbled for a handkerchief. The carpet ... he'd damage it! Another Aubusson.

The girl was laughing.

Bonny didn't smile. The squat figure with its squat neck, wide head and face sat so still. The dark eyes were sad and empty and slanting slightly away from the nose to take him in. Not a word of greeting, just hatred seething behind that look.

At fifty-seven, Pierre Bonny was his senior by a little more than five years. The greying hair had receded well back of the broad, flat forehead. The heavy cheeks were tightened to single creases that ran straight up the middle of each cheek. An ox of a man. Round-shouldered, the dark blue-black serge suit new but the fit still too tight; the silk tie a wash of pearl-grey, pink and white. The neatly cornered handkerchief in the jacket pocket was white.

Bonny sucked on a tooth. Louis hadn't changed. He was still the prick he'd always been. 'So, my friend, what brings you to us, eh?'

There were three card-index drums to Bonny's left, a bank of them behind him. He was famous for them. His own little file on everyone and everything he thought of importance.

St-Cyr set the glass down on the desk. The urge to tip it over was strong but he resisted doing so.

One single droplet of blood marred the stiff white collar of that too-tight shirt.

Bonny had thrust his face at that girl upstairs. He'd grabbed her by the throat or blouse. There was blood on the cuffs of his shirt, but like Nicole de Rainvelle, he'd yet to notice this.

So many things surfaced in that instant. The years of being subordinate to him, of having to say good morning and have him look over the reports; the years of secretly questioning things that hadn't looked right even though a colleague had been behind them, then the accusations, the evidence that had been patiently and secretly gathered, finally the destruction of that colleague.

A file card, together with a head-and-shoulders photograph of the girl who'd called herself Christiane Baudelaire, was flattened beneath those pudgy hands.

'What have you to say for yourself?' asked St-Cyr with barely controlled fury.

'You're shaking in your fucking boots, Louis. Fill that pipe of yours. Sit down and shut up.'

'Never.'

Cops could breathe that way. 'Suit yourself. The cockerel still wants to crow, Henri. Shall we bring on the hen for him to shag?' he called out.

'Show him the photos,' came the answer from the other end of the room.

Bonny's look never varied. The widely spaced eyes beneath dark, greying brows took St-Cyr in again.

Christiane Baudelaire had visited one of the flea markets – the Saint-Ouen most probably. The photographer had caught her unawares, not once but many times over several weeks or perhaps even months.

Had she been trying to sell something? wondered St-Cyr. He had the idea they'd keep this from him, but that they'd have photographs of the items the girl had clutched in her coat pockets.

Small things. She'd been afraid.

A last photograph showed her naked on the floor of that room at the Hotel of the Silent Life. Quite obviously the rue Lauriston had managed to get there before Hermann and himself. Ah yes.

In the top right corner of the card-index file Bonny had written: '*A Big One.*'

'Seen enough?' he asked, not showing a ray of sunshine.

'Yes. Yes, I've seen enough.'

'You can take these with you. I've copies.'

'That won't be necessary.'

'Suit yourself. You always did think yourself better than the rest of us.'

The crooks that had been in the Sûreté and still were! 'Not better, my friend. Just more dedicated.'

Nicole de Rainvelle had joined them. Leaning over to expose even more cleavage, she plucked one of the photographs from among the litter.

'Take this one. Henri says you should. Me, I will escort you to the elevator.'

'I'd prefer the stairs. My partner, Hermann, has learned the hard way not to trust the elevators in establishments such as this.'

The stairs would be better. 'So be it then, Monsieur the Chief Inspector. Allow me . . .' she indicated the door, handing him the shabby hat he'd somehow forgotten.

'Next time you must wear your rubbers. We don't want you to catch a cold.'

Out in the hall she breathed in quickly, the excitement building. It was always like this, the smell of danger, the smell of blood. Of perfume. Of Mirage. Fingertips lingered lightly on his neck. His skin was hot. 'Adieu, my poor inspector. Please do not forget to come to see us soon.'

'Who was she?' He tossed his eyes to indicate the floor above.

He'd break to pieces. For a moment she was tempted to tell him. 'Just someone who wouldn't co-operate.'

'Why are you wearing that scent?'

'You know you should not ask such a thing of a woman such as myself.'

He shut his eyes. He clenched his fists, crumpling his hat and mangling the photograph. It was exquisite to see such pain. It made her body crave rapture. Henri would be pleased.

Gabrielle Arcuri, a *chanteuse* with a Russian past and an evident interest in Jean-Louis St-Cyr, had worn the perfume Mirage.

Giselle le Roy, the young prostitute from the rue Danton and the house of Madame Chabot, was Hermann Kohler's latest girlfriend.

With just such strings were detectives pulled and made to dance.

The butterfly pin was of silver, its enamelled surface smooth, the street ahead narrow.

Kohler sat alone in the car. Giselle would have liked this little thing, but the girl was nowhere to be found and he had the uneasy feeling he'd never see her alive again.

She'd not been in the Red Room at Madame Chabot's, not in the Easter Parade or in the Forest Glade with its battleship-grey bathtub that had been made over into a grotto pond with silk water lilies that seldom stayed in one place or held their shapes for very long.

She'd not been in there with someone else, not on her hands and knees or on her lovely back. Not in the schoolroom either, with the other young girls who played at being teenagers for older men who liked to think of things like that.

Giselle le Roy, age twenty-two, half Greek, half Midi French, a perfect hourglass when standing or bent over fake Empire tables in the Red Room, she throwing him that little look of hers. Stockings of black mesh or Prussian blue right up to her working parts; all the rest of her clothes gone. Damn it, where the hell was she?

Not in the Bal Saint-Séverin, the dancehall she liked to dream in, which was just around the corner from the house on the rue Danton and not too far to walk.

She hadn't been in the Odéon either, soaking up a tired bit of unwanted culture to get in out of the rain, nor in any of her three most-favoured movie theatres watching ancient reruns in hopes there'd be a banquet scene to drool over. Hell, the whole of Paris did that now and then. It was the only way they got a decent feed.

Kohler's fingers shook. She hadn't been happy to see him back in Paris. Come to think of it, she'd been damned worried and distracted.

Had she bolted from the car in fright? Had that been it?

The butterfly took wing and he cursed himself for being in love with man's worst enemy, a young and very vibrant hooker.

Gerda wouldn't like it, but then Gerda was back on the farm and this was Paris. Besides, he hadn't seen the wife in nearly two and a half years, not since his transfer here. Well, once a quick visit to settle her fears about the boys, but that had been so long ago, he couldn't remember exactly what she looked like any more. Besides, she'd only laugh at him and double her fists!

The butterfly lay in the crumbly mud on the floor beneath his shoes, the mud of Vouvray. Louis would be needing him. He would have given the Frog the butterfly along with the other things but the insect had become tangled in the lining of his pocket. Threads still clung to its tiny claws – did butterflies have claws?

The Fabergé wings played their greeny-blue iridescence on the mind when he turned it this way and that. The eyes sparkled as tiny, well-cut sapphires should. Giselle would have been quite taken with it, it would have gone with the colour of her eyes, her hair, her smile.

Thumbing the jet-black body, he heaved the sigh of a wounded detective who was getting just a little too old for this sort of thing. Records had turned up nothing. Only acid had greeted his request. The photos of the corpses hadn't yet been sent over. They'd virtually nothing to go on.

The same with the operator of the carousel, but there he had the feeling that once they'd tied a name to that one, they'd find his file missing.

When gangsters ruled, they always cleaned the nest.

Christiane Baudelaire had been murdered between 9.00 and 9.30 last night, Thursday; the mackerel at about the same time the night before. And very early today, or late last night, a Wehrmacht corporal had been killed in the rue Polonceau. And now thirty hostages had been taken.

A priest had reported that last murder. Somehow they'd have to get stays of execution and deportation. They couldn't have potential witnesses vanishing before they should. Besides, thirty was far too many for a lousy corporal who probably shouldn't have been there in the first place. It implied that Boemelburg had been told precisely how many to choose, and that could only mean Oberg had known the exact number of coins in that room and had said 'Or else.'

The gear shift was sticky, the Benzedrine still hammering in his veins. He'd best be careful. Taken with alcohol, that stuff didn't go down so well. He wasn't as young as he used to be, and he wasn't getting any younger. Crime didn't pay. He should have been a farmer like his father and grandfather before him.

'Up to my ears in shit, no matter what!' he snorted, goosing the Citroën. He'd find the Church of Saint Bernard in Montmartre, he'd hear what the good father who reported the corporal's body had to say.

But had he forgotten something to do with that dead girl? Had Giselle's disappearance made him forgetful?

All Germans were tourists. To treat them any differently was to admit they existed for purposes other than tourism and that they wouldn't eventually go away.

Father Eugène Delacroix rubbed his hands in anticipation of payment. 'The chapel of our patron saint lies on the hallowed ground' – he ducked his head to indicate the very place – 'of the much smaller edifice that was first erected here, monsieur, in the twelfth century.'

Kohler took the bandy-legged little bastard in. Seventy-two, if a day, with narrowed, watchful eyes, a grey brush cut and a grizzled beard that showed the severe shortage of razor blades in bloodied nicks and bits of sticking-plaster.

'Listen, you ragged little bag of bones, your history's a little too old for me.'

Delacroix ignored the warning. 'In 1852, monsieur, the Baron Lepic laid the first stone even as the nuns of the Josephine mixed the Holy mortar.'

A heavy door slammed. The priest went on anyway. 'The Monsignor Christophe, the Bishop of Soissons himself, has consecrated this house of God not three years later, monsieur. Three!' as if it had been Rome itself and built in such a shortness of time.

'Father, I'm here on business.'

The distant steps had grown nearer but now paused. 'What sort of business?' shot the priest, raising his voice to sound a warning.

'Murder,' breathed the detective.

Kohler moved swiftly. He hit the vestry door and shrieked, 'GESTAPO, FREEZE!'

The novice flattened himself against the far wall and went as white as a sheet.

'Kohler of the Gestapo, my fine young sackcloth. A few questions or would you prefer the ashes?'

The old priest came to stand in the doorway. 'It's all right, David. You may go now. Do the silver. See if we haven't enough wafers – perhaps you could break them in half. Yes, yes, that would be best. The shortages,' he clucked his ancient tongue. 'Leave the wine alone. I'll take care of it.'

'Just a minute. No one leaves until I'm done.'

The vestry door closed. The young priest couldn't seem to pull himself off the wall. The older one scratched the three-day growth, opening a wound and flaking off a bit of sticking-plaster that wanted to go somewhere else. 'David, *sit* down. It's all right. God will protect you.'

Kohler knew he ought to ask, why he needed God to protect him. 'Which of you reported the body of that corporal?'

The novice swallowed hard, glancing to the elder priest for reassurance. Receiving none, he said, 'I did. It was me,' and, shutting his eyes in a grimace, thrust out his arms for the handcuffs.

Well now, how about that? 'Start talking. We'll see about the bracelets later.'

'One of our parishioners called David in, Inspector. Me, I was indisposed at the time.'

'Drunk and sleeping it off, eh? Let him sing his own song, Father. Yours is too rich for the blood.'

'Monsieur, your people have taken thirty souls from my parish. Is that not rich enough for *your* blood?'

'Stung, eh? Let him tell me himself. I'll get to you soon enough.'

The young priest was now sitting on the bench, wringing his hands in despair. 'It's all over, Father. I knew they'd come for me.'

'David, God will guide you. Put your trust in Him.'

The tears were very real, the face was pinched, the forehead high and narrow so that the rampart nose gave steep access to the close-set blue eyes and thin, fair hair.

A cigarette might help. Kohler shook one out, only to have the old priest accept it on the novice's behalf. 'I've warned him, Inspector. It's a penance. These days the young should not smoke. It's bad for the lungs and too expensive.'

Father David's voice was toneless. 'I found the body in the

courtyard. Someone had dragged it in from the street. They'd stolen his boots and socks but had left the rest.'

There, he'd said it at last and God would have to answer for him.

'Where had he been shot?'

'Right between the eyes. It . . . it was not so pleasant to look at, monsieur.'

Fair enough. 'How long had he been dead, do you think?'

The novice shrugged.

They'd find out soon enough. 'Who told you where the body was?'

'M . . .'

'The person was taken away in this morning's *rafle*. To the rue du Cherche-Midi, Inspector. I have only just discovered this.'

Kohler ran his eyes over Delacroix. 'There's nothing wrong with your tongue, Father. Is it that this one might choke if he used his own?'

The old priest gave a deferential nod. 'So be it. Let God decide.'

'Madame Ouellette. It . . . it was in her courtyard. She . . . she is the one who told me of the body.'

'Her husband, our horse butcher, is in a prisoner-of-war camp in Germany, Inspector. David, he is young.'

'I think I get the picture. Come on, son. Come and show me.'

'I'll come too, just in case you have need of my tongue.'

They were a pair, these two, and as sure as that God of theirs had made little green apples, this Madame Ouellette hadn't been carted off this morning. She and the young priest had been up to something and hadn't heard a thing in that courtyard.

With the two of them hurrying before him like rooks, Kohler went through to the back of the church and from there stepped on to the rue Saint-Luc, a short bit of nothing.

The house with its shop and golden horse's head above the door was nothing much either. The shelves were bare. Madame Ouellette didn't take to butchering and when he saw the woman, he instantly knew it wasn't just because of the shortage of horsemeat.

She had a child at the breast and that kid could not possibly have been the husband's unless their God had made it by mail.

The woman's hair was long and brown. The doe eyes were full of alarm and likely to beg forgiveness.

Apparently the penance didn't just extend to cigarettes but to

76

twenty-six-year-old war widows with earthy minds and needs below the waist.

'Marie, you must forgive us the intrusion,' managed the young priest. 'The Inspector is here to find out what he can about the body of that German soldier.'

Satan had many forms. The breast was being clasped by the greedy tyke and the milk was dribbling down its little chin. Father David brushed a fond hand over his child and in that instant, Kohler knew he'd witnessed a rare and resigned bravery.

The old priest had let the young one continue in his priestly duties even though he'd broken his vows on the altar of this one's bed. It was that or forced labour. Of just such things was Paris made.

'You have thirty, my friend. Try to spare us this one.'

The eyes of the old priest revealed the bond he felt for his protégé. Kohler nodded. 'Just tell me everything you can about the corporal, most specifically who might have killed him.'

'It was not a Resistance killing, monsieur. Of this we are certain, but,' Father Eugène gave a shrug, 'you may choose to think we would not say otherwise.'

'If not the Resistance, then who?'

The child was switched to the other tank, the woman not bothering to cover either of them, her dark eyes watchful now.

It was the young priest who said, 'Someone who wanted the authorities to take hostages and who didn't care how many your people took.'

'The killer of that girl?' asked Kohler incredulously.

The old priest nodded. 'Word was left on my doorstep, monsieur, that the Resistance had nothing to do with the killing.'

From the folds of his cassock he drew an envelope and, opening it, handed the Gestapo the note. 'Read for yourself, since you are one of the few who bother to speak our language.'

Look not to the Resistance for this one. Try the rue Lauriston and if not them, then the rue de Villejust. Those bastards must have killed the girl as well.

'Show me where you found him. Tell me how he was.'

The coins had been scattered about the girl's room but one had been dipped in blood and left in the centre of her forehead as a warning.

Louis should have got clear of the rue Lauriston by now. That left the rue de Villejust, the Intervention-Referat, the shock troops of the avenue Foch, who used them when they didn't want to become involved.

The dead corporal had just taken on another meaning, but had he been killed for what he knew or simply because he'd happened along at the wrong time and had, perhaps, called out in alarm, in a drunken stupor?

Blood marked the paving-stones near a side-entrance to Madame Ouellette's house and empty shop. 'I thought he was drunk,' said the woman. 'I didn't know what to do, so I went to find Father David.'

Even now she'd cling to calling the young priest that. And at the height of passion too? wondered Kohler.

'I touched him. I knew he was dead, monsieur. I . . . I went to fetch Father Eugène,' said Father David.

'Did the corporal have anything with him?'

The three of them exchanged rapid glances. The baby had to be burped and brought up a mouthful which hit the paving-stones.

'A small thing in his fist, monsieur. A dragonfly.'

'A brooch,' said the woman, finally thinking to cover herself while at the same time wiping the child's lips with a corner of her blouse.

'A dragonfly,' breathed Kohler. 'Was it like this?'

They studied the butterfly. They hid their thoughts. It was Father Eugène who said, 'Madame Ouellette has it in her house, monsieur, because I gave it to her for safe keeping and the authorities who came to remove the body were far too busy to ask, just as were those who removed the hostages.'

'You were there. I saw you,' accused the woman.

'Only as an observer. That's not our department. We're strictly murder.'

'Marie, please go and find the dragonfly. Here, let me hold Jean-Guy,' said Father David.

The child had the young priest's eyes and hair, though both might darken with age.

'God help you if the husband comes home,' breathed Kohler. 'Don't try to leave town until I'm done with you or I'll hound you to the ends of the earth. Keep quiet about this too. Don't even confide it in that God of yours. The Corsicans of the rue de Villejust and the other boys of the rue Lauriston both have direct pipelines to Heaven.'

Father Eugène knew only too well what he meant.

Louis would be intrigued. A dragonfly and a butterfly. The

poor Frog would be pounding the beat, trying to figure things out and biting the bullet with good reason!

'The Préfet has a cold, monsieur. He extends the regrets but suggests your health is foremost in his mind and that he would not wish for you to catch it.'

There was no sense in arguing with the housekeeper. To ask for help had been a mistake, an act of cowardice. Talbotte had the shutters closed.

'Extend to him my sincere condolences, madame, and tell him, please, that Chief Inspector Jean-Louis St-Cyr has paid his respects. From now on I wear my muffler and gloves, eh, to keep the influenza at bay.'

All of which made the woman toss her head before closing the door in his face.

'Horse hamburg steeped in bouillon is supposed to be good, madame!' he called out for the sheer pleasure of it. 'I always knew the Préfecture was a draughty place. Beware the currents of air, madame. Keep him away from the rat-holes!'

Like those of the rue Lauriston and the avenue Foch! Currents of air that would blow over a dead girl's naked body or brush a carousel into motion.

The Préfet's house was one of two that overlooked the boulevard du Palais on the Île de la Cité. Behind it rose the massive stone edifice of a former barracks, the Préfecture. He ought to see about the carousel licence. He ought to force them into doing something.

Talbotte *had* sent his chief coroner to the carousel. That *was* something. But now the draught was too much. Word must have got round that St-Cyr and Kohler were dead.

Shunning the quays, he tried to find a bit of solace in the Flower Market nestled between the Préfecture, the Tribunal of Commerce, and the Hôtel-Dieu. The stalls were empty. Few people were about and those that were appeared nervous.

He touched the canary in his pocket. He remembered the coin in the centre of that girl's forehead . . . a warning, ah yes. *Maudit*!

Beyond the mist of condensation there were a few tired poinsettias in an otherwise empty shop. Distraught, St-Cyr stared at the plants. Where once there would have been a riot of blooms, a jungle, there were now only these and a single rubber plant that should have stayed at home.

Henri Lafont was capable of the utmost cruelty yet loved with the passion of an innocent child, all types of flowers. He had them in his office – there'd been hothouse begonias on a corner of that desk. White ones. A mass of red roses over by the windows. A lemon tree.

Every day the flowers were changed no matter the season. Orchids were a favourite. Orchids and women like Nicole de Rainvelle.

He pushed open the shop door.

'M'sieur?' asked the startled reed in glasses who was warming his hands by furiously rubbing them with cat's fur.

'Ah yes. I'd like a cactus. The pricklier the better.'

Alphonse Bilodeau didn't like the look in this one's eyes. Taxes – were they after him again for the taxes?

'A cactus?'

'Yes. *Cleistocactus strausii* perhaps.'

'Something with spines. These days that's about all we have.'

Bilodeau motioned him to follow. Behind the shop, which was less than three metres wide and four in length, a thin partition separated the living quarters, some three metres by one and complete with larder, hotplate, cold-water tap, sink, clothes rack, chamber pot, et cetera, et cetera.

'My apartment,' said the florist apologetically. 'These days . . .'

'The Thirties too, and the Twenties,' said the detective, taking it all in. How in the name of God had he managed to sleep and cook under that thing without hurting himself?

The pot was huge, the main column of the cactus bent where the ceiling had given it no more room. A secondary column leaned directly over the unmade bed. Another scratched the wall; a third caressed the photograph in glass of a dancer who'd forgotten her clothes and had shyly turned her back to the camera.

'*Cereus Peruvianus*,' enthused St-Cyr with admiration. 'It's perfect, my friend. Perfect!'

'You can't mean that. You're just saying it. You *flics* are all the same! None of you buy a thing but you all come here . . .'

'Please, I did not hear that, monsieur. If I buy, I pay.'

'You can't want my Titan.'

He'd even named it. 'Oh but I do.'

'It'll take four men to move it,' seethed cat's fur. 'Men are in short supply these days and costly.'

A real tiger. St-Cyr drew out the black leather billfold his mother had given him thirty years ago. 'I have little time to negotiate. Here is three hundred francs. Deliver it to Number 93 the rue Lauriston, and see that you do or I will come back to haunt you.'

Number 93 the rue Lauriston ... 'I will need the vélo-taxi, monsieur.'

'Keep it warm. Enclose a card. Say it's from Louis. Use two vélos if necessary but don't break it. Me, I want this thing just as it is.'

He pulled out a further hundred-franc bill. 'Does stroking cat's fur really help to make the hands warm?'

The man tucked the finances away. 'The plants used to, but now . . .'

St-Cyr thought to ask him if it had been his cat but left it unsaid. There was no sense in pushing his luck. 'Use a couple of blankets to keep the cactus warm in transit. If anyone bitches, tell them you're doing a little job for the Sûreté as it used to be.'

Bilodeau watched the cactus-buyer walk away. There was a briskness, a looking-up to see his God perhaps. A smile, a wave to the heavens. All the world was crazy these days. Cat's fur! Of course it helped to keep one warm. How the hell else could half the population of Paris exist and half the cats have died if not to be eaten?

Locking the shop, he prepared to go and negotiate the help, but the cactus-buyer came rushing back.

'Talbotte – you know him?'

The Préfet, the sourest bastard in France! 'Of course, m'sieur.'

There was one poinsettia that had lost all but two of its leaves. 'Send this to him. Gift-wrapped! Say, I hope you're feeling better.'

'A coffee without milk or sugar, please.'

A polite one at last, a man of great sensitivity.

St-Cyr threw his hat on to a chair, then dumped his overcoat on top of it. Pipe, tobacco and matches were arranged. The view was suitable, the water of that grey-brown shade it always seemed to acquire in winter. Silt from Troyes, from Châtillon-sur-Seine, from upstream anyway, and more murders, rapes, muggings – crimes of passion than he'd care to remember.

There were no barges and the river, with but a few old men breaking the law along the quays to fish, looked desolate and empty.

He wondered if he'd ever see it from freedom's eyes again. In the autumn of 1940 the Germans had taken the barges and the larger of the tour boats for the invasion of England that had never materialized.

Russia would be their nemesis as it had been Napoleon's. Winter was everyone's curse in these wretched latitudes; ice and snow, the punishment rain had forgotten.

The tobacco was good – pre-war and Belgian, a gift from Hermann, for whom he could not, even with all his inner rage against what had happened to France, find in his heart of hearts anything but a wary affection. But would Hermann be forced into choosing loyalties again, as he himself had been forced?

It was a particular punishment God had laid on detectives these days.

The coffee wasn't ersatz, and the taste brought tears to his eyes. Ah Mon Dieu, what were they missing?

He knew the waiter would be watching for some sign and that he'd have seen the cup hesitate and been held out as if a chalice of holy wine or water.

Nothing more was needed, no further demonstration of appreciation.

The spires of the Church of Saint-Gervais-Saint-Protais were just visible, submerged and set against the ramparts of the rooftops. The Hôtel de Ville flew the German flag of course, but if one did not look that way it was almost as it once had been, except for the absence of the barges.

The table was reasonably private. The canary would cause some notice but the desire for a quiet think was too much.

Little birds were among the hardest to mount. This one had been done by an expert who knew both taxidermy and his birds. The feathers were all in place. There'd been a few bald spots – all birds had them. These spots had been carefully hidden as they would have been in life.

The wires that held the skeleton and filled out the shape in unsupported parts had been implanted properly. There'd have been no flesh left to putrefy after mounting. The bird smelled clean but of lavender, and he wondered then if it hadn't been kept in some other bureau drawer for years.

Taxidermists were not having an easy time of it these days. Mementos of household pets were not in fashion but consigned instead to the stew pot and the fur made into gloves and hats or used to rub oneself to keep warm.

There'd been an elastic band around the bird, a reminder

perhaps, something with which to hold a little note that was now absent?

The possibilities were there. Always questions and more questions.

The choker of pearls was very fine, from the Belle Époque, that period before the last war. There were six strands of perfectly matched pearls, five millimetres in diameter, all of them curved outwards from a hinged plaque of silver on which were opposing poppies that had lost their petals. The fruit of the opium poppy? he wondered, alarmed, only to remember the avant-garde of that period had often played with it to their detriment and disgrace. The stems of the poppies were sinuously curved and folded in upon each other, though juxtaposed so that the seed heads faced away from each other at the top of the plaque.

Why had the girl had it in her room if not to wear when her clothes were absent, if not to remind some successful middle-class roué of his daughter or his grandmother perhaps? It took all types and a young woman's body usually brought out the worst in most men.

The single strand of pearls was of an even finer quality but much older. Perfectly matched and sized, the stones began with one superb pearl of five millimetres in diameter and then diminished to those of less than two. It made one think of the South Seas, of native girls and cannibals, of drums and rum and firelight and sweat in the night, of mosquitoes, of so many things.

The emerald earrings were indeed from South or Central America, Peru or Colombia perhaps. Very, very old, taken from some tomb perhaps.

Had all the pieces of jewellery belonged to the same person? Had they been from some legacy to the girl who had called herself Christiane Baudelaire, or had Madame Minou's Monsieur Antoine brought them to her?

Pierre Bonny's card-index file on the girl had held the notation, '*A Big One*' – lots and lots of loot to be gained. Ah yes.

The crumpled photograph showed the girl anxious and yet entirely unaware that she was being followed. She'd been in a hurry and had turned away from a cluttered table in the flea market, perhaps to see if the next bus had come in, and if she could possibly catch it.

St-Cyr glanced at his watch. Ah Mon Dieu, it was almost four and he had one further thing to do before the morgue.

With the Benzedrine still floating around inside him, he felt as though he could go on for another forty-eight hours.

The canary lay atop the counter beneath which a lynx from Canada held a Hungarian partridge in its jaws while clinging to the branch of a birch tree.

The taxidermist, M Édouard Verdun, was thin and lofty and not inclined to inspect the work of others, no matter how good. It had been a long time since this one had paid him a visit. A dog that time, a pink ticket for a beagle bitch that had been left for mounting in the spring of 1937, the 15th of April to be exact. Number 603. A wealthy widow in her eighties from Chartres, a customer for years.

The woman had been murdered in her bath and the Sûreté had never paid up. He still had the dog in the window.

'Look, I know all about it, eh?' grimaced St-Cyr. 'I put it in my report, an absolute recommendation that the estate be made to pay you, but', he shrugged, 'such things take time.'

Verdun drew himself up. 'Patience is not bought with words, Inspector.'

'It's Chief Inspector.'

'No matter. As I was saying . . .'

'Yes, yes, get on with it.'

'Do you want my help or not?' snapped Verdun, defying answer until an apologetic nod was received. 'These days no one hunts or fishes. There are no safaris, Inspector. Only German generals bring me their pets.'

St-Cyr ducked his head subserviently. Why was it that taxidermists – this one in particular – always engendered a whining servility?

The shop was full of lions and tigers, the heads of zebras and Thomson's gazelles, their skins, their pelts and more of them, all left to be picked up later. After the war, after the Occupation, or not at all. Out on the rue des Lions a few bicycles passed by and then the staff car of a German general, but it continued on and he heard the sigh of disappointment the taxidermist gave.

'Look, I will personally see that you get paid for that other job.'

The slender fingers hesitated as they delicately felt the bird. 'Five thousand francs, with interest.'

Ah Mon Dieu, the pinch was excruciating! 'Tell me who did this one.'

'First, the consultation fee is one hundred francs, Inspector. Out of necessity our prices have risen.'

In the name of Jesus, why must God do this to him? St-Cyr smoothed the bill but continued to hold on to it. Verdun moved the canary out of the detective's reach. 'Usually I can tell whose work it is – *if* he's been in Paris and is long established. Usually, too, there is some sign. A tiny initial on one of the claws perhaps. Birds like this aren't easy, Inspector. If one takes pride in one's work, one likes to leave a little something.'

St-Cyr was impressed. 'Like the hallmarks on old silver?'

'Ah yes, exactly. The set of the eyes is another way; also, did he use stock eyes and hand-paint them, or take the trouble to have them custom-made?'

There was no stopping him now.

'Then, too, is the body padded out with well-chopped tow? Cotton wool is no good, Inspector, and this one didn't use anything but the best.'

He put the bird down. 'Without opening it up, I can't say more. There's no mark. The work's excellent – so good I have to feel the twinges of envy. Was he not in business here in Paris?'

Meaning he hadn't been. 'Why would there have been a heavy elastic band around it?'

Verdun shrugged. 'To remind the owner of something or to hold its ticket, but we would not do such a thing, nor do I think this one would either. No, someone else must have put the elastic there, someone who didn't know, or didn't appreciate fully, the quality of the workmanship, the hours, the labour of love, the . . .'

'Good! Enough! So, for now that's sufficient.' St-Cyr swept the bird away and started for the door.

'You can leave it here. A thought might come. I might be able to sell it for you. I have a general who is very partial to canaries.'

The pavement was narrow. There were two women coming towards him. 'What general?' he asked, darting back.

'He's actually not a general. He wears the blue uniform.'

'Luftwaffe? Their airforce? Come, come, I'm in a hurry.'

Verdun knew he'd missed another 100 francs. 'It has the anchor. Their navy.'

'The Kriegsmarine?'

'Stationed in Paris. The Hotel Lutétia, I think. A moment, please, Inspector. Yes . . . yes, here it is.'

He held up a white card. 'The Vice Admiral Guenther Heinrich von Lion.'

Von Lion in the street of lions! Ah Mon Dieu ... **The Hotel Lutétia** was the headquarters of the Abwehr, the German military intelligence service – arch enemies of the SS and their Sicherheitsdienst, the SD, the secret service of the SS over on the avenue Foch!

The *pissoir* was rank. A plugged drain gave fjord to the yellow slime that had collected. A few cigarette butts, smoked down to their last toothpick, floated about giving tendrils of nicotine. Some bastard had jerked off against the flaking iron of the trough.

The Abwehr ... the Abwehr ... the Sicherheitsdienst ... A canary.

'Louis, what the hell's happened to you?' The morgue was freezing.

'Me? I have just lost my lunch. The Abwehr, Hermann. The canary ... It's just possible our Monsieur Antoine is an Abwehr agent.'

'Jesus, you'd better read this then. It was left on the doorstep of the head juju man up at the Church of St Bernard, Father Eugène Delacroix.'

Louis read the thing, the pallor deepening as the blood drained completely away. 'Is Christian Masuy also involved?' It was a cry, the bleat of a goat in trouble.

Masuy was also the Belgian, Georges Delfanne, who had invented for the Gestapo and their French counterpart the infamous torture of the bathtub.

'Paul Carbone is enough, Louis. He and Lafont have been at each other's throats for years, or hadn't you heard, seeing as you were the one who told me of their feud?'

Carbone, a notorious Corsican gangster, worked out of Number 48 rue de Villejust, the Intervention-Referat that was mentioned in the priest's note.

'But ... Carbone and Lafont both work independently for the avenue Foch, Hermann, not the Abwehr any more?'

'This thing goes round and round, Louis.'

'Why the Abwehr's interest in the canary, Hermann, unless the girl had been about to sell out to them?'

There were gangsters upon gangsters interlayered with the many layers of the Gestapo, the SS and the Abwehr too. What treasures one didn't get, another took, and quickly. Each was jealous of the others; Henri Lafont *did* hate Paul Carbone with a passion, and the Carbone gang *was* the leading edge of the Intervention-Referat.

'Let's have a look at the bodies, Louis. Something might have turned up.'

There were two empty pallets beside the three occupied by the girl, the mackerel and the Wehrmacht corporal.

'Are those for us?' asked St-Cyr. 'Have we stepped into a vendetta, Hermann?'

'I wouldn't want to bet against it, Louis. The shit's always deepest in the centre of the sewage lagoon.'

'Then take a look at this. Lafont's latest pigeon insisted I bring it along for company.'

St-Cyr handed him the crumpled photograph. 'Search the faces of the crowd, Hermann. See if the mackerel isn't among them, or the other one. Me, I'm open to all possibilities but must take an immediate look at the girl's ears.'

The photo was grainy and the girl anxious. Both hands were in the pockets of her overcoat. The collar was up. She wore a kerchief and a frown. A nice kid, a kid out to flog the loot she'd stolen from her grandmother's jewellery box? Was that it?

That and forged Roman gold coins.

Kohler fingered the butterfly which had become entangled in a death's grip with the dragonfly.

At peace, the mackerel didn't look pleasant. They'd had to break the rigor just to lie him on the stretcher. The face was still frozen in its hideous grin. He'd bad teeth and snot in his nose. Snot and dried blood.

The girl was standing in front of a stall on which were arrayed the leavings of several lives – books, lamps, dishes. He thought of that room and the little things he'd seen there. The vase of artificial flowers, the porcelain figurines.

In profile, she looked as if she'd had more taste – wealthy perhaps, but down on her luck. Of breeding anyway, the brows, the forehead and the eyes told him that. The way she stood and looked over her shoulder.

A girl who had dyed her hair even in the warmer climates.

There were several faces in the crowd – men, women, even a child, a baby in a German corporal's arms. A baby . . .

Kohler bent over the jerk. Powder-burns tinged the skin around the bullet hole. The eyes were closed, the grin still there as if he'd only just said, 'So, what else is new?'

Kohler soaked up the photograph, concentrating on the child and on the corporal's face.

It was him all right. Grinning then as he was grinning now. A blocky, square-jawed Pomeranian. Aged thirty-two to thirty-five and still a corporal. A randy bastard of medium height and stocky build. Two small scars on the right cheek – a fight probably. Brown hair and a dick that would have made a schoolgirl scream.

'Louis . . . Louis, I think I've been had.'

'Hermann, what is it? Can't you see I need to be left alone?'

With a corpse! 'Is this one the father of the child I saw this morning drawing on its mother's breast?'

The Frog left the girl to move swiftly between the pallets.

'The young priest, Louis. I . . . I thought he was the father.'

'Most priests are.'

Hermann shook his head. 'The father of that.' The child.

'Perhaps you'd better explain things, Hermann.'

The insects were tangled but when separated, the dragonfly found its rightful owner.

There were three blood spots on the corporal's left hand where the brooch had dug in its feet at the moment of death. One wing was slightly bent, as were the feelers, but with these an attempt had been made to straighten them.

'The corporal could simply have been minding the child, Hermann, while the mother made a purchase?'

'Then what's the mackerel doing over there?'

It was true. The mackerel was watching the girl from the vantage of another stall. He was screened by a man in his sixties and a woman in her forties.

Had the old priest been completely fooled by the young one, or had Delacroix known of it all along and lied with such dexterity?

'Concentrate on the mackerel, Hermann. Did they bring his little finger?' asked St-Cyr.

'You know I don't like this sort of thing.'

'But you'll do it anyway. Here, give me the photograph for safe keeping. The insects also.'

St-Cyr moved back to the girl. The ears weren't pierced so she could not possibly have worn the earrings. Perhaps she had not worn the pearls either? he thought, wanting desperately to be alone with her.

An attendant in a blood-smeared labcoat and filthy cap cracked a grin. 'You two chicken-pluckers back?' he crowed. 'Ah, my fines, she's a nice bit of stuffing, eh? A virgin until the moment of death. Who would have guessed?'

A virgin . . . 'That's impossible,' stormed Kohler. He'd show the –

'Hermann, wait! Perhaps it's not so impossible. The autopsy, please. Quickly, quickly, my friend, if you value your life.'

'In this place? You've got to be kidding. I only work here because I have to.'

'You're Féloux. I knew your father. He worked at the old place over on the Île de la Cité.'

'The autopsies have gone to the Préfet. My lips are sealed and no amount of money will open them.'

'But you've just said she was a virgin.'

'That much I saw for myself when they first brought her in. Torn like a rapist's souvenir.'

'So much for privacy. When the dead are carted here they become common property.'

The mackerel had been one of the *durs*, one of the hard ones, but had chosen not to wear the three dots in a row on the backs of the middle three fingers of the left hand.

Instead, he had the five points of the dice tattooed on the web of skin between the thumb and the forefinger of the right hand.

' "All alone between four walls", Hermann. This one has spent time in solitary.'

'Then Records might have a file on him, and if not them, the Santé or some other can.'

'Why would Madame Minou think it was her son who'd been murdered?'

'Aren't most mothers like that?'

The attendant watched in silence as the two cows chewed their cud. A dope- or tobacco-sniffer, the *dur*; the girl a virgin before she'd been taken; and a corporal who'd received the bullet but who continued to smile as if from satisfaction.

The girl was in good company; comfort even after death.

'Louis, it's suicide for us.'

'Hermann, it must be done. I need time with that girl. The mackerel is nothing; the corporal little else, but she can tell us what we need to know.'

'The dead can't talk.'

Hermann would never understand the need for silent communication with the victim or victims. 'In their own way they can. Now put your foot to the floor. Me, I'm getting sleepy. A few more minutes . . . Please do not crash into anything with my car.'

'Your car! You French don't own anything any more! Besides, you never had the ownership of this one. The Sûreté did.'

The Kommandantur was on the place de l'Opéra. The bicycles and vélo-taxis scattered at the Citroën's sound. Kohler clipped a couple, sending shrieks into the crowd.

Darkness was descending on the city.

Von Schaumburg, well past retirement and a Prussian of the old school, hated two things more than interruptions. The French and the Gestapo!

'It's on your head, Louis. Just remember it wasn't my idea.'

Champagne flowed. Old Shatter Hand himself, Rock of Bronze to his staff, was glad to see them.

Kohler's sagging jowls and shrapnel scars were marred by one half-closed eye and the nicest duelling scar a rawhide whip could give.

St-Cyr looked pale.

'Gentlemen, your health.'

The Krug went down like broken ice. The orderly refilled their glasses then, at a toss of the General's hand, left the bottle and evaporated.

'So, gentlemen, two more murders for you to solve, and the death of one of my corporals.'

He offered cigarettes. Taller, bigger in every way than Hermann, he had the sternness and expeditious mannerisms a general should have. The grey hair was close-cropped and bristly, the eyes were very blue.

No fool, von Schaumburg knew they were on his side, though it would cost them dearly. Vouvray had left its stamp on them.

'You will want my order staying the execution of the hostages pending your questioning them and the outcome of your investigation.'

He'd had it all figured out. There'd been no need to even ask.

'Corporal Schraum has been a burden for some time, gentlemen. Frankly, I am not sad to see him depart this world, but I must be satisfied as to who was responsible for his death. I can't have our men being killed in the streets. You do understand?'

The look was one of apology, a puzzle. The champagne burst against the roof of the brain, keeping the eyes open but only just.

St-Cyr drew in a breath. 'General, might I ask if you would

order also, that the bodies not be released for burial until we request it?'

The nod was curt. The explanation followed. 'Schraum had relatives in the Reich. Some minor SS bigwig, the Gauleiter of Stralsund, his home town. Berlin are demanding retribution and full military honours. There's even talk of awarding him a medal.'

For one whose horse had fallen so low, the General had taken it pretty well. A medal...

'Refill our glasses, Kohler. So, gentlemen, the Oberkommando der Wehrmacht and myself find ourselves in debt to two detectives from unlikely sides and I must ask that you again offer the army your assistance. Kohler, you will be excused your affiliation with the Gestapo; St-Cyr, you will make sure he behaves himself and that I have the answers I need to justify the stays of execution. This office, gentlemen, is at your service.'

'They all know more than we do, Louis.'

'Especially the dead ones.'

'You want a room at the Boccador? No one will mind.'

'After what that one just said about the Gestapo? No, my friend. I will sleep at my house in my own bed.'

'Enjoy the rats. If I see Gabi, I'll tell her the deal's off.'

'It has to be, Hermann. As in war, so in sleep; let the warmth of valour offer its slender reprieve. I can't have her hurt.'

'Seven will come too quickly.'

'Not soon enough. The sifting must begin, Hermann. Let's start with the carousel, eh? and go on from there.'

'I'll pick you up.'

'No, I would like to walk over. It's not far from the house and it will give me time to think.'

They parted at the foot of the rue Laurence Savart, and he walked up the street alone.

The boys were playing soccer in the dwindling light but when they saw him trudging wearily towards the house, they stopped to watch.

He waved a tired, sad hand. Hervé Desrochers said, 'Send him the ball.'

Antoine Courbet, who lived across the street from Number 3, said, 'No. The explosion smashed all the windows in our house. My father would beat me.'

'First they took his car, his beautiful big black Citroën,' said Dédé Labelle, whose mother took in laundry and did odd jobs.

'Then they took his revolver and only let him have it *after* the shooting had started,' said Guy Vachon, whose sister had been brought home from the streets by that one, and whose father had then miraculously found a very good job in a garage.

'Then they demoted him to inspector with the consequent loss of wages.'

'And killed his wife and little son.'

'*And* blew up the front of his house, instead of letting the Resistance do it for them!'

'Give him the ball. He looks as if he needs it.'

'He'll *never* see that we get our windows back. My father says he's not long for this world and that the Resistance are bound to get him the next time, if only God would give him the smile.'

Dédé dropped the ball and kicked it. They all watched in silence as it hit the road and started to bounce and roll towards the detective.

His vision blurred, St-Cyr missed the kick and they knew then that he must be really sad and very preoccupied with another case.

'I hope he doesn't start playing that horn of his,' said Guy Vachon. 'My mother says he will.'

'His *euphonium*,' said Antoine Courbet. 'It drove the first wife to madness. She had to leave and married a railway worker from Orléans.'

'It was the crime, the long nights without passion,' said Hervé Desrochers. 'A woman requires regular thrusting to keep her happy.'

'That's why the last wife took up with a Kraut.'

'A house without a woman is a house without a soul.'

'Or bread in the oven.'

'Or buns.'

The detective retrieved the ball and worked it up the street towards them. He seemed to falter, to stumble – was he a little drunk perhaps? – but then he had a burst of energy, showed real skill, and took the ball through them all before collapsing into sleep.

'We can't leave him there. Someone might steal his wallet.'

'I'll get my father. You get your uncle. *They'll* put him to bed.'

'He's not drunk. He's just tired.'

'Detectives need their sleep.'

4

Mirrors turned, lights flashed, stallions galloped madly. He tried to leap aside. A rabbit rushed him, bumping a shoulder and screaming: 'Why don't you look where you're going, St-Cyr? I've got to hurry . . . hurry . . .'

A rooster was right behind, then an elephant that lifted its trunk in the stampede, then a lion, the music blaring – trapped, he was trapped! He'd be trampled to death!

Sprays of blood marred a sequined sky-blue sheath. Everywhere there were swastikas, everywhere flames, and through the flames the faces of the crowd.

The harnesses were bright, the music ribald, playing high, playing low as the animals rose and fell and the corpse of the woman of the sheath came round, she naked now and riding a camel. Her skin pale, her eyes wide and empty, she hanging on to the pommel as the beast kicked and bucked. He thought he knew her, thought he should cry out a warning to her.

She threw an arm back, her pale breasts tightening, rising, falling . . . blood . . . blood all over her chest and slender waist. Not the girl of the room . . . Not that girl . . .

Blue harness, red harness, green and gold . . . the sound of coins intruding . . . hundreds of them being flung about, the naked girl now reaching for them as she raced around and around, the floor rising and falling under her. She beckoning to him now, her long legs spread, her knees up, the eyes, those violet eyes . . . The beckoning becoming a plea for help as someone . . . someone came at her with a –

'Watch out!' he cried in panic and blinked. His heart was pounding.

Something had awakened him. Lafont? Had Oberg sent the bastards so soon?

'Gabrielle . . . Gabrielle . . . Ah, Mon Dieu, you're safe! I had thought ... Listen, please. You and me, it would never work. This place ... the life I must lead.'

She got up from where she'd been sitting on the edge of the bed. The house was a shambles. Jean-Louis had a good day's growth of whiskers and crusts in the corners of his eyes. The covers were thick and up to his chin. He'd a knitted toque on his head and earmuffs as well as gloves. 'You'll find me at the club if you need me.'

'Yes ... Yes, of course. The club.' He wet his throat.

She tossed her beautiful head, tossed the mane of hair that was not blonde but the fine, fine shade of a fine brandy.

'I've a general waiting, Jean-Louis. I only stopped by to see if you were here. I had a premonition you would be.'

'What time is it?'

'0800 hours Berlin time. I am just on my way home. We had a good crowd last night. They had missed me.'

'How's René Yvon-Paul?'

Her son. 'Fine. Yes, fine, Jean-Louis. He has asked about you, and I have explained things to him. Think about it, eh? It would mean a lot to me.'

'Me also, but it cannot be.'

She left him then in the cold and paltry light with the faint allure of Mirage in his nostrils. Gabrielle Arcuri, the *chanteuse* in a sequined sheath. A general was waiting.

Flinging himself over on to his left side in anger, St-Cyr saw that cracks had made pleasure with the wall on which had once hung an enlarged portrait photograph of his mother. The frame had been broken, the glass shattered by the blast. The photograph was now in shreds and he knew there'd be no sense in trying to glue it back together.

Gabrielle had made him an offer to stay at her place, an offer he dared not accept. Ah *merde!* why had he dreamt of her like that, and naked too?

The house was draughty but by some trick of fate or act of God, the lavatory he'd installed with plumber's tools and flames had been spared, the kitchen too. They were enough. Once Hermann and he had settled the murders, he'd start in on the repairs.

The nightmare continued to haunt him. Some of the animals had not risen as high as others. The High Court Jester had been trying to tell him something.

When he came out of the house, Hermann was waiting in the

car. 'Louis, I still can't find Giselle. No one's seen her. Madame Chabot is bitching about lost income.'

So much for the leisurely walk up to the carousel, the quiet think!

A cinematographer at heart, the film of Nicole de Rainvelle passed frame by frame before St-Cyr. He knew he should tell Hermann that Giselle might well have been worked over by Lafont and Bonny but ... ah, *Nom de Jésus-Christ!* he didn't have the courage.

'Have you not slept a wink, Hermann?'

'Not yet.'

'More Benzedrine?'

'Louis, I'm being torn apart. I can't get it out of my head that something's happened to her. I'm missing her like crazy.'

Was Hermann really in love? This thing, this case ...

'You drive. I hit someone's black cat, Louis. It's custard for the crows.'

Was he getting superstitious too? 'Climb in the back, my old one. Go to sleep. I'll wake you when we get there.'

'Breakfast?'

'Let's do the carousel first, while it's still fresh in my mind.'

The greyness of the early morning filtered into the carousel through its canvas roof, and the wind, tugging at some bit of bunting, played mischief with the silence.

Not a thing inside moved. The elephant still had its trunk lifted in the stampede that had stopped. The lion still chased the lioness; wild-eyed, the zebra followed white stallions whose nostrils flared and whose eyes shied away in fright.

It was at once a moment profound and one he felt deeply. Here was the essence of the carousel, the lively colours that even in the subdued light of morning had lost none of their vitality. He was glad he'd left Hermann in the car asleep. Even the intrusion of packing a beloved pipe might be too much.

The carousel seemed as if each of its animals wanted to cry out, For shame, Chief Inspector! A killer, monsieur. Help us before it is too late. __, though we hated him, need not have died here, at least not here. __ was good to us – you can see that for yourself. Look at our paint, look at how well kept we are. We're still good some two and a half years after he left us. After the Defeat! __ is in trouble. __ is in danger. __ are to blame.

Clément Cueillard popped his grinning head out of the inner workings. 'You've turned to salt, eh? Good morning, Chief Inspector.' He gave a cheery wave of his straight razor before disappearing to whistle up some lively tune, thus interrupting time and thought. Ah Mon Dieu . . . son of a bitch!

There'd been a towel folded jauntily about his scrawny neck. Cueillard had made himself at home. The place was warm. 'Would you care for a coffee?' the man sang out. 'It'll have to be in the monkey's cup, but I'll give it a swish if you like.'

A swish of soapy water? 'Did the monkey come back?' shouted the detective.

'Late last night.' The head popped out again. The razor glinted. 'The little bastard woke me up. Bitching, swearing and banging things – leaping from animal to animal expecting a free ride and climbing all over the place. When it saw me, it gave a yelp and buggered off. Me, I could not catch it in my long johns. The grass was too cold and wet. Besides, there were stones.'

So much for monkeys at night. 'Any idea where it's holed up?'

'The Temple of the Sibyl at Tivoli. Monkeys like height. Besides, there's no food in the kiosks and restaurants. They're all closed. He came back to get some. He'll come back again if you leave a few bananas out.'

Bananas at a time of war, with most of Europe under naval blockade! Bananas from a former banana merchant?

'Carrots will do,' Cueillard sang out. 'Or oranges. Personally I think he bitched because I ate the last of his stuff, except for the apples and pears. The chestnuts were excellent with the salt and a little butter. Roasted right in here.'

The ostrich grinned, the giraffe did too. The razor flashed.

'The Préfet himself has given me the orders, Chief Inspector. I am to stick around until the case is closed. I am to report anything suspicious directly to him in person, and I'm to report in detail all developments. They are sending me a scaffold of paper.'

'A scaffold?'

Cueillard examined his chin in the mirror that hung from a post. 'Of paper, yes, monsieur. That is what I will construct for him.'

'Let's hope it doesn't fall down. Hold the coffee. Don't wake the sleeping beauty in the car.'

Armed with two apples and a pear, he set out. Footpaths led uphill through the trees. The smell of decaying leaves was in the air, the sound of water in some gully not far away.

Prior to 1867, the Buttes-Chaumont had been a stone quarry, the refuge of petty thieves and beggars. Though Baron Haussmann, the Préfet of the Seine, had got all the credit, it had been someone else who had put the place right. And wasn't it odd, or a coincidence, that Talbotte, yet another Préfet, was involved today with the park, and that Talbotte, being Talbotte, would reap all the credit and none of the blame should a successful conclusion come to this whole affair.

Ah, Mon Dieu, what were they to do? Instead of witnesses, he was trudging after a monkey in the faint hope the creature could tell them something.

He'd take the long way round. The lake itself was fed partly by natural springs and partly by a diversion from the Canal Saint-Martin. Access to the island was by a brick footbridge and an iron suspension bridge, or by the simple and pleasurable act of hiring a boat and rowing across.

Which would the monkey look most favourably upon?

Lindens crowded the grassy shores. There were flower-beds now put to sleep, park benches, one old gentleman sitting patiently waiting for a bit of sun to warm the old bones should God be so kind.

Ripples on the water and peace, absolute peace.

The temple was perched high atop cliffs of flat-lying rock in the centre of the lake. Ivy and wild grapevines clung to the unscalable wall. Trees and shrubs, now bare of their leaves, sprouted precariously from the many vertical cracks.

There were eight round columns with ornate capitals to the temple, with what were perhaps acanthus leaves beneath the volutes. An iron railing was inside the columns to keep visitors from defying death, a leap of some twenty metres. In all it was a pretty thing, but still there was no sign of the monkey and he hesitated to ask the old man. Such frailty – that little bit of sun. Could God not grant such a trifling wish?

'He's not up there,' came the acid from beneath that black beret. 'He was, but he's gone. He's seen you.'

'Pardon?'

'The monkey. Now buzz off, you parasite! I've almost got him to the point where he'll eat out of my hand. Another day and he'll be in the oven.'

The man had a burlap sack partially hidden under one hip, and a small wooden club, the last leg of a chair. There was a chunk of bread in his hand.

So much for monkeys on the lam.

'He's not yours!' hissed the man. 'I saw him first, damn you! He belongs to *me* now that the operator of that devil's machine has been murdered. The monkey will only die from the cold, so don't get holy and spoil it all. My wife and I are going to eat him, or I'll drown myself.'

So much for frailty. 'That monkey is a witness to murder, monsieur. Might I suggest that you do not trouble yourself with drowning at this time of year, but attempt the leap.'

'*Bâtard!* I knew you were a cop! The gravy, monsieur. Think of the gravy from such a roast.'

In spite, and in tears, the old man wolfed the last of his bread. 'I hope the monkey doesn't tell you *anything*,' he shrilled, 'and that you do not catch him! A witness to murder, he says. Hah! my ass, you fine detective shit!'

The monkey was busy exercising on the suspension bridge. It made no attempt to approach, seeming only to retreat with each hesitant offering of fruit.

It was a spider monkey. The wizened little face had a jet-black muzzle and dark, sunken eyes that were ringed with light amber fur as if by a mask.

'Chew, chew, come on, my little friend. Never mind that old boy down there. He'd only have done you mischief.'

Another wedge of apple would do, a generous one. He'd lay it on the railing and back away. He'd wait and watch as the monkey did.

The thing swung out of sight and for one mad moment he thought it might have fallen into the lake. But then there it was, coming along the railing to hesitate while still a metre or so from the fruit.

'You saw the mackerel's killing. Is it that the man who killed him frightens you, or is it that you knew and loved him and therefore are shy of me?'

If only he could catch the thing. If only there'd been a name tag around its neck.

'Ah Mon Dieu, please don't be afraid. Here, have two slices of apple and one of pear.'

Only when he took out his pipe and tobacco pouch did the monkey break the rule of caution and come closer. Closer still. Sniffing now. Waiting . . . the eyes beseeching.

'To hell with fruit, eh? You like tobacco.'

Its teeth were sharp, the lips wet and clinging. Saliva oozed as the thing climbed into his arms and the detective hooked a secretive Judas thumb through its little neck chain.

'So, my friend, you've acquired a new master, eh, and since we are so close to the temple, we'll take a little walk. Please don't spit tobacco juice on my coat. It's shabby enough.'

There was no sign of the old man. Perhaps he'd left in disgust to try his hand at pigeons.

The views of Montmartre and Saint-Denis were breathtaking; the dome of the Basilica white and crystalline under thin sunlight. Down from him, the forests, ponds, little rivers and ravines fell away to the carousel. A long red pennant flew from its pole. The canvas roof sagged but in the early light, the carousel looked the place of magic it must once have been.

An Abwehr vice admiral who collected stuffed canaries. The gangsters Henri Lafont and Pierre Bonny. 'A Big One'. Paul Carbone and his gang over on the rue de Villejust. The SS of the avenue Foch. Talbotte keeping his hands clean of the affair; the General von Schaumburg wanting to help. Gold coins and bullion, the Corporal Schraum, ah yes, and corruption within the ranks.

The mackerel might well have contacted Lafont and Bonny, he might have tried his luck with Paul Carbone, or simply have wanted all the loot for himself but found it absolutely necessary to go along with Corporal Schraum.

The coal the carousel used had had to come from somewhere, and he thought then that he knew exactly where.

Fingering the canary helped, but as with the tobacco so with this. At once the monkey took the canary from him to play mother, cradling the bird in its tiny arms, fussing with delicate little hands, even to lifting the bird to a tired and withered breast.

Down on one of the wooden paths, far below them, an old woman strode along, hand in hand with a young boy.

For a moment St-Cyr watched them, and when certain they were headed for the carousel, he said, 'Let's go, my little friend. I think this thing is about to break. You're the first witness, eh, and soon we'll have the woman who found the mackerel's body, but more than this, she'll tell us what we need to know. She has that stride only those who've been forced to survive can acquire.'

'Joujou! *Grand-mère*, it's Joujou. She's come back!'

The kid was jumping, the grandmother less than happy.

'The filthy thing should be in a zoo! Chain the beast and *don't* give it tobacco!'

The woman was of Belleville, all seventy-eight years of her, and not inclined to have much patience.

'Why isn't the machine running, eh?' she shrilled. 'Monsieur Audit would never have left it idle, not for a moment. "It's for the children", he'd say. The children were everything to him, poor man. He'd lost the wife, you understand, Inspector. He'd only the granddaughter to keep the soul together, she and his "children". Five sous, no more, and plenty of rings for the little ones to catch the free rides. So,' she huffed, 'get it going, eh? or else my Robin will burst his breast and drown his bed again!'

Hermann had appeared in the doorway. Clément Cueillard had poked his head out from the machinery. The monkey's tin cup was steaming.

'Start her up, Louis. It can't hurt anything but my ears.'

'Take the coffee and go back to bed. I'll wake you when it's necessary.'

'No, I'm okay. I want to see the fireworks.'

'Then hold the monkey. I think it wants to shit.'

Cueillard found the creature's chain which had snapped during the murder perhaps, and which he'd wired securely together. 'I was going to repack the main gearbox this morning,' he said testily. 'That bastard, the mackerel, hadn't done it in ages.'

'Not since he took over, eh?' snorted the grandmother, pushing her glasses well up on the bridge of her nose. 'Just like a turd of the streets without a mother to call his own, or a father. A wipe of the cloth, that one, but seldom deep. It just goes to show you both how well maintained Monsieur Audit kept this thing.'

'A ride for the kid,' said the Gestapo's detective, the pouches under his eyes sagging to the tin cup. '*Salut!*'

The coffee was good, the monkey content not to defecate when chained to one of the horses.

The boy took his place atop the seagull, excitement glistening in his deep-brown eyes. '*Grand-mère*, did you pay?' he asked.

'She doesn't have to. All rides are free today,' announced the Gestapo, reaching for his cigarettes only to desist under the old dame's glare. 'I forgot,' he said lamely. 'Monkeys aren't supposed to smoke.'

'To chew,' she said darkly. 'It makes the creature's stools runny.'

The carousel began to turn, the boy to hang on and rise up, his feet jammed securely in the stirrups.

The monkey let go of the brass pole, waiting to be jerked out of the saddle perhaps.

'Madame, a few small questions, eh?'

The dark button eyes swept callously over him. 'The Sûreté were always sour, m'sieur. So, I am to be denied the pleasure of seeing that my grandson does not forget to hang on?'

Kohler knew he'd have to do it. 'Okay, okay, Louis. I'll watch the kid.'

The woman gave the orders. 'Get behind him on the seagull.'

'Not on your life. I'll sit the goose next to him.'

'Don't spill your coffee then. Monsieur Audit would never have allowed food or drink of any kind on his magic machine.'

'It's all in the line of duty, Hermann. Don't fall asleep. So, madame,' he indicated the doorway but she shook her head.

'In the centre. At my age it's nice to be warm. Monsieur Audit always kept a drop of cognac in there and he was not impartial to me if approached in the correct manner.'

Ah, was that so? The thing began to gather momentum but the old girl was steady on her pins. The music of 'Daisy, Daisy' started up as they threaded their way towards the centre.

Cueillard made room for them beside the boiler and its firebox. The place was self-contained, complete with bedroll et cetera, et cetera. St-Cyr sat on one of the sacks of coal, the woman on a butter box.

There was a five-star cognac. The *flic* had even found three thimble glasses.

'This Monsieur Audit, madame. Tell me about him.' Cueillard had already begun to make notes, the date, the time, that sort of thing. All scaffolds must be properly constructed.

'Monsieur Charles Audit was not always the owner of this thing, monsieur. That one once had money but he lost it all and went away. When he came back, after the years of absence, he bought this carousel in 1926 for his little granddaughter. He had it shipped all the way across the seas from Rio de Janeiro, though it had gone there first from New York City in America. The granddaughter became the light of his life, that one. Oh for sure he made money, but not all that much. Enough to keep the house perhaps, though me, I think the brother helped him out.'

'The brother?'

'Ah yes, Monsieur Antoine. Explosives, glass, wine and truffles, the silk too.'

'Monsieur Antoine.'

'Is it that you have met him, Inspector?'

The Sûreté had forgotten his cognac. The one from the Préfecture held his pencil poised.

'In a way, yes. Yes, I have met him a little,' murmured the detective. 'What was the granddaughter's name, madame?'

'You've not even asked madame her own,' sniffed Cueillard, fingering the left knee of his trousers.

'Madame Lucienne Giroux of the rue Piat, Number sixty-three upstairs at the front, never the back. Everyone knows me.'

St-Cyr nodded to Cueillard. 'I'd like a copy.'

'I've already got the carbon in place.'

Again there was that nod but still the look of one wanting to be left alone with his thoughts.

'The granddaughter, madame. Please, her name, eh?'

'Why, Audit, of course. Christabelle. She used to take the tickets here before the war.'

Yet again there was that nod, this time as if the detective had known it all along.

'Her address, madame? And that of this Monsieur Charles Audit?'

'Number twenty-three the rue Polonceau, a villa, or so he once said.'

It was all fitting together. The selling of the trinkets to buy food or medicines, the suspicions of gold coins, the panic, the forgeries that were not very clever but done perhaps on the advice of the brother, Madame Minou's 'Monsieur Antoine'.

How many times had he seen it before, the successful brother, the businessman, and the down-on-his-luck brother, the family's disgrace? A carousel for a living, a love of little children and a granddaughter that was the soul of his life.

The body too? he asked, hating himself for doing so.

'The mackerel, madame? How did he come to take this thing over?'

The woman gave a shrug; the music changed again, a march this time. 'He took over. His type always do. Monsieur Charles or his brother must have sold it to him for a song even as the Germans were shouting at the gates of the city.'

'Could they have retained a piece of the action?'

'Never! That is,' she gave a shrug, 'not Monsieur Charles. Not him. Maybe the brother, maybe Monsieur Antoine. That one was shrewd. No heart. Me, I think he laughed at Monsieur Charles for running this thing at a loss and for taking such passionate care of it.'

'The mackerel must have been running it for someone else. Even at depressed prices, that one would never have had enough cash.' St-Cyr dragged out the crumpled photograph. 'Just for the record, Madame Giroux, is this the girl you knew as Christabelle Audit?'

At first the woman vehemently shook her head, but then she said, 'What has she done to her hair? It is dark, is it not?'

He acknowledged that it was.

'That one, the German soldier with the child in his arms, he came to see the mackerel many times. They always came in here and left the machine running.'

Again things seemed to be fitting together, almost too well and too rapidly.

'He used to come here in the early days, the mackerel. I remember him as a boy when Christabelle was perhaps ten or twelve years old. He was arrested for stealing chairs from one of the cafés and selling them to another, only to steal them back for a price.'

'Henri Chamberlin, alias Lafont, got his start that way, madame. It's an old game. Nothing surprises me.'

'How long have you been a detective?'

'Too long.'

'The mackerel's name, madame?' asked Cueillard, as quietly and unobtrusively as possible. Police work bothered him. Details, always petty details.

'Victor Morande. That's what the other one called him. Either, "Hey, Victor, you fish in olive oil", or, "Morande, it's time to take a walk and find our little pigeon". Monsieur the Detective, has anything happened to . . .'

Madame Giroux couldn't bring herself to say it.

'She was murdered two nights ago.'

'And violated?'

'This one could not possibly have done it, madame, but it's interesting you should think it possible that he would violate her.'

'Idiot! I meant the brother not the mackerel! The brother was always after her skirt!'

'Monsieur Antoine Audit?' asked the startled detective.

'Who else? The big car, the birthday cake and barley sugars, then the clothes and the jewellery. Ah, that one had his eye on her. Monsieur Charles knew it too, and so did she. Fifteen and a new pair of red leather shoes. High heels. The lipstick. Sixteen and the black underwear if you ask me, Inspector. The pigeon beneath the loins of a relative! Every girl must pay her price, isn't that so?'

Especially if you were beholden to your grandfather's brother.

'You have exhausted me, madame. For now that is enough. Cueillard, you may stop the machine and start servicing the main gearbox.'

Talbotte's chief scribe set his clipboard aside and went to man the controls.

As Madame Giroux watched, the detective from the Sûreté tore off both copies of the notes and several pages as well, before tucking the original away and throwing all the rest into the firebox, including the carbon paper.

'Shh! Don't breathe a word of it, madame. The Préfet has a direct line to God, so there is no problem since the smoke will reach Him and it contains the notes. Please don't concern yourself. When one gangster kills another it is always best not to let too many know who might have been helpful to the investigation.'

'Louis, we should have pumped her dry.'

'Not with Cueillard listening in. So, my friend, we have a name to attach to the mackerel's big toe.'

'You didn't really mean that about gangsters killing gangsters, did you, Louis? Madame Giroux's insisting you're full of cotton wool. She says Schraum must have done it and if not him, then Monsieur Antoine Audit.'

'She's really got it in for the brother, hasn't she?'

Louis was at the wheel and enjoying it. The streets of Montmartre were easing past. Traffic had more than enough chance to get out of the way. The Citroën was purring.

'So, how does a mackerel like Morande come to be running a carousel?'

'Precisely, Hermann. It's not exactly the racket one would expect of him.'

'At least he found himself a place to live rent free.'

'But when, Hermann? When?'

'Just after the Defeat. Within a week of it, he was here. I asked her.'

The Defeat? Were Hermann's sympathies making him careless? 'The Conquest, Hermann. Must I correct you, for your own sake?'

'I still say Morande had no business wasting time with a carousel. Seven long years in stir, Louis. The Santé and then Fresnes. Nineteen thirty-three to 'forty for armed robbery and assault. Ran two girls on the side, but that was a secondary matter. Got out in June, in time to meet the New Order. That old dame's a Bible.'

'Maybe the carousel suited him?'

'At five sous a ride? Come on, Louis, you know better. Even with the depressed market, he'd not have had the cash to buy it. The Préfet's boys recovered the loot before they put him away.'

'Then maybe someone told him to stay off the streets?'

'Ostracized, was that it? He spent fourteen weeks in solitary for hitting a prison guard with a shovel in an attempt to escape.'

'That should have earned him more than five dots. Perhaps his attempted escape was the act of a desperate man. Perhaps our friend Morande had to get out before someone killed him.'

'If so, then that person waited for two and a half years.'

'Revenge is sweet, Hermann. Like the carbuncle, it is best squeezed when full of pus.'

To that there was no answer. The car had stopped in front of the entrance to a courtyard. A small bronze plaque, now covered in heavy black paint to protect it from thieves, gave Number 23, the rue Polonceau.

'A villa just like the grandmother said,' sighed the Sûreté.

'It's too close to the Hotel of the Silent Life, Louis. Too close to the Church of Saint Bernard.'

'My thoughts exactly. Madame Minou would have known the girl by her real name.'

'The girl wouldn't have chanced a liaison in such a familiar neighbourhood.'

'Then why Number twenty-three, Hermann?'

'Madame Giroux would not have made a mistake, Louis. She sucked on her eyes every time she mentioned Charles Audit.'

Number 23 was one of those delightful little surprises so typical of the city. A quiet, walled courtyard, a bit of peace from a troubled world. Chestnut trees, lilacs, rose-bushes, wisteria and trumpet vine, all without their leaves. A scattering of brick-red paving-tiles among the limestone flags. A small fountain, a faun with cloven feet, the pipes of Pan. A bird-bath.

The shutters were open. Two low steps led to the entrance path that ran through clipped box and Yew towards a terracotta urn.

The curtains were drawn. There were scrolled, Louis XIV iron-work grilles on the lower part of the tall windows. Not a sign of anyone.

'Very nice, and very private, Hermann. Very bourgeois too. The businessman in retreat.'

There was a bell – tidy links of wrought iron and a ring to grasp. Kohler yanked it down. Louis told him to turn his bad cheek away. 'We don't want to frighten the mistress of the house unduly, eh?'

'The stitches don't come out for another three days. They're beginning to itch.'

He gave the chain another yank. Somewhere beyond the door, the faint sound of ringing came to them.

'There's no one home, Louis. The place is empty.'

'Try your fist. They might be hard of hearing.'

'Want me to break it down?'

'No. No, we'll leave it for now, but it isn't right. Something's wrong.'

The Hotel of the Silent Life was just up the street and across from the bakery; the Church of Saint Bernard was down the street and around the corner. 'It's all too convenient, Hermann. Did the girl know of the district and come back to use it, hence the dyed hair, or did Madame Minou's "Monsieur Antoine" know of it and wish to use it for purposes of his own?'

'Don't forget our Christiane or Christabelle took the trouble to dye her locks below the waist.'

'A virgin, Hermann. It is a puzzle, unless, of course, the room was only made to look as if it was for that purpose.'

'Then why the jewellery, why the canary? Things from M Antoine for her to sell, or from her to him *if*, my fine Frog friend, if selling at the fleas wasn't working out to her satisfaction?'

'Then Antoine was the buyer, she the seller and the gold coins, eh? What of them?'

'This thing goes round and round.' He'd open the hotel's courtyard door for Louis, he'd show mutual respect and let the baker who was hanging on to his window glass see that the Gestapo could back off when it suited them.

Madame Minou was in her cage and nervous. The coffee

wasn't ersatz but black and strong. A sacrifice. Pre-war and hoarded, and therefore against the law, leading not just to confiscation but to incarceration.

'Me, I have passed the miserable night, messieurs. I'm an old woman. God should be kinder. Word of the murder has now got round to all of the tenants. The hotel is abuzz.'

St-Cyr crowded in after Hermann. The woman was forced by the lack of space and nerves into the sagging armchair that had always given comfort in troubled times.

Arfande, the cat, disappeared under the narrow cot she used as a bed.

Hermann offered a cigarette but it was refused, then taken at his insistence. 'For later, yes, *merci*.'

She avoided looking at them and gazed perhaps into a finer, more distant past.

'Madame Minou, did you know the girl who was killed –'

'Murdered! Violated! In my hotel! As tenants die, messieurs, others will not come to replace them.'

So much for the future, bleak though it was. 'Madame, did you know her by any other name than Christiane Baudelaire?'

The grey eyes swam. 'Why should I have?'

St-Cyr hushed her with a gesture of his hand. 'Was the girl new to your neighbourhood, or a resident from before the Defeat?'

The Gestapo had taken out one of the coins. Now a toss, now a fall. He had that look about him, that one had. 'New, of course. I would have known otherwise. Since 1912 I have been concierge of this place.'

Thirty years . . . To live like this. Hermann was still flipping the coin. Good! 'Then what about Monsieur Antoine?'

'No. With that one I would have known from fifty years even though he is like so many men of his age and station in life. The big shot, isn't that so, Inspector? The young girl naked and on her knees between his own.'

Kohler nodded. The coin went up a little higher. 'There's more than one way of using a young girl, eh, madame?' he taunted, flustering her.

'You men are all the same! Filthy minds when your buttons are undone and a girl, a wife is –'

Louis lit her cigarette. She drew in, but coughed. A glass of water was needed.

Again the questions started up. The one from the Sûreté would not be distracted. Ah *merde*! what was she to do? The Gestapo had seen it too. They were a pair of shit-miners!

'Madame, we have an informant – no, please do not distress yourself, eh? Hermann, a little more water for madame. The ashtray, my friend. Yes, yes, that one will do nicely. The one with the broken parrot.'

He'd not stop now. 'Madame, our informant tells us that a Monsieur Charles Audit had the villa at Number twenty-three. Do you remember him?'

Questions – always they would ask her questions. Roland would come to mind. They'd find out. Was there nothing she could do to stop them?

'How should I know who owned that place, eh? I do not push open doors I should not push open. It's rented perhaps, or perhaps the owner is in the South for the duration. Many left the city before the Defeat, monsieur. The streets . . . such emptiness. Ah Mon Dieu, it was like walking through the Devil's shadow and coming home to cancer.'

'Then you did not know of this Monsieur Charles Audit?'

'She's lying, Louis. Let's call up the salad basket and have her over to the rue Lauriston for a bit of undressing.'

Her eyes leapt. Her cigarette fell from quivering lips and began to burn a hole in the flowered dress that had seen too many years.

Kohler picked it out of her lap and put it back between her lips. 'Three coins, madame. Three deaths. I'm holding the fourth.'

'They were all fake. Take them, damn you!'

'They're like your son, eh, madame? Phoney beneath the wash of gold. Where is he?'

Hermann had a way with him when he wanted it. The rue Lauriston . . . Her eyes began to drain at the thought.

'I do not know, monsieur. Roland, he has . . . he has stolen my purse and emptied my savings box too many times for me to care.'

'When was the last time?' asked the one from the Sûreté, brushing a knuckle across his thick brown moustache as if he'd just taken custard.

'Not since the day of his call-up for the army.'

There, she'd said it, and they would not think that Roland had come back to steal more, not once but four times.

'Two and a half, maybe three years ago, Hermann. It's a mother's love that makes her search for him and think bad thoughts.'

The Bavarian sucked in a breath as he caught the spinning coin. 'They'll sort her out, Louis. We haven't time for wind. We'd better get to work.'

The Gestapo collected the coins from beside the parrot ashtray and she knew then that he'd meant exactly what he'd said.

There was only one thing to do. She could not give up Roland so easily, not even after all he'd done to her.

'This Monsieur Charles Audit, messieurs. I have lived in the *quartier* all my life. I have not seen him in years, not since he lost the villa in 1905 to his brother for debts and went away. Colombia, Brazil, Peru, those distant places where there are jungles and . . . and the monkeys.' Had she said too much?

'And his brother, madame?' asked the Gestapo with tired breath.

'I have never seen him. They say he lives in the South, in Périgord, in Lyon and Saint-Raphaël. But all that happened many years ago. Now no one talks of it.'

'Does Antoine Audit still own the villa he squeezed out of his brother?'

'That I would not know, Inspector. Father Delacroix might.'

She would give them a shrug, may God forgive her. But Delacroix might not say the right things. A soldier had been killed. A German corporal who'd been seen with the horse butcher's wife enough times to make one wonder whose side that shameless slut was on. Had Roland put the bullet into him, eh? Had her baby done a thing like that? To kill one German was to be killed in turn. All members of the immediate family, regardless of whether they'd stolen from their mother or not even seen her in years except for those few times. All would be taken. It was the rule.

Pity was not for situations like this, yet St-Cyr could only find that quality foremost in his heart. 'Madame, is there anything else you can tell us? Some little thing perhaps forgotten but now needing desperately to come to light?'

'Louis, you're being too kind.'

'Hermann, the warning is taken.'

The rue Lauriston . . . People went there never to return. Madame Minou swallowed. The coin had stopped flipping. 'There was a note, a letter for Mademoiselle Baudelaire but . . .'

'But what, madame?' demanded St-Cyr impatiently.

'But this one took it, monsieur.'

'Hermann?'

'Yes.'

Kohler dropped the coin and it rolled about the carpet among the cat hairs. He fished for the note in a pocket and finally trod on the coin. 'Sorry, Louis. The lack of sleep. The loss of my dinner. That girl . . . her black hair, the look of her . . . Giselle, I . . .'

'Just let me have it, Hermann. Quickly.'

The envelope hadn't been sealed. ' "*Christiane, leave the hotel immediately. Don't go up to the room.*" It's not signed.'

The girl had been late and in a hurry. Madame Minou had not been able to stop her long enough to give her the note.

'Who left this with you, madame?'

She knew they'd ask! 'Monsieur Antoine. The one she was to meet.'

'When? When was it left?'

'At eight o'clock. No, eight-twenty. I have noted the time in my ledger. You may check if you wish.'

The ledger was open on the tiny desk. All comings and goings were to be noted.

'Louis, he must have known the hotel was being watched. He played it smart and came by an hour early to check out the ground.'

This was standard Abwehr, Sicherheitsdienst or even Resistance procedure, but there was no point in mentioning it in front of the woman. Still, it was a thought. 'Then why didn't he try to stop her at the *métro*, Hermann, or watch for her from some small café, eh? There are a thousand whys with nearly an hour to back them up. "*Christiane, leave the hotel immediately. Don't go up to the room.*" '

'They must have been on to him, Louis. He must have taken it upon himself to give them the slip in the hope they'd follow him and she'd get away.'

'One doesn't write notes like this on the street, Hermann. One uses a desk and a fountain pen.'

Hermann pocketed the coin in order to examine the note and its envelope. 'Borrowed, eh, Louis? The pen even has a bent nib just like the one that's squeezed in the centre of a certain concierge's ledger.'

Together they turned on the woman, who had caught herself by the throat. 'All right, all right, messieurs! It is my envelope and paper but I swear I did not see who wrote the note, only that it was left on my counter.'

'And the time?' breathed the one with the terrible slash. 'Just for the record, eh?'

'Eight ... eight-twenty. I ... I was in the toilet – even a concierge has to go!' Ah *Mon Dieu*, what was she to do? 'It ... it is at the far end of the corridor, messieurs, beside the tradesmen's stairs. It's Turkish,' she sweltered. 'I have not had the opportunity to modernize. I have always had the trouble when they flood.'

She was practically blushing. A hole in the floor over which one had to squat, a chain too far to the left, a rush of water et cetera often covering the cubicle's floor as the chain was finally yanked.

No escape. Kohler grinned hugely but he'd be kind. 'The truth always hurts, madame. Now give us the key to that room up there and tell us who else had a key besides the girl.'

'Hermann, let her think about things, eh?'

'They both had keys, messieurs, but Monsieur Antoine always came after.'

'Did you read it?' asked Kohler, waving the note at Madame Minou.

Her expression hardened. 'No I did not.'

'It's good of you to have said so, madame, because otherwise we'd have had to charge you with being an accomplice.'

'Hermann, Madame Minou knows all about such things, don't you, madame?'

She wouldn't sing like a canary for them, not even after that! 'Please do not disturb my tenants unduly, messieurs. They are upset enough and threatening to move elsewhere if I cannot guarantee them the peace and quiet I have advertised for so many years.'

The forensic boys, such as they were these days, had chalked the position of the body. Otherwise, the room had been left much as they'd last seen it. The curtains were still drawn.

One after another Louis began to open the bureau drawers, leaving each of them partly closed.

Kohler went over to the bed to look at the position of her scattered things.

'So, what about the girl, eh?' asked Louis, more of himself than of his partner. 'There are still plenty of undergarments. Silk and Chantilly lace, meshed stockings, two garter belts, a rose-red chemise and teddy. Lots of things for a girl who must have been playing a very dangerous game.'

'She threw her underwear the farthest, Louis. It's my guess, more in anger than in fear.'

'Did she know her assailant then?'

Kohler lifted the plain white briefs that had been worn only once. 'He'd found her out perhaps, but then . . .'

'Ah yes, why dye the hair below the waist as well unless, perhaps . . .'

'One feared arrest or being caught up in some *rafle* and then strip-searched at the préfecture to give the boys a bit of fun.'

'These days it's best to be on the safe side.'

'Most French girls don't shave their armpits, Louis. She did.'

Good for Hermann. 'A girl of some distinction.'

'Well educated?'

'Schooled perhaps in something, Hermann, but alas naïve when it came to gold coins unless, of course, she knew only too well they were forgeries.'

Kohler examined the lie of her belt. In anger, her cheeks hot with embarrassment perhaps, she had made a clumsy flick of it and the belt had landed half on the bed and half off it.

'She knew him, Louis. She'd been expecting something like this.'

St-Cyr ran a hand in under the silks and satins to the far corners of the drawer. 'It can't have been the mackerel. By then he was dead.'

'It can't have been her M Antoine either, so who the hell was it, seeing as she might quite possibly have known him?'

Louis was smelling a crushed fistful of pink satin, a chemise. He took a grab of silk – a half-slip – then a black, see-through brassière.

'There is some bitter orange, Hermann, a little lemon grass and rosemary, the touch of coumarin. The scent is not common, not cheap either, and she did not use much, so she knew of its value. It is very faint, my friend, but still very much alive.'

'Just a touch or two then. Try the briefs. I won't mind.'

'You should have left everything here for me!'

'Sorry, Louis. Was it Madame Minou's son, Roland? Was he the one to make her undress without too much of a fuss because she thought, my fine Frog friend, that if she could but distract the bastard long enough, her pal Monsieur Antoine would come along?'

'Hermann, you are absolutely brilliant. Of course that is how it must have been! She took off her things in hopes of rescue.'

'Then M Antoine was not just a successful businessman, eh? but also good with his hands.'

'Or the pistol or the knife.'

'And she knew this, Louis – knew she could count on him.'

'Did M Antoine kill the mackerel?' asked the Sûreté.

'Perhaps, but then why stick around, eh? Why meet so soon afterwards?'

'A last meeting, Hermann. An emergency – the crisis, no? They had to agree quickly on a course of action.'

'He tried to warn her off; she believed he'd be coming here.'

'She was late and in a hurry. Madame Minou could not stop her on the stairs to pass her the note.'

Kohler went over to the windows to part the curtains a little and look down at the rue Polonceau.

The street was empty. The black Citroën engendered only terror, as did all such vehicles.

He hated himself a little. 'When I was a kid shovelling shit on the old man's farm, Louis, I dreamed of being a big-city detective, not this.'

The dresses bore traces of the scent. 'Is it that you are trying to apologize for the present state of things, Hermann?'

In other words, the interference of criminals who could no longer be brought to justice because they were now above the law. 'You know I am, Louis. We'll have to question the hostages. Von Schaumburg will expect us to.'

'It will be painful for me, Hermann, and this I freely admit.'

'Maybe we could get them off if we could prove beyond a shadow of a doubt that Schraum didn't deserve a medal but only the proper end of a burial shovel, and that the Resistance had nothing to do with the killing.'

This was heresy coming from Hermann. St-Cyr let go of the red dress. 'And if that proves impossible, what then?' he asked quietly.

The Bavarian was grumpy. 'Maybe we'll just have to find another way. Maybe we won't. Lots of good men are dying on the Russian Front, Louis, on both sides. I'm no judge.'

They went back to work in silence. Hermann was always very thorough when goaded by guilt and ashamed of his fellow Germans.

The girl and M Antoine had spent no more than an hour or two at a time in the room, once or twice a week for nearly a year. Always from between eight and nine o'clock in the evening except for Tuesday when they'd met at four.

M Antoine hadn't stayed long then and afterwards she'd been

most distressed. She hadn't changed out of her clothes, nor had she washed herself.

She'd been the one to pay the rent and each week she'd done so in advance.

A girl who'd known her own mind? Had she been an equal partner in this thing, this scam, or the innocent and naïve accomplice?

St-Cyr took out the canary to replace it in its nest of velvet. The box was beautifully made and of some type of gumwood, very light in colour and weight. There were no designs, no initials. It was just a simple box, perhaps once intended for cigarettes but with its lid missing now and so made into a little bed for a little friend.

He could see the girl as a child in her cage taking tickets for her grandfather; he could hear the music of the carousel.

'Louis, there's something I should have told you. Madame Minou was not all that sure the client's real name was Antoine. Maybe we're not dealing with the brother at all but with the girl's grandfather.'

'M Charles Audit?' It was a thought. 'Madame Minou hasn't seen him since 1905. He must have changed a good deal.'

'I wish we could find the girl's identity papers, Louis. I wish we could find her purse.'

The light had shifted a little and now there was not so much shadow in the courtyard of Number 23. Louis stood just inside the door, breathing in the essence of the place. Kohler knew he had to leave him to it, that at times like this the Frog was best on his own.

To the left, a slightly raised kerb of cut limestone separated a metre-deep strip of garden and its wall from the flagstones with their brick-red tiles. To the right, across a space of no more than twelve metres and the width of the house, there was a somewhat deeper strip of garden, another wall of equal height, and a sycamore now bare of leaves like all the rest.

St-Cyr shut his eyes and breathed in deeply. Without motorized traffic, the city had a hush like no other. He could smell the bark of the sycamore, the dead leaves and round, tassled, prickly seed pods that always reminded him of Christmas-tree decorations in some ancient and far-away land. The chestnuts, too, and the rhododendrons.

It was at once that kind of garden and he had the thought that it hadn't changed much in the last thirty or more years.

The night would have been dark, the girl afraid but more than this, in a great hurry. She'd have slipped quickly into the courtyard and would have closed the door quietly behind her.

Then she'd have stood here trying to remember through the darkness the locations of things, and listening closely to hear if she'd been followed or if someone had come out of the house. Her heart hammering.

Christabelle Audit ... Had there been time for her to walk across the courtyard and up those two low steps, then along the path to the doorstep? He thought not, and he reminded himself that the girl could not possibly have lived here, but then she might well have visited the villa as a child, especially as it had once been the house of her grandfather's brother.

She'd have played in the courtyard all by herself perhaps, been very busy in her own little world of make-believe.

When he saw the rustic birdhouse hanging on the wall not two metres from the courtyard door, he knew he had found her secret place. It was just large enough for a small purse – not a regular handbag, ah no. She'd not have carried one on such occasions.

Kohler watched as Louis lifted one half of the hinged roof of the birdhouse.

The purse was of dark blue, very soft and well-tanned leather. Not deerskin or cowhide but snakeskin. Anaconda perhaps. The photograph was good, the head and shoulders face on. The hair was black, but then that would have been necessary.

'Christabelle Audit, Hermann. Number ten rue Bènard, apartment six. Here are her residence permit and ID, a few of this week's yellow ration tickets in case she got hungry and went into a café. A lipstick, compact, pair of tweezers, eyelash brush and small bottle of black dye, no label, a few francs and sous, two safety pins, six hairpins, a handkerchief and two keys.'

'Which one?'

'Both are of brass and much worn. Take your pick. Neither may fit.'

'I'll try them both just in case.'

St-Cyr let him go ahead. It was always best this way. The present owner or occupant might now be at home and wondering just exactly what the hell the two of them were up to.

But had the sense of something wrong emanated from the girl's simply having left her purse and identification here, or from something inside the house?

One thing was certain. The girl had lived in Montparnasse, not all that far from the girlfriend of Georges the baker. A widow, just as Georges had said he was a widower. The same cemetery, the same purchased stones, the same empty graves, the bodies of their loved ones elsewhere.

He'd have to talk to this Marianne St-Jacques alone just in case the Resistance was involved. He owed that to Hermann, one could only ask so much.

And he remembered then that other young girl from that other case and how her lips had been pressed against his own.

That house, too, had been in Montparnasse. Where was she now? In Dachau or Mauthausen? Ah yes.

'It's this one, Louis. Our girl had a key to the front door.'

Toadstools, peonies and the ripening green heads of waving poppies covered the fabric of the *chaise longue*. The designs were at once bold; the colours of mauve, blue, yellow, red and green subdued yet vibrant.

The *chaise* was against a wall. There were two throw cushions propped against the corner so that the bather might well have stretched out after a bath or before it to read, meditate or simply relax.

The floor was bare, but there was a dressing-screen, one of those Art Nouveau pieces fashionable around the turn of the century. Nothing expensive – something picked up in one of the fleas or at auction. It had been painted a beigy-cream to match the background of the spread on the *chaise*. Blue irises had been sketched on its panels.

St-Cyr breathed in deeply. The irises were exceptional.

Storklike ibis waded among the marshes of the Nile on the exposed side of the bathtub. There was a rectangular, bevelled mirror without a frame above the bronze taps and shower head with its coiled brass tube.

The mirror was large enough to see the top half of oneself when standing in the tub. But that hadn't been enough for the former mistress of Number 23 the rue Polonceau. Ah no. With outspread, batlike wings, a Bird of Death clung to the top of the mirror to stare back at whoever thought to examine themselves in that glass, reminding all that age soon overtakes.

There were tulip lamps on either side of the mirror above the sink, which stood against the far wall between the end of the tub and the cushions on that *chaise*. Everywhere there was Art Nouveau – songbirds on the walls, a bronze soap dish in the shape of an outstretched lily pad.

For some time now Hermann and he had been moving quietly about the house, and always there was this sense of its being a time capsule. Used but then not used continuously, not any more. Not since perhaps before the Great War.

And like the rest of the house so, too, this bathroom. Things picked up for a song and tastefully done over – artistically, yes. She'd had a fabulous sense of colour and design. A bird entrapped by marriage? he wondered.

Quite obviously there was a housekeeper who came in to dust and air the place. Yet there was this sense of its not just being left unused but left that way on purpose.

Behind the dressing-screen there was a small stool and a table with an oval mirror. Shelves of books were ranked on either side and above the table; no space was wasted. Proust, Baudelaire, Guy de Maupassant ... books on existentialism, the roots of Symbolism and its art.

Books on flowers. Sketches of them. The sketch, in charcoal, of a young woman in her early twenties lying naked on that *chaise*.

An arm supported her head. She'd lovely legs, a lovely figure, and she looked up at the viewer quite boldly, as if to challenge that person into embarrassment or the honesty of carnal lust.

He knew she'd done the sketch herself, just as he knew that though the house would have been in her husband's name, it had been hers to decorate in the style of her choosing.

A dark-haired woman with a penetratingly frank gaze. Had the eyes been violet? he wondered.

A pearl-handled mirror, comb and brush set lay to one side of a dressing-table that had been painted an antique white with gold threads in Celtic swirls and spirals. Two snakes faced each other with fangs bared and bodies entwined. She'd have sat here looking at herself even as her elbows had rested on the snakes she'd drawn and painted so well.

There was a box of face-powder, some rouge, tints to accent eyes and lashes, all these things from at least thirty years ago.

Gingerly he drew open the middle drawer of the dressing-table. There were the usual things of that period. Buttonhooks, corset stays that had been removed in anger perhaps, or in

117

freedom's relish. Some hatpins, a cushion for them in the shape of a pomegranate. Calling-cards embossed with the motif of a hand-painted peacock fanning its tail. Letters in gold, and others in silver.

Michèle-Louise Prévost, and underneath this, in brackets, as if it had been important but not the most critical thing in her life, *Mme Charles Audit*.

A lipstick, very new and incongruous because it shouldn't have been there at all, lay next to the lock, in the centre of the front of the drawer. Pre-war and of very good quality.

There was also a crystal vial of scent, half full. Had it been forgotten by the owner of the lipstick?

The perfume was the same as the one Christabelle Audit had worn and he thought then that the girl had come in here, not to leave her lipstick, ah no, but to 'borrow' some of the forgotten perfume. But why should she do such a thing? To remind her Monsieur Antoine of this other woman, the owner of the lipstick? To hope he'd notice, eh?

Christabelle Audit; Christiane Baudelaire.

In a far corner of the drawer, wrapped in thin tissue, was a small, dried contraceptive sponge attached to its thin length of thread.

A handkerchief smelled faintly of the scent, and he thought then that the owner of the lipstick had left these four items here quite recently. And he wondered who that person could have been and if the vial of perfume had really been hers?

Unfortunately, though of silk, there were no monogrammed initials on the handkerchief, but he thought that it had been made in Lyon.

Pocketing the lipstick, bottle of scent and handkerchief, he softly closed the drawer.

Hermann was in the kitchen at the back of the house. He'd a wicker hamper on the marble-topped pastry-cutting table that was near the cast-iron stove.

'*Pâté de foie gras aux truffes*, Louis. *Vraie truffe avec pâté de poulet jeune aux champignons* – young chicken and mushrooms, what will they think of next? The dishes are for two, my old one, the silver also and really quite nice for a picnic. One bottle of raspberry liqueur, made on the premises of Antoine Audit and Sons. How's that for detective work? One also of apricot brandy and this one,' he held up a bottle, 'the local specialty, Cream of the Walnut! My guess is that a certain M Antoine Audit or one of his sons packed the happy couple the hamper, which they then lunched on in bliss as they drove to Paris from Périgord.'

'The girl – the woman with the lipstick and the scent,' muttered the Frog, withdrawing the same from a pocket and dropping the handkerchief which then had to be retrieved.

'One half-smoked excellent cigar, Louis. One pair of forgotten black leather gloves, Kriegsmarine issue, no less, their owner with hands much smaller than mine unfortunately, but larger than a woman's and definitely of the officer class.'

'I'm liking this less and less. Was there anything else?'

Hermann shook his head. 'The housekeeper was too tidy. The pair of them could have stayed here a week or a month ago, maybe more. The cigar was considered too valuable to throw out or steal.'

Together they went into the sitting-room. Again there was that clutter of made-over, second-hand things. The divan was covered with fabrics bought in the bazaars of Marrakesh perhaps. There was a round, brass coffee table on ebony legs with a border of green Art Nouveau leaves she'd hand painted, a hammered brass urn with a beautiful globular shape. Candlesticks in brass with white candles, sprigs of dried flowers – those would have been replaced, but had that been done by her, or by Antoine Audit in her memory?

Potted tree-ferns appeared to be exceptionally healthy, as did the rubber plants that grew about the room. There was a green Tiffany cobweb lamp, a gorgeous thing that didn't look a bit out of place if one threw oneself back in time at least thirty years.

There were books, books and more of them, scattered about as if Michèle-Louise Prévost had but left the room to make a cup of coffee.

'Three women, Hermann. The one who decorated this house and painted the pictures, the granddaughter who left her keys and identity papers outside, and a visitor.'

'And that last one's boyfriend. The Kriegsmarine, Louis, but there aren't any ships or submarines in Périgord.'

The room was at once comfortable and intimate, but crowded, too, with easy chairs, cushions for sitting on the floor if that seemed best, a sofa, prints on the walls, bits of sculpture – strange, surrealistic fish, Lalique-like girls and peacock feathers. Dashes of colour, whole blendings of it.

St-Cyr pinched his moustache in thought. 'This place must be registered, Hermann.'

'On loan to the Great and Glorious Third Reich, but to whom, eh, Louis? The Abwehr, my old one, since they share the same uniform.'

The Abwehr, ah *merde*!

In the hall there was a woodcut of a nude done in the style of Félix Vallotton. The woman was lying on her stomach on a divan, reaching languidly out to a black cat.

'She was better than Vallotton, Hermann.'

There were Gauginesque things, again symbolistic and surrealistic. Hibiscus claws in flower, wrapped around a sleeping girl who'd somehow lost her clothes; the lover sitting cross-legged in studious, loinclothed contemplation of her.

An earlier study, perhaps, was exactly of the Carrière school, and showed in brushed gossamer a mother and child.

St-Cyr found himself thinking of his wife and son. He was deeply moved by the picture.

'Michèle-Louise Prévost, Hermann. The wife of Monsieur Charles Audit copied many of the French masters of Symbolist and Surrealist art, but even better, I think, than they could have done themselves.'

It was when she got to Gustav Klimt that she had showed she'd been a master of them all. Her study of his *Female Friends* was more than equal to his own.

'Did she forge coins?' asked Kohler, fingering the sculpted study of a nymph who was trying to reach the ceiling but was being shy about it because she'd lost the towel she'd been wearing.

There were several fired-clay tablets on yet another bookcase: bison in full flight, in ochrous hues of rusty red and reddish brown; ibex and horses running across some Neolithic plain; a superb study of a giant black bull, done simply in outline.

'Les Eyzies or Font-de-Gaume, Hermann. She's done these from some of the cave paintings in Périgord. Wait here, I won't be a moment.'

St-Cyr went up the stairs two at a time and when, rising through the trap door he reached the attic, he found the dust of ages in her studio. It was all a clutter just as she must have left it in 1905, some thirty-seven years ago. A sculptor's pedestal held the half-finished bust of a commission – a banker perhaps – so she'd had to do some of her work just to earn a bit of cash and Charles Audit really hadn't been all that well off.

Her easel was there, the paints and brushes all laid out on

trestle-tables among frames and sketches, bits of fabric she'd been designing, a model's stool – everything.

He could smell the turpentine and the oils, even the dryness of the clays that had gone so hard in their tin pails.

There were three trunks that had been hastily stored in the centre of the room, near the trap door, and on the floorboards near these, where a candle had been fixed, there were the burnt stubs of two forgotten matchsticks.

Someone had knelt beneath the skylights that had given the artist the north light so necessary to her work.

The trunk nearest the match stubs was full of her clothes from that other era and, beneath these, on the left side at the bottom, he found her jewel case – a made-over thing that had once held silver cutlery.

She had left everything and had gone away or died, but now her granddaughter had come back to take some of her things and try to sell them.

There was one more butterfly brooch, a superb thing in the style of Gaillard, that master of enamelled Art Nouveau. Even with this she had dabbled. Gold and enamelled silver and tiny diamonds – God knew where she'd have got those, but they were real, not rhinestones. The figure of a young and slender woman was wrapped in its golden sheath, her body that of the butterfly, her outspread wings green, blue, black, gold and pale shades of rose enamel.

He held it in his palm. He knew the girl would not have wanted to sell such a thing, not even if it had meant starvation.

There was a coiled serpent bracelet in the style of Georges Fouquet, circa 1890, with opal platelets forming scales on its head and tiny ruby eyes – they would be rubies, he knew this now. She'd have settled for nothing less, this Michèle-Louise Prévost.

Beetlebug pins and caterpillars, haircombs, strands and strands of beads, and earrings to dangle from pierced ears – she'd made some, bought others no doubt, and been given still others.

There were no emeralds that he could see and he had the thought again that the emeralds must have come later, that everything here was from the time before Charles Audit had gone away.

Hermann had selected a half-dozen photographs from an album in the woman's bedroom. 'Charles Audit and his brother. The three of them together at those caves. Then a shot of them hunting truffles – that's Antoine holding the loot. Two of the woman bathing *à la* buff. Those must have been taken by Antoine, eh? And one of him fully clothed and out for sport with his shotgun.

'Oh, there's one other, Louis. A shop on the rue du Faubourg-Saint-Honoré. Our boy Charles sold shoes and wasn't too happy about it.'

5

'M Charles Audit! Yes, yes, monsieur. I knew him well. A brave man. Killed like all the rest.'

The old soldier looked away in sadness at the thought. St-Cyr heaved a detective's sigh. The room in the Hotel of the Silent Life was far too stuffy for health and badly in need of cleaning. There were ribbons on the lapels of the blue blazer. The thin red of the Legion of Honour, the yellow and green of the Military Medal. The medals themselves were on prominent display in a locked *vitrine*, along with the splintered remains of the shell that had killed his comrades and some bits of china and silver still too precious to sell.

'This war, it is nothing, monsieur. Nothing! No spine, do you understand?'

The voice had leapt with accusation. It would be best to offer a cigarette and wait while those vibrating fingers took their nourishment.

Major Fernand Corbet gave a dignified sniff of thanks, then, as if the record was broken, for all invariably said the same these days, he spat, 'They ran, monsieur, when they should have stayed and held their ground as we did.'

Corbet lived in 4-9, next to 4-7. A little man with cigarette ash and dandruff on his jacket, tie and beret, he'd been about to go out for his afternoon *apéritif*. 'A simple glass of the *vin ordinaire*, the white you understand. These days the red's too acid for the digestion.'

St-Cyr drew up the only other chair. 'M'sieur –'

'Major. Please, I must insist. These days one *has* to do something.'

'Major, the girl who used the room next door to you?'

'A student. No spine. She should be making bombs or seducing Boches so that real men could cut their throats, not fucking some fat windbag of commerce!'

'Yes, yes, Major, but she's dead.'

'Dead? What is this, eh? A murder in the hotel? *Nom de Jésus-Christ*, I'll get that bitch this time! Calls herself a concierge! Can't keep order in this place. *Order*, do you understand?'

He was quaking with rage. 'Yes . . . yes, of course I understand, Major. Later . . . we'll both speak to her later.'

'You're from the police, aren't you?'

'The Sûreté.'

'Who let you into my room, eh? That bitch . . .'

Corbet had a coughing fit. It was several moments before he had fully recovered.

'That girl . . .' he began. 'Yes, yes. Always at it, the two of them. Naked . . . naked on that floor in there.'

Though it was useless to ask, St-Cyr had to try. 'Did you see anything, hear anything? It happened Thursday night, at between nine and nine-thirty.'

Thursday . . . Thursday . . . They'd been waiting for the shells. Paul Tremblay, the one with the hollow eyes and the look of death, had said, 'It's my turn. Today I'm going to get it.'

'Pardon?' asked the cop.

The Major tossed a tired hand. 'I heard nothing of that affair, monsieur, nor did I see anything untoward.'

He sucked on his cigarette as one accustomed to the trenches. 'Dead,' he said, tossing his head in acknowledgement. 'All of them, Colonel. I am the only one left. Why did God spare me and yet take them?'

To his dying day he'd ask the question all survivors of such things must ask.

St-Cyr patted him on the shoulder. The elevation in rank to colonel from a mere sergeant in the Signals Corp had said it all. 'Take care, my old one. I'll drop in again.'

Out in the hall it was the thigh wound that gave the first twitch of sympathy to strip away the years, then the one in the shoulder that had knocked him off his feet and made him ask that same question himself.

Always it was like this, old wounds, old battles, old memories he'd sooner forget.

His left side had always been the vulnerable one, ever since he'd broken that leg as a boy while scaling his Aunt Jessie's barn near Beaune. It had been one of those rare incidents when his mother had lost her temper and had slapped him across the face, the left side, always the left, ah yes, for disobedience.

Never mind that his leg had been hurting like hell!

'The girl next door ... Yes, yes, I remember her well, monsieur. Always in a hurry, that one, and not wishing to come in even for a moment. I have even left the door ajar so as to watch for her and call out, but', the man gave a shrug, 'she has ignored me. Not out of unkindness, I assure you, Inspector. Out of haste, always haste. She did not wish me to know she met another in there.'

Alphonse Dupuis had been a captain, a sapper who'd lost his right leg but who otherwise appeared quite debonair in spite of his reduced state of being. A man of some fifty-eight years perhaps. Not too thin. Still with a little paunch.

He readily accepted a cigarette but flicked his own lighter, the one he kept for special occasions when he wanted to impress. 'Don't believe a word of what Corbet has told you, Inspector. That one's so touched he still doesn't think it possible there were men below the rank of major.'

The little joke went well, the one from the Sûreté had understanding in his eyes, instant rapport. So, good! Yes. Now the interview could begin.

'She was quite pretty?' he hazarded. 'Dead, I understand, from garrotting with the wire? Violated as she lay beneath her assailant, eh? My poor little bird.'

'Did you ever talk to her?'

'Me? Ah no. She was, as I've only just said, far too embarrassed. She'd have seen the truth of her life in my eyes – they're like a father's, is that not so, Inspector? It would have been too much for her.'

The paunch rose to press against the buttons of the green silk vest Dupuis had had for years. His hair was thin, the head nearly bald over the crown, the eyes of a deep and intense brown but constantly on the move.

'What about the one who visited her?'

Had the Sûreté seen the truth? Did he know that the dreams of the little one had hurt almost as much as the nightmares? 'That one has a moustache much wider and fuller than your own, Inspector. Brown and greying. The well-pressed suit, the corpulent, well-fed bastard's son of a shopkeeper's whore.'

'His age?'

'Madame Minou will have already told you. Me, I haven't time for trifles, Inspector. I'm busy writing my memoirs. The publishers, the bloodsuckers, they're always pressing me for deadlines yet still refusing to pay their advances.'

'About fifty-six or fifty-eight?' *Nom de Dieu*, don't get bitchy on me!

'Yes, yes, all right! Of almost your age, but with more vitality for a man with two legs, more zip to his step.'

'I'm only fifty-two.'

'You look eighty but never mind. I suppose it's all that sitting you people do.'

'Just tell me about him, eh?'

A ten-franc note was parsimoniously fingered in a black leather pocketbook that would have shamed a priest.

The note was placed on the desk. A cloud of exasperated smoke enveloped the Sûreté's gumshoe. Good! 'Another, Inspector. There is much that I can tell you.'

'Withholding information is a criminal offence.'

'Arrest me then. Jail would be preferable to this hole.'

Twenty more fell and then a further twenty to bring it up to fifty.

'He was from the provinces, from the south-west. A bourgeois up to Paris to see his mistress. He brought her things, little favours. Chocolates, several jars of pâté at different times – I'm certain of it. Once two bottles of liqueur, once four bottles, usually only one.'

'How can you be so certain?'

'Because she left them outside my door when she went away.'

St-Cyr laid another fifty on the desk. 'Antoine Audit and Sons of Périgord?' he asked. 'A *pâté de foie gras aux truffes*?'

Dupuis grunted. 'It was exceptional. I looked for more.'

'She spoiled you, monsieur. Any ideas what went on in that room?'

This from the Sûreté! 'Of course. She took off her clothes while that one watched, then they did it, not once but several times, after which he always left the room first and went down by the tradesmen's stairs.'

'How long did he stay?'

'The half hour, the hour, as long as it took.'

'And the girl?'

'She always washed herself afterwards. Me, I've seen her many times carrying the basin to the lavatory. There is a tap in that place. It drips constantly. We all have to get our own water for such things.'

'He came once or twice a week, always at the same time?'

'Between eight and nine in the evening, yes.'

'Except for last Tuesday.'

'Yes, he came then at four, and he did not bring her anything that time.'

'How was she when she left the room on Tuesday?'

'Upset. She touched her hair at the back, like this, like a young girl in distress. I think she must have informed him of her pregnancy, and that one told her to get lost. So much for the pâtés, eh? and the strawberry liqueurs!'

Things no one in their right mind would give away these days unless they had a damned good reason for not wanting to be seen with them. 'Do you think she loved this Monsieur Antoine?'

'She was not a prostitute, not that one, Inspector. Kept – of course he gave her money for the use of her body – but love? Who's to say what that is? She enjoyed it, this much I do know, though it grieves me to have to mention it. On several occasions her step was very light and quick as she left the room, and twice when I called out to her, she smiled at me and I saw the happiness in her lovely eyes.'

'Did you ever leave money out for her in hopes she'd come in?'

'Money? There's hardly enough of it to get by.'

The cop said nothing. He was too perceptive, too difficult and not so easy as some others had been. 'Of course I did not leave her money. That would have insulted her. Besides, Madame Minou's son is not to be trusted.'

St-Cyr thanked the boyhood that had taught him to question so as to elicit those answers that were vital to an investigation.

'Madame Minou's son?' he said blandly, reaching for his hat.

'She never knows when he'll come back. He still has a key to this place, though she will deny it to God on her day of judgement.'

'Such is the love of a mother for her son, eh?'

Long after the detective had taken himself away, Dupuis sat in his chair going over things. He'd said everything as it should have been said, even to that bit about the old shrew's son, Roland, and to that bit about the girl's M Antoine leaving by the tradesmen's stairs. The Sûreté would go out that way to see for himself. He'd notice that the door opened only from the inside, that there was a bellpush to wake the old slut in her cage. He'd realize that the door could be left open a little with a stick or a pencil if one wished to come back in again unnoticed.

So, it had gone well enough and now he would sleep a little. Later he'd go out for a drink to celebrate. Yes . . . yes, he'd do that, but he must hide the money from prying eyes so that Madame Minou would not get wind of it and demand it all in payment of the rent.

Kohler pushed a dozen of the coins across the inlaid fruit-wood of the coffee-table. There wasn't any sense in beating about the bush. A visit to the Abwehr's headquarters in the Hotel Lutétia had turned up nothing but the stone wall of interservice rivalry. He'd had to leap it.

'The girl did a deal and the deal went sour.'

Hermann 'Otto' Brandl smiled as he rubbed his hands together. The slightly scented cocoa butter had been good for them. It had a nice smell and wasn't too greasy when worked into the skin.

'All things are of interest to the Bureau Otto, Hermann, but why show me these?'

'I thought you might like to help me find the real ones.'

Brandl affected delicacy as he smoothed his silver locks. 'Since when does the Gestapo seek to help the Abwehr?'

'Louis and I are being given the run-around by Lafont and Bonny. Rumour has it Carbone's involved.'

The puffy eyelids lifted. At the age of forty-six, Brandl, a captain in the Abwehr, headed up the Reich's huge and complex purchasing office in France. Supreme power, supreme graft and everything else that went with it. A real producer.

Supplies from all over the country poured through his fingers – iron, copper, coal, manganese, potatoes, leather, chemicals – whatever the war effort and the Reich needed, and in plenty. Silk from Antoine Audit, of course, ah yes. Gold and diamonds, stocks and bonds, fine wines and paintings – enough for him to have syphoned off ten or twelve personal fortunes.

The coins were good imitations but not good enough. 'What does Boemelburg have to say about your coming to me?'

'The Sturmbannführer's a busy man. He doesn't like to know the fine details, just the big things.'

Again the puffy eyelids questioned. In spite of the immaculately tailored naval uniform and the polished mannerisms of the best salons, Brandl remained a toad in oil. A Bavarian schmuck.

who might, at best, have run a steel mill had his mother slapped his wrists.

'Schraum worked for me.'

'I rather thought he might have.' This would have been the order of the day, in any case.

The pale-blue eyes in that round and pasty face narrowed. 'Did Carbone kill him?'

'We don't know that.'

'What about the mackerel, Victor Morande?'

'We don't know that either.'

'You don't know much then, do you, Hermann?'

'Enough to ask for help where it can count. Look, we know the girl was flogging bits of jewellery in the fleas.'

'Lots do that. It's nothing new.'

'Lafont had her followed. Bonny had her tagged as a big one. You used to have Lafont working for you. You know he's got a nose for stuff.'

'And you want my help.'

The rubbing had finally ceased. Now the backs of his fingers were being smelled again. 'Von Schaumburg's behind us. Anything we want we get. The full weight of the Kommandant of Greater Paris. He's a stickler for law and order, Otto, and he's out to strip your gears. Schraum was one of his men who had been assigned to carry coal and other things for the Bureau, not filch whatever sidelines he could. A corporal no less. No discipline, chasing after the wives of others, dabbling in a little gold.'

How could Kohler dare to say such things? 'Your boss won't like this, Hermann, and neither will Osias Pharand.'

'Our superiors needn't know unless you tell them.'

'Okay, so I'm listening.' Brandl snapped his fingers, motioning to one of the club's stewards. 'Two whiskies on ice, none of that lousy *gazeuse* you bastards think is soda water. Put it on my chit and don't cheat me.'

'Make mine a double, will you? I've not had any breakfast or any sleep. I have to take my pills. Doctor's orders.'

The Traveller's Club was on the Champs-Élysées. Brandl had a particular affection for it and for doing business in such places. The busty, life-sized girls on the richly carved chimney-piece were aimed over their heads. Far above them in the centre of the ceiling more painted nudes cavorted or lay about with bare-assed cherubs scrambling over walls to duck the arrow of some strong-armed hunk of virility.

'Nice . . . this is really nice, Otto. I like it.'

'Oh do you? This "partner" of yours, Herr Kohler. We of the Abwehr don't like him. The SS don't and neither should the Gestapo.'

'Louis is useful. He'll lead you to the loot if you let him.'

The toad rubbed the oil in his palm with a thumb. 'Rumour has it he's dead meat.'

Poor Louis . . . 'The coin that was left in the centre of the girl's forehead?' asked Kohler. Lafont, ah Christ!

It would be best to affect a rather bored air. 'We could help you a little, perhaps. I'd have to see about it.'

'Did Victor Morande get the coal to run that carousel from Schraum?'

'Of course. Who else?' Brandl thought about lifting his glass and taking a small sip. Perhaps it would be construed as a toast to their mutual business, perhaps not, and Kohler would have to worry about it. Yes, that would be good.

The single malt whisky was excellent, and the Gestapo took to it as the desert rodent to the oasis.

'Careful, my Hermann. Careful. If you're going to work for the Bureau, we shall have to insist on a modicum of . . . what shall I say? Not total abstinence. Nothing so harsh. Merely prudence.'

'I was just taking my pills. They're for the digestion.'

'Have you ulcers?'

'A few. They're not bleeding, not yet.'

'Then perhaps I can help them. Schraum's uncle, the Gauleiter of Stralsund and SA-Obersturmführer, is an avid coin collector who writes to others of the same interest. He's also a distant relative of Goering.'

A storm trooper . . . a relative . . . The pills caught. Kohler choked. Moisture rushed into his eyes as he swallowed hard and forced himself not to reach for his glass.

The Benzedrine stung. 'A coin collector?'

'And a relative of the Reichsmarschall and Reichsführer himself.'

'Who also collects coins.'

'Roman ones, my Hermann. Things like those with Nero's head and those of Caesar Augustus and all the rest.'

'Sestertii and aurei.' Brandl already had someone working on it! The bastard was even competing with the SS and the rue Lauriston on this one too!

'Have a little sip. It'll help. Then tell me about the girl, about the room and about the villa at Number twenty-three.' He'd see how much they knew, then call him my Hermann again to see if the bait had not just been taken but the hook set deeply.

Another whisky came for the Gestapo's warbler and then a plate of Norwegian smoked salmon with little wedges of toast, which he wolfed as only one of the Gestapo's most disloyal men would wolf.

'Common crime, my Hermann. It's with us every day and must be cleansed from the streets, but what's this? Your eyes keep straying to the ceiling. Is it because of your little pigeon – what was her name?'

'Giselle le Roy.'

A fist had clenched, a slice of the salmon had fallen on to the carpet. Good, very good. 'Yes, yes, Giselle. Perhaps you cannot find her and wish the assistance not just of the Kommandant of Greater Paris but also that of the Bureau Otto?'

'Who's got her?'

'Really, Herr Kohler, the darkness you betray so willingly is admirable. Not the Bureau, I assure you. Pigeons are only of interest if they can lead us to gold that others want and are too greedy to share with the proper authorities.'

'Morande?'

'He offered Schraum half of what the Audit girl could bring and the Corporal bit, as corporals like Schraum will do who are eager to impress their uncles back home in the hopes of being given a step up the ladder by a certain Reichsmarschall.'

'Was Morande connected to any of the gangs?'

'To Lafont or Carbone or any of the others? Really, Herr Kohler, for a detective and a fellow Bavarian you surprise me.'

'Talbotte's washed his hands of the affair. Even records down at Headquarters are being tight.'

'They've clipped your wings, have they?'

Kohler's head was singing. The girls above were beginning to dance. His heart was pounding. Brandl was blurred.

'Really, my Hermann, do you not know the mackerel made himself unwelcome in the Santé by coughing up a name he should never have mentioned? That someone paid him back. It's that simple. Find out who he is and you'll find the forger. Then bring me the loot so that the Reichsmarschall can gloat over his newest coins and we can have all the rest.'

'What makes you so certain there are any coins – any real ones?'

Brandl savoured things. Baiting Hermann had had its

moments. Henri Lafont should never have gone over to work for the other side, for the SS of the avenue Foch! The rue Lauriston was getting far too greedy for its own good and meddling in things it should never have meddled in.

'Industrialists who have found favour in high places, my Hermann, should always make certain they have declared every last sou of their valuables.'

'M Antoine Audit? The silk, eh?'

'Explosives, glass and wine, truffles and, yes, the silk.'

Just like the old grandmother had said, Antoine Audit had had to sell through Brandl's Bureau Otto.

'It's only a thought,' said Brandl. 'After all, Bonny, your partner's former colleague did mark the girl down as being a big one, right?'

'Who told them about her?'

'Find the mackerel's killer and you'll find out. He must be a fund of information, that one. A bank.'

Lagace, the baker, brushed flour from his forearms. The one from the Sûreté had come across the street to ask more questions; the one from the Gestapo had taken the Citroën and driven away some time ago.

Merde, it was like waiting for death and not knowing what went on behind the scenes to influence the decision one way or the other. Still, it would be best to put on a brave face.

'Inspector, I must thank you for what you did for me the other day.'

St-Cyr raised both hands in a gesture of Hold it, my friend. Enough said.

There were two customers in the shop, plus the woman who helped when the thrice-weekly bread ration was to be distributed.

'Georges, a few small matters. Little details. Nothing important. We've all but wrapped the thing up and are just tidying.'

'Mademoiselle Rose-Eva, did you hear that?' shouted the bearer of glad tidings. 'No more rapists or sadists in the rue Polonceau. You and your sister can breathe a little easier.'

They were both in their eighties, timid, frail bits of dust with black biscuit hats, black shawls and coats, black everything.

The woman who had been handing them their ration of bread

repeated the news in an equally loud voice, then warned them of theft. 'You must guard your bread with your lives this time. We cannot give you any more if it's stolen again.'

'Give? Who gives?' shrilled the older of the two.

'He did it. We both know he did. He undressed her and then he violated her.'

'Jeanne, shut up! Madame, you owe us bread for last week. I'm not leaving until we get it!'

'He split her hymen even as he strangled her. It's the God's truth. I have heard this straight from the horse's mouth!'

The younger one hastily crossed herself before wetting her thin lips in expectation of some further development.

Lagace heaved a sigh. 'Come into the back, Inspector. It'll be quieter there.'

'No . . . no, a moment, Georges. Mesdemoiselles, who was the killer of that girl?' he shouted.

'Killer? Killer? He wants to know who the rapist was, Rose-Eva.'

'The rapist, yes. The killer. He's a detective, Jeanne. Let him find out for himself. Let him "tidy" his own little details since they have not yet arrested the villain.'

'Who?' asked the detective.

'Who do you think?' demanded the older of the two hotheads.

Snatching their thin stick of bread, the sisters headed for the door.

'Later, Inspector. Later. Please, I can explain. Those two, they've been talking about that sort of thing for years. The younger one reads the papers and dreams of it; the older one rejoices at the trouble the dreams are causing the younger one. It's nothing but the air of two old women whose moment has long passed.'

A poet, eh?

They went into the heart of the bakery where empty cutting and pastry tables gave the lie of commerce and cold ovens that of plenty.

'Two sacks of flour arrived today. Some salt and sugar. I can't understand it, Inspector. A Wehrmacht truck? An order for six hundred loaves of bread to be delivered to the local barracks of the German Army on Monday morning at 0600 hours.'

St-Cyr told him not to worry. 'You've just earned yourself a job courtesy of Sturmbannführer Walter Boemelburg.'

Lagace's face fell. 'The one who came to choose the hostages.'

'It's his little joke on me. Don't worry. I told him you had the job and he just made certain that you did.'

'But it will take at least another sack of flour and the gas to heat the ovens?'

So much for a baker's sense of humour. There were two chairs pulled up to the front of one of the ovens. He seemed turned to stone. 'I knew it was too good to be true. Now they'll come for me and that will be the end of it.'

Had he no thoughts for Marianne St-Jacques, his girlfriend?

'What is it that you want of me, Inspector?'

'Merely your silence.'

'My silence?' Ah Mon Dieu, the grave! The one from the Gestapo had left the Sûreté to give the *coup de grâce*!

'First, the villa at Number twenty-three.'

'That place?' he shrilled.

St-Cyr nodded. 'Tell me about it.'

'There's nothing to tell. No one comes and no one goes. It must be leased to the Boches – ah, excuse me, Inspector. Those two old ladies, they've got me rattled. The Germans. The Nazis.'

'Was there a housekeeper?'

'Madame Gilbert, a widow. She was one of the hostages taken to the Cherche-Midi. We have only found this out last night, quite late.'

St-Cyr said 'I see,' but wondered, After curfew? The Resistance, eh? and wanted to add, You should not have been so careless, idiot!

Boemelburg could not have known of the housekeeper but, then, Walter hadn't chosen all of the hostages himself. She could have been taken away on purpose.

'Anything else?' he asked.

There'd be more and more questions now. Lies would have to pile upon lies. 'Occasionally there are guests but myself, I have never seen anyone go into or out of that place in years.'

'What sort of guests?'

'Germans. Who else?'

Hermann would find out the rest. 'How's Marianne bearing up?'

'Fine. She's fine. I've told her not to come near here until . . . until things have cooled down.'

You're a damned fool, he wanted so much to say but knew he couldn't. 'She'll be expecting a visit from me, will she?'

'Yes, yes, she'll be expecting that.'

'You must have talked to Madame Gilbert several times, Georges. Surely the villa at Number twenty-three would have come up in your conversations?'

'Never. That one knows her duty is to the hand that pays her.'

Fair enough. 'Now tell me about the two sisters. Who did they think might have killed that girl?'

'Captain Dupuis. The one who has lost a leg.'

'Why him?'

'How should I know? Inspector –'

'Yes, yes, I know you have six hundred sticks of bread to bake. Good luck. I'll be in touch.'

'I still meant the thanks I said when you first came into the shop, only now I'm not so sure it was such a good idea for you to have saved me.'

'Don't worry. Just do as the Gestapo Chief has asked and keep the army happy. They'll love your bread and soon you'll be able to skim off a little to augment everyone else's rations. Sturmbann-führer Boemelburg will know I have suggested this but do it anyway.'

Both old ladies were still on the street. The younger one clutched the arm of the older one. The bread was gripped between them and both had canes no one would dare to argue with.

The sitting-room was small and from another time, with faded wine-red velvet, yellowed lace and flowered chintzes that spoke not just of passing fancy but of missed careers, failed attempts and partial successes.

Four cat baskets lay about: one on the floor by the end of the plush but faded blue sofa, another on the carpet in front of the tiny stove, a third up by a vase of dried asters in the curtained window, the last under a chair.

There was only one cat, and this was asleep in the middle of the sofa. But had there once been four cats or had that cat but four places in which to sleep? And if the former, which of the sisters had killed the others and hidden the truth? One could not afford to keep four cats these days – four roasts, four nourishing stews that could, if stretched, last at least three days apiece.

St-Cyr decided it would have to have been the older sister, Rose-Eva, who took care of such things. The younger one was too delicate, too timid. That one had been the orchestrator of the chintzes. The room bore the stamp of a spark caught in mid-flight on a cool summer's evening some fifty or sixty years ago.

He accepted the tiny glass of 'juice', a loganberry cordial perhaps, but set it aside out of politeness as one would and should. The French didn't readily invite people into their homes – the Sûreté had special privileges they could invoke and did – but always, as with all others, there was this formal offering of the 'juice'.

One seldom drank it and when one did, the regrets inevitably followed.

'Mademoiselle Rose-Eva Gagnon, permit me, please, to ask again who you and your sister think is the killer of that girl and why you feel so certain of this?'

'If you'd been doing your job . . .'

'Mademoiselle, I assure you I am and was, but I make no apologies for the overwork, the lack of sleep and the pitifully low wages.'

She tossed her head but was too polite to think or say, Suck lemons! monsieur. 'We told them. We pleaded with them, but they would not listen.'

'He'd done it before, you see,' offered the quiet meekness of the younger sister, sitting bolt upright to one side of the cat while her sister sat on the other side of it.

Was she protecting the cat, that last vestige of sensibility, from the older sister?

'Who had "done it before"?' he asked politely.

'The Captain, the man without the leg.'

'Captain Alphonse Dupuis,' whispered the younger sister. 'Me, I have had the . . .'

'Jeanne, that is enough! Don't start again.'

Chastized, the younger sister timidly reached out to the cat only to withdraw her trembling hand, knowing the gesture would bring rebuke.

'What my sister wishes to say, Inspector, is that on the evening of the day before the Defeat, there was a similar murder in our *quartier*. A young girl – Jeanne, stop it immediately, do you hear?'

The cat slept on as the hand desperately stole its way across the blue velvet of the cushion in spite of the warning.

Rose-Eva sensed the need in her young sister and, in a rare moment of resigned weakness, said, 'Oh it's all right. Go on, you silly thing. Take Muffti into your lap. Just *don't* become too attached to him.'

'I won't! I won't even touch him!'

Again they were at an impasse. 'This other murder . . . ?' he hazarded.

'In the courtyard of the house next to that wretched draper's shop on the Pas-Léon, not a stone's throw from the Church of Saint Bernard.'

'It's not a "wretched" shop,' whispered Jeanne. 'Anyway, it was closed and I only went there after my prayers to remember a little.'

'Ladies, *please*! I want to help. It's my job.'

'We're trying to tell you. She's *trying*,' said the younger one in a rare moment of defiance.

'Perhaps it is yourself who should be telling me,' soothed St-Cyr, throwing up a cautionary hand to silence the older sister.

Jeanne Gagnon composed herself. 'Very well, it is I who shall say it.'

The other one held her breath but gave him the sabre of dark-blue eyes that had lost none of their will to fight.

'I went to church to pray for the deliverance of the city and of France in her hour of need. So few were there, monsieur. Empty – I have never known the streets or the church to be so empty.'

'Everyone had fled the city,' said Rose-Eva. 'I was ill in bed, a bad fall –'

'You had *drunk* too much, Rose. The Inspector will know this. The Defeat, if nothing else, has cured you of your affliction because now it is rationed, *if* one can get it! So, where was I? Yes . . . yes . . . Father Eugène and Father David were both at the church – they'd been on call all the time. It's a priest's duty, isn't it?

'They blessed me. Father Eugène heard my confession. He always has, that one, since the years of my original sin, my small sin, which was only to be of hope, you understand?

'I left the church but did not want to, Inspector. I was afraid. I was alone.'

'At about what time would that have been?'

'At about eight o'clock in the evening.'

'Still plenty of light. I remember the city well, mademoiselle.'

'I started home. I crossed the rue Saint-Luc and came to the Pas-Léon, which joins the rue Polonceau at the foot of the street next to the square. I was tempted. I needed to see the shop again, Rose-Eva. I was so afraid the city would be completely destroyed.'

A moment was called for.

'The courtyard door was open, Jeanne.'

'Yes . . . yes, it was. I'd gone to see if Monsieur Paul's son had placed anything new in the windows but . . . but of course he and his wife and family had fled the city.'

A draper's shop. A lost love perhaps – the father, Monsieur Paul senior?

'The girl was lying in the courtyard between two trash barrels, partly beneath a carpenter's workbench. Her clothes had . . .'

'Inspector, must you?'

'Please, it is necessary.'

'Her clothes had been pulled down around her ankles and pushed up above . . . above her breasts. I could not see her face, only a portion of her hair.'

'What colour?'

'Blonde, not black. Ah yes, I have even thought of that, Inspector. Though the age was the same, the hair colouring was different.'

'She'd been strangled with a silk stocking, Inspector, but it hadn't been one of her own.'

'She'd become separated from her family – they'd all left the city without her. There was such confusion, such fear, such terror, no people to cry out to, no people to hear her screams for help, for mer –'

'Jeanne, stop it! Stop it!'

'Forgive me. Please forgive me.'

'The Captain Alphonse Dupuis had not left the city in the exodus, Inspector. Indeed, he had not left the *quartier*.'

'I had met him earlier on his way back to the Hotel of the Silent Life as I went to church. I did not know then what he'd just done. He was afraid to face me, Inspector, and when I came along the street, he turned away to hide his face by searching in a shop window. He was trembling. I spoke to him. I asked him how he felt about things and was there anything the matter, could I help him in any way? He gave no answer. There . . . there was . . .'

'There was blood on the collar and one cuff of his shirt, Inspector.'

'Blood!' exclaimed the younger one, bursting into tears.

'After she had found the body, my sister hurried to tell Father Eugène, Inspector, but could not find him at first.'

'He . . . he was in the sacristy talking to someone. I did not see who. I was too upset. Deranged!'

138

'And the authorities, the police?'

'They did not come until the next day. They didn't believe me. They said it must have been done by the Germans, by a drunken soldier. That soldiers rape and pillage in conquest, that no one is safe, no woman no matter how old or young, but of course, there were no German soldiers in the city at that time.'

Jeanne tucked her handkerchief up a sleeve and strained for breath. 'The Captain swore I was mistaken and ever since then has hated me.'

'How long have you lived in the *quartier*?'

It was a question of much kindness. 'All our lives. Jeanne wanted so much to become an interior designer, to have a shop of her own. Madame Audit . . .'

'Mademoiselle Prévost, Rose-Eva. Michèle-Louise.'

'Yes, yes, I know, my dear one, but as I've told you many times . . .'

'I'm *sick* of hearing it! Sick, do you hear? She was good to me. She was someone I could talk to who understood what I felt inside. She was my friend.'

'An artist of the avant-garde, Inspector. A charlatan who copied the works of others. A much younger woman than Jeanne, one who thought the barriers of age should be broken and not allowed to segregate people.'

'Michèle-Louise said I had promise, that if she could decorate her beautiful house with nothing, surely I could do wonders with very little.'

'But then her husband went away, Inspector, and the woman left the house without even saying goodbye to my sister.'

'She was expecting a child. It was his child. I know it was.'

'He had a shop, Inspector. He sold shoes. The woman was never satisfied with this. For her, to spend one's life selling shoes was to spend it in the grave.'

'Someone had to pay the bills. She did love him. I know she did! We were two souls crying out to be heard, Inspector,' said the younger sister but with such frankness in her sensitive eyes he thought he understood.

'There was a brother?' he asked.

'Monsieur Antoine Audit. Yes . . . yes, there was a brother. He lived in Périgord. An estate or a farm – an industrialist, though. Yes, yes, he was an industrialist.'

'Did Monsieur Charles ever come back to the street?'

Rose-Eva shook her head. Jeanne stared emptily at the carpet.

'The cuckold can't, Inspector. Me, I have never before this day spoken of it, but as God is my witness I say it to you now. She was unfaithful to him and that is why he went away.'

'He was arrested, Jeanne. He tried to kill his brother and for this they sent him to where he could do no more harm.'

'When?' asked the detective.

'Why, in 1905, in the spring,' said the older sister.

'May the third. It was a Thursday. We . . . we were going to do over some cushions using a metre or two of the blue silk she had received from Monsieur Antoine.'

'Mesdemoiselles, my thanks. You have been most helpful.'

'And the Captain? Monsieur Alphonse Dupuis?' asked the butterfly.

'We will take him away for questioning as soon as my partner gets back with the car.' Hermann . . . where the hell was Hermann?

The house was nothing – five floors of flaking stucco under cluttered chimney-pots, broken slates and skylights that gave all-too-easy access to the rooftops.

Kohler was impressed. In just such little things were there answers, and Christ they needed them! The new operator of the carousel had looked to his future. If necessity had demanded escape, he had had it in plenty. A warren of forgotten streets, a trap for the unwary, and the rooftops up there.

The quai Jemmapes was silent in the mid-afternoon. The Canal Saint-Martin had the colour of used crankcase oil. Two old men, bundled in filthy blankets, fished for God alone knew what. A nun pushed a foundling's pram towards a priest whose flat, round hat miraculously refused to blow off.

So far so good. Everything ordinary. No one taking any notice.

He'd left the car well out of sight. He'd seen them watching the house.

Some of the shutters were crooked; others lacked all or a part of their louvres. The Café du Paradis, while it might once have provided a passable living, now looked cheated and angry.

A lone girl on a bicycle passed by. A coven of four housewives stopped to stare at her while a portly shopkeeper with nothing better to do clung to the walls behind them, using the impasse to slip along to the café.

The girl disappeared round the corner, up the avenue

Richerand towards the *Hôpital* Saint-Louis. Kohler pulled his gaze back to the house. It'd be the room at the top to the far right, just below the dilapidated dovecote whose wire cages would most likely be empty. All eaten by now, but excellent cover for a first dodge across the roofs or a nice little watch of the street and the quays.

Again he drew in a breath. The Benzedrine ... he couldn't afford to take any more. He'd become addicted if he did. He had to sleep, but how?

Hurriedly crossing the bridge, he went along the quay until he came abreast of the café. They'd have seen him now. They'd know he was going up to the room. They'd tell Lafont or Bonny and the rue Lauriston might or might not be happy.

The concierge was a surprise, a tall, winsome blonde with large blue eyes, her hair in a braid down over the left shoulder. 'Monsieur...'

Dutch and an illegal immigrant. *Gott im Himmel*, well what do you know? About forty and still a fine-looking woman. Married too.

Again he was impressed. The choice of room had included a concierge who'd be certain not to question things and would also not know a hell of a lot about the French, or even the city for that matter. One hundred per cent.

'Kohler of the Gestapo.'

The fair cheeks tightened. In fear or hesitation, she touched her slightly parted lips with the tip of her tongue. 'Herr Kohler. Yes ... yes, they did say you might come. I'll take you up to the room.'

'Who said I'd come?'

'Those ... those who came and took my husband away.'

Ah, *merde*! Not the husband!

There were two sets of stairs and a lift that looked doubtful – three exits. More potential. Again he had to be impressed.

She opened the lift cage. He thought to object, but already she'd stepped into the thing.

As they went up, they were crowded face to face, her chest all but touching his, the clench of death, eh? Her choice; she could have faced the other way. Often women chose to do that. Back to front. Did the frankness of her gaze betray something other than fear? She was almost as tall as himself and knew he was studying her.

'Where are you from?' he asked.

Right away she'd known he'd ask it. 'Rotterdam. Our papers are in order. The Kommandantur...'

Kohler stuck out an arm and jammed his hand against the far side of the cage door, barring her escape when they reached the top floor. 'Don't give me any of that shit. You left Rotterdam in a rush, right? and you got here just ahead of the Panzers.'

'Was that a crime?' she asked, not altering her gaze.

'Only if you're here illegally.'

'We're not. Our papers are in order but ... but they've taken my husband away. I want him back.'

Kohler nodded. The couple would have bought the papers, good ones too, probably, but they'd only be good for so long and she damned well knew it.

'Let's go up to the roof first. I want to have a look at that dovecote.'

The eyes never wavered. They were so clear, so blue. 'The elevator only goes to the fifth floor. From there we'll have to climb the stairs.'

Good again. *Mein Gott* the man was a marvel! Exits like he couldn't believe. Skylights and now even a staircase.

'Tell me about him. Let me have the name he gave you, then his age, weight, et cetera, and everything else just so we can tell whose corpse it is.'

'Was he killed?'

A cool one. Not even a quiver. 'Not that we know of. Not yet.'

The Gestapo's swollen eye was badly bruised, the stitches inflamed. He had been in a fight, yes ... yes, but would he really help her to free Martin?

Kohler saw her looking at him and grinned. 'What's your name?'

'Madame Oona Van der Lynn.' They were jostled. Always it was at the fourth floor that there was this catching of the cable. 'It will pass,' she said. 'It's nothing. Don't worry.'

He let go of her. She smelled nice, had that very Dutch smell about her. Clean as a whistle, not perfume, just soap she'd scrounged from some place.

Again he heard her telling him not to worry. 'I wasn't,' he lied. 'Why not give me his name, eh? The look of him.'

'Réjean Turcel. He was about sixty-three or maybe sixty-six, so a little older than yourself but very tough. A hard man, a...'

'I'm not that old.'

Again her gaze was steady, a momentary pause.

'Turcel was short and stocky, swarthy, yes,' she fingered the braid in doubt. 'With ... how should I say it? Very quick, dark-brown eyes.'

Always watchful then. Again it fitted. 'A business-like walk? Fast, very fast?'

'Yes ... yes, he did walk like that. He was always going or coming. A man with a purpose.'

'A man with a carousel.'

'Pardon?'

Kohler told her but all she did was shrug. 'I never knew what he did for a living. He never said.'

Had she been a little lost by the question? he wondered. 'What about his skin? Did he look as if he'd spent his life in the sun?'

They had reached the fifth floor. His arm still barred the way.

'Yes ... Yes, he was like that.'

'A Corsican?' It wasn't so much a question as a statement of fact, and she knew then that his thoughts were racing ahead to other things. 'Dots – did he have three of them on either of his hands? The backs of the middle fingers?' he asked.

He looked quite ill at the thought, but perhaps it had only been the ride up in the lift that had made his stomach turn. When she went to open the lift door, her left shoulder and hip would have to brush against him, but would it help her? Would it really? 'Yes, Turcel had three faded dots on the backs of the middle fingers of his left hand, the first joint; five in the web of skin between the thumb and forefinger of his right hand.'

Squeezing round to face him again, she showed him her hands and he felt her middle as it came against his own and he wondered exactly what kind of pressure the rue Lauriston had put on her.

Her finger kept tapping the web of skin. She'd a nice thumb. 'The tobacco pouch,' he said, a whisper. 'One of the hard ones, a Corsican.' A friend of Carbone, an associate, a member of that gang? The rue de Villejust? Lafont's arch-enemy? The hit men.

Oona Van der Lynn flashed him an uncertain smile. 'These things have hardly any room,' she said not moving her middle.

Kohler ... his name was Hermann Kohler of the Gestapo.

They went along the corridor to the far end of the house until they stood outside Number 5-13. The stairs to the roof were as close as spit, the tradesmen's set a fraction closer. The woman hesitated. When her eyes dropped to the floor, she touched the top button of the grey-blue cardigan she wore. Her braid had fallen forward a little, and he wondered again what the hell she was really on about and he felt the blood pounding in his veins. 'You first. There's no danger. It's better this way.'

'For what?' she asked, knowing all about it.

There was hardly light enough to see her and when she stopped once in the middle of the staircase, he was reminded again that she smelled nice. 'My husband. They . . . they took him away.'

'Where to?'

'The Vél d'Hiv. They said . . .' She began to climb the stairs again. 'It . . . it doesn't matter.'

'The Vél's not being used any more, is it?' She had reached the door to the roof. No key was needed; he was impressed again. Réjean Turcel or Réjean whatever had chosen well.

The Gestapo was standing on the step below her. She could feel him against her. It was dark. He'd . . . 'The door, it always sticks a little, monsieur. Could you . . . ?'

Kohler felt the fit of her. It was nice, really nice. His chin brushed against the back of her head. Her skin was cool but then, it was winter.

He gave the door a shove and miracle of miracles, it opened at a touch.

The dovecote was made of weathered boards that had been salvaged from some dump. The cages were arranged in tiers. There were about thirty of them and all were empty. 'Who lived up here?'

There were blankets on the floor, several books, the stub of a candle and a washtub to hide the light.

'My husband.'

'A Jew?'

The blue eyes sought him out. They didn't waver, they didn't beg.

He'd not help her. He couldn't! She saw this come into his eyes, saw him silently curse and then clench a fist. 'The Vél d'Hiv, eh?' he said. 'But first the rue Lauriston. What did your husband know that you didn't?'

'Martin never said, but I think he may have talked to Monsieur Turcel, for that one often came up here.'

'At night?'

'Yes. To . . .'

'To avoid going out the front door? What'd he do, madame? Threaten the two of you, eh? Did he buy your silence by not asking us Germans for the hundred marks reward turning in your husband would have brought?'

She didn't flinch. 'He "bought" more than that, much more.'

'How long has he had the room?'

'For nearly a year now. Yes, yes, it's been that long, though it didn't start between us until . . . until last Spring.'

The shit! Kohler swept his eyes over her, a damn fine-looking woman. How had she and her husband stood it?

'My husband wanted to kill him. I . . . I said that was not possible, that these days, one had to . . .' She gave a shrug, a small smile, one of loss perhaps. 'One had to go along with such things.'

'You're not Jewish. You can't be.'

'Not all Jews have black hair and dark eyes, monsieur, but no, I'm not. I loved Martin dearly and still do. We . . . we lost the children on our way here. I . . .' There was another shrug. 'I tried to find them – it was my fault. I went to get some water. They were so thirsty, there were so many people milling around the well, fighting to get a drop, screaming at the farmer who controlled the pump and demanded payment. The Messerschmitts and Stukas came. They – Look, I know my children must be dead and now it doesn't seem such a bad thing any more. Half-Jews are just the same as whole ones, and if not, they soon will be.'

'The Vél d'Hiv . . .' Kohler took out his cigarettes and offered one, which she readily took. Louis and he had been in the Free Zone when the *rafle* of last July had seen five of the Paris *arrondissements* sealed off by 9,000 French police – Talbotte, yes, and Pharand. Belleville had been one of those districts, the poor Frog's precious Belleville.

Over 12,000 Jews, many of them women and children, had been arrested. The sports stadium of the Vél d'Hiv had become a filthy hell-hole during their eight-day stay without water, food or toilets that worked.

Louis had gone all to pieces at the news. They'd argued, they'd fought and then they'd got drunk and ever since then neither of them had mentioned the thing again.

But now Lafont and Bonny had taken this woman's husband and locked him up in that stadium. After questioning.

'Come on, let's take a look at the bastard's room.'

'There's nothing. They've already searched it. There was a woman with them, a young one, a dress designer's mannequin.'

Nicole de Rainvelle.

'She laughed about it. She . . . she said they'd come back for me if they didn't find out what they needed. My husband couldn't have told them anything, Inspector. Turcel would have been too careful.'

Kohler held the door of the dovecote open for her. Madame Van der Lynn went ahead of him across the short span of roof that lay between the dovecote and the door to the stairs. Even up here Turcel had kept his options open. A Jew in hiding – he'd have flung the poor bastard down the stairs as they rushed to get him. He'd have gone any of six different ways across the roofs and he'd have had them all mapped out long ago.

'He had a knife, this I do know,' she said, pausing at the door to Number 5-13, her forehead touching it. 'A switch-blade. It was never far from his hand. He used to keep it under his pillow. That's . . . that's how I found out about it.'

They went into the room: two good-sized windows overlooking the canal and the quays, the curtains offering discreet cover to the not so passive observer. A chair, a table, an armoire and bureau, a washstand – a repeat almost of Christabelle Audit's room in the Hotel of the Silent Life, except that the stuff was a shade better.

Oona Van der Lynn went over to the bed. Kohler saw her begin to unbutton her cardigan. His voice level, he said, 'Don't. Please don't. They . . .'

'They have got someone else?' she asked, still touching a button.

He clenched a fist. 'That I don't know. I wish I did.'

Giselle . . . Her name had been Giselle.

He began to search the room, was very patient for a man so in doubt and afraid.

'How did you manage to find this place?' he asked.

Would he arrest her after all? 'So many had left the city, the owner was in a panic. Looters, arson, so many things were on his mind. He found us quite by chance, or we found him. Even now I can't decide. His concierge had gone to Provence to stay with her brother. He asked few questions. Then he too left the city.'

Kohler opened the armoire to run his eyes over its emptiness. 'And you haven't seen him since?'

'I do the rents, pay the bills – everything. I send him the balance.'

He moved the armoire out from the wall a little to look behind it. 'Give me a hand, will you, while I tilt it? Look for anything other than dust.'

She got down on her hands and knees at his feet. 'Nothing . . . there is nothing. Monsieur Turcel had very little. A suitcase, one jacket, a coat, a few jerseys, a dark-blue turtle-neck sweater and soft-soled tennis shoes. He said they helped his feet.'

'I'll bet they did.' Kohler set the thing back down. She stood up but didn't move away.

Stepping round her, he parted the curtains a little. Lafont and Bonny's men were now standing out for all the world to see. Hands in their coat pockets, the snap brims new. They were waiting to see what he'd do.

The woman went over to the bed again but now sat on its edge. There was nothing in the washstand, under or beneath it, nothing in the bureau either.

The cardigan was almost undone. 'He came back. I'm certain he did,' she said.

'When?'

'On Wednesday night, at twelve-fifteen, maybe twelve-thirty. I'd gone up to see my husband after the curfew had started. We had to talk. Lately it had become so hard for us to even speak to each other. The house was locked. I . . . I thought I saw someone cross the roofs. I went downstairs but didn't go into the room. Instead, I waited in the hall, at the other end. It was him. I know it was. He'd come back to see if he'd left anything.'

So much for visiting his 'dying' mother. More likely he'd slit the throat of a certain mackerel.

'Did you tell the rue Lauriston this when they came to take your husband away?'

'I . . . I forgot. Look, I really did. I was terrified. We both were. Besides, I was afraid that if I did, they'd kill us.'

'Would your husband have known he'd come back?'

'No, no I don't think he would have. Turcel would not have let himself be seen. I was just lucky. A chance, that's all. A glimpse.'

There was a burnt match in one of the geranium pots, a last cigarette before the killing could begin, or one taken afterwards? He'd have stood in the darkness carefully going over things, trying to figure out where whatever it was he'd left in the room had been misplaced.

She'd have stood out there in the corridor listening for him.

Oona felt her cardigan fall open. Now she could start on the blouse. They'd said this one had an appetite for it and that maybe if she let him do it to her, he'd help free her husband.

Kohler knelt on the bed to search behind the headboard. There was something lying in the fluff – yes, yes there was. A tool of some sort.

As he clambered off the bed, she stood up and he caught a glimpse of unbuttoned things and of moving fingers that were long and slender. 'Don't. Please don't. Hey look, I'm on your side. It isn't necessary.'

'They . . . they said . . .'

'*Ja*, I know what they said. They think I'm a son of a bitch and they're out to prove it, so *don't*.'

He pulled himself under the bed and strained to reach the thing. Ah *merde*! This thing, this case . . . A man who was good with the knife, a Corsican – *Gott im Himmel*!

It was a small, handmade tool with a flattened wire loop at one end that was not circular but bent out for a couple of centimetres. A blunt point, with a sharper, more circular curve to the right.

The wire was bound to the short wooden shaft by tightly wound string that had first been soaked in salt-water to make it shrink on drying. Then grease of some sort – tallow perhaps – had been applied. It had the look of long usage, was something kept as a memento perhaps, but of what?

Lying there on his back, with the sagging springs just above him, he tried to think. Réjean Turcel . . . One of the hard ones. Three killings – had they been in sequence and had they all been done by him? The Ré and the Tu would fit the real name. The rest would be make-believe, but why rape the girl? An act of vengeance, violation to pay someone back? Antoine Audit, or Charles, his brother?

Thirty fake gold coins and the promise of far more. Find the forger, find the new owner of the carousel, the previous one too, find out what went on. Never mind the killings. Killing was an everyday affair these days.

Oona Van der Lynn's skirt hit the floor, then the slip cascaded about her ankles, lastly her underpants. She'd nice ankles, nice calves. A very stubborn woman.

'Look, I told you not to do that. Put your things back on, and that's an order, eh? You're far too nice and I'm not like those bastards think I am.'

'They will kill me if I do not let you have the use of my body.'

'Then I'll tell them it was great, madame, and so will you.'

148

Getting down on her hands and knees, and then on her elbows, she peered uncertainly in at him. It was cold and she gave a little shiver as he stared back at her.

'Can you think of anything else about Turcel?' he asked. She had such clear blue eyes. They were so large.

Doubt clouded the eyes and he wondered then if she would still try to force herself upon him. But no, she was honestly searching her memory just as a Dutch maiden would. Perplexed and earnest and wanting to help.

'Once he laughed about the crows. He said that now that the city was starving, there was so little food they would have to go back to their old ways of raiding the farms, only they didn't know how to any more. Generations of sponging had spoiled them. He'd seen three dead ones that day. All had been too ravaged by hunger to have survived. Not even good enough to stuff.'

'To stuff?'

'To stuff, yes. To mount, I think.'

The draper's shop on the Pas-Léon was empty but Father Eugène Delacroix had a key.

'There is nothing in here, Inspector. Nothing, as I've said! The Nazis came and took it all away. Looted – that one looted the place! Monsieur Paul junior and his family did not come back from the South after the Defeat, so by the decree of August 1940 all such businesses and their contents became the property of the Third Reich, and I have failed to protect what I had said I would.'

'I'm not working for the Germans, Father. I'm as French and as patriotic as yourself.'

'I didn't say you weren't.'

'Then please don't become so irritated by a few simple questions. After all, there have been two murders in the rue Polonceau, and one of them very near to your church. My partner and I . . .'

'Your "partner" – ah that one's as Gestapo as all the rest! And you . . . your *few* questions, eh? They'd flood the place and cause the ark to founder.'

The grizzled chin was belligerent. The shabby black beret looked as if pigeons had not just roosted but had left their prayers for a fertile earth.

'Father, your secret is safe with us. Herr Kohler and I understand the needs of the flesh, eh? We're both detectives of long-standing. You need have no fears.'

'As God is my witness, I wish that were so, but I am afraid for that young couple and their child. Father David has sinned many times with her – ah, Madame Ouellette seduced him, of this I'm certain. Marie . . . I've known her since she was a child. Always after the boys, that one, always up to mischief and at confession, the most lurid of thoughts, shameful in a grown woman, wicked in a girl! But', he gave a shrug, 'it became a game with them, and then I became a party to that game.'

'Relax, eh? Have a cigarette and take your mind back to this other murder but first tell me who cleaned out the shop and when?'

The Sûreté had been kind but would he now leave things well enough alone? 'The Corporal Schraum, the one who took his pleasure with Madame Ouellette whenever he wanted. It was he who cleaned it out last summer. In passing through the district on his way to her, Schraum saw a shop forgotten and decided it was too good to leave. Marie swears she tried to stop him. Father David . . . It was all I could do to restrain him.'

The priest paused, but pausing would do no good. 'I argued with the Corporal but they loaded everything on to their trucks, even the furniture. He gave Marie two bolts of cloth with which to make new dresses – just flung them off the back of one of the trucks. He had so much of it. All his, all those things. The accumulations of two generations, father and son. They're bastards. Bastards!'

The cigarette did little to calm the old priest's nerves. Indeed, tobacco seemed only to make him more agitated and angry. The acid of the years came forward.

'The sisters Gagnon,' he spat. 'They are lying. *Lying*, Inspector! The Captain Dupuis is innocent of such a hideous crime. I've warned them repeatedly. I've told them both they must stop picking on a man with one leg, a veteran! But at the ages of eighty-seven and eighty-three, God could tell them and they'd still turn the deaf ear!'

Delacroix took a quick drag. '*Merde*! must I go down on my knees to those two old bitches, eh? Dupuis is nothing!' He tossed the hand of insignificance and spat tobacco from his lower lip. 'Oh, for sure he looks at the girls – which of you doesn't, eh? and the younger, the prettier – you can't tell me you haven't ravaged a few in that mind of yours, eh? But the Captain is incapable of killing anyone.'

St-Cyr took out his pipe and tobacco pouch. 'He was a soldier, was he not?'

'Verdun. Yes . . . yes, he could have killed. Does that make you feel better?'

The pipe was forgotten. 'Why not say the Captain was incapable for other reasons?'

He'd show the Sûreté! He'd not let up now, not when things were going so well! 'Dupuis often frequented the houses – Mme Lauzon's, Mme Belle's . . .'

'Yes, yes, but was it always the youngest he chose?'

The Sûreté's eyes sought him out. The pipe, tobacco pouch and matches had yet to be put to use. 'He . . . he had strange tastes, Inspector. They had to be suitable, you understand, but those two old women are wrong. They're simply being vindictive. It wasn't Dupuis. It was Charles Audit if it was anyone from around here.'

The pipe was packed but the effort took time. At last the match was struck. 'M Charles Audit?'

Delacroix drew deeply on his cigarette to let the impasse grow. The further they got from discussing Father David the better, but should he air the parish linen, should he not listen to God?

'I've no proof, except that I saw Monsieur Charles early on that evening coming out of the courtyard of the Villa Audit. I'd gone to have my supper but, of course, the cafés were all closed, the streets so empty it was not difficult to notice a man in great haste who was afraid he might be caught.'

'Are you certain it was Charles Audit?'

'Positive. I've known the brothers for years. He was some distance ahead of me, carrying two suitcases which he left behind those barrels in the courtyard out there.'

Two suitcases . . . St-Cyr hesitated. Why had the priest not called out to Charles Audit? Why hadn't he offered to help carry the suitcases? 'And you didn't tell the police?'

Delacroix again tossed a hand. 'I had no reason to. At the time I didn't suspect him of the girl's murder. Besides, the police had better things to do and so did I. Two suitcases are not much, even though Monsieur Charles did not own the Villa Audit and should not have been taking things from it.'

The Germans had been at the gates of the city, Paris all but deserted but what had happened to now make him suspect Charles Audit? 'Tell me about this other girl.'

Father Eugène looked away. Was there sadness at the memory of her, or relief that they'd passed beyond Father David and the murder of Corporal Schraum?

'Her name was Mila Zavitz. She was a Polish refugee, a very pleasant and presentable girl from Cracow. M Paul junior took her into his shop over the objections of his wife, to which, I must confess, I agreed. The girl was quite attractive, not what you'd think at all. The wife had reasons enough to worry.'

'When would that have been?'

Such eagerness for the sordid. 'In the late spring of 1938. Mila was only seventeen. She and her family lived over in Belleville, in a cellar off the rue Armand Carel, near the parc des Buttes-Chaumont. The father was a shoemaker. Mila spoke delightful French. She was a very well-educated girl. The parents could speak so little of our language, but she . . .'

Father Eugène drew on his cigarette and held the smoke in for the longest time. 'She played the piano – classical things. I let her . . . I could not have kept her from the instrument in our parish hall even though she was a Jew.'

And one whose murder on the eve of the Defeat would have counted for little?

Saddened by the thought, St-Cyr drew on his pipe. He'd leave Charles Audit for the moment, would keep his voice very calm, for the death of this other girl was hurting the conscience of the old priest in more ways than one. Delacroix had been forced to face up to his anti-Semitism. 'Did Mademoiselle Jeanne come to tell you of the body she had discovered?'

Delacroix blinked at this but did not turn from gazing sadly out at the street. 'Yes. I asked Father David to look after her and I went to see if it was true. Mademoiselle Jeanne has always been afraid of men, Inspector. Ever since I have known her it's been the same. When one is a priest, one bears the agonizing of other souls, even their darkest secrets and, yes, desires.'

'And the girl? How did you find her?'

'Dead, as Mademoiselle Jeanne will have told you. Ravaged, strangled.'

Was Father Eugène not lying a little? 'How certain are you that she was in fact "ravaged"?'

Ah damn! The Sûreté's detective saw more than he let on. 'Her clothes . . . the attitude of the body . . .'

'Yes, yes, but was there anything else?' He'd push the priest now. 'Semen? The ejaculation?'

St-Cyr waited. A cloud of pipesmoke would be useful perhaps. Delacroix was struggling with his own soul for he knew only too well what the 'ejaculation' looked like. All priests do.

'It . . . it was on her pubic hairs, on her stomach. Some . . . some of it had collected in her belly button.'

Then the killer had withdrawn himself at some sudden noise – footsteps perhaps, in fright perhaps, or had it simply been because of guilt, because of a realization of what he'd done?

Mila Zavitz, age twenty, a Polish refugee, a Jew.

'What makes you now want to accuse Charles Audit of this girl's murder, Father, and that other killing, that of Christabelle Audit, his granddaughter? Please, I know you are linking the two deaths to him. Just give me your reasons.'

Delacroix crossed himself and muttered a prayer of absolution. 'Monsieur Charles spent fifteen years on Devil's Island for the attempted murder of his brother, Inspector, nearly six more years in the jungles of Brazil and Colombia. He was a man who had been betrayed by a brother seven years younger than himself.'

'M Antoine Audit.'

'When Charles returned to Paris in 1926 he was a changed man, no longer the bourgeois shopkeeeper. Though I saw him rarely, there was much hatred in him. Oh for sure, he lived for his carousel and his granddaughter, but he hated also and myself, may God forgive me if I am wrong, believe he waited only for the moment to repay his brother.'

'Revenge is at the heart of darkness; vengeance is its sweet success.'

'He came back for his suitcases only to find Mila in the courtyard. Since he'd stolen the things from the villa, he had to kill her.'

'Why?' The priest was edgy.

'Because she knew him, Inspector. Mila often went to the parc des Buttes-Chaumont on her afternoon off and on Sundays. She would have seen him at the carousel. She spoke of him and of his granddaughter. I remember her once saying, "Those two, they are so close. It's as if the one loves the other and she reminds him of her grandmother."'

'Michèle-Louise Prévost.'

'Yes, yes, that one.'

'Could M Antoine have withdrawn the charge of attempted murder he brought against his brother?'

'He could have. A misfired pistol – myself I have prayed for this at the time. But he chose not to. Instead, at the age of thirty, M Charles went to the tropics, to hell itself, and Madame Charles left the house and went to Périgord with M Antoine.'

'She was expecting a child.'

'Yes . . . yes, a girl – Christabelle's mother. That one died in childbirth at the age of fifteen.'

'Did Michèle-Louise raise Christabelle?'

Father Eugène shook his head. 'Not after the age of six. That's when Charles came home and bought the carousel. From then on he raised Christabelle himself with the aid of a housekeeper. They didn't come here to this *quartier*, not to my knowledge, and I hear most things that happen sooner or later. Michèle-Louise could not have been much of a mother. She was not a good woman, Inspector. She was too loose, too busy with her "artwork" and her friends.'

'And you're certain the Captain Dupuis could not have killed Christabelle any more than he could have killed Mila Zavitz?'

'Lonely men are always suspect, Inspector, but fear is a terrible thing. The few droplets of blood Mademoiselle Jeanne saw on the Captain's shirt could just as easily have come from these, the cuts and nicks of shaving. There weren't many of them – I examined the shirt myself at the local préfecture. The sisters have had it in for the Captain ever since he got the better of them in one of the shops. A last two bottles of sherry, I believe, or was it Madeira?' He gave a shrug. 'Of just such little insults are mountains made and the avalanche of nightmares begun again.'

'Was there no blood on the girl?'

'A little. In . . . in the area of her . . . her sexual parts and on the legs, the thighs.'

'So M Charles could have killed her to protect himself for having robbed the house that had once been his own?'

'Yes. The law had been broken.'

How close to the truth was the priest treading? 'Did you see the contents of those two suitcases, Father? Did you open them?' he asked harshly.

'*No*, I did not open them. They were locked, but I can tell you that they were heavy.'

'And when you saw Mila's body, they were no longer there?'

'That is correct. He'd pushed the trash barrels back. He was

154

quite strong. The years on Devil's Island had changed him, as I've said.'

St-Cyr nodded. There was so much more they needed to know, but one could ask only so much at any one time. 'Why is it that you feel M Charles Audit could also have killed the granddaughter he loved so much?'

The priest tossed his head and shrugged. 'It doesn't make any sense but me, I feel he did.'

'Could it have been Madame Minou's son, Roland?'

Delacroix fingered the crucifix he carried in a pocket. He'd come to the end of the cigarette, must remember to save the butt. Always these days there was something to remember, and the wine . . . he'd have to have just a little of it. 'Roland Minou . . . Yes, yes, I suppose if you could find him, that one might well have done it too, but he'd have had to have a good reason.'

'Cheating?'

Father Eugène's gaze narrowed. 'Yes. Yes, cheating. If he'd thought he'd paid good money for something that wasn't what he'd been told it was. He's a mean-minded little gangster, a young man without a conscience. That silly woman dotes on him but he's played her for a sucker once too often. Still, you might have something there, Inspector. Yes, you certainly might!'

The old priest grinned with relish at the thought. Belligerently the back teeth were ground. 'If he ever shows his face around here, send him down to see me, eh? I'll teach him not to rob the parish poor-box. I'll teach him not to steal my wine and silver.'

I'll teach him. Yes, yes I will, as God is my witness.

God and the Devil.

6

The dream was different, the dream was very real. Another nightmare! Incongruously the carousel had been transported to what must be Devil's Island. The galloping stallions slavered. The ducks cried out for water. The heat sucked the moisture from their wild dark eyes, deadening them to wicked slits as the thing came round . . . round, the animals all going up and down, faster, faster, the music jarring, jarring . . . A girl in a cage of bright-red iron and gold wire, a laughing girl who took the money in, the money. Naked . . . naked, so young and beautiful and lying on her back. An arm unfolding, the slender legs parting, she taking her breasts in her hands to wet their nipples with her fingers. Nipples . . . nipples . . . A panda – why a panda? The thing chasing the girl . . . The thing rising and falling . . . Slow . . . too slow . . . The girl . . . the girl . . .

St-Cyr awoke in a panic. Ah, Mon Dieu, must he have constant nightmares about this case? They were in a terrible fix. The rue Lauriston . . . the avenue Foch . . . the Abwehr . . . Gabrielle Arcuri and Giselle le Roy . . . Hermann . . . ah yes.

Christabelle Audit's mother had died at the age of fifteen while giving birth to the child. Antoine Audit and Michèle-Louise Prévost had raised the girl until the age of six. Then Charles Audit had returned to take her from them. He'd bought the carousel for her – bribery, had it been bribery?

Ah *merde*! The Île du Diable. Two square kilometres of barren rock and scrub and more than a thousand convicts. Nothing but the hardest of them and the immenseness of trackless jungle lying across but a few kilometres of ocean.

The coast of French Guiana would have beckoned with the lure of a naked harlot who carried syphilis and cried out as a leper, 'You can't! You mustn't! There is no escape from here. Absolutely none!'

He wet his lips. 'The villa,' he said. 'It all began at the villa so long ago. A touch of lemon grass, a whisper of rosemary, a suggestion of coumarin.'

Had the panda really been about to rape that girl, or had his subconscious been trying to tell him something?

Swallowing with difficulty, St-Cyr lay back as the whisper of her perfume mingled with the heady scent of Cream of the Walnut in his mind.

Christabelle Audit had shaved her underarms and had dyed her hair, but why? To please her grandfather, or to please his brother, or to hide herself from one or both of them, or neither, but someone else?

She'd lived at Number 10 rue Bènard, apartment six.

Fumbling for his cigarettes, he took one and lit it, let the darkness of the bedroom he'd once shared with Marianne close about him.

To go from shoes to utter desolation to a carousel and a granddaughter one loved so much one put her in a little red-and-gold cage to take the tickets as the thing went round, was something. A cage within a cage, the canary singing its lungs out in competition or chorus with the calliope.

M Charles Audit and his granddaughter. Around those two elements the carousel had revolved, the years from 1926 until the day of the Defeat seeing the girl grow into womanhood.

Then the carousel is sold – quickly, decisively. Charles Audit goes where? To Number 10 rue Bènard, apartment six, in Montparnasse?

Perhaps, but then...

A year later the granddaughter has good false papers in the name of Christiane Baudelaire, a name she must have chosen herself but one so close to what a criminal might choose, it has to make one wonder. Change it only a little, eh? That way if someone calls out to you or questions you, the name is almost as natural as your own and causes no difficulty. Ah yes. A criminal.

She meets M Antoine – was it really her grandfather's brother? A man of some fifty-six to sixty years of age from Périgord, a bourgeois who brings her gifts of pâté and liqueur from one of his businesses. Presents which she leaves outside the door to Captain Alphonse Dupuis' room as if, though in need of money and food, she still cannot bear to bring herself to touch them.

For nearly a year she meets with this M Antoine once or twice a week in that room, always at about the same time, between 8 and

9 p.m. The Captain Dupuis is driven crazy with thoughts of her naked body and what the two of them must be doing in there.

She has been taking pieces of her grandmother's jewellery from the Villa Audit on the rue Polonceau and selling them in the flea markets, or trying to.

Then she is killed – forced to strip naked before her killer. Why?

She knew him. She expected help to come from M Antoine, who'd left a note for her but she hadn't picked it up. Did Dupuis take it, read it and put it back? The envelope had been unsealed.

And why should M Antoine know what to do? Had he training in such things?

She'd taken off her clothing garment by garment in the hope that help would soon come.

Then she'd been killed – garrotted, savagely raped, a virgin all this time – and left to lie on the floor with thirty forged Roman gold coins scattered about her body and no answers. Only a warning that this detective from the Sûreté had instantly taken to have been left for himself. Ah yes.

Did the killer throw the coins or did someone else? Lafont perhaps? Nicole de Rainvelle or Pierre Bonny? They'd visited the scene of the crime, they'd photographed the body. Any one of them could have placed that coin on her forehead.

Talbotte had washed his hands of the affair. Boemelburg, Oberg and Knochen had insisted on Hermann and himself. Lafont and Bonny had offered help, he himself suffering the humiliation of having to go before them or else.

All of them believed there were real gold coins to be had, loot in plenty.

Find the forger, find the loot. Never mind the killings.

And two and a half years before these killings, another young girl, another strangulation, rape and withdrawal during ejaculation. Mila Zavitz.

Two heavy suitcases. M Charles Audit.

He'd been sent to Devil's Island in 1905 at the age of thirty. This meant that he was now sixty-seven years old, still spry perhaps, tough perhaps, and well able at sixty-five to carry two heavy suitcases *if* he'd wanted to.

But he'd left them hidden in the courtyard beside a draper's shop that was not very far at all from the place where Schraum had been shot, and not very far either from the Church of Saint Bernard.

Antoine Audit was seven years younger than his brother. In

1905 he would have been twenty-three years old and now he was sixty.

And Michèle-Louise Prévost? he asked, flicking ashes into the darkness. The sketch of herself on that *chaise* had shown her to have been about twenty or twenty-two. The same age as the granddaughter.

But if twenty-two in 1905 when Charles was sent away, then forty-three in 1926 when he came back to buy the carousel, and now fifty-nine years old if still alive.

A woman of great determination, one so skilled she could copy the works of others far better than they could have done themselves.

Prévost ... Prévost ... It didn't ring any bells in the male-dominated art world he knew. And certainly to make it as an artist was still exceedingly difficult for a woman. The copying could simply have been an act of rebellion.

Four killings all linked to the villa on the rue Polonceau or not linked to it at all. Each one done by the same person, or by separate individuals, or two by one, three by one ... It was just guessing, but ...

Find the forger, find the loot, find Charles Audit who'd been so financially in need his brother had 'helped' him out and had possessed the villa *and* the young wife in payment of those debts, not to mention having consigned him to Devil's Island for fifteen years on a charge of attempted murder.

It made one thankful one had no brothers or sisters, no grand-daughters either.

Or sons like Madame Minou had.

Christabelle Audit's 'lover'. A successful businessman of between fifty-six and sixty years of age. Pâtés and liqueurs from *Antoine Audit and Sons of Périgord*.

Charles Audit was sixty-seven. It had to be the brother of Charles Audit, or someone using his name so as to implicate him.

The girl might well have undressed in front of her great-uncle for reasons financial or otherwise – relatives were always the first to take advantage of the young. She might not have known the coins she was trying to sell were fake; alternatively she might well have been in on the swindle.

In any case, she must have let him see the jewellery she'd taken from the villa. He'd have known about it. He'd have paid the rent by leaving the money with her.

But why, if it *had* been Antoine Audit, would he not have used the villa?

Because it was rented to the Germans. Because it was occasionally being used and he didn't want to chance being seen there with her or anyone else.

Dragged out of sleep at 3.15 in the morning, the concierge of the house at 10 rue Bènard in Montparnasse had nothing but venom on his tongue. A scarecrow in faded flannel and nightcap.

'The Sûreté, eh? Well suck lemons, my fine. You'll find no tits to play with here! The house you want is next door!'

The door began to close . . . 'Monsieur, please! The Sûreté, eh? A detective – a chief inspector. Please permit me to put the bicycle inside, eh? *Don't* crush the wheel! Ah! In the Name of Jesus, my only mode of transport!'

'CRUSH? I'LL CRUSH YOUR TESTICLES, YOU BASTARD!'

'No . . . no. Ah *merde*! Now look what you've done!'

St-Cyr wrenched the bicycle back from the gap in the door and flung the thing aside. 'The boot, the whistle or the fist, *mon ami*?' he shrilled. 'I'm on a murder investigation and even an old stick like yourself will not stand in my way!'

His shoulder hit the door. The chain snapped, the bolt was torn free. All bones and knuckles, the concierge grabbed him and stumbled backwards. Jesus, the fists! 'MONSIEUR, STOP IT THIS INSTANT!'

So much for the quiet word, the unobserved journey.

Amber eyes threw daggers up at him, accompanied by the hot wind of garlic. 'The Sûreté, eh? you dog's green offal! I'll show you!'

He'd the strength of ten! Several of the tenants had come rushing to the rescue. St-Cyr let a rush of breath escape as he tried to hold the raft of bones down. 'Okay . . . okay, you win, eh? *Did you hear me?*'

He dragged him up. 'That bitch!' sang out the concierge. 'I'll show that bitch! This is the last time, I tell you. The very last time!' The man sucked in his grizzled cheeks and spat.

The crowd of tenants cautiously approached. Some were armed with brooms, others with chairs, one had a cricket bat, another a butcher's knife. Sleep is so deceptive, the ravager of us all. 'Go back to bed. That's an order, do you hear me?' shouted St-Cyr.

'Your badge. Your papers. Quickly, quickly,' rasped the concierge. 'Don't give me the shit, monsieur. I, Phlegon Yvode, know very well what you were after.'

'But that's next door.'

'Yes. Did your mother suck all the goodness out of your father's prick before he penetrated her to breed you, eh? Or did neither of them have any brains?'

Hermann should have been with him. 'My chest is hammering, monsieur. It's the Benzedrine – no, please, do not trouble yourself. Merely an after-effect, I assure you. The heart ... I'm afraid for my heart.'

'Fuck your heart! With brains in your ass, it must be in your boots!'

St-Cyr drew himself up. He'd give the bastard a moment, he'd allow the tenants one more chance to bugger off. 'Monsieur, you remind me of my days with the cape, eh? Ah yes, me I came up the hard way. I know very well how to deal with turds like yourself but please don't force me to violence. You're too old to have a broken nose and six caved-in ribs. Those teeth of yours would be hard to replace.'

A *flic*, a cow! He might have known but had best give the rush of breath defeat would bring.

With a yank, Yvode hitched the torn nightgown back over a bare shoulder. 'Well, I am waiting, my fine Inspector. What is so important that you should awaken the whole of a decent, respectable house at this ungodly hour?'

'Shh! Don't start the engine again, eh? Please, the key to apartment six and everything you can tell me about its tenants. The girl was murdered – strangled. Raped.'

'Ah no. This ... this cannot be. Me, I have thought...'

Devastated and suddenly spouting tears, the man turned away to search the corridor and the stairs down to the entrance. To the stragglers he said, 'Mademoiselle Audit, my friends. Christabelle.'

'Monsieur, what was it you thought?'

'Nothing. My lips are sealed. You may see the flat but you will find nothing there either, Inspector. They came and took it all away yesterday.'

'Who came?'

'The Gestapo, who else?'

'Which Gestapo?'

'The French ones. Those of the rue Lauriston. Monsieur

Charles has gone to see his brother. Mademoiselle Christabelle ... Ah that one, to think she is dead. Never the unkind word, always in such a hurry.'

St-Cyr found his cigarettes crushed in the tussle. He tried to take two of them out but gave it up. 'When did Monsieur Charles leave?'

'On Tuesday. He ... he has said he would return in a week, that Lyon would be a pleasant change at this time of year but that Saint-Raphaël would be even better. His brother had places in both and in Périgord.'

'How long had they lived here?'

'Since a few weeks before the Defeat.'

His slippers flapping on the tattered runner, the concierge reluctantly led him up one flight of stairs and along the hall to Number six. 'The curtains are gone. Everything is gone. We cannot show a light. The regulations...'

A little kindness wouldn't hurt. 'We'll leave the door open. I just want to see it. Come ... come ... you first, monsieur. You've nothing to fear from me.'

There were several rooms and, as their steps took them farther from the door, the darkness increased. 'Tell me about the ones who came to clean this place out.'

'Must I?' Yvode saw him nod. 'There were ten of them, with two trucks and a white car – a huge car. Never have I seen such a beautiful thing as that car.'

The white Bentley Lafont always drove. 'Pistols? Revolvers? The...'

'The swastika armbands, monsieur, and the black uniforms, as I have said, of the French Gestapo. Everything ... My curtains – *mine*, monsieur – even my register. Me, I have only a tired memory. The authorities, they will...'

'Yes, yes. I'm sure you'll get it back. They'll have given you a receipt.'

'Of what good is a piece of paper when a valued tenant returns to find his possessions gone?'

'Perhaps he won't come back.'

'Was he murdered too?'

'We don't know that yet. We hope not. Now where did they take the things? It'll have been on the receipt.'

'The rue Lauriston, as I've said.'

'Tell me about the possessions, the things in this flat.'

'Stuffed birds, stuffed animals – strange creatures from the jungles, monkeys, snakes, seeds, beans, plants, books, leather-work . . . a few photographs taken in South America, I think. He never said much about it. He has assumed I would know about such things and me, I have not thought it correct to ask.'

Yvode sucked in a breath. 'A photograph of a carousel. He had raised his granddaughter from childhood, you understand, mon-sieur. The carousel was his heart and soul, his present to her but . . .' he gave a shrug . . . 'Monsieur Charles, he had to sell it.'

'What did he do for a living?'

'He had a little money. He did not work any more, not that I knew of. He was past this. Some of us are.'

'Lonely?'

Yvode was quick to catch the drift. 'Self-contained. Absolute. Just him and the granddaughter.'

'And the girl?'

'She was a student, an artist and an artist's model. She posed in the nude. M Charles was very much of the old school, Inspector, but Christabelle said she had to, and that one knew he'd have to let her but he did not like it. Ah no, that was most evident. Monsieur Charles was very strict, very possessive.'

'Unnaturally so?'

The Sûreté, always the filth! 'They did not have much money, monsieur. She had to work so as to get enough for her share of the rent and the food. I sometimes wondered how they managed but these days we're all in the same bucket, except for those who have become friends of the Boches, eh?'

'I'm not one of them, Monsieur Yvode. I am merely a detective who is trying against formidable odds to do his job.'

'Did she die in agony?'

How was the body, eh? Parisian to the core, the man wanted to know the most intimate of details and he hated to rob him of these, but he gave only a curt nod. 'She knew her killer. At least, we think she did.'

'We?' asked Yvode, only to hear the Sûreté say he had a partner, a German, a Nazi, a Gestapo.

'I'm forced to work under him. It will pass in time but for now I must tell you that I know the rules and that my partner has been only too forceful in telling them to me.'

Don't forget anything then. Ah *merde*, Monsieur Charles would never forgive him. 'He had a friend, a Corsican. One of the *durs*, monsieur. I myself did not see him here, you understand. There were never any visitors. But I have a sister in Belleville, near the Parc des Buttes-Chaumont. Quite by accident I saw them in a pavement café last summer. I –'

'Excuse me, monsieur, the name of this café, its location? Everything . . . we need to know everything. It's important.'

'The Café Noir, it is on the avenue de Laumière, not far from the park. A little place much frequented by those I would not wish to know. I was surprised to see him in such a place and when later I have mentioned that I saw him, Monsieur Charles he has denied it most emphatically and offered instead ticket stubs to the races at Longchamp as proof. The granddaughter has held her breath, Inspector, and given the grandfather the quick and doubtful glance. Me, I think she was afraid.'

'Did the girl and her grandfather come in together that day?'

'Yes, as I've just said, she . . .'

'Would she have met the two of them at that café?'

Yvode gave a shrug. 'I really do not know, monsieur. She might have, but then again she might not have and he could just as easily have told her of the meeting later on when they met up some place else.'

Matching the register with Madame Minou's would be an almost impossible task, given that Lafont had taken this one. 'Tell me what Monsieur Charles looked like.'

'A swarthy man of some muscular strength. A man of medium height like yourself but strong, you understand, like the Greek peasant I once had as a lodger in the old house. A labourer. The black beret, the thick grey-white hair over the tops of the ears, the narrow eyebrows, not bushy, the sad grey-blue eyes deep in thought, the pipe – a long, black-stemmed thing, something from the old days, I think. A favourite in any case.'

'Yes, yes, I know the feeling well. The face, monsieur? Please, it is very important. We have photographs of him when he was much younger.'

'Then that one will have changed a great deal. There are crow's-feet at the corners of his eyes and these have made their criss-crossing inroads well on to the grizzled cheeks. Always a morning's shave followed by two or three days of respite. A creature of long habit, perhaps, but myself, I think he didn't care much for barbers. Perhaps he was just saving money, perhaps he wanted the stubble to shade him from the sun but now, of course, there is so little of that, it would not matter.'

'A man of sixty-seven?'

'A grey man, monsieur, so sad at times he didn't realize others might notice. But sometimes a twinkle of laughter. A man who understood a great deal about life and accepted the sins and desires of others with a certain resignation and ... yes, yes, compassion. His face not round but a little longer, the chin fleshy, with creases curving up on either side from the round line of his jaw. A nose that was wide and flared, with large nostrils from which unclipped hairs would sprout until his granddaughter got at them with the clippers.'

The concierge was a treasure. The darkness had worked its miracle, the absence of light negating distraction and offering its own sharp illumination to memory. 'Anything else?' asked St-Cyr pleasantly.

'A red polka-dot kerchief knotted at the throat, an open corduroy jacket of a deep plush black, much worn, much loved for its comfort. The blue denim shirt, faded like most. Corduroy trousers and the shoes ... ? Sometimes the leather sandals, sometimes the tennis shoes. Monsieur Charles always maintained that canvas breathed and was good for the feet. Sometimes the leather shoes but these he tended to save and me, I think he had grown accustomed to the others.'

Again St-Cyr asked if there was anything else.

'A flowered carpet-bag, dark wine-purple and very shabby. Monsieur Charles often used it when going to and from the shops – a bottle of wine, a stick of bread, though now there is so little. He ... he has taken this bag with him when he went to see his brother on Tuesday.'

'And the other one, the man he met, the Corsican?'

'One of the *durs*, as I have said. It's not too hard to tell with those, is it? Younger by a few years, swarthy too, and very tough. Me, I don't remember anything else about him, monsieur.'

A killer then. 'One last question, Monsieur Yvode. Did Charles Audit frequent the house next door?'

Ah *merde*, could there be no secrets from this one? 'Yes. Yes, sometimes he went there. He used to laugh about it. He used to say it's always wisest for a man to live next to a bordello, then he can see when the doctor comes to screen the girls and will have the first crack at the cleanest. His granddaughter would only smile sweetly at this, monsieur, a puzzle in one so pure.'

They went down to the entrance. The rue Bènard was pitch-dark. The bicycle, though badly damaged and unridable, had been stolen. So much for the curfew, for the lateness of the hour. Paris had become a city of the hidden.

There were no air raids, no sirens. From the roof of the house overlooking the quai Jemmapes, the city lay in darkness. Unearthly because there were so few sounds, and yet the depth of its silence could be broken at any moment by the tramp of hobnailed boots, the screech of brakes or scream of burning rubber.

Kohler chanced a cigarette. He'd fallen asleep. Lafont and Bonny could think what they liked.

When Madame Van der Lynn came up to him in her nightgown, he saw her clutch her shoulders for warmth. 'What's the matter?' she asked.

He drew on the cigarette then passed it to her. 'Nothing. I just couldn't sleep any more.'

'You were worried about your partner. You cried out "Louis, don't!" Is he out there some place?' She indicated the darkness of the city.

'In my dream Louis was being followed. He hasn't got his gun, madame. I've got it in the car, under the front seat.'

'Won't someone steal it?'

'They'd better not. Neither of us have had the time even to think. I forgot about the shooters. I'm the one who's supposed to keep track of them. He's French and not to be trusted. It's an order from above.'

'We could go down to the car. You could take me to the Vél d'Hiv. We could get it over with, protect the guns and see what's happened to your friend.'

'I want to think for a moment. Put something warm on. It's too cold for you up here.'

He felt her uncertain fingers touch his cheek. He heard her saying, 'They will ask if we had sex. I will try to lie but must confess I don't think they will let me.'

'Look, your husband will be okay. They'll not have killed him.'

She wished he hadn't said it! 'You could have made love to me. I needed to forget. I'm so afraid of what we'll find.'

Kohler took the cigarette from her fingers. 'Okay, get dressed and I'll take you to him.' Louis . . . where the hell was Louis?

The rue Bènard was not so wide that one could not worry about the doorways. The thin blue lamps on the corner of the rue des Plantes had been conveniently extinguished. Not two minutes ago St-Cyr had heard the breaking of their glass.

So, my friends, what's it to be, eh? A death on cobblestones still slicked with the afternoon's rain? One to come from behind; the other from the front? They'd probably been holed up in the house next door. That racket with the concierge would have wakened the dead, but these two would have been light sleepers in any case, and only one of them would have been asleep.

What had Hermann and he got themselves into?

Straining, he listened to the street, smelling the dankness of Paris in winter, the Occupation. He'd no knife, no pistol, only his precious bracelets. Would one of them remember these, would that one be out for vengeance, or would both of them?

A warning. A fake gold coin, dipped in a murdered girl's blood.

He owed it to her to find her killer or killers. These two? he asked, stepping quickly to the left to feel for and duck into the doorway of a shop, café or house. It was so dark.

No steps came on. If he could get to the rue des Plantes, he could go up it to the avenue du Maine. He could lose himself among the tombstones of Montparnasse. He could go to ground there.

Not with these two. They were out to kill him. He could only wonder what he'd done in the past, could only think, Why is it that they do not want Hermann and me to learn anything more about this case?

As carefully as he could, St-Cyr opened the box of matches in his pocket and, feeling for their heads, arranged the ten or so that were left into a small bundle.

The stones were wet. The heads would only smear with the dampness.

He'd have to take that chance. Something ... he needed something they wouldn't be expecting.

These two will be expecting everything, he said. Was it Charles Audit and his Corsican friend? Devil's Island would have taught Audit many useful things.

They'd have no fear of the Germans.

The Carbone gang? he asked, stepping quickly back on to the narrow pavement and then on to the street as if off the edge of the moon.

He floated down on to the cobblestones and went quickly up the street at a run, only to stop suddenly. Ah Mon Dieu, they were so good.

When the knife flashed, the matches tumbled from his fingers. He gave an instinctive cry that echoed up and down the street.

'Jesus ... Jesus ... In the Name of Jesus, why are you after me, you bastards? I can help you.'

It wouldn't have worked. He clutched his bleeding left hand. They waited. They watched. They circled him. 'Who are you?' he cried out again in anger now, in fear, in so many things, the wounded stag baited by the hounds of the night.

Two men, two dark silhouettes, a slotted glimpse of the sky beyond the edges of the roofs.

The sound of a single car now, the screeching of its brakes, the leaping throttle of its engine. He tried to hold his hand up. One of them was behind him again, the other in front. Both would have knives, but which would rush him first?

The one behind him leapt! The knife ... St-Cyr turned, pivoted again, ducked again, twisted aside. The knife flashed and flashed, tearing his coat.

He threw his back against a wall, licked the sweat of fear from his lips. 'All right, my fines, all right, eh? Come at me as men. My revolver is out!'

They melted away and they left him there with water in his shoes, ah damn! Two wise men who were not afraid, who would have known he could not have hit either of them in the dark. But they had no need to gamble. There'd be another time and they'd left him with that thought, as with the smile of cruelty.

St-Cyr clamped his eyes shut and tightened the grip on his injured hand. They'd cut it right across the back. It would be stiff for days.

Pressing a thumb against the wound, he continued on up the street. Twice more there was the sound of that car. Hermann, was it Hermann? Then a convoy of trucks started up, and when he reached the rue des Plantes, there was the sound of a patrol.

Had this been what had deterred them the most? Had their hearing been so good, their instincts so much better than his own?

If they had wanted to kill him why hadn't they simply come to the house, to Belleville and the rue Laurence Savart?

It was damaged. They'd not thought he'd go there to sleep.

They had also known the address of Christabelle Audit's residence. They'd been waiting for someone to show up.

Kohler finished the last of his cigarette. Oona Van der Lynn waited beside him in the Citroën, where Louis usually sat if not sleeping in the back.

'Look, I know how you must feel, Herr Kohler. I'm sorry we could not find your friend.'

They'd been to a carousel, to a villa, a small hotel, a church, a house whose front had been blown to pieces by the Resistance. They'd been to so many places. Now the dawn had come and there was nothing more to be said except, 'You needn't worry about me any more. I can manage on my own.'

'You're a good woman, madame, and I'm sorry for what's happened to you. Louis wouldn't want me to leave you in the lurch, not with those bastards holding your husband.'

'Your friend must be exceptional.'

'He is, or was. Come on. I'll take you there.'

The Vél d'Hiv, the Vélodrome d'Hiver, looked shut up. The wind fluttered a poster, years old, for a cycling race. The stadium needed a coat of paint.

To the north of them the Eiffel Tower would be flying the flag of the Third Reich. Here on the rue Nélation there was only the reminder of what that Reich could do and had done.

The doors were locked. He raised a fist. They could hear the pounding echo inside the empty stadium. 'God damn it, open up. Gestapo!'

The *flic* who unlocked the door from inside had been sleeping in the straw but managed a grin at the sight of them. 'Ah, the one with the slash. Good morning, Inspector. Your fame, it has spread even to this small corner of the earth.'

'Go fuck yourself. Where's Martin Van der Lynn? He's wanted for questioning in connection with a murder case.'

The turd ducked his pumpkin head in deference. 'Of course, Monsieur the Inspector. Please come this way. I, Claude Poirier of the fifteenth in the *Quartier* Grenelle, will escort the Inspector and madame to the gardens, eh? Number . . .' he consulted a notebook . . . Number 100312, Yes . . . Yes, that's him.'

Kohler gripped the woman by the arm. 'Hey listen, eh? Things will be okay. Once we've got him out, I'll see what I can do. Don't worry.'

They went through to one of the concrete staircases and up this into the grandstands. The cycling track looked bleak and empty under the washed blue of the glassed-in roof high above them. It made one feel lonely to see no one else about. It made one hear the shouts, the cheers as the cyclists hurtled themselves round and round the track in suicidal clusters at the bends.

It made one hear the cries of little children, the hysteria of their parents who'd been taken from them. Cattle trucks to the concentration camps at Pithiviers and Beaune-la-Rolande, the adults straight to Auschwitz, the kids to the one at Drancy and then finally to the same and bugger that crap about no one knowing a thing. Only one of those 9,000 French cops who had rounded up the Jews of Paris had resigned in protest. Only one. Poor Louis.

The 'gardens' were several rows of crosses tucked away in a far corner next to latrine pits that had overflowed this past summer but were now awaiting the annual rise of the Seine.

Kohler realized the joke of a fresh grave was on him but had no liking for it. Lafont and Bonny had accused him of being a lover of the French, their Jews included, and so had thought to show him the truth. They couldn't have known how badly Louis had taken the whole thing but had guessed at it. And they did hate Louis with a passion even though they wanted the poor Frog's help.

'Oona, come on. It'll do no good to stay here. Look, if it means anything, I'll make certain you don't come to any more harm.'

'He was a nice man, a good man, the father of our children.'

Taxidermists who slept behind their shops slept late like the exhibits in their windows. Chez Rudi's offered an interlude: Black Forest ham, two eggs on horseback, coffee and rolls.

Awakened, Verdun, the stuffer of birds and animals who smelled of lye as if he drank it, examined the tool with the care of a demolitions expert.

Kohler breathed impatiently. Out on the rue des Lions, Oona Van der Lynn sat in the car, his mascot now.

'Look, I'm packing two guns so don't fart about. Just tell me what it is.'

'It's a modelling tool, for pushing the chopped tow in under the skin and around the skeleton when mounting small birds or animals. Sometimes it is used for sculpting in plaster or paraffin wax, though we do not recommend the use of such things.'

A taxidermist's tool, but had Réjean Turcel been the one to drop it or Charles Audit? 'It's been well used,' said Kohler, glancing up to see Verdun drag his eyes from the car. 'Handmade years ago. What's that one?' He pointed to a case beneath the glass. 'The one that looks like a flattened dental pick, an earspoon?'

The eyes settled back into their lofty perch. 'A skull-emptier. Has the tool anything to do with the Chief Inspector of the Sûreté who came here, monsieur?'

'St-Cyr? That schmuck? Not a chance.'

Verdun gave a shrug. 'I could have sold his canary. I told him so. I offered.'

'You didn't! Did he really have a canary?'

It would be best to be truthful. 'A beauty. A Clear Border Yellow cock, perhaps the commonest of canaries, but a superb job of mounting, considering the primitiveness of that tool. He wanted to know who'd done it. He asked about the elastic band.'

'And you could have sold his canary?'

Verdun drew himself up. 'Yes, to the Vice Admiral von Lion. Me, I have told the Vice Admiral of the bird. He was most disappointed to have missed it.'

Kohler gathered in the tool. 'I'll bet he was.' Tracking down stuffed canaries instead of gathering military intelligence! Hunting for gold coins and girls who sold them. What would the Abwehr think of next?

The empire of Hermann 'Otto' Brandl never stopped. That huge purchasing company the Abwehr had set up in France had its head offices in two fine old period houses at numbers 21 and 23 square Bois du Boulogne. This was money. This was power and class. The air fairly breathed of it. Even the rain that was pissing ran cleanly to the sewers.

Oona Van der Lynn stirred uncomfortably on the seat beside him as the Citroën's engine began to cool. 'Relax, eh? This is where it's all at. If you want to get ahead in business today, you have to come here to Brandl or see that one of his minions comes to you.'

'And if you want to hold on to your wealth?' she asked.

She wasn't dumb. She'd begun to figure things out for herself. Kohler knew he was impressed. 'You make "friends", madame, and you hope you've hidden that wealth so well they won't get a sniff of it.'

'And if someone else knows you have that hidden wealth and doesn't particularly like you?'

'Then you're in trouble.'

'This place is too close to the avenue Foch. The rue Lauriston is practically around the corner.'

Kohler grinned to ease her mind. 'Boys with their toys have to gather near one another, madame. The trouble is, they seldom play together. One always wants what the other has and, like boys everywhere, they often get nasty.'

'Do you want me to wait in the car?'

He shook his head. 'I've already lost someone that way. I'd just as soon not lose you as well.'

She seemed to take frugal nourishment from what he'd said, and he knew she'd asked herself, Does he really mean it? Was she safe with him? Could *anybody* be safe these days?

'The rue Lauriston will want to question me now that Martin is dead.'

'Not if you're with me. Just try to keep that in mind and *don't* bolt until I can find a safe place for you.' She flashed him an uncertain smile that was at once sad and realistic. 'Look I really will see you're okay. I mean it.'

'For your partner's sake?' she asked, not looking at him but at those two fine houses that flew no flags, remaining unmarked except for a small bronze plaque: *The Bureau Otto.*

'For Louis' sake. Yeah, that's right. I owe the Frog. Now come on. Look your best. Let me do the talking.'

A grey mouse, one of the fräuleins who had volunteered back home for the typing pools and the sacks of their bosses, held fort at the outer desk of the string of offices they were ushered to. Abwehr blue was everywhere. Telephones, teleprinters, secretaries, accountants, purchasing agents, two rows of stiff, unsmiling businessmen sitting with knees together and briefcases hiding them. Hats in their hands and goods to sell. After all, this was practically the only place a fellow with a couple of factories could keep hand to mouth short of the black market, which they'd dabble in anyway. And money they made. Lots of it. Buckets. One Frog trying to outFrog another, the little flies that were so tasty being tossed to them by the Chief Toad, one Hermann 'Otto' Brandl.

The grey mouse looked up sternly. 'Herr Kohler?' she said, distastefully fingering his Gestapo's shield.

'A collector of stuffed canaries,' he grinned. 'They said you'd know where he was, seeing as he's the one who's in charge of silk, glass and explosives, and as his office is empty.'

Kohler drew her attention to a fact she already knew. The offices she guarded were posh, nothing stinted. Leather and antiques and lots of them, all tastefully arranged.

'Kapitän Offenheimer is *out*,' she said, consulting a diary.

'Didn't Brandl tell you to open your lips?'

The buttons of her zinc-covered bosom were tight. Her blue eyes didn't leave his. 'Look, your boss collects stuffed canaries. He's got a passion for this one. I'd like to give it to him.'

'A moment then. I will see if Kapitän Brandl is still willing for you to be tolerated.'

She rang through and listened sharply as a tadpole should. 'He asks if you know who killed the mackerel Victor Morand.'

Blandness would be best. 'Réjean Turcel, a Corsican, the new owner of the carousel. Address changed, the new address not yet known but we're working on it. He's the prime suspect but there are others.'

This she relayed to Brandl, who replied that they must be getting warm. 'Kapitän Offenheimer and his personal secretary are at one of the warehouses in Saint-Ouen. You may see him there.' She scribbled the address on a slip of paper. 'Is this the canary?' she asked of Madame Van der Lynn. 'I thought she was already dead.'

Outside in the car Kohler said, 'Don't let her bother you. It's a world in which no one tells anyone anything more than they absolutely have to, madame. A world of lies, half-truths and utter deceptions, where greed is conqueror and petty jealousies reign supreme.'

'Did Réjean really kill this . . . this mackerel?'

'Like I just said, I don't know. Let them *think* he did. For now that's good enough. Don't panic, eh? Just try to keep calm. I think we've made a tiny breakthrough. We've let Brandl's side know that we'll play by their rules.'

'But you won't.'

'Not really. No. That's half the fun of it, but it's also what they'll be expecting.'

The sounds of charcoal being scraped on drawing-paper came up to St-Cyr, here a cough, there a muted exclamation that served only to emphasize the intensity with which the various pieces of work were being executed.

The studio, one of several in the École des Beaux-Arts, was cold and poorly lit. From the observers' balcony he had the best of views. He'd been to the hospital, had had his hand stitched, had had a little something to eat.

Among the students there were several Germans on leave, corporals, sergeants, even a lieutenant or two. The Kriegsmarine, the Luftwaffe, the Wehrmacht, all dedicated to improving their talent.

The French students were a mixed bag, some old enough to be grandfathers, others young enough to have been their grandchildren. There was a noticeable lack of young men, painful because the war had stripped the youth of France of them.

Marianne St-Jacques sat on a *chaise longue* on a small dais in the midst of the students. There was a white woollen blanket under her. The ankles were crossed. One arm rested casually over the back of the *chaise*; the other hand held a red silk rose.

This she was smelling.

St-Cyr looked down on her as that God of his looked down on him and the dice of fate were thrown in the back alley of life.

The urge to photograph her was overpowering. The cinematographer had to start the cameras but he took the film back to the rue Polonceau, to the morning after they had found the body of Christabelle Audit. 0500 hours and darkness, the end of the curfew.

And he heard this girl saying to Georges Lagace, the baker, 'Until tomorrow, my love, I die with waiting and hunger.'

She was not overly pretty or striking in any particular way but had many positive anatomical attributes. The brown hair was thick and cut short, bobbed in waves and curls with one pronounced wave over the right side of the brow. The legs were not too long or too slender, a girl of perhaps some fifty or so kilograms with small but nicely shaped breasts, the nipples turned slightly outwards. A slim waist, good hips that would grow bigger with time – in many ways a lot like Christabelle Audit. Very positive, very proud shoulders, high collar-bones, a slim neck and sharply jutting chin, a chin of character. Ah yes, this one would not take no for an answer.

The face was on the narrow side and very much of the middle class but with suggestions, in the sharpness of the features, of misadventure among her ancestors with the aristocracy.

The rose was tickling her nose. The cold made her shiver until at last she saw him looking at her and came to look up at him.

So many seconds ticked by, the drawing mistress, a woman in her mid-fifties, said, 'Oh, all right. Take another break. This lack of heat! If any of you could assist, it would be most helpful.'

They were there to draw, not to arrange for coal to bypass the authorities who had none to give unless they got something in return.

The girl's voice came softly up to him. 'It's all right, madame. I will continue to sit.'

St-Cyr began to study her as the cinematographer would, dredging character, motive and action from her very pores.

The thighs were not heavy – a girl who walked a lot and rode her bicycle. A girl who had once been married, so Georges had said, and who had purchased a tombstone in the cemetery of Montparnasse to mark what had to be an empty grave.

They'd met by accident in that cemetery. Love takes all angles, but had it been love, eh?

He didn't think so.

Her knees were dimpled. She'd a small scrape on the inside of the right calf – an episode with the bicycle perhaps.

There was a small brown mole to the left of her navel and near the hip. No stretch marks that he could see. Had she wanted children only to find the war had interfered with that dream? He thought not – not yet in any case. Not with this one.

The pubic hairs were curly but there was not the breadth and thickness of hair Christabelle Audit had dyed black.

The left breast seemed as if in need of suckling, for its nipple had stiffened under observation from the balcony's brass viewing telescope which stood on a little tripod by the railing.

The lips were wide and sensuous when in repose but tight now in the grim realization of what must surely lie before her.

'Monsieur, *do you mind*?'

It was the drawing mistress. They must get all types coming in here. 'Ah, *pardon*, madame. Forgive me. I was but thinking of Renoir.'

The girl's eyebrows were thick and pleasing but would cause concern as she grew older. The frown that furrowed her clear wide brow was earnestness itself. At twenty-eight, a girl could still frown like that.

'If you do not desist, monsieur, I shall have to ask you to leave the studio at once!'

'Forgive me, please. I will cease in a moment.'

He had to have one last look and began it at her ankles, running it up the length of her until he found the rose and found Marianne St-Jacques looking at him. Her eyes were of a greeny-brown with amber flecks, and they did not waver as she held her breath.

They were good eyes, lovely eyes, but he could not help but see them as in death.

The mannequin's dressing-room had a tiny stove and she saw no reason to wrap herself in anything.

'What is it you want with me, Inspector?'

'Merely a few questions.'

'Are they about that girl who was murdered?'

St-Cyr took out his pipe and tobacco pouch. What would the cinematographer have done? Asked her to put something on, or merely told her, Yes, yes, that's what it's all about?

He helped her to feed some of the fist-sized balls of dried papier mâché into the stove and stood beside her as she warmed her hands.

She couldn't look at him now, knew he'd find out the truth, but when his voice came, it was gentle. 'Mademoiselle, what is it you are trying so valiantly to hide from me? A chance encounter with that murdered girl, a few words passed in haste, in the darkness after curfew? Come, come, I know she was an artist's model, a student here. You met, you talked, you shared your meagre lunches, and if I am not mistaken, you have never had a husband to bury under a "purchased" stone in the cemetery of Montparnasse.'

She clasped her shoulders. She *wouldn't* look at him. The stove . . . the stove . . . she must concentrate on it.

He struck a match and she shuddered, gripping her shoulders more tightly. 'Please, it is essential that you tell me everything and quickly. Your life is in danger. This . . .' he thrust his bandaged hand in front of her – blood had seeped through, 'is but an example of what they can and will do to you. Now come, please come, I am not a lover of the Nazis, Marianne. You can and must trust me.'

It had hurt to use her name. It brought back memories of his wife and son . . .

Her shoulders were unclasped. 'Please, your nakedness won't deter me from asking you the things I must in order to save your life.'

'How did she die?'

Her breasts were firm, the skin clear. Her underarms had not been shaved or clipped.

'How did she die, damn you!' cried the girl.

He would give her a whisper, though it would distress him to deal with her in such a manner. 'Terribly.'

She burst into tears and he hated himself for having had to do it, but . . .

Her nose was quickly wiped with the back of a hand, her eyes with the fingers. 'It's true I knew her a little, but we were not working together on anything.'

'Then you had been following her?' he asked.

'Yes . . . Yes, I was following her. Sometimes.'

St-Cyr reached out to the stove to strike the match. A cloud of tobacco smoke billowed about him; he waved it away. 'For the Resistance?' he asked sharply. 'Come, come, Marianne, to me you can speak the truth and it would be best if you did so that I can help you and the others if necessary, and keep my Gestapo partner or anyone else from learning of your connection with the case.'

The Resistance! *Maudit*! What would they think of next? he wondered.

Her backside needed warming. She would turn to face him boldly now, this detective from the Sûreté whose shabby over-coat had been ripped and whose hand had been cut.

'Christabelle wasn't the target, monsieur.' She gave a brave smile. 'He was. The man she had been meeting for sexual favours, the one who had bought the use of her body. M Antoine Audit, the industrialist and the maker of explosives, Inspector. *Explosives* and parachute silk for the *Nazis*!'

Her breasts heaved with the force of her young words. Her fists clenched.

'We . . . our group . . . myself . . . that is Georges and myself . . .'

It would do no good to try to hide the truth from this one. *Merde*! Had he no sympathy for tears, no interest in her naked body, nothing in his heart for a young girl in distress and trapped by him? Had he only the cold brown eyes of a whoremaster choosing his whore?

'Your group? Come, come, out with it, Mademoiselle St-Jacques.'

He would hit her now, slap her, tear her by the hair and beat her! 'We were going to assassinate him. Georges –'

'Georges Lagace is nothing, mademoiselle. Nothing! A baker trapped by the dough of your stupid, stupid scheming. Now quickly, the rest, before madame the drawing mistress begins to pound on the door.' Assassination! *Merde*! Did they not know the SS and the Gestapo would most certainly have caught them?

She would lift her eyes proudly to his, she would let him see how brave she was. 'Georges was my dead sister's husband. He's weak and yes, you are correct, he is innocent. He didn't want any part of things, but we forced him into letting me stay with him when . . . whenever the girl . . . whenever she went to be with her industrialist.'

'Are you a Communist?' he asked. The answer was fiercely given in the affirmative and he gave a sigh at the stupidity of the young, for the Nazis hated the Communists almost as much as they hated the Jews. 'How did it all start?' he asked.

She gave a shrug, unconsciously rubbing the base of her throat and between her breasts. 'We'd been kicking things over – the need to do something. *Anything*! The topic of those industrialists who are co-operating so well with the Nazis came up. I'd been to visit Georges a few times. One night I met Christabelle quite by accident. Things began to fall into place. Last summer I saw Audit for the first time in the rue Polonceau and then my friends showed me photographs of him and some of his factories. He . . . he was to have been our choice.'

Antoine Audit. 'Did he ever suspect this, do you think?' he asked, letting her detect the note of caution that had crept into his voice.

She shook her head. 'I was very careful, as were the others.'

I'll bet you were! he said to himself with a sigh. 'I don't suppose you possess a gun, a pistol perhaps – a nine millimetre Luger, eh?'

His shoes were muddy. One lace had come undone. If he was Gestapo-friendly, he'd have arrested her by now.

She filled her lungs. 'I . . . I do not do such things. I'm only used as a courier or to keep a watch on someone. It's better for a girl. There's always less suspicion.'

St-Cyr gently lifted her chin. The skin of her throat would be so soft. The wire would cut into it. Why . . . why must he see her as in death? Was there nothing he could do?

'Please don't lie to me, mademoiselle. You left Georges just as the curfew ended. You rode down the rue Polonceau on that bicycle of yours. Schraum, a corporal in the German Army, accosted you. He was drunk. He caught hold of your bicycle. You fell, you cried out as he came at you. You had no choice – no choice, eh? It was kill or be taken!'

He dropped his hand. 'You've a scrape on your leg. It's evidence enough.'

The misty eyes were steady. 'I did not kill him. I did not see him. I did not even hear the shot, monsieur. We weren't involved in that business.'

Merde! she was still being difficult! 'Who left the note for Father Eugène?'

'A friend. All right, one of us, but only after the hostages had been taken.'

The hostages ... The drawing mistress was standing in the doorway, waiting for the girl. They'd not heard the knock the woman must have given.

'A moment, please, madame. *Please*. Get out!'

The impasse fell back on them. 'A last few questions, Marianne. The Captain Dupuis, the veteran with one leg. Did Christabelle ever mention him to you? Was she not perhaps a little afraid of him?'

The girl shook her head. 'She said Dupuis was obviously quite interested in her but that he could never get up the courage to speak to her. Me, I think his attentions mildly amused her. I had the feeling that she knew all about men and what they wanted of a girl.'

'And Roland Minou, the son of the concierge at that hotel? Did you ever see him lurking about? Did she ever mention him?'

Again she shook her head. 'This one I do not know. Christabelle came always in the evening, at around eight or nine, so he could have been some place else.'

Or was simply too clever to have let himself be seen.

'What about a Corsican? A man of sixty-three or so? Please, it is vital, mademoiselle. *Think*! You must remember.'

'A Corsican ... ? But she has met only the industrialist?'

The frown deepened, the left cheek of her seat was unconsciously scratched, first towards the hip and then a little further back.

'Well, what is it?' he asked.

'The villa at Number twenty-three. I ... I saw her stepping out from its courtyard once. As I came along the street, she turned quickly away towards the door, but did not touch it, monsieur. It closed by itself, and when I asked her who she'd met in there, she said no one, that she had simply gone into the courtyard to see what it looked like.'

'Did this occur before or after her meeting with the industrialist?'

'Before. At . . . at about eight-thirty. It was warm. There were still lots of people about. They would have taken no notice of her, they would have thought she'd simply got the wrong address.'

But you knew she'd left her purse in there, didn't you, eh? and you're not about to tell me this.

It made him sad to think she still didn't trust him. 'That place used to be her grandfather's house. Did she ever mention him or the carousel?'

'No . . . no, she never mentioned those. A carousel . . . ?'

'A canary?'

The girl looked away. 'A canary. Yes . . . yes, I once saw her with it. A little bird that had been mounted by the taxidermist, you understand. She was stroking it, so lost in thought she did not hear me and when she did, she put it quickly away in a pocket.'

'Take Georges' advice. Don't go near him. Do absolutely nothing but your work here and in the hat shop. Stay indoors after curfew. Keep out of draughts and tell your friends to do so as well. The heat is on. I'll be in touch.'

Only then did she clasp her breasts to feel them rise and fall in the sigh she gave.

He'd closed the door behind him. He'd given her a few brief moments in which to compose herself.

He'd not asked if she had ever been in that room of Christabelle's or inside the Villa Audit, or why the girl had met her grandfather and the Corsican at the Café Noir on the avenue de Laumière near the parc des Buttes-Chaumont.

Or why the girl had taken the canary out of her pocket and had quietly stroked it as the two men had talked so earnestly to her about things. A young girl, a dark-haired girl who had dyed her hair like that – why, why had she done so?

Christabelle Audit; Christiane Baudelaire. Two sets of papers, the one correct, the other false, but the occupation of art student and artist's mannequin the same, as if pride could not let her make some more sensible choice for at least one of them.

The dressing-room was small. The stove had gone out and the door was still closed but would it open suddenly some day, would he come for her also, this murderer?

A Corsican . . .

Gripping her shoulders, she rubbed them for warmth but

stood alone wondering ... wondering ... How did she die?
Terribly.

The warehouse was one of hundreds in the bustling dock area of
Saint-Ouen to the north of the city near the Seine. The faded
yellow logo of a hand of bananas was just visible on the rusting
corrugated iron above the main shipping door and entrance.
Kohler was struck by the thing. It could not possibly have anything to do with Oberg, the Butcher of Poland, but was it a
reminder that one should never forget one's bosses?

The noise was unbelievable. Donkey engines, overhead
cranes, pneumatic drills – three, no four shunting locomotives,
gangs of French labourers pulling track and laying down others,
gangs of the Wehrmacht's finest too, soot and coal dust in the air
and everyone pausing to get an eyeful of Madame Van der Lynn,
who didn't like it one bit.

There were mountains of coal, stacks and stacks of firewood,
steel drums that carried labels of all kinds. Kerosene, alcohol,
glycerine, liquid fertilizer (i.e., pig shit), concentrated apple
juice, a real cocktail.

The collector of stuffed canaries had been forewarned. Offenheimer avoided looking at Madame Van der Lynn and concentrated on him instead. 'Herr Kohler, as you can see I'm very
busy.'

Kohler gave the Abwehr's man a Gestapo's 'Heil Hitler!',
crashed his heels and shook hands formally. One had to do
things like that. 'Brandl said you'd co-operate. It's good of you to
see me.'

'Yes, yes. Oh, very well. Sit please. You may not smoke. I
would prefer it if you didn't.'

Well, what do you know about that? In these days of high
anxiety tobacco was out and that could only mean real coffee was
in. Lots of it and strong. He indicated the cup on the desk and
asked if they could have some.

Karl Ernst Offenheimer was forty-four years old, of medium
height, light build, wore unrimmed eyeglasses that didn't do
anything for the round and unhealthy face whose pallor spoke of
too many late nights but doing what?

The naval uniform was far too tidy. The short black hair was
heavily pomaded and parted in the middle. He'd shaved but
already near noon there was a blueish shadow.

'Tell me about Schraum,' said Kohler.

The dark eyes glistened with barely suppressed anger. 'There is *nothing* to tell. As you can see, I have been going through the accounts. Kapitän Brandl is convinced we will find something. Myself, I think we know enough.'

'And have for some time.'

'I don't like your manner, Herr Kohler. I resent your coming here. It's *my* job to find the coins, not yours!'

'The coins are only a part of it. What we want are the murderers.'

'Yes, yes, the killers. Schraum ran this warehouse for the Bureau and had, as I'm sure you can well surmise, a direct pipeline through to his uncle in Stralsund.'

'The Gauleiter, the SA-Sturmbannführer and collector of coins. A distant relative of the Reichsmarschall Goering.'

The dark eyes flicked to Madame Van der Lynn but raced away to the ledgers as if guilt had slapped a wrist and mummy had said no.

'Yes, the Reichsmarschall. He is himself somewhat of a collector.'

'Aren't we all,' breathed Kohler. The bastard was up to something. 'Brandl operates the Bureau Otto on the principle of the barracuda in thin waters, Herr Kapitän. He lets the little fish fatten among the coral heads until they make mischief. Then he eats them. Right? So what's your game?'

Kohler was the nuisance who had embarrassed the SS and Himmler himself. 'My *game* is this. The coins, though forged, are copies of real ones that must have been syphoned from a substantial hoard of undeclared valuables. Schraum should have brought the matter to our attention but chose not to.'

And got eaten by the barracuda? Was it that simple?

'He bit off too much, Herr Kohler. All little fish must understand that the reef is controlled by the big fish.'

'Meaning me? Come off it, Herr Kapitän. I can't even swim. How long have you been working on this?'

'Since long before the murders.'

'What's stored here? What kind of goods did Schraum handle?'

'Coal, firewood – don't tell me you haven't noticed?'

'Bananas?'

'Bananas?'

'Yeah, there's a logo above the door.'

'Oh that. It has nothing to do with us. It must be something from the past.'

No sense of humour at all. 'Oberg was a banana merchant. Oberg, my fine Abwehr twit! *Oberg*. Now give.'

The shadowed cheeks quivered. The dark eyes flicked to Oona, to her legs, her chest, her face and hair; they made the trip and came right back to settle on the ledgers, thus avoiding a confrontation. 'Otto said you would help us. Is this the help of one who says he is a friend?'

'And needs his friends right now?'

With a supreme effort of will, Offenheimer pulled his gaze from the columns of figures. So many tons of coal, so many cords of firewood. Even a donkey could have written them.

'No one crosses Otto Brandl, Herr Kohler. The reef is to be kept peaceful at all times for the good of us all.'

Out of a corner of his left eye Kohler saw Madame Van der Lynn tug her skirt down and smooth it over her knees. 'Tell me what happened with the coins; let's begin with them.'

It would be best to appear judgemental, to place his fingertips together and bring them to his lips in thought. 'Ten days ago Schraum's uncle received the coins in a consignment of liqueurs, old silver, tapestries and wines. Schraum was apparently confident he'd scraped the surface of something big. We have since learned that the uncle wasn't happy. The coins didn't get past his scrutiny, Herr Kohler. Unfortunately, Reichsmarschall Goering's appetite had already been whetted.'

'Only duds turned up and the uncle turned nasty, that it, eh?'

'In so far as the deaths are concerned, yes. The uncle was embarrassed, and when you are an SA-Sturmbannführer and Gauleiter you can't afford to be embarrassed by a careless nephew, even though he might have been useful to you in the past.'

'Someone was hired? Sent straight from Stralsund? A debt-collector perhaps, assuming cash had been paid for goods received?'

'Precisely. Victor Morande had been Schraum's source. They'd been working on the deal for months. Morande was forced to tell the killer of the girl's whereabouts, then she was killed and finally Schraum.'

'The knife, the wire and then the pistol,' oozed Kohler with feigned wonder. 'You should have been a detective.'

The mackerel, the girl and then the corporal. Offenheimer

polished his glasses. 'The Reichsmarschall is, of course, insisting we locate the real coins. Apparently the gold sestertius is of some personal interest.'

Their coffee came. Oona clutched her cup with both hands. As she took a sip, she chanced a look across the desk at Offenheimer. She would not wish to be left alone with this one, ah no. There was something wrong with him. Sex . . . had it to do with sex?

Kohler took out his cigarettes. In alarm, Offenheimer's spoon stopped stirring. 'Oh, sorry. I almost forgot. It's a good thing Louis isn't here. Then there'd be three of us to one of you.'

'Will there be anything else?' asked Offenheimer.

He'd ignore the hint. 'Schraum was approached by Victor Morande. They'd had the coal and firewood exchange going for some time but now it was fifty-fifty on a deal Victor thought he could deliver.'

'The hidden wealth of Antoine Audit.'

'Of Périgord, Lyon and Saint-Raphaël.'

'The same, but you won't find any of Audit's silks here. Schraum was too careful for that.' Offenheimer ran a finger across the ledger. 'He swapped coal with an accomplice in Saint-Denis who was in charge of the warehouse where the silk is stored. There's only the requisition for the coal, nothing else, but I know silk changed hands. It was sold to some of the dress designers. Another deal gave him access to the foodstuffs of Audit and Sons.'

'Pâtés with truffles and walnuts,' said Kohler. 'He got to know his man a little better. Did he send samples to the uncle?'

Men like Offenheimer cannot shrug; it's a gesture that would only have been punished. Instead, the Captain settled for a sip of coffee.

'The uncle passed the word back to the avenue Foch when the coins turned out to have been forged.'

'After having first hired a hit man to do away with a nephew who'd turned troublesome? A Corsican? Hey, I didn't think they had any of those in Stralsund. Dumb of me, I guess. It just goes to show you what can happen when a fellow's overworked.'

Kohler was trying to make a mockery of things! Very well, it would be best to teach him a lesson. 'The avenue Foch could have supplied the killer, Herr Kohler. The rue Lauriston are not always as tidy as they should be, nor are the Intervention-Referat.'

Paul Carbone then, was that it? 'Where's this put Antoine Audit?'

'Under suspicion for not declaring what he should have, but he has friends in high places so one must go carefully. It's a little like hunting for Easter eggs. There's a crowd of others to be beaten. Each leaf must be carefully turned and none of the eggs trampled until they've been examined to see if they are to taste.'

'Lest the wind of the Gestapo blow all of the leaves away, eh? Hang on a minute, will you? Where's the head? I have to drain the battery.'

Oona choked. The coffee scalded her throat and made her eyes water. Herr Kohler had left her alone with him!

The Kapitän Offenheimer refused to look at her or speak. He broke off a piece of cookie and dunked it in his coffee. Then he ate the thing fastidiously, rubbing his thumb and forefinger together quickly as if in guilt and under watchful eyes.

He was staring at the left corner of his desk. The hackles on the back of her neck began to rise, the muscles in her legs to tighten. She was making him nervous, afraid . . . 'Have you been in Paris long, Herr Kapitän?' she hazarded, trying to break the silence. A mistake.

Ignoring the question, Offenheimer reached for his coffee and blew on it before taking a sip. 'Have you slept with him?' he asked, still not looking at her.

'I beg your pardon? Paris . . . I asked you about Paris.'

'And I *asked* if you'd slept with him.'

An avalanche of coal outside jarred her nerves. 'Yes . . . yes, I've slept with him.'

'Did you enjoy it?'

Why in God's name couldn't he look at her? 'My husband was arrested by the rue Lauriston. I thought . . . Herr Kohler asked . . . He demanded I undress. I – I had to! Don't you see, I had to?'

The coffee was perfect. Five teaspoonfuls of the finest grind to three cups of boiling water over the filter, then one and a quarter teaspoons of granulated sugar, a touch of cognac to sharpen the taste, and cream, rich cream. Just as at home, just like auntie used to make it and grandmother too.

Deep in the warehouse behind them, Kohler was impressed by what he'd found. There were tins of tomatoes, pears, peaches and peas, bottles of pickled walnuts *à la* Périgord, tubes of walnut cream, or was it paste? Truffles in wine and in honey – Christ, Audit and Sons must have been desperate to think up something new. What hadn't they tried?

Behind the coal and under canvas there was enough pâté with

truffles to keep the hogs at home happy for years. Cases of Bordeaux, bottles of walnut liqueur. Gifts from Antoine Audit to keep a certain corporal quiet, or merely samples to be sent home to the uncle?

By the look of the loot, Schraum had shown great promise, a real wheeler-dealer in his element. A pity to have been such a disappointment.

Shoes, good ones, too. All size ten and a half. Uncle had big feet. Luggage, cosmetics, perfume and soap – friend Schraum had used his authority over the lifeblood of coal and cordwood to choke the pipeline to his uncle.

There were small antiques, even a cluster of oils on canvas in gilt frames. Porcelains in straw. But did the corporal really have any taste? Louis would have known. In any case, the bugger had had deals with everyone who had counted. No wonder the barracuda had got uptight.

But the barracuda had been caught sleeping all the same. There'd be questions now and that's what Old Shatter Hand, the Kommandant of Greater Paris, had wanted. Questions, questions and more of them. Another scandal.

This one on the Abwehr, which didn't make a lot of sense on von Schaumburg's part unless someone in the Bureau Otto was also working for the SS over on the avenue Foch and hadn't said a thing about it. Oh yeah.

Snorting at the thought, Kohler pocketed a jar of pickled walnuts for Louis just in case the Frog was still around and pounding the pavement. A crock of the famous pâté went into the other pocket. The guns were getting in the way and were too heavy, but he'd manage somehow to swipe a bottle of the Cream of Walnut liqueur. Just a taste. What the hell.

The woman who had made the coffee was Offenheimer's personal grey mouse and by God she was grey! A grandmother from the Teutoburger Wald yanked out of retirement. They couldn't have come of sterner stuff. She'd be well into her sixties and she had to make him wonder.

'Tell Madame Van der Lynn that the Inspector Kohler is finished here for the time being. Extend my thanks to the Kapitän. Sorry about the canary, but she's spoken for.'

Son of a bitch! Louis . . . where the hell was Louis? He'd not believe it either! A granny, when everyone else voted for the young ones and saw that they got them.

7

By mid-afternoon a light mist had replaced the rain. Round the Étoile and the Arc de Triomphe the traffic had the sound of wet cornflakes in cream.

German direction signs were everywhere. Bicycles ... there were so many of them. Vélo-taxis pedalled by eager young girls or grim-faced men in their middle fifties and older. Now a Daimler edging through the cream, now an army truck coming abreast of a cornflake, a blonde in a red coat and matching beret pedalling like the damned. German officers laughing at her. German corporals looking on with lust or disinterest, the whole mass swirling in the mist, undulating as it went round and round ... The Benzedrine? asked St-Cyr. The panic? The carousel of what Paris had become? Ah Mon Dieu, this thing was fast becoming a nightmare!

He squished his toes together. Memories of the rue Bènard kept coming back. Memories, too, of that girl Marianne St-Jacques and her foolish, foolish bravery, and of thirty hostages. Thirty of them!

He'd been to headquarters in search of Hermann only to find closed doors. Osias Pharand, who should have been screaming with territorial rage, had *refused* to see him. Walter Boemelburg had been 'busy'.

Reports seemed unwanted, advice not freely given, the streets of Paris left waiting only for the assassin's knife. Vouvray had made them outcasts. Hermann and he had been pitched into the maelstrom and told to find the loot or else! Never mind the murders. M Antoine Audit must be running scared *and* not just because of an insignificant Resistance cell of young and dangerously careless hotheads.

No, my friend, he said as the hard-boiled eggs of the vélo-taxis passed through the eerie mist, Antoine Audit has much to lose.

The traffic took on more motion, the speed increasing as a horn blared angrily and he thought, he hoped that it was Hermann. But it was a white Bentley, and when it passed, showering a wall of water over him, Nicole de Rainvelle smiled and laughed and left her silk handkerchief in the gutter.

St-Cyr picked it up. Mirage . . . the perfume of Gabrielle Arcuri. 'BASTARDS!' he screamed. 'YOU LEAVE THAT ONE ALONE!'

Still quivering, he threw up a hand and whistled sharply. The vélo-taxi skidded as it swirved to avoid a cyclist and swung in to the kerb. 'The corner of the boulevard Raspail and the rue du Cherche-Midi, and hurry,' he said. '*Hurry*! I have to get there.'

'The prison?' gasped the girl, dismayed by the fare.

'Just do as I say. Don't argue! I'm from the Sûreté. It's a matter of life and *death*, mademoiselle. *Death*!'

'Ah no, the rue des Saussaies?' The dreaded rue des Saussaies! She swallowed. Drenched red curls were matted to her brow.

'Look, just take me to the convent, eh?'

'The convent! The *prison*, monsieur! Four hundred and sixty francs.'

Forty times the going rate! He thrust his bandaged hand at her and shouted, 'It's getting wet, eh? I'll give you ten francs and that's an order!'

Gestapo! she said to herself. *Merde*, what was she to do?

The vélo was a converted antique settee of little value on wheels that wobbled. The cushions were, of course, soaking!

'Drive on. Relax, eh? I'm sorry if I've upset you, mademoiselle. I'm on a murder investigation. Assassins are out to kill me and I have, alas, no weapon.'

She began to peddle much harder and, as they joined the flow, the casserole of the settee floated well enough.

Hostages . . . potential witnesses. Lafont and Bonny – had they killed those who might count, thereby eliminating critical information they themselves already knew?

Four murders . . . and where was Hermann? Had he followed up on Schraum? Had he found the warehouse where the corporal had worked? Had he managed anything at all on the collector of stuffed canaries?

Christabelle Audit could well have been killed by Captain Dupuis. The girl Mila Zavitz lent weight to this. Had her death not come to light, things might have been more difficult. Hers was the wild card every criminal dreaded, but it didn't quite fit. Ah no, it didn't.

Yet Mila Zavitz could well have looked in those two suitcases and been caught in the act by Charles Audit, Roland Minou or someone else. Except that Father Eugène had said the cases had been locked . . . But had they really been so? Had they? Ah, *Mon Dieu*, why couldn't this girl hurry? If only God would not mock His lonely detective so much, if only He would give but once, the kind whisper, the little benediction, not the sacrament of death by assassination! The witnesses . . .

'Monsieur, we . . . we are almost at the corner of the boulevard Raspail. Could you . . . Would you, for my sake? I . . . '

He blinked. He saw the girl straddling her bike, still holding on to it by the handlebars and turned so as to face him.

They were on the rue du Cherche-Midi. 'Monsieur . . . ?' she said again.

St-Cyr heard himself saying, 'Drive on. Don't be afraid. I won't be long and when I come out, I hope my clumsiness has not made me too late and that there will be two of us and one hundred francs for yourself.'

His rumpled fedora was soaked. The Sûreté looked like a tramp, except that the Nazis had all but 'cleansed' the city of such people.

The rue du Cherche-Midi was in the sixth *arrondissement*. In better times St-Cyr would have thought it a pleasurable journey back into the seventeenth century and if he could but shut his eyes as a cinematographer would, the tumult of those times would come readily enough. But, ah! one had so little time for life these days. The pleasurable lunch had practically vanished except from the lies of the cinemas where the crowds gathered to watch in rapture celluloid diners eating celluloid meals. The better the banquet, the greater the rapture.

The Prison of the Cherche-Midi beckoned. Even the blush of exertion had disappeared from the girl's cheeks. 'Wait for us, please,' he said grimly. 'We shouldn't be long.'

Her green eyes glanced uncertainly at the heavy door and though he hated himself for saying it, he felt he had to. 'Please do not run off, mademoiselle. I have taken down your licence number.'

She crossed herself and he left her to the mist.

The prison had been a convent in the days of the Sun King. Its airless, windowless cells had found another use during the Revolution and ever since then it had kept that use, God having deserted the place along with the nuns.

'St-Cyr of the Sûreté to see the prisoner Madame Gilbert. She was one of the hostages taken from the rue Polonceau after the shooting of the Corporal Schraum.'

She was the housekeeper at the Villa Audit.

The *flic* on duty took in the clothes, the rips in the overcoat, the leaking shoes. 'Gilbert . . . Gilbert?' he said. 'I seem to remember seeing that name, monsieur.'

'It's Chief Inspector St-Cyr.'

'Don't they pay you people any more?'

'Not the honest ones, so don't get wise.'

'Pneumonia then.'

'The rue Lauriston?' *Nom de Jésus-Christ!* could nothing go right?

The *flic* got stiff. 'That name does not pass my lips, Inspector. It was simply a case of double pneumonia. Paris in winter is the shits!'

'Chantal, you must excuse my appearance. I have come the back way so as not to bring trouble to your door.'

She touched a blonde wave delicately, so delicately. A flutter. 'But my poor Louis, you have hurt yourself! Ah, there is blood . . . '

He swept the hand behind his back. 'My pardons, my pardons, please forgive me.'

That little bird from yesteryear, vivacious as always, had to fan herself as she sat down. St-Cyr said, 'Please don't let it upset you, Chantal. A cat after a canary. Nothing more, I assure you. Merely a scratch.'

'You are *wrong* to come to me in this . . . this state, Monsieur Louis! Your shoes, your trousers – that coat. Muriel . . . Muriel, a moment, please,' she called out urgently. 'Ask one of the girls to join us. Louis, you must remove those things at once. Hurry! Hurry, I say. They stink. You need a bath.'

His 'Forgive me,' sounded weak and lame. Unable to shrug out of the overcoat with ease, he was clumsy. 'The hand . . . it really is nothing.'

A scratch! 'What *have* you been doing?'

Chantal Grenier and her friend Muriel were both over seventy and had run their shop Enchantment on the place Vendôme for almost fifty years. Lingerie – silks, satins and lace, perfumes, bath oils and soaps.

'Another murder case,' he apologized, handing the girl his coat but telling her please to empty the contents of its pockets on to the desk for him. 'I must lose nothing, you understand.' She was really quite obliging, but then they all were.

The office was cluttered with bolts of material, books of fabric designs and samples, perfumes from everywhere, so many things the years had brought to light and they had stored. Muriel, in a severe grey pinstripe with wide lapels, smoked one of her endless cigarettes, did the designing, the buying and made up the perfumes; Chantal, in flowered silk today, handled the sales, helped pick the trends, fought off the creditors when Muriel couldn't, which was seldom, and managed the staff, though Muriel always got to choose the girls.

'Now the tie and shirt, Louis. We will find something to keep you warm.'

'Me, I will retire to the bath, please. Your hospitality is more than I deserve but,' he gave the shrug of a vagrant on the run, 'I have no place to call home at the moment.'

'No place . . . ' Those large brown eyes flicked apprehensively to Muriel's stern grey gaze. 'You shall stay here, Louis. It is the least we can do.'

'Make sure you clean the tub.' Muriel puffed on her cigarette. '*Don't* use the bath oil. It always leaves a ring.'

His wallet, keys and Sûreté bracelets were placed on the desk, his pipe, tobacco pouch, et cetera. 'Shall I send the clothes out to be cleaned, Mademoiselle Grenier?' asked the girl who doubled, as did all the salesgirls, as lingerie mannequins.

'Discreetly,' said the detective, Muriel giving her a nod that would have splintered a bank robber's knuckles.

A slightly wheedling tone entered Chantal's voice as the pencilled eyebrows took on what might have been construed as a frown if frowns had not long ago been known to be damaging. 'I will make us some tea, Muriel. Let us send out for sandwiches and a little something to sweeten his tooth. Louis will want to talk to the both of us this time. He will need the knowledge you alone possess.'

Those clear brown eyes that missed nothing and were so sensitive, had already noticed among the trash of his pockets a half-filled crystal vial of perfume and a lipstick. Ah yes.

Muriel snorted. 'When he's ready, dearest, and not before then!'

The bath was heaven. St-Cyr lowered himself into the suds and when, at a discreet knock, one of the mannequins asked if he would like his tobacco pouch and pipe, he said dreamily, 'Yes . . . yes, you may bring them in.'

Muriel had lit the pipe for him. The girl wore nothing but Chantilly lace, an apology of sorts. She was not plump except in those parts where a little plumpness suited. 'There is a cognac, too, Monsieur the Chief Inspector, a double.'

She touched the tip of a forefinger to remove a spilled droplet. 'Please enjoy the bath for as long as you wish.'

Chantal and Muriel occupied the flat directly above the shop, as they had all these years. They owned the building, had lived through the times of war and those of the Depression, the inflation and the repeated devaluations of the franc. They had weathered a lot of storms together, those two, and they had done it exceptionally well.

He knew the shop would be full of high-ranking Germans and their French girlfriends and that neither Muriel nor Chantal would approve, but business was business and the Decree of 1940 had spelled out the rules. Business was, of course, booming, though many things were now becoming quite difficult to acquire. Silk especially unless, of course, one bought it on the black market or from German corporals who might fiddle on the side.

If, of course, Schraum had really been involved in such things to any great extent – Hermann would find that out. Hermann . . . where was he?

St-Cyr waved the pipe smoke away, reminding himself that Schraum must have been involved with coal and firewood and that these would have been how Victor Morande had first made contact with him.

Then why in the Name of Jesus did Lafont and Bonny have to question the housekeeper of that villa? Why had they had to kill her?

'They don't trust us any more than we trust them. They must have wanted to silence her, or perhaps things simply went too far.'

'Pardon, Monsieur the Chief Inspector?'

This one wore black right from her silk-stockinged legs to her garters, briefs and brassière. She had a generous smile and raven hair to match the undergarments that were not, of course, under anything!

'Muriel has thought you might like another cognac, Monsieur the Chief Inspector. Please forgive us for disturbing your thoughts.'

Another apology? 'Please thank her for me. She's being very kind.'

Perhaps an hour passed, perhaps a little more. Yet another mannequin, an auburn-haired girl this time, ducked her head discreetly round the door to inquire if a salmon pâté would suit?

She laid a pair of flecked beige tweed trousers over the back of a chair, then a new shirt, new woollen socks, a new tie and gold cufflinks.

She was wearing nothing. Another apology from Muriel! 'Ah, Mon Dieu, you are like a gift from heaven, mademoiselle.'

The girl let him feast his warm brown eyes on her body as Muriel had requested. 'You are to be forgiven, Monsieur the Chief Inspector. New shoes are on their way and should arrive after you have had your tea. The overcoat and hat will also be replaced as they are considered to be beyond repair and unworthy of a man of your calibre.'

A new man but one who was getting sleepier by the moment!

Muriel Barteaux laid the experience of her perfumer's eye on the vial that was nothing exceptional in the world of Laliquesque and showed a naked girl scenting her body in frosted glass among some leaves. 'It is not new, Jean-Louis,' she said, and he thought he detected a speck in her eye.

The cigarette smouldered in its ashtray – the tenth or was it the twentieth? He had opened his heart to them, had told them everything connected with the case, well, almost everything. A few details here and there had been left out to protect Chantal's great sensitivity. Only by winning their absolute confidence could he ask what he needed to know.

'I think it is one of Cartel's, or perhaps it is one of M Coty's earlier works. A perfume of . . . ' She unscrewed the silver cap and removed the tiny glass stopper.

'Lemon grass,' breathed the Sûreté with excitement. 'Rosemary and coumarin.'

'Yes, yes. Don't trouble me,' she scolded.

The nose was flattish, the cheeks still strong – indeed all of Muriel's features exuded strength. But in perfumes and their concocting she had perhaps her only sign of weakness, apart from her friend and lifelong companion. The voice was one of gravel and incongruous in a perfumer. 'There is musk and civet in this and it has the anger, Jean-Louis, of a woman who knows her own mind and body. What we used to call a "fast" woman.'

'Sex ... sex with many men,' whispered Chantal with great modesty.

'The civet is subtle, the musk has been used mainly to accent its sharpness. There is some Balsam of Peru, some sandalwood – she wanted those elements of mystery – the wildness of thyme as well. A woman of much abandon, Jean-Louis. One who teases, or did so, since she can no longer be so young and foolish.'

'The cloves of Bourbon and a touch of sweet fennel?' he said, watching her every expression with all too evident admiration.

So loyal! Ah, Mon Dieu, it was at once tragic and elevating to see Monsieur Louis and Muriel exchange views like this. A sensitive man, an unmarried man now, a widower. Childless too. Another tragedy but for the best. Ah yes.

'The lime is for the acid with which she would turn each of her love affairs into bile.'

'Are you certain?' he asked. One could have heard a pin drop.

Muriel took a last breath of the scent. 'It was called Revenge, Jean-Louis, and it was made by a German in the rue du Faubourg-Saint-Honoré. Gerald Kahn. He died in an automobile accident in Cannes in 1926.'

'He didn't. Tell me he didn't.'

Muriel reached for her cigarette. 'Your woman was with him.'

'Michèle-Louise Prévost?'

'We followed the shooting in 1905 with much interest. Everyone did. It was idle chatter to while away the parties. Even a cuckold of a Parisian shoe salesman was of interest in those days. Chantal will have the newspaper clippings in one of her scrapbooks.'

That one ducked her lovely eyes away and into the past. 'She had been having a running affair with this Kahn for several years, Jean-Louis. Now on, now off. He was much younger. They'd been staying at a villa near Saint-Raphaël. M Antoine Audit did not take a very nice photograph.'

'Revenge?'

'Michèle-Louise had a daughter by Monsieur Charles, his brother. Your Christabelle was the daughter of that girl, but they did not name her father, Jean-Louis. It's all so sad, Muriel. The past should never be scraped in such a way! Me, I shall shed tears. Tears! Muriel. A father whose name was not given.'

Chantal was stricken. Muriel made her blow her nose. 'Be strong, little one. Be brave. Jean-Louis does not mean to torment us.'

The brown eyes beseeched her companion of so many years. 'He will know we have bought silks from the Corporal Schraum, Muriel. Jean-Louis is no fool.'

'Now, now, he's been bribed enough, if one could ever bribe such a man. You need have no fears of the Gestapo.'

It made one feel guilty, and he took several cigarettes just to prove it and was glad Hermann hadn't heard things. He'd have to be stern with the two of them. 'How did the Corporal Schraum get the silks? Straight from M Antoine's mills in Lyon, or via some friend of a friend in the Bureau Otto's warehouses?'

'The warehouses, of course,' said Muriel sternly. 'M Antoine would not have dealt directly with such a one no matter if he was German or not. I paid the Corporal in perfume and in francs. Fifty-fifty.'

'Mirage?' he asked of the perfume, remembering the Étoile of this afternoon and the handkerchief of Nicole de Rainvelle, remembering the rue Lauriston and the scent the woman had been wearing.

The scent of Gabrielle Arcuri.

'Mirage of course.'

A second pot of tea was necessary, another plate of cakes and more cognac. At just which point he began to doze off was anyone's guess but when he slipped away from them, Muriel put his feet up on the *chaise*.

'He'll keep. I hope he doesn't snore. Snoring's bad for business.'

'I will give him just a touch to make the subconscious guide his dreams, my Muriel. A little of the Revenge yes, on the pillow by the nostrils that are so bold and Roman, and a suggestion of Mirage. If he does not fall in love with the present, then the past will claim him.'

'Or the truffles and the walnut liqueur. Do you think he has guessed that M Antoine bought our lingerie for that poor unfortunate girl?'

'For Christabelle? Ah yes, he has guessed it. My poor Louis, my poor hero of the *crime passionnel* and otherwise. My knight, Muriel, in his new suit of armour. And very handsome too, don't you think?'

'For a man, yes, and for a detective particularly, but we will share the expense and charge it to the shop.'

'And to the future, lest he come here looking for the gold coins we have not declared.'

195

'Those are napoleons and louis d'or, Chantal, not sestertii and aurei of the Roman emperors.'

'Gold is gold and to the Nazis it is all the same.'

'No, no, you are wrong, little one. Some of it is worth far more than others.'

'She was a pretty thing, this Michèle-Louise Prévost. Perhaps it is,' Chantal ducked her eyes away in hesitation, 'perhaps it is that you have once noticed this, my Muriel?'

They kissed, they brushed cheeks and held each other for a moment. Then they parted, Muriel to go in search of silk to replace that whose source had suddenly dried up; Chantal to attend to the shop.

Blue pot-lights intermittently led the way across the Seine to the Île Saint-Louis. Through the darkness and the fog the lights appeared ethereal.

Kohler folded his arms over the steering-wheel. 'He went this way, Oona. I know that bastard did.'

'A black Mercedes in a black night. You should have let me take my chances at the house.'

'Not on your life. You stick to me like glue and you'll be okay, right?'

She didn't answer. They'd spent part of the afternoon in the flea markets of Saint-Ouen dodging the footsteps of this Captain Offenheimer. He'd bought a green ceramic tortoise, a duck in the same, two crocheted tea cosies and a tarnished tin of marzipan that had looked suspicious.

The car crept along the quay. Herr Kohler began to search the houses, the grand mansions of the seventeenth century with their steep mansard roofs that could not possibly have been seen because of the darkness and the fog.

When the car stopped, she heard him say, 'This is it. There's his car.'

And some others.

The 'house' was next to the Hôtel de Lauzun on the quai d'Anjou and when he'd rubbed a sleeve across the bronze name-plate, she read the names of poets and writers, that of Baudelaire.

'Well, what d'you know about that, Oona? Baudelaire, a fellow I'd never heard of until this case.'

A small sign on a discreet door to one side of the main entrance said: *Enter without knocking*.

They stepped into a parlour of plush wine damask, Turkish carpets, brasses, dusky, tassled lamps and small crystal chandeliers with lozenges of ruby and amber glass.

Another sign said *Please wait. The house is fully occupied at the moment.*

Kohler rang the bell several times. At last a bustling matron in her early sixties, all weight, wind and business, came through in a rush. 'Monsieur, such impatience! Ah, Mon Dieu! you cannot bring that one in here! Out . . . out, I say. Get her out of here at once!'

The fleshy hands made brushing motions. He pulled his Gestapo shield. Her face-powder began to crumble, her eyes to moisten. 'But . . . but why?' she asked. A raid . . .

'Your name?' he demanded.

'Joyeux, Henriette, Madame. I am the sous-maîtresse, the submistress of this house, monsieur. The House of the Silver-Haired.

Kohler gave her a wolf's grin as he breathed, 'The Silver-Haired.' He'd quicken his voice now. He'd catch her on the run. 'You've a Kapitän Offenheimer here, madame. A regular. Eyeglasses, navy-blue uniform, a real sea captain of about forty-four, eh? He'll have come bearing little gifts for your girls. A turtle, a duck . . .'

The woman's eyes darted away. The plump bosom hesitated. 'What's he done?' she asked sharply, turning on him now. 'We have had no trouble with that one. An angel, monsieur. An angel, I assure you. This is a very respectable house, very clean.'

Her gaze swept furtively over Oona who was trying not to be too evident.

'Which room?' breathed Kohler. 'The glass of the invisible eye, madame. This one comes with me, so don't argue unless you want me to close you down.'

'But . . . but you cannot do that! We have the Germans, the generals, the . . .'

He summed her up with a look. 'The Wehrmacht doesn't recognize you even exist. Of the one hundred and twenty brothels in Paris, forty of which were reserved for the Reich, there's not a mention of this one.'

The stitches were very black and where the flesh had puckered, it was puffy and red. The one eye was terrible. 'We are known by the word of mouth, monsieur.'

'So, what else did the horse drop when it passed by?'

'Men from all over Europe come to us. We fulfil their needs.'

'I'll bet you do. Now come on, let's have a look.'

'Please, you . . . you must remain quiet at all times. He mustn't be disturbed.'

Offenheimer and three old dames were playing bridge. Kohler glued himself to the eyepiece. The room unfolded, starch and linen, lace doilies and damask, heavy . . . heavy . . . The Berlin of the 1910s perhaps, the parlour of the Captain's granny.

'What the hell's going on?' he hissed. 'They're all wearing clothes? Those old dames have dolled themselves up for formal company?'

She could not see him through the darkness, she could only feel the nearness of him. 'It is what he desires, monsieur,' she whispered. The closet, it was so small. The woman this Gestapo had brought had squeezed herself back into a corner. 'You must watch and be patient. Life will unfold. It takes a little time.'

The 'ladies', all well into their seventies, wore staid, matronly dresses, one a light iron-grey, with a cameo at the throat – her severe hair had a slightly blueish cast. Perhaps it was the lighting. The plumper one, her partner and shorter by far, wore black, a widow? he wondered, only to remember a maiden aunt of his own who'd always worn that colour. Lost opportunities. Love passed by.

Offenheimer's partner was a fine, stiff-backed woman, taller than the rest and wearing a soft blue chiffon in which there were parallel lines of white. She'd a choker of pearls at her high-collared throat, earrings of the same, and though age had taken its toll, there was yet a certain beauty.

The talk was formal but also animated. There were little asides, little lectures which the Abwehr's captain always accepted with shyness, he the grandson and the nephew, they the grand-mother and maiden aunts, well, at least one of them.

As for sex, there was none. They'd had their coffee – he'd given them the gifts he'd found in the fleas as a boy of ten would do. The tin of marzipan had been opened, the tea cosies lay neatly in a forgotten pile on a forgotten table near a forgotten sofa that should have been put to better use had the 'girls' been a lot younger.

Kohler studied the table on which the things lay. There was something under cover, a lamp perhaps. A beautifully crocheted white woollen shawl all but hid it and he could see his own aunt's swollen knuckles as she'd patiently made some similar thing and he, too, was taken back to his boyhood on the farm.

Oona Van der Lynn nudged him and reluctantly he let her have an eyeful. Lost in thought, he felt her backside pressed firmly against his middle, a good fit but strangely, though he was finding her increasingly attractive, he'd lost all desire, had been robbed of it.

They had wrinkles. They all had them. It was a fact of life and yet . . . his stomach turned at the thought.

'How often does he do this?' he asked of the *sous-maîtresse* against whose generous bosom his arm was solidly squeezed.

'Twice a week. Always twice, but never on the same nights. He telephones ahead but sometimes is forced to cancel at the last moment.'

'What about last Tuesday?'

'He was here. Yes . . . yes, a good session.'

'And Thursday?' he asked, holding his breath.

'Thursday is always busiest. Many of our clients have to go home to Berlin for the weekends. He knows this but insists. We – ' The Gestapo was deliberately squeezing her against the wall. 'Yes, he was here on Thursday night.'

'At what time?'

'At just after eleven. Monsieur the Captain has come in great agitation, you understand. Me, I have had to tell him the ladies were occupied but he has insisted on the calming. He has said he had to see them.'

'I'll bet he did. Was there any blood on him?'

'Blood?' He felt her bosom rise and hold itself in dismay. 'Blood? Ah, no, no, monsieur, there was no blood on him. Only a lost button which I have sewn back on to the jacket of his uniform.'

Kohler felt Oona stiffen. 'Herr Kohler . . . ' she began. He shifted her out of the way.

The game of cards had speeded up. Offenheimer had insisted he and his partner had won the hand. The two old aunts were objecting. One of them went so far as to slap the back of the little boy's hand.

Stunned into tears, the Captain got all choked up.

Then someone must have interrupted things, only no one had come into the room. The one in black pushed back her chair and said something sharply to the visitor. Offenheimer blanched. Anger made him quiver and clench a fist. So much for politeness.

The maiden aunt got up and went quickly over to the table to yank the cloth away. *Gott im Himmel*, it was a white porcelain nude, a lovely thing, a gorgeous bit of behind with high breasts and splendid young hips.

Shouting erupted. Offenheimer flew into another rage. His chair fell over. The cards were scattered. Tears rushed down the little boy's cheeks. The old girls were all aflutter now but had stepped back as the captain seized the statue with both hands, only to withdraw from it at once.

He grabbed a hammer! Giving a cry of anguish, the bastard smashed the porcelain to smithereens. Not one blow but several. A real tantrum in which, at the last, his glasses were knocked askew.

Then the aunts and the other one fell on him in a rush of kisses and commiserations and he had it with the grandmother on the sofa in an orgy of lust and ripped chiffon that should have given her a heart attack!

'Jesus, if I hadn't seen it, I'd never have believed it. What'd he do? Kill his older sister or something?'

'It is harmless, is it not, monsieur? Twice each week, always the same thing. First the coffee and the cakes, the tête-à-tête and the exchange of gifts, then the game of cards that is always interrupted by the statue.'

'Never the real thing?' he asked, a yelp.

'Only once. We first tried it with a young girl I had hired especially for the task, but he became . . . '

'So violent you had to restrain him?'

'Yes. Insanely jealous, but with the statue it is much better. When clothed, the thing took too long, for he had to get up the courage to undress it. Naked it is very fast, is it not? He smashes her. The rage is spent and the session exquisite in its completion.'

A grandmother fixation. Offenheimer's face was still buried in her bosom. The aunts had retired from the room. 'Those statues must cost him a lot.'

'Five thousand francs each. Me, I . . . I have arranged their purchase for him.'

'And the house fee?' Oona was trembling.

'Another two thousand since he requires the same three of our ladies – never any of the others, monsieur. He has chosen them himself.'

From the line-up. 'And if I were to put this one in there with him, naked?' he asked.

'I . . . would not wish to do such a thing, monsieur. Who knows what he might do.'

'Strangle her, eh?'

'Yes . . . yes, he might do that.'

'Violate her?'

'Yes, yes, he might do that also, but' . . . may God forgive her . . . 'only after he had slain her.'

'How many others have watched him at it?'

When there was no answer forthcoming, Kohler leaned against her.

'Two men, monsieur. One French, the other from the SS.'

The rue Lauriston and the avenue Foch.

'The French one brought the SS, and like yourself, there was a young woman with them.'

Nicole de Rainvelle. 'Okay, I've seen enough. When will he leave?'

'In another twenty minutes, after . . . after first trying to have it again with his . . . '

'His grandmother.'

She'd try for sympathy. It would be expected of her but useless, of course. 'Some men require the attentions of older ladies, monsieur. It is entirely a matter of taste.'

'Did Baudelaire really come here?'

The woman sucked in a breath.'Baudelaire . . . ? Ah no, monsieur. That plaque belongs to the hotel next door as . . . as does this building we are in.'

The fog was thick and they were both freezing. Oona clamped her knees together. She'd known it would end this way for her, that ever since they'd met Kapitän Offenheimer at the warehouse this morning Herr Kohler would use her as bait. It was nothing personal. It was simply necessity.

The Seine lapped against the quay, sucking at the stones as each small wave withdrew. The city was so quiet.

A car door slammed! Herr Kohler stiffened. 'Just stand beside the light, madame. Let the bastard see you. Tell him you've lost your way.'

'And if he won't stop?' she asked, bursting into tears.

'Step in front of the car and make him. Look, I've *got* to know. Thirty hostages are at stake, yourself as well, damn it! Oona, it's the only way. I'm sorry.' He gave her a shove and she knew again that Martin was dead and never coming back, that their children had died and that she was now completely on her own. And she wondered, What if Offenheimer tells me to get into the car?

Herr Kohler had parked the Citroën up a side-street. He'd never reach it in time to follow them. God . . . oh God but it was cold.

She pulled her collar close and, slipping her hands back into the pockets of her coat, began to walk away from him, only to turn to search the darkness and say his name at last. 'Hermann, must I?'

He gave no answer. He was already lost to her. Droplets of mizzle kept striking her face, each one bursting as it hit her skin.

The smell of the river was rank. The pot-light hissed, and when she reached it, the car came slowly along the quay towards her. Late . . . it was so late. She threw a terrified glance upriver. There were a few small blue lights, well spread out and far too distant to matter. From the other side came the tramp of hobnailed boots.

Offenheimer had not yet turned on the headlamps. He was afraid someone might see him leaving the House of the Silver-Haired. Kohler held his breath. Suddenly the headlamps were switched on. Oona threw up an arm to shield her eyes, a blonde-haired young woman obviously in distress.

The Mercedes crawled to a stop. The window was rolled down.

'Your name?' asked Offenheimer. He'd not yet recognized her but his voice . . . it was like something out of nowhere. Mist continued to fall through the beam of the lights. Oona forced herself to step closer to the car.

'Please, I . . . I have lost my way in the fog, monsieur. I know I should not be out after curfew but my aunt, she is very sick, and I had to sit with her until . . . until it was too late. Now I must get home. My husband . . . my children . . . '

Offenheimer switched off the headlamps but said nothing. The seconds ticked away and she knew he was struggling with himself, that something dark and evil must have happened in his distant past.

'Where do you live?' he asked at last. Had he really argued with that conscience of his or with the regulations? Had he recognized her?

'In Auteuil, on the boulevard de Beauséjour. My husband, he will be so worried, monsieur. I . . . '

'You should not be out after curfew. It is against the regulations

202

and punishable by a sentence of no less than three months if . . . if all other questions are resolved.'

She was lying and he knew it.

'Please, I will find my own way, monsieur. Forgive me for having stopped you.'

Afraid . . . she was so afraid of him. 'Let us walk for a little. Then I will take you home, Hilda.'

Hilda! Jesus Christ! The car door opened and was shut. The fog soon closed about them. Their steps came and went as the Seine sucked at the stones and gave back the laughter of a river that had seen it all.

Kohler tried not to listen to the river, tried not to think of what he'd done to that poor woman. Where . . . where the hell had they gone? 'OONA!' he called out in desperation. 'O . . . O . . . N . . . A!'

Their steps came again and he heard them faintly, just a whisper, just a throb.

Then the music came to him from across the river and the tramp of hobnailed boots returned.

The dream was very real, the dream was most intense but the perfume of Revenge kept intruding into that of the Mirage. St-Cyr saw the carousel in midnight blue as if the lights had all been dimmed and the animals, favouring this blue, charged wildly through the night losing all but a little of their own colours. Now the elephant with its trunk high, now the zebra, the camel and a stallion or two. Now a bird in a gilded cage, a rain of female clothing that turned into one of gold coins in sprays of blood . . . blood . . . the stallions all snorting wildly at the sight of her naked body as they raced away, the monkey chattering excitedly. Monkey . . . monkey, blood and gold and wild-eyed creatures crying, 'Hurry . . . You must hurry.'

Revenge! A woman . . . the scream of a motor car out of control . . . an accident? A mirage? Faster . . . faster! A young girl's eyes, her naked breasts sagging as she stared blankly up at him, her lips moving . . . moving . . . ' Revenge . . . Revenge . . . Mirage . . . Mirage, monsieur.' The carousel flying round and round, the light changing to a rainbow of colours under court jester's eyes that flashed in the mirrors over a naked, strangled, violated girl. 'Gabrielle! Gabrielle!' he cried out in despair and sat up suddenly. The face of Marianne St-Jacques dissolving into that of Gabrielle

Arcuri. Ah Mon Dieu, Mon Dieu! The scent of Revenge so strong in his nostrils, the intrusion of Mirage was fretful.

Christiane, leave the hotel immediately. Don't go up to the room. Why had Antoine Audit not tried to warn the girl better than that?

The Resistance had been after the industrialist. The Resistance . . . the Café Noir.

One of the mannequins, a brown-haired girl with nothing on but flimsy, coffee-coloured undergarments, was standing just inside the door looking very worried.

'What time is it?' he asked.

'Just after curfew.'

'Good. I'm going to have to do something about these night-mares. I am distressed to have frightened you.'

'Chantal says she is very pretty, this Mademoiselle Arcuri, and very close to your heart, but', the girl gave a shrug, 'she is untouchable at the moment.'

'I did not say she had the curse, did I?' he asked anxiously of the dream.

'The curse? Ah no, Monsieur the Chief Inspector. Chantal has said it is because of the rue Lauriston that you have come here. The French Gestapo! But that you *must* go to Mademoiselle Arcuri, since she is the Mirage of your dreams.'

'And the Revenge?' he asked. 'What does Chantal say of this?'

'That you will find the answer, Monsieur Jean-Louis, because you are her knight in shining armour, but that if there should be any leftover silk you will know where to leave it.'

Kohler breathed in carefully. The fog was thick, the night like ink, the quai d'Anjou and the House of the Silver-Haired now behind him. Once across the boulevard Henri-IV there was a small park, the square Barye, chestnut trees, lindens and a few shrubs.

A single pot-light on the pont de Sully appeared frosted through the mist, its light suffused too quickly. They'd not have crossed that bridge. He knew it, knew Offenheimer was forcing him to follow them into the park.

Oona Van der Lynn hadn't cried out in a long, long while, which could only mean the Captain had a knife or pistol. Regulation issue, nine millimetre. A Luger, Mauser or Walther P-38.

Schraum had been killed with one of those. The poor woman would be naked now, lying on the wet grass, her clothes every-where. Son of a bitch, why had he thought to use her as bait? Had he no feelings, no humanity? Had he sunk into the slime of this merry-go-round?

It took him back to Munich, to the banks of the Isar; Berlin, too, and the Spree, and not all of the victims had been women and young girls, ah no. Lovers lost were target enough; lovers taken quickly in the heat of the moment were often best dispensed with.

Not so tidily either, especially when it came to young boys. The penis and testicles of one had turned up later in a box.

He stepped into the tiny park, could hear the lapping of the Seine from both sides and from straight ahead, for the park occupied the upriver point of land.

Droplets fell from the branches, mist broke against his face and he was cold. He knew he mustn't think of Oona Van der Lynn any more, that she was just another woman in trouble. That Offenheimer would kill him and then kill the woman if he hadn't already done so.

Where . . . where were they?

The grass underfoot changed to gravel and he cursed himself, for the sound of the stones rumbled like thunder against the patient dripping and the fetid lapping of the swollen river.

The Van der Lynn woman had been wearing a trenchcoat with a belt. There'd been a scarf – the one to tie the hands and ankles, the other to gag the mouth. Then the clothes cut off by the knife and the breasts fondled as they became wetter and wetter, the blood mingling with the water from the branches and the slowly falling mizzle.

Would he shove the knife up inside her as some had done? Would he cut out her eyes or drive the thing up her seat as others had done after first having slashed the buttocks in a rage?

When you hate, you hate with a vengeance and God alone probably knew what had really set the bastard off in the first place. An older sister who'd found him playing with that limp thing between his legs and had never let him forget it, eh? A sister who had tied him up and taken down his pants to find out more about the male anatomy.

Where . . . where the hell were they? A bench, right out on the very point? Offenheimer behind her, the Van der Lynn woman on the grass in front of it?

So many ways, so many combinations. One shot. One dead Gestapo detective that was not wanted any more by his superiors. A naked 'prostitute' violated, ravaged – who'd care a damn if there was evidence so long as he himself was found with her, having 'shot' himself.

The bench was empty! Wet under the hand. The laughing of the water as it sucked at the quays was all around him.

Calm ... he had to keep calm. Offenheimer, in spite of his having called the woman 'Hilda', had realized this and had used her for bait of his own. He must have killed the Audit girl. He must have raped her afterwards because a guy like this wouldn't have had the guts to have done it while she breathed.

When his hand closed about her underwear, Kohler knew her clothes were scattered. He found a stocking, a garter belt ... drew his pistol only to remind himself that if he killed Offenheimer he was as good as dead himself. Even von Schaumburg, much as he wanted to stop corruption in the ranks, wouldn't come to the rescue.

Her ankles were tied. He touched a bare foot and felt the woman stiffen. Damn! She pulled away, struggled!

The bastard was sitting with his back to a tree and the woman firmly between his legs. Offenheimer would have a hand in her hair, the gun to her head, or the knife at her throat.

Quivering, Kohler backed away. The Captain cried out shrilly, 'That's enough! One more move and she dies.'

From out of the fog he snorted, 'She's nothing to me, you sap. She's just another cunt to ram it into. Haven't you realized that yet?'

Warm blood trickled down her throat to run between her breasts and she felt this through the waves of panic. The killer had twisted her hair, had twisted it and twisted it until she had had to arch her back and draw up her knees. Now this ... this ... A cunt!

The knife moved against her throat, the voice was shrill! 'We have to talk, Herr Kohler. I did not kill the Audit girl. Brandl assigned me to the Schraum business. Lafont and Bonny found out about the House of the Silver-Haired and forced me to co-operate. An exchange of information. They were to get everything, all the loot.'

There was no answer, no sound from Kohler. The woman shrieked, 'Gestapo pig, you Nazi bastard! Ah my hair ... Hermann, my hair!'

'I DIDN'T KILL HER, KOHLER! SHE WAS DEAD WHEN WE GOT TO THERE!'

Kohler steeled himself to give the Captain time. 'Who threw the coins?' he asked calmly from somewhere in the fog.

'Lafont! In a rage – he always gets into them. The coins had been sent back to the avenue Foch by special courier from Stralsund. Oberg and Knochen got after him and told him to bring the girl in for questioning.' The Captain dragged in a breath.

'But she was dead when you got there,' said Kohler from off to the left.

Offenheimer savagely yanked the woman's head back. 'Someone got to her first, I swear it!'

'Who?'

'We ... we *don't* know. Lafont blamed Paul Carbone, the Corsican from the rue de Villejust.'

Kohler's voice now came from the right perhaps. 'Who left that coin on the girl's forehead? Hey, I don't believe you. I think you killed her and then you raped her dead body. Was it fun, eh? Still warm.'

The hair was tightened. The woman stiffened in panic. 'I DIDN'T!' shrieked Offenheimer. 'I SWEAR I DIDN'T! Nicole ... Nicole de Rainvelle, she ... she dipped the coin in the girl's blood and ... and placed it on the forehead.'

'Why?' The bastard was crying.

'Because ... because Pierre Bonny told her to do it, damn you! They *knew* by then that Oberg and Knochen had insisted you and St-Cyr be given the case. Bonny wanted to leave your partner a warning. Lafont is insanely jealous of Paul Carbone and would not listen to reason. I ... I kept trying to tell him I didn't think Carbone was involved, that it ... it must be some other Corsican.'

'And how did word first get out about the coins?'

The Captain sucked in a ragged breath, the woman gave a stifled gasp as pain leapt through her. 'The girl must have shown one of them in the flea markets. People go there to – '

'Ja, Ja, I know. To flog their valuables on the quiet. You turds all have informants in the fleas. It's one of the ways you nail the big ones, eh?'

Where was Kohler now? 'We ... we think that at first the price wasn't good enough, that the Audit girl really believed the coins to be of great value.'

Oona gave a piercing cry! He must ignore it! 'When would this have been?'

Offenheimer lowered the knife to a breast. 'Last summer. Early in June. She ... she then showed three of the coins and ... and that's when Schraum first got acquainted. They must have argued, for the girl got angry with Schraum and was afraid he'd arrest her but . . . '

'But the good Corporal let her go on the condition she agreed to meet him again.'

'Yes . . . yes. He must have examined her papers. He . . . he must have been satisfied.'

Oona gave a sigh – one too deep, too deep! Kohler moved swiftly away. The bastard had to have a knife, otherwise he'd have taken a shot at him by now. 'Did the Audit girl show Schraum her false papers?' he sang out.

'False papers . . . ?'

'She had an alias, *dummkopf*!'

'I . . . I don't know if she used it. I . . . I think she must have. About a month or so later he made contact with her again and this time she must have told him there was a very large collection and that her friend wished to part with all of it, preferably to one buyer.'

Kohler waited. Offenheimer continued. 'Early in September he met with the girl again in the flea markets of Saint-Ouen and this time she agreed to part with one of the coins as a sample. No money changed hands. The coin, we think, was to be returned if the price could not be arranged.'

Kohler cut the belt from Oona Van der Lynn's ankles and this time she didn't flinch, a bad sign – was it bad? Ah no . . .

Offenheimer stiffened. Kohler . . . Kohler . . .

Again the Gestapo's voice came from a distance. 'How many coins were there supposed to have been in the collection?'

'Four hundred and eighty-seven. Enough to fill one of those Empire coin cabinets – we know this from the uncle in Stralsund. Schraum . . . Schraum must have told him of the cabinet.'

'The coin went to Stralsund, to the uncle, eh?' asked Kohler from off to the left again. 'News of a fabulous collection that had never been reported to the authorities.'

'That . . . that is correct. The uncle wired back that the coin was genuine and in excellent condition. Schraum was to enter carefully into negotiations.' The woman gave a sigh and then a gasp.

Again Kohler steeled himself to her. 'Did the uncle send the coin back as agreed or did greed get the better of him?'

Dealing with Kohler was like dealing with *death*! 'The . . . the coin went to Reichsmarschall Goering.' Where was Kohler now?

'Then what happened?'

'They . . . they met, they negotiated. Again and again the girl said her friend wanted to be careful about things, that it wasn't easy to get him to commit to a price but that he would be willing to part with a further sample.'

'The thirty coins?'

Offenheimer yanked the woman closer. 'Yes . . . yes, the thirty coins. By then we had all independently begun looking into Antoine Audit. We knew he had declared some of his valuables – a few paintings, some antiques. Most of his wealth was in his factories and in property. Bonny . . . Bonny thought Audit had hidden a great deal and wanted to search the caves in Périgord. Brandl felt there was much to be gained, but then the coins came back and Victor Morande was killed. We closed in on the girl only to find she'd been silenced, then . . . then Schraum himself was killed and . . . '

'And Antoine Audit?' asked Kohler from very near.

'AUDIT HAS POWERFUL FRIENDS!' shrilled Offenheimer. 'Laval, the Premier; Lindermann a cousin of Martin Bormann, Herr Kohler. *Bormann*! Von Lindermann is the naval attaché in Bordeaux. Périgord is . . . is in his department.'

The Abwehr then, but another branch of it. The visitor and his girlfriend who had left the pâté et cetera at the Villa Audit. 'Anyone else?' he asked suddenly.

Offenheimer pushed the woman's head forward. He'd shove her aside as Kohler came at them. 'Hogenburg, a nephew of the Minister of Armaments. They are all friends of Audit, Herr Kohler. They all think very highly of him and that is why the avenue Foch turned the matter over to the rue Lauriston.'

So much for 'delicate' matters. Antoine Audit must damned well know of it too.

Kohler teased the knife from the Captain's hand. 'Two last items, my fine. First, are Lafont and Bonny still holding Giselle le Roy?'

Oona Van der Lynn began to sob with relief; Offenheimer hardly breathed. 'Yes . . . yes, they still have her. She . . . she was too badly beaten to release.'

'Did the kid refuse to co-operate?'

The pistol was pressed harder. 'Yes, she . . . she wouldn't spy on you.'

'I'm not worth it. Now, did you smash this "Hilda" or not?'

Granny's boy broke down completely. Kohler yanked Oona to

her feet and wrapped his coat about her. She couldn't find her voice, went all to pieces.

'Yes . . . yes, I killed my sister, damn you!' shouted the Captain. 'She *deserved* to die!'

The urge to be his executioner was there, a foolish thought. 'Then live with it. Go and smash another statue.'

'YOU'LL PAY FOR THIS, KOHLER! THEY'LL NEVER LET YOU AND ST-CYR LIVE, NOT AFTER WHAT YOU DID IN VOUVRAY!'

'Oona . . . Oona, hey *listen*. I'm sorry. I didn't mean it to go that far. Honestly I didn't. Look, I'm going to take care of you. I really mean it.'

She could not walk, she could not talk. Kohler swept her up into his arms and carried her back to the car.

The Club Mirage was on the rue Delambre in Montparnasse. At 2.47 a.m. behind locked doors, the place was jumping. Kohler breathed in the syrup of tobacco smoke, beer, wine, sweat and brandy, and grinned with relief.

Louis was tossing dice up at the zinc. From the balcony there was an excellent view. Eight hundred of the Wehrmacht's finest laughed, jeered, whistled and clapped or beckoned as they swilled their collective booze and eighteen naked girls and mothers who should have known better stomped, kicked and jiggled their way through the number and the band let them have it!

Oona still shuddered at the memory of what had just happened to her. Hermann Kohler's coat was rough and far too big. Cringing in her nakedness under it, she looked down to see watermarks where her bare feet had trod.

'Relax, eh? Hey, try to forget it, Oona. Louis' girlfriend will have a little something for you to wear.'

'None of them have,' she said blankly.

Kohler chucked her under the chin and gave her a grin. 'She's not one of those. Just give me a moment, eh? I've got to scan the horizon.'

Louis swept up the dice and raised a fist. Once, twice – three times he shook them. There was that little flick of the wrist and crash! the bones hit the zinc to scatter and run. Then the process began again. He was completely oblivious to the racket and to the clamouring herd that tried to reach the watering-hole while thrusting out their fistfuls of bills.

Blind to the eighteen beauties. Crash again. Now the sweep, now the first – always the right one . . . a taunt, a threat, a toss.

Kohler dragged his eyes along the line of threat and when he found the table, he picked out Henri Lafont, Pierre Bonny and Nicole de Rainvelle.

Giselle was with them. She'd been badly beaten – had had a 'fall' as the madams say in the trade. Bruises marred the fresh young cheeks, yellowing up into half-closed eyes. Her nose had been broken, her lips were swollen.

'Herr Kohler, what is it? What's wrong?' Oona yanked at his jacket sleeve, only to hear him swear.

'Look, I'm sorry. I've just seen someone.'

The girl clutched a grey fox-fur coat under her chin just as she was clutching Herr Kohler's coat. The racket came to an end and the place erupted in a deafening roar as the dancers romped away and the house lights were dimmed.

Then she saw, as all of them were breathlessly seeing, a mirage walk on to the stage in a shimmering sky-blue sheath that was covered with tiny pearls. Tall, willowy, a gorgeous figure, a blonde with shoulder-length hair and what appeared at this distance to be absolutely stunning blue eyes.

There were diamonds on her fingers and wrists. Diamonds at her throat.

'My dear, dear friends, a little song for you.' The voice had warmth, depth, resonance and power. Not a man in the place stirred and even Hermann Kohler finally had to tear his gaze away from the little one in the fur coat, and Oona saw the tears running down his sagging cheeks.

A lion in its winter; a man in torment with himself.

She slid an arm through his but he had no time for her, only hatred for himself.

Crash! The dice hit the zinc in irritation. Crash again.

'This is a song of lost love, my friends. Of a home that is far away, and of things we all wish and hope for. It is of a girl who has lost her lover and yearns for him with all her tender years. Letters do no good – isn't that so?'

Eight hundred men, many of them sailors on leave, some from the submarines of the North Atlantic, held their collective breath. Gone were the floozies, the big-breasted laughing girls who had sweated and kicked their legs so high. In their places, this one's voice lifted. It struck to the heart, the soul. It was bell-like, crystal clear, sweet, so sweet and earthy too.

It sang in French, it sang in German and once, just for a few brief seconds, a little Russian slipped in and Hermann Kohler knew the woman had done this especially for his friend.

Kohler wet his throat and tried to think. The song went on, lifting everyone. Not a man's glass was touched, not an eye wavered. Bonny sulked, Henri Lafont beamed, Nicole de Rainvelle sipped champagne while Giselle lowered her swollen eyes.

One sailor wept openly. Another held him by the shoulders. Shell-shock? Lost comrades? Battle fatigue?

A boy in the olive-grey of the army stood out as if the *chanteuse* was singing only for him and he'd never been in love before that moment and would die for it.

'Come on. Let's find Louis. He and I have to talk.'

'Is that her?'

'Yes, that's her. She gets ten per cent of the gate and she packs them in like this every night of the week.'

'I meant the other one. The little one.'

They went downstairs quickly, too quickly, but the crowd was jammed and no one would let them through until the song had come to its close on a high, sad note. Hermann dragged her by the hand. He hit the first of the men as they cheered and applauded. He was shouting now. 'Gestapo! Gestapo! Get the fuck out of my way!'

They reached the bar and he swung her in front of him. 'Louis, what the Christ is up?'

St-Cyr tossed his head to indicate the table. The Corsicans – the Rivard brothers who owned the place – were keeping their distance.

'A scratch!' leapt the Frog. 'A *cat* in the dark, Hermann. A *Corsican* cat!' He threw the dice at Remi Rivard, the one with the face of a mountain, the one with the dark eyes that were so swift.

'Sealed lips, eh?' shouted Kohler angrily.

'*Eighteen* stitches, Hermann. My left hand. Always the left side.'

'Louis, this is Oona. Oona, meet Louis.'

St-Cyr brushed momentary eyes over the woman, nodding sagely. 'We'll discuss it later, madame, but for now, my partner and I have things to settle!'

It was a hiss, that last word. Hermann Kohler laid a revolver on the zinc. The one called St-Cyr swept it up and cocked it.

'*Don't!*'

Both of the Rivard brothers had spoken at once. 'So, okay, my fines. First the dice are to be returned from your floor, and then a few small words of answer to the question I have been asking you for far too long.'

Kohler downed a nearby beer and wiped his lips with the back of a hand. 'Louis, I think I know what you want. His name's Réjean Turcel or something very close to it. About sixty-three years of age and tough as hell, good with the knife and good on his feet. He was shacked up with Madame Van der Lynn in the house on the quai Jemmapes. He's the new owner of the carousel.'

'Réjean Turcel?' shrilled the Frog. 'Réjean Tourmel perhaps, EH?' he shouted fiercely at the Rivard brothers.

They didn't even flutter. All grace and fluid motion of their own, they continued serving up the drinks, taking the cash and running their swift dark Corsican eyes over the crowd.

'Réjean Tourmel, so what's he done, EH?' answered the one with the face of a mountain.

These Corsicans were all related. 'Slashed my hand, I think,' mused the Frog, now somewhat subdued and trying to figure things out.

Kohler plucked at the mountain's leather jerkin. 'Give him another pastis and a little more water. Make it two of them, then leave us alone or we'll torch the place. I'd like another beer.'

'Steal one then.'

He took out the Walther P-38. 'Louis, ten francs a bottle, eh? and fifty says the place will empty in less than five minutes.'

'Too many would be trampled to death, Hermann. It's all right. Me, I think I know what's up.'

Kohler added a touch of water to that filthy yellowish-green muck Louis drank. Insipid, cloying, the taste of liquorice that, after indulging only once, some two and a half years ago, had stayed with him ever since.

Oona watched as the liquor became milky. St-Cyr made room for her and when she hesitated, he noticed she was wearing nothing under the coat.

'Louis, we had a bit of trouble over on the Île Saint-Louis. A collector of stuffed canaries. She's okay now, I think.'

'Good!' The pastis vanished. The glass was slid the length of the bar. 'Another,' said the Sûreté.

The cheering and the applause had subsided again into that breathless hush of expectancy. Again the voice of magic came. 'My friends, I have a little something for you now that is very dear to my heart. It is a song of a boy in the trenches of that other war. He is standing watch, is he not? He knows the battle will come and that in the morning he and others will die. His thoughts are therefore of home, of a girl he once knew. If only he could have made her understand, if only he hadn't said what he did.'

Louis grimaced and shut his eyes as he gripped the edge of the zinc.

Oona Van der Lynn tried to understand these two men. Quite obviously there was a bond between them that went much deeper than that of mere friendship.

The pistol was put away. The song reached into their hearts. All around them fistfuls of new francs which had to be spent in the occupied country were lowered into waitfulness.

The zinc was wiped. The taller of the two Corsicans let his eyes sift over the crowd, looking always for trouble.

'Réjean Tourmel, Hermann. Now I know why that coin was left on Christabelle Audit's forehead. I put that one away for seven years. Robbery with violence and extortion. The attempted murder of a police officer and a detective from the Sûreté. This one!'

'Devil's Island?' asked the Gestapo.

St-Cyr shook his head. 'Not me, someone else. Ten years, from 1905 until 1915, Hermann. I put him in the Santé.'

Right here in Paris. 'Along with Victor Morande?'

'Perhaps. In any case, Lafont and Bonny both knew of Réjean's association with me. Pierre will have been the one to leave the coin. He'll have thought it funny.'

'Actually, he got Nicole to do it for him.'

Louis clucked his tongue and downed his pastis neat. '*Salut!* my old one. Let's go and have a little talk with them.'

To approach the table was not easy due to the crowd, but as they neared it, Hermann Kohler automatically went to the right and the one called Jean-Louis St-Cyr went to the left. There was no signal, no word or sign one to the other. They simply moved as extensions of one being.

Oona did her best to follow first Kohler, then St-Cyr, only to find they had left her to approach the table on her own.

They had their hands on their guns. Because they and she were standing, they blocked the view of some and there were objections. One soldier said, 'Here, you can sit on my lap'; another pulled at the coat and she had to wrench it away from him.

The spotlight was concentrated on the stage. The *chanteuse* sang her heart out.

When Oona reached the table, Hermann Kohler was still some distance to the right; St-Cyr well off to the left.

'You . . . you killed my husband,' she said, but knew her words could not possibly have been heard. He was incredibly handsome, this man she'd spoken to. Tall, virile, clean-cut and well groomed. A film star, a banker . . . polished, so polished but with small, dark, round eyes that were hard and glistening with hatred.

'Sit down,' he said, indicating a chair that had been taken at another table but whose owner now stood giving applause.

She hesitated. The German owner of the chair would not know it had been taken . . . Lafont gave a high, falsetto laugh that startled her and made her skin crawl. 'Take it!' he hissed, and the girl in the canary-yellow dress who sat beside him, the girl with the shaggy mop of curls and the lovely eyes, watched with a tenseness that was both carnal and demented.

The pasty-faced older man, the one with the receding hair and the heavy cheeks, had no interest in this . . . this Madame Van der Lynn. To him, she was already dead.

The battered girl wept and cowered in her overly large fur coat. Kohler took a chair; St-Cyr, one also.

'So, my friends,' began the one called Henri Lafont, 'a little progress report, eh, Louis? Then the latest ground rules.'

St-Cyr cocked his revolver and took aim at the banker. Kohler pressed his pistol into the fleshy stomach of the balding one.

'No rules, no game,' breathed the Sûreté's detective. 'Hands off, or you get nothing. I know where the gold is hidden.'

'Louis . . . ?' began Hermann.

The falsetto laughter was harsh against the songbird's voice. There were angry shouts – threats from the audience.

Lafont pushed St-Cyr's revolver aside, leaning heavily over the table as he did so. 'Listen, my fine, you hold no cards. That one', he indicated the stage, 'is mine. Cough up and we'll see if we can find the right syrup for you.'

The one called St-Cyr could barely contain his rage. Hidden beneath the table, the battered girl's hand reached out to hers and Oona took the trembling fingers into her own.

The guns were put away. The Corsican brothers fluttered closely. Two magnums of champagne had been brought. 'They're on the house, Monsieur Henri,' said the one with the

215

face of ground meat. 'If anything else is required, just ask,' said his brother.

Lafont smiled at the homage. 'I hate all of you,' he said of Corsicans, 'but some I hate more than others.'

'Then *listen*,' hissed the Sûreté. 'Paul Carbone is *not* involved.'

Rage leapt into those little eyes, a magnum swung and smashed on the floor!

Leaning over the detective, Lafont held a spine of glass at St-Cyr's face. 'THEN TALK, COW! TALK!' he shrieked.

The song kept on. The song did not stop. It was about a man who had lost his wife and only child, a little boy, but had found quite by chance someone else who had lost a husband but had a son. They could not meet; they could not even be seen together.

The ring of angry servicemen who had gathered to silence their table cautiously withdrew as Henri Lafont put down the spine of glass and settled back into his chair. 'So talk, then, talk,' he said.

The other one, the older one who had the look of an accountant on trial for fraud, had watched with hatred and . . . yes, she had to say it, hope that the glass would be shoved into St-Cyr's face.

The girl in the yellow dress had held her breath with excited anticipation. The battered one's thigh had come closer so that now Oona could feel it pressed firmly against her own for comfort.

When he next spoke, the Sûreté's detective was calm, and she had the idea he knew very well how to keep control in situations like this. 'What did the contents of Charles Audit's flat turn up?'

'Nothing but a lot of stuffed birds and animals,' answered the accountant, watching him darkly. 'We had to burn the crap after we'd ripped it apart.'

St-Cyr ignored his former colleague. He'd stick to Lafont and try to get him angry again. 'Where are Charles Audit and Réjean holed up?'

Again it was the accountant who answered. 'We don't know. They've gone to ground. When they surface, we'll get them.'

'How much did Schraum's uncle have to advance on the thirty coins?'

Louis was playing it tough, but then he had always done so. 'Five thousand marks. One hundred thousand new francs, but the girl would accept only old francs,' said Bonny.

'Which, of course, was illegal and subject to imprisonment, a fine and deportation to forced labour in the Reich,' replied the Sûreté. 'One hundred thousand new francs is 31250 old ones.

That just goes to show you what devaluation will do, Hermann. But it's still a tidy sum for two old residents of the Île du Diable.'

Lafont grinned. The woman in yellow glanced repeatedly from one to the other of them, touching the crowns of her perfect teeth with the tip of her tongue.

'Their retirement pensions,' offered Kohler.

'Or money with which to travel light,' said his partner.

Lafont could not tolerate being ignored. 'Réjean hates your guts, St-Cyr. Rot in hell. Bring us the coins and you can rot in heaven.'

'Where's Antoine Audit?'

'Staying out of harm's way.'

'Collecting truffles?'

'Perhaps. It is the season for them.'

St-Cyr leaned forward. 'Then listen carefully, my fine. We have four killings. One which is separated from the others by two and a half years, eh? It is in this first killing that the answers lie.'

'What killing? There was no other killing. You are crazy.'

Lafont glanced uncertainly at Bonny, who refused to take his gaze from St-Cyr.

'What's it all about, eh, Monsieur Henri?' asked the Sûreté. 'Coins for Goering or else the rue Lauriston suffers a reversal from which it can never recover? What did Victor Morande have to say before you cut his throat?'

The little eyes were livid, the sound of the laugh so out of place in a man like this that the battered girl cringed and wept.

'Not even a charge of murder will stick on us today, Jean-Louis, so don't get your ass in a knot. We didn't kill him.'

This had come from the accountant.

'Carbone did,' seethed Lafont, working himself quickly into another rage. *'That bastard Réjean is with him in this. I'll tear his heart out. I'll –'*

St-Cyr let him have it. 'They've got you just where they want you, eh? Réjean has never worked with anyone before. Charles Audit is his friend, idiot! The code of the Island is at work and nothing you or I can do will break it.'

'Morande ratted on Réjean while he was in the Santé,' snorted Pierre Bonny. 'If you want the mackerel's killer, Louis, find Réjean Tourmel and you've got him.'

'The new owner of the carousel hires the ex-convict who fingered him in stir to run his pleasure machine?' snorted Kohler right back at him. 'Come on, my fine. You can do better than that.'

Hermann would never understand the logic of the French let alone that of the Corsicans, but for now it would be best not to enlighten him. 'Those who search for gold, Hermann, search not for the truth unless they find it in the dross.'

'Fuck your philosophizing, Louis,' seethed the accountant. 'We've come to renew our insurance policies and to take out others.'

The song had come to its end. 'I never liked you, Pierre. As a chief inspector and divisional head you were always too high-handed. I don't need you to tell me how to solve this little puzzle any more than I need your threats.'

'Then look!' hissed Lafont.

The girl, Giselle le Roy, burst into tears and shouted that she would not do it. Lafont told her that she would. Nicole de Rainvelle wet her hesitant lips, watching the girl and watching the others until Giselle finally stood up.

'The table,' ordered Lafont, a whisper through the hush as the audience awaited another song from the stage.

Reluctantly the girl stepped on to her chair and then up on to the table. The fur coat was unbuttoned. 'Hermann . . . Hermann,' she began.

Kohler reached out to her but Nicole de Rainvelle tugged at the coat and it slipped away to a rush of sucked-in breath, a chorus of gasps.

The spotlight left the stage to settle on them. The hush became a murmur, one of puzzlement and growing discontent, one of horror now but of lust, too, in broken laughter and whistles that were silenced swiftly by others.

A switch was to be made and Kohler knew it only too well. Oona Van der Lynn for Giselle de Roy. 'Kid, I can't do it,' he said, reaching up to help her down. 'You know nothing; she knows far too much.'

'Then they will kill me, Hermann, unless you do exactly as they say, and they will kill that one up on the stage.'

'Who did that to her, Jean-Louis? *Who* beat her with a belt so hard the welts will never be erased?'

The dressing-room, off the narrow corridor behind the stage, was very small, but they were alone.

'Why can't you answer me?'

The eyes were of that deep fullness of colour violets get when in the shade of new leaves. The hands were slender and pressed together on her lap so that the diamonds, the seed pearls and the chatoyant, shimmering blue of the sheath were as one and in prayer.

'Gabi, listen to me. Lafont and Bonny are untouchable. The rue Lauriston holds – '

'Such power they can tear a young girl's buttocks and back to pieces and bruise her breasts like that, eh? Me, I have thought you *better* than to be afraid of such as they! We agreed, did we not, to do something together for France?'

The moisture of shame was in his eyes. He had to let her see it. 'Please don't say anything like that. Don't even think it. You're Russian, Gabrielle, an illegal émigré for all they care. You can go to dinner at Maxim's, the Ritz or the Tour d'Argent with any or all the German generals you like, but none of them will stand in their way if Lafont and Bonny really want to kill you, because they *are* the Gestapo, they *are* the tools of the SS. Just give me time. Let me settle this in my own way.'

She tossed her hands, was through with him. 'I can't go with you and Kohler to Périgord. It's impossible. Me, I refuse absolutely this "protection" you offer. I've too much else to do. Besides, there is the club to think of.'

'And all the money you're raking in, eh? Ah! forgive me. I shouldn't have said that.'

'We hardly know each other. Perhaps it is best we don't.'

'Yes . . . yes, that would be best but they would never believe it.'

'So what do we do?'

'We find the gold and we find out who did the killings.'

'And then?'

'We let them have the gold because that is all they really care about.'

'And what if someone tries to stop you?'

'We kill him, Gabi, or he kills us.'

'And this gold?' she asked hotly. 'These louis d'or or whatever. Where are they hidden?'

'That I wish I knew.'

'To hide best is to expose the things you value most to view. Ah, don't tell me you didn't notice the furniture in that place of mine? A small fortune under heavy paint. Things bought for a song and kept because they are hidden so well and . . . ' the eyes were lowered, for he had the gaze of a saint at times like this, ' . . . and because I am content in knowing I have saved a few of them, the paintings also.'

'Don't give me the heroine's tale, Gabrielle. Me, I know only too well of your shrewdness and much admire that quality in a woman. What you do both here and with those things you keep in that flat of yours is no concern of mine, eh? But please, please, madame, don't tell me you do it for the good of France.'

'Ah! don't be so wounded, idiot! I'm trying to tell you something. *Look* where others have looked but failed to see.'

He drew in a breath. 'Anger makes you even more beautiful.'

'Compliments won't hide the truth, Jean-Louis. Take care of yourself.'

St-Cyr got up. She turned away to the mirror. Thoughts of what had happened to Giselle le Roy intruded. He knew she was weakening, knew any signs of weakness would be rapidly overcome.

'What will you do about the hostages?' she asked. 'The twenty-nine who are still left?'

'Who told you one of them had died?'

'No one. It's of no consequence. I only ask because one has to ask such things, isn't that right?'

Someone connected with the Resistance must have told her. Ah, Nom de Dieu . . . He let a hand fall to her shoulder. 'Von Schaumburg will release them if we find Schraum's killer, but me, I greatly fear that that one will turn out to be as French as all the rest so they will be lost in any case.'

'Please close the door and tell them I will be a few more minutes.'

'Gabi . . . '

'*Don't*! Please don't. Just go.'

Ah *merde, merde*! Why would she not listen?

8

Mist crept up the forested slopes to be caught by the wind on the heights above the rocky gorge. There was snow in the air and water dripping from the branches.

'It's beautiful, is it not?' croaked the Frog with all the hushed reverence of a monk.

'Piss off. I'm catching my death. Goose shit and worry in the eyes of that little one who was force-feeding the feathers between her thighs. No one in his right mind would be anywhere but by the fire.'

Kohler eased the stiffness in his back. Eighteen hours in the saddle and for what? A glimpse of Périgord at dawn, the finest scenery in France?

'You should have stayed at the château, my friend, or at the walnut mill. But ah no, you had to force yourself upon my patience! Kindly shut up and leave this to the French who understand such things.'

'Don't get your ass in a knot, Louis. Gabi will be okay.'

'And Giselle, eh? What of her? Antoine Audit is out here somewhere, Hermann. Find a man in his element and you understand him best.'

'Find a girl like that stroking geese like that and ask her to join you in the hay, my old one. You need it, Louis. You're becoming bitchier than usual.'

'That girl is *nothing*, Hermann! Just a diversion the latest Madame Audit tolerates but barely. If one knows where to look, one finds.'

The road south from Limoges had been a bastard. Once through St-Yrieix-la-Perche they had hit the kaolin pits, then wound through the hills and valleys to a doubtful crossing at Muquet. After that Louis had tried to alleviate things by going on and on about the cave art of Upper Palaeolithic man as if the heart of Périgord were at once the heart of humanity and the River

Vézère the Nile of that dawning age some 40,000 to 10,000 years ago!

There were caves in the yellowish limestone scarps at Les Eyzies, La Mouthe, Font-de-Gaume, Les Combarelles and Lascaux, the latest and most spectacular find of all. The last ice age had still been very much a fact of life when those caves had been occupied. Swollen rivers here and rains.

'Food-gatherers, Hermann. Is it not odd that Périgord should be the cradle of modern man and of the black truffle?'

'I just hope we haven't made a mistake leaving Oona at the château.'

'She'll sleep as long as Madame Audit allows her to.'

'So what gives then, eh?'

'What gives is that the goose girl said our Monsieur Antoine would take the pigs with him today.'

Kohler found the crushed remains of a last cigarette but there were no dry leaves to offer help as paper. 'The pigs,' he said.

'Female pigs are used on level ground, mongrel bitches on the slopes.' A self-evident, if grumpy fact.

'From here I see lots of slopes, my old one, but level ground that's far too distant for my lack of boots and wings.'

The opposite side of the gorge! 'If I remember correctly, Hermann, I warned you to equip yourself accordingly.'

Still bitchy, still worried, eh, and in need of a damned good lay. 'Since when did that God of yours grant you wings?'

St-Cyr heaved a sigh. 'The *Tuber melanosporum* favours the moist areas near the roots of the oak, Hermann. We look for oaks and we look for ground a female pig would not have too much difficulty traversing.'

'The pig gets the scent, the gatherer digs for the fungus, so we look for the holes, right?'

Sometimes the Gestapo tried so hard to be helpful. 'The holes are carefully covered over, Hermann. The whole thing is done in great secrecy since the black gold of the Périgord is exceedingly valuable.'

'And mid-December's the best time, right?'

'You're improving but please, don't try my patience. Me, I have had enough of your terrible driving. I will take my chances here because I must.'

'A walk to where, then?' asked Kohler, dumfoundedly looking around at the woods.

'Where the scent would lead a man whose fortune began with

the fungus, Hermann. A man who must return to its hunt each year as the pilgrim seeks the spiritual nourishment of Jerusalem or the Shrine at Mecca.'

'You're too deep for me, pal.'

'Then leave me to the truffle-hunter and go back to that girl with the geese. Sweet-talk her a little, find out what you can. Already the empire of Antoine Audit is far more extensive than I had imagined.'

'That château up on the rocks?'

'Purchased for a song from a departing Jew unless I'm mistaken.'

'Take care of yourself, Louis. Don't get lost.'

'Don't get shot at either, eh? Can't you feel it, Hermann? Can't you sense the tensions of these hills and rocky valleys? Generations of feuds and petty jealousies going well back before the Romans, each landowner fiercely guarding his holdings against all poachers, yet coveting the land of his neighbours? The pigs will be doing their work while the hunter watches with more than half an eye for other game and listens lest his secret be discovered.'

'He'll hear the car as it leaves.'

'You impress me, Inspector. For you there's still hope.'

'Since when would the Reich allow them guns?'

'If you've friends in the right places, Hermann, all things are possible. In any case, who's to know out here?'

He had a point. 'Shall I come back for you at noon?'

St-Cyr shook his head. 'That's too early. Once the sun is fully up, the frost will leave the ground and the hunt will go on in earnest until darkness. He'll have transport back to the mill. I'll hitch a ride.'

'We'll have to find us a place to stay.'

'I'm sure Madame Audit will be more than willing to oblige a member of the Führer's Gestapo, Hermann.'

A hint, eh? Kohler gave him a handful of slugs for the Lebel. 'Fire three in sequence if you get lost. The sound will carry down the gorge.'

'Enjoy the girl's fist. Don't slip in the shit.'

He ignored the jibe. 'You watch your back, eh? Remember brother Charles and friend Réjean could just as easily have taken a little holiday.'

'By train?'

'Or truck, especially as M Antoine has them running to and

from Paris on a more or less regular basis. Wine and pâté, remember? Silk and Cream of the Walnut.'

'The more there are to hunt, the richer the harvest.'

'The better the omelette, eh?'

'They won't leave Paris, Hermann, because they can't.'

'If I were you, I'd not be so sure of myself.'

The Citroën dwindled from sight, but just before it turned down into the gorge, Hermann stopped and got out to look back at him. Mist trailed across the road. The forest, naked of its leaves, seemed to frown as they walked towards each other, two lonely men with their cross.

'It's merely a matter of deduction, Hermann. Antoine Audit holds answers his brother Charles and Réjean Tourmel want desperately to keep hidden as does he himself. Why else the girl in that room at the Hotel of the Silent Life, why else this butterfly or these gold and emerald earrings she could not possibly have worn?'

'Why else the coins that were forged, eh, Louis? Why else the carousel? Do as you're told, my fine Frog friend. Watch your back because I won't be around to watch it for you.'

'Then you do the same for yourself.'

The man they had come so far to see was not easy to find. Though barren of its leaves, the forest all too often hid things. Always the smell of damp, rotting leaves was present, warmer now perhaps because the day had grown and the mist had begun to clear.

Since leaving the road, St-Cyr had climbed to the heights, for the Périgord was an old and much dissected plateau where the elements of karst topography had been played in collapsed sinkholes, scarps, abandoned river gorges and flat-lying uplands. Not always were there oaks. Spasms of misguided plantation fever had seeded pines for lumber but they'd not had a decent time of it. Too much lime in the soil probably. The chestnut trees had fared better, the poplars, of course, much better still, and some of these had retained a few recalcitrant leaves on branches that had been broken during an early ice storm or by the winds.

Those leaves tended to stir, and long before he would come upon the poplars, he would know where they were. But, ah Mon Dieu, where was Audit? To come so far, to leave loved ones behind in grave danger, twenty-nine hostages also, was unforgivable.

Just when he realized he was being stalked was not quite clear. There'd been a shallow dip in the crown of a hill, a grove of magnificent walnut trees, quite unexpected, for he'd been amongst them before he'd noticed a few stray nuts and had stopped to gather them.

The undergrowth had been sparse. Had he heard something? The distant barking of dogs, the flight of a partridge? A step perhaps?

Never the grunting of a sow upon which he had, at first, depended as much as on the flatness of the land.

Going from tree to tree, he'd suddenly stopped. Yes . . . yes, there'd been a half-step.

This one was of the forest.

Now a flat-floored, empty gorge opened into a former plunge pool where once there had been a waterfall. Oaks grew in profusion among the blocky boulders. The scree was thick and of that yellowish, buff tint, invariably stained by oxides of iron like the walls of the gorge that rose perhaps to a height of 20 metres and just above the crowns of the trees.

He knew he had walked right into it – he'd been making circles, trying to come up behind his starting point, only to find the circles had become spirals that had taken him farther and farther from their start.

When he turned, a single-barrelled 10-gauge shotgun was levelled at him. An old gun, much used and therefore reliable.

'Antoine Audit, I presume,' he said. 'Jean-Louis St-Cyr of the Sûreté Nationale.'

Audit would have fitted well into any of the local farm markets. This was not the successful businessman who would dally with a young mistress, this was the truffle-hunter.

The high leather boots were tightly laced about rough brown corduroy trousers that bagged at the knees and sagged at the crotch. The jacket, of the same, had leather patches at the elbows. The sweater, of a coarse brown homespun, made the chubby girth of the businessman, the barrel chest of the goatherd.

Only in the carefully brushed moustache was there vanity.

'Monsieur, the gun is not necessary. I'm here merely to ask you a few questions in the matter of Christabelle Audit's death.'

The dark-brown eyes in that large round face were watchful, the flecked tweed cap hid all but a slice of the brow. The thick, bushy eyebrows were greying.

Though the barrel of the gun never wavered, some of the

suspicion seemed to ebb from Audit. 'I tried to warn her. I knew there was trouble, but why her? Was she to be an example too?'

A boy of twelve now came into view. Two black-and-white sows, healthy bacon and ham but worth far more, roamed about on tethers of rope. Wicker baskets were crooked in each of the boy's arms. Mattocks were gripped.

The boy was every bit as watchful as his father.

'It's all right, Armand. Leave me my basket and mattock. Take Benedictine and Mathile up to the wash, eh? Work the hollows. I'll join you in a few moments.'

'Please permit me the experience, eh?' interjected St-Cyr. 'The secret is safe. Let us simply pass a little time more profitably. A detective's life is seldom offered such reward.'

Audit took in the well-worn hiking boots with their sturdy tread soles. The boots were in complete contrast with the rest.

The Sûreté brushed the thought aside. 'The suit, overcoat and hat are, I'm afraid, quite new and not my usual.'

'But the boots are?' How much did this one know?

'Boots are second only to the wearer of them, monsieur.'

'Armand, this one tells me he's of the salt of the earth. So, we will allow you to join us, monsieur, and we will see if you really are what you say.'

The boy and the pigs led the way out of the plunge pool and up to the plateau above it. There was a 'wash', the bed of an ancient tributary now long since gone and forested over. The oaks were old, the humus deep.

Antoine Audit's eyes remained swift and narrow as he searched among the trees for evidence of poaching. The pigs went to work, rooting in the rich dark earth that lay beneath the autumn thickness of leaves. The ropes that tethered them were liberal and the boy quite capable – indeed so much so St-Cyr had the idea, and the admiration for it too, that Antoine Audit had started the boy off at a very early age and would impart all he knew to him.

'Armand is a natural, Inspector. To be successful with the truffle, one has to know intuitively where to look. The female pig has an insatiable appetite for the *vraie truffe*. Every once in a while we give them a taste.'

When a truffle was located, the pig would be pulled away and tethered to a tree or led elsewhere while the father or the son used the mattock. First the topsoil was cut away – two or three quick chops – but then great care was taken to remove the earth down to the roots. Like black walnuts without their husks but still in their shells, the truffles clung to the roots upon which the fungus had fed. Most were of the size of a single walnut, occasionally two or even three.

Audit and son would carefully break off only the largest. Always some were left to produce spores for next year's crop. Each hole was carefully covered and disguised with leaves, even to removing traces of their footprints.

'To understand the truffle, monsieur, one has to comprehend that the land has changed. Here there was a streambed. Underneath the soil, the capability of carrying moisture is still retained. The best truffles are always found in the moistest soil and often on the shady side of the tree, so one has to think of the angle of the sun as well.'

They'd been going deeper and deeper into the forest. No hope of finding his directions, eh? Already their baskets were half full. When brushed of its humus and soil, the surface of the truffle had a coal-black, finely ribbed appearance.

Audit scraped a bit of one away to show him the net of white veins that marbled the black flesh. 'If these are grey, the thing has lost its essence, its odour and taste, monsieur, and is of no use.'

St-Cyr brought the truffle up to his nose, breathing in the heady aroma of imagined omelettes and pâtés. 'They must feel solid, isn't that so?' he said watchfully. 'The rounder the better; the blacker the better.'

'But always with the white marbling. Monsieur, what is it you really want of me?'

St-Cyr glanced uncertainly towards the boy, who was digging nearby. 'Merely a few questions.'

'How did she die?'

Audit set the truffle carefully back in the basket and, thinking the leaves not hiding the recent excavation well enough, tidied a few of them. 'I don't need to do this sort of thing any more, monsieur. I buy most of the two hundred tonnes we process or sell but,' he gave a shrug, 'one has to come back for a few days at least. One can't forget. One mustn't.'

'She was garrotted with wire and savagely raped.'

The narrowed eyes didn't flicker. There was such control. Ah, Mon Dieu, it was magnificent. The shotgun still ready at a moment's notice.

'I see,' was all Audit said.

Some moments passed. The boy put a little distance between himself and his father, but was it deliberate or merely that he'd best get on with the hunt?

The two sows were grunting softly among the underbrush.

Audit stood up. 'I knew I had been targeted by those idiots in the so-called Resistance. Thugs, students, *imbéciles*, dodgers of the call-ups of 1939 and '40, cowards.'

'Hotheads,' said St-Cyr, taking out his pipe and tobacco pouch, his hands still steady.

'*Fools* who think men like myself are traitors. If I did not co-operate with our German friends, monsieur, you and I would not be here.'

That was fair enough and admirably cautious for one who'd benefited so well from dealing with them. 'Just tell me what happened on Thursday night.'

The Sûreté's detective would take a half-hour to pack that pipe. No chance to reach for that revolver, eh? Ah *merde*, what was he to do? 'I came a little early – it's become a habit these days, eh? One checks the ground first. The street made me edgy. In business, as in anything, Inspector, one develops a sixth sense. There was a girl I'd spotted several times before. She watched for me. Sometimes by that bakery, sometimes from inside it. Often she would be just down the street, pretending to fix her bicycle.

'I left a note for Christabelle, warning her to leave the hotel immediately and not go up to the room, because that is where they would have tried to get at me.'

A few oak leaves were taken up to be felt by Audit's strong fingers. Had he needed the reassurance they would bring? 'Why would they have come for you in that room, monsieur? Why not simply in the street?'

Only frankness would suit. 'Because they would have thought me in bed with Christabelle. She can't have received my note. Why didn't she?'

St-Cyr struck the match but allowed a moment's pause. 'That we do not know yet, monsieur, but we think the note may have been taken by someone and then put back later.'

Audit gave an understanding nod but added, as if puzzled, 'Who would have done such a thing?'

Drawing the flame into the bowl, St-Cyr let the smoke billow around him. The boy was now out of sight. Ah no! 'The killer perhaps, or someone else.' He extinguished the match with spittle out of habit. 'Tell me, monsieur, why she used an alias.'

228

The leaves were tossed aside. There was no sense in denying he'd known about the name. 'Because it was best that way. Though our meetings were harmless, Inspector, Christabelle wanted her identity protected. There was also the very real problem of her having two places of residence when only one is allowed.'

That seemed to suit the Sûreté. Audit drew out the silver flask he always took with him in the woods. 'It's plum brandy, Inspector, one of our own.'

'My thanks.' The brandy was fiery and excellent, the very essence of the fruit, and in better times it would have been much appreciated. 'You knew she was living with your brother Charles, monsieur. Did you not question why she was meeting you?'

There could be no smiles, no grins. 'Why should I have, eh? I understood her, monsieur. Men like myself do. Besides, my first wife and I had raised her from birth until the age of six. When one does such a thing, one comes to know a person best since all else is dependent on those first tender years.'

'Perhaps, but then . . . ' He'd leave it at that and see what happened.

'My first wife was killed in an auto accident in 1926, Inspector. When my brother learned of this, he returned to France to look after his granddaughter. I hoped for a reconciliation and allowed him to take Christabelle away, since she was no relation of mine. Well, not really.'

Thus does the close relative excuse himself, thought St-Cyr. 'You advanced him money with which to purchase the carousel?'

'He was strapped for funds and had wired me from Rio de Janeiro. A small loan, which was repaid with interest. The thing was harmless and it offered my brother a modest living.'

'Did you see each other at all?'

Audit held the flask out to him again. 'Did the reconciliation work, is that what you mean?' It was. 'Then no, Inspector. The wound was too deep, so', he gave the shrug of one who had tried, 'I left them to themselves.'

It would be best to suck dreamily on his pipe. The boy and the pigs had still not returned. The shotgun now rested against a nearby boulder but well within easy reach, ah yes. 'Tell me about Christabelle, monsieur.'

'There's little to tell. I paid for her studies, if that's what you're asking. In return, we agreed to meet, and I took her a few little things from time to time.'

'Was she the one to come to you for money for her studies or did you . . . ?'

'Yes . . . yes, she approached me. Charles would have no part of it – we both knew this. Christabelle agreed to meet once in a while, just to talk, to have a coffee or an *apéritif*. Later, she suggested the hotel and I, well what would you have done, what would any man have done, eh? I agreed.'

'Why did she dye her hair like that?'

They'd have seen the body in the morgue. 'Her hair, ah yes.'

Audit found papers and tobacco and proceeded deftly to roll himself a cigarette. A man of millions who chose not to show it here but to live as he'd first lived before the fortune had come.

'She said she had done that because as an artist's model she wanted to protect her "real" self.

'You accepted that answer?' breathed the Sûreté with surprise. 'Come, come, monsieur, the girl bore a striking resemblance to her grandmother, Michèle-Louise Prévost; so much so you could not face up to the lie of what she'd done to you.'

Audit kept his eyes from the shotgun. 'And what was that?' he asked cautiously.

'She forced you to see the resemblance – forced you to agree to meet with her once or twice a week because, monsieur, you could not have said no.'

It would be best to tough it out, best not to deny everything. 'So we met. What harm was there in that?'

'You bought her things, monsieur,' reminded St-Cyr gravely.

Was this idiot a saint? 'Some lingerie. Ah, Mon Dieu, Monsieur the Inspector, you're a man of the world, eh? You know how it is. Young girls, pretty girls . . . All right, I bought them for her, but at her suggestion.'

'Did you fall in love with her?'

'Love? A man like myself? In the Name of Jesus, have I taken you for a realist, Inspector, only to have uncovered a romantic? I *understood* Christabelle, just as that one understood me. About six months ago she asked if I would like to see what the artists saw. Oh she knew I'd been to the studios. She knew I'd already seen her like that. Of course I said I would like to see her undress – you'd have done the same, eh? But I also told her only if she wanted to. There was to be no pressure – none whatsoever. It was a game we played. Nothing happened. A harmless hour or two, never more. A room to which we both went. Myself for the look; she for the tease. Of course I asked for the use of her body. I suggested we might ... I offered to pay her, but she ... '

'Did you know her father?'

Irritably Audit flicked cigarette ash to one side. 'Kahn ... a German who lived in Paris, a perfumer. He and Michèle-Louise ... All right, you have me, Inspector. Eventually Michèle and that bastard ran away together and were killed in a road accident, leaving Christabelle in my care.'

'The girl's mother was very young. Fifteen, I believe.'

'Kahn couldn't have cared less, Inspector. Michèle-Louise was a wild woman. Crazy! Fantastic, but ... ' His eyes strayed to the shotgun.

'But not to be trusted even when her own child was concerned?'

Audit's gaze was unwavering. 'Totally unreliable. I wouldn't have put it past her to have given that fifteen-year-old to Kahn as a present, and then to have climbed in with them. She could never accept the staid life my brother had imposed on her, Inspector. Ah, what can one say about such things? Charles ... Charles tried to give Michèle-Louise the freedom she required. She furnished their villa to her own taste, painted, sculpted – '

'Made forgeries of the coins you once had?'

'Pardon?'

'The coins, Monsieur Audit. What really happened to them?'

The cheeks were blown out in exasperation, the hands were tossed. 'They were stolen from my house here. Of course I reported the theft. The local Préfecture were as thorough as they could possibly be. Lyon was called in and Bordeaux, but, ah! they turned up nothing. No leads. Just nothing. Why do you ask? What have the coins to do with ... with ... '

'Christabelle's death? Thirty of them were scattered about her body.'

'But you have asked about forgeries? My coins were very real.'

'And stolen when, precisely?'

Audit picked up the shotgun. 'A month before the Defeat. I was in Paris at the time. Things were chaotic. When I returned to the house, my present wife informed me of the theft.'

St-Cyr hefted a few of the coins as one would a handful of loose change, before extending his fist to Audit and opening it.

'Rubbish. It takes but one glance, Inspector. They're too round, too perfect. Half of those were struck from iron dies when bronze ones were still in use.'

'But are the copies exact?'

Audit shifted the shotgun awkwardly into the crook of his other arm then fanned the coins out in his palm. 'I have not got my reading-glasses with me but yes . . . yes, I'd say they were. Augustus established mints here in Gaul and in Spain, as well as in Rome. During Gallienus's reign mint marks were shown. The ARL on this one', he tapped the coin, 'means Arelate, or Arles. The LVGD is for Lugdunum – Lyon. Yes . . . yes, they're good copies, Inspector, but ones that would fool no one but the stupid and the gullible.'

So much for the necessity of reading-glasses. 'Could Michèle-Louise have made them?'

'Michèle . . . ? Why? Whatever for? How could she have? That one was dead before I ever had the coins, monsieur.'

'Then could it have been Christabelle who made the dies from which these coins were struck?'

Audit saw the detective's gaze drop warily to the shotgun only to return. 'Why would she have done such a thing, Inspector?'

'Why indeed?'

Up in the loft of the barn beside the walnut mill, Kohler knew there could be no immediate danger to himself, yet he felt it. *Gott im Himmel*, it made his hands clammy. Was Louis in trouble again? Was that it?

The girl with the geese sat below him on a block of wood amid the littered straw. Wisps of fine flaxen hair trailed over the fresh-faced brow. The bright bandanna was only of so much use. At eighteen years of age a girl had no right to look like that while doing such a domestic chore. The geese crowded. She snatched another, clamped it between her warm thighs, jammed the funnel into its uptilted beak and proceeded to force-feed it. Thrust, thrust with the short wooden plunger, then the fist wrapped around the neck and down, down, the strokes firm and sure, the glance up at him, she knew damned well what he was thinking.

A tidy household. The château, the manor and the walnut mill. The hunt, the living in the rough while that was on, and a little something to warm the toes on frosty nights, ah yes.

In a way he envied Antoine Audit, but why did he feel the way he did? The loft had the usual paraphernalia, if one was in the walnut trade and making pâté as well. Baskets by the dozens, sacks, rakes, ladders, saws, bits of machinery, replacement paddles for the water-wheel, barrels for the walnut juice, the oil and pulp, screens, sieves, et cetera.

The canvas was dusty and when he'd got it off the thing, he stood in awe of it and knew immediately why the place had made him uneasy.

The rich deep tones of mahogany brought out the gnarled grain and beaten silver inlay. It was a cabinet, perhaps a metre and a half high and built in the shape of a truncated pyramid. Falcons with outspread wings hovered at the top of each of the four sides while lesser ones formed the handles of the tiny flat drawers; serpents with crowned heads were poised atop bamboo poles in silver that wrapped the edges of those same sides.

He pulled out one of the drawers. Another and another revealed the same. Each drawer was empty and lined with dark-blue felt.

Lost in thought, he didn't hear the voices until they rose to shouting. There was a slap – a stinging smack across the face! The girl with the geese had fallen off her block of wood and now held her burning cheek.

Madame Audit stood over her. 'Fool! *Idiot*! How could you have let him . . . '

The woman looked up to see him in the loft and, trembling, lowered her hand. The sound of the geese returned. The girl still lay sprawled among them, clasping her cheek.

Nice . . . it was really nice. Madame Audit was in her early thirties, wore a leather hacking jacket, whipcord jodhpurs and riding boots. A not unhandsome woman whose thin face served only to emphasize the rage and uncertainty in her hard brown eyes. 'Monsieur, what right have you to search this place?'

'None whatsoever,' he heard himself saying. She hadn't used the flat of her hand but the riding crop.

Sensing that he'd seen this, the woman turned quickly and strode from the barn.

The girl still lay in the shit and feathers looking up at him. Her fine young breasts pushed at the heavy shirt and sweater, then gradually settled down.

Gestapo, he heard her saying, though no words passed those fresh young lips. You're from the Gestapo.

When he reached the floor, he stretched out a hand to her. 'Relax, eh? It's not you we want.'

'What's he done?' she asked, giving out a fresh well of tears.

'Nothing that I know of. Simply enjoyed himself making money and playing with the locals.'

The blue eyes blinked as if slapped again. 'He's got a mistress in Paris. I . . . I know he has, though he has denied this to me on the grave of his father.'

'Hey, come on. Don't worry so much. It'll all sort itself out.'

'Madame Audit knows about the girl. She has followed him to Paris with . . . '

'With whom?'

'The . . . the Major, the Count Felix von Lindermann. He . . . he is the one who comes from Bordeaux to . . . to stay with Madame and Monsieur Audit.'

The naval attaché and overseer of Bordeaux and Périgord, the Abwehr . . .

'When's the baby due?' he asked, hating himself because it would only make her cry all the more.

'In July, after . . . after the strawberries have been taken.'

The mare, a dappled grey, stood with its reins drooping in front of the main entrance to the château. Accustomed to the manor house, the Audit woman had chosen the newly acquired premises as her defence.

The horse had been ridden hard, but why the hurry? Why leave a fine animal to catch its death?

Getting angrily out of the car, Kohler started across the lawns. The château's blue-slate turrets and yellowish buff stone walls half enclosed the courtyard.

The horse was dragging in the air. Sweat streaked its neck and flanks.

Without another glance at leaded windows he knew must be watching, Kohler took up the reins and led the poor thing in search of the stables. Built in medieval times as a river fortress high on limestone bluffs, the château was self-contained. The stables would be off to the left. When he found them, he helped the stable-boy to rub the horse down.

The latest Madame Audit was waiting for him in the library, had been pacing irritably back and forth before the windows, smoking cigarette after cigarette.

'Why have you come here?' she shrilled, not turning to look at him, but pausing to cup her left elbow more firmly in her right hand and suck on the cigarette as if she just couldn't get enough nicotine into her.

Kohler didn't answer; it was always best this way. He gave the crone who had announced him a nod and indicated the madame and he were to be left alone.

The doors closed. An antique table held drinks. Vermouth, whisky, cognac, vodka and all of the many Audit specialities. The strawberry liqueur then? A toast to a certain goose girl's lost maidenhood?

Glassed-in bookcases held leatherbound tomes. The floor was a mosaic of verd-antique. Nice ... yes, it was very nice, and Jewish of course.

He handed her a cut-glass tumbler of strawberry liqueur. 'The view of the river's great from here.'

'WHAT THE HELL DO YOU WANT?'

Up close, she was modestly pretty. 'Just a few questions.'

'That ... that woman you brought with you says Christabelle was murdered?'

'Raped and murdered, or vice versa.'

'What's that supposed to mean?'

The nostrils were pinched. The hand that held the strawberry liqueur trembled.

'Antoine would not have done it, monsieur. He ... he is not the type to have done such a thing.'

'I didn't say he was, but if I have to, madame, I'll see that the boys at Headquarters take you apart piece by piece.'

'*Bâtard!*' The dark-brown eyes flicked away to settle on the windows and the river that lay far below them in its gorge.

Kohler took a sip of the liqueur. 'Permit me, madame, to advance a theory that's fast taking shape. Is it not correct that you went to Paris on a number of occasions with the Major, Count Felix von Lindermann, and that ...'

'That little bitch, I'll cut out her tongue!'

He grabbed her by the arm but kept his voice calm and hard. 'You stayed at the Villa Audit on the rue Polonceau primarily with the intention of checking up on your husband.'

She yanked her arm free of him. The cigarette was finished, the butt crushed out. 'Yes, that is correct, but neither Antoine nor Felix suspected it.'

'And what did you find?'

Her snort was very quick and very real and it lifted the narrow chin, giving a touch of regality. 'That he was meeting a young girl in a nearby hotel. Look, I've had two sons by him. I . . . ' She indicated the château, the manor house, the walnut mill . . .

'Did you or did you not meet with that girl?' he asked.

She would have to answer readily to allay suspicion. 'I did on . . . on two occasions. I caught her in the courtyard of the villa one evening after dark. It . . . it was in summer, in August. Felix – the Major – hadn't come back, a meeting, I suppose. I was sitting under the sycamore where it was a little cooler. She said she'd just stepped into the courtyard to avoid someone whom she'd thought had been following her. I took her at her word but then discovered she'd been meeting my husband in that hotel.'

'And then? The next meeting?'

Some of the strawberry liqueur dribbled from a corner of the slender lips.

'I . . . I caught her stealing things from the villa.'

Kohler scoffed. 'Yet you didn't inform the police?'

Damn him! 'No . . . no, I did not do so. She didn't threaten me, Inspector. Oh, she could so easily have said she would tell Antoine about Felix and me, but . . . but the girl was really very shy, and . . . '

'And what?'

She would let a faint smile brush her lips. She would leave the liqueur on her chin, since it seemed to trouble him that she'd forgotten it. 'And *odd*, Inspector, if you know what I mean. It *pleased* her to know that I was being unfaithful to my husband and I got the feeling, too, that on more than one occasion, the girl had listened to the Major and I making love in that villa.'

Louis should have been with him. 'Does Count von Lindermann have other women?'

'Probably. Oh I see what you're after, Inspector. Yes, yes, Felix could quite possible have used the villa to entertain others. He's really very good as a lover, but I have no illusions. Antoine robbed me of those.'

Gott im Himmel, where was Louis? 'Would the girl have been afraid of your husband?'

The chestnut eyes were lowered in a touch of shyness or doubt.

'Why should she have been?'

'Because she'd been raised by him, madame, until the age of six. Because she was Charles Audit and Michèle-Louis Prévost's granddaughter. Surely you must have realized this when you caught her stealing things?'

She wouldn't turn away. She'd face him! 'We didn't discuss it.

236

At the time I thought she'd got into the villa through one of the windows.'

He'd let her have it quietly. 'But you met her more than twice then, madame, and you did ask her, and she told you who she really was.'

'Yes . . . yes, she did.'

'And realizing that the bits of jewellery should have been hers, you let her have them and did not inform the police because, madame, you needed her silence.'

The gorge was deep, the walls across the river were stained with rust. 'Yes . . . yes, that is true. Antoine . . . Sometimes a woman never really knows the man she marries, Inspector. Antoine has always had a thing about his older brother. He took Charles's wife and drove him into debt so that he could have her.'

'Then he made certain the poor bastard went to Devil's Island.'

The villa, the room, that bed, Michèle-Louise's perfume, the sketches of her lying in the nude . . . 'She was wild, but . . . but Antoine still thinks of her.' She gave a shrug. 'Again you see I have no illusions. The girl was the absolute reincarnation of the grandmother. Christabelle looked exactly like Michèle-Louise must have looked.'

And had dyed her hair to do it. 'What did you think went on in that hotel room?'

'Sex, what else? He bought her things. He took her things from here, never much, but I know they went to bed. Why else would he have gone to her so many times and she to him?'

It made her nervous to have to stand under scrutiny. It made her wipe the liqueur from her chin at last.

'Would it surprise you, madame, if I were to tell you the girl was a virgin?'

'A *what*?'

Anger, rage – jealousy, for she'd been cheated of the one thing she'd wanted so much to believe – so many things flashed before him in that moment.

The woman conquered them by vehemently shaking her head. 'He *loved* the girl – did you think I wasn't aware of this, eh? The trips to Paris, monsieur. They were more than just for business and to play with a new mistress. Ah, yes, he's had several. Antoine is like a boar in rut. It's the *vraie truffe* he hunts so avidly. An aphrodisiac, Inspector, as well as a major source of income.'

She tossed a hand. Another cigarette was found and lit. her

head tilted well back as she drew in and blew smoke towards the ceiling. 'Just how certain are you that girl was a virgin?'

'Let's be brutal about it, eh? Is that it?'

'Yes, that's it!'

'Reasonably.'

'Pardon? *Reasonably*? Surely the coroner's report would have spelled it out for you, Inspector? Did you not look for God's sake? Ah, you *did*, eh?'

'Yes, we did. At least, someone did.'

The cigarette was crushed into the ashtray with a brittleness that surprised. 'Then she held out the offer of it to my husband, monsieur, and he's an even bigger fool than I have given him credit for!'

At dusk the yellowish hue of the limestone deepened and the walnut mill with its turning water-wheel exuded that quiet sense of timelessness for which Périgord was justly famous.

St-Cyr drew on his pipe. There was a small wooden bridge across a turning of the flume and he'd chosen this as his point of observation. The boy had led the pigs away. There'd been other hunters working designated parts of the region, but they'd long since left. Even the truffles had gone off in the truck to Sarlat to be made into pâtés, sorted, shipped to Paris, Berlin and elsewhere. One day's haul had more than equalled a Sûreté detective's annual stipend. So much for making money by solving crime!

Something had happened at the mill. The girl who tended the geese had come out only to be told sharply to disappear. Now, again, she timidly approached Audit. They talked in earnest, the girl broke into tears. An angry word was said. They looked his way.

He drew on the pipe and waited. Antoine Audit had lived up to his every expectation. The man was wily, exceedingly shrewd and, at times, ruthless. Ah yes, my old one, he said. Witness the killing of that rabbit and how the glint of triumph and greed came into your eyes on seeing its struggles and hearing its last high-pitched screams.

The wire had been tight around a hind leg – not new wire, ah no, nothing like that, but very finely braided, very flexible steel. Quite unlike – and he must remember this – quite *unlike* the wire that had garrotted Christabelle Audit.

The boy had found a suitable stick, then he, too, had watched with rapt attention the rapid strangulation, the deftness, the flinging of the little corpse to the ground on release of the wire. The patient resetting of the snare. The lack of comment as if the whole thing had been as nothing.

At a shout, he crossed the bridge, but took his time so as to cause impatience.

Audit and the girl led him to the barn and up into the loft. The girl handed her employer the lantern and Audit hung it from one of the beams. 'That friend of yours,' he began.

'My partner, yes.'

'He had no right to search this place or to question my wife.'

St-Cyr lifted a tired hand of apology. The girl stepped aside, the lantern-light burnishing the swollen welt on her cheek. Ah now, Hermann, what has happened here?

'It's magnificent,' he said of the coin cabinet. 'French Empire, monsieur, but why have you put it away like this? A priceless antique . . . ?'

Why indeed. 'Out of sight is out of mind, Inspector. Ah, you know the Germans. Questions, always questions.' Audit gave a shrug. 'Sometimes our friends are hard of hearing. Jeanine, you may leave us now.'

'But – ' began the girl.

'I said *go*, Jeanine. I will be staying at the château tonight. The Inspector – I must walk back with him. I've things to do, eh? Don't provoke me at a time like this.'

A last glimpse of her climbing down the ladder revealed the desperate uncertainty of a young girl in trouble. St-Cyr glanced questioningly at Audit, who gave a shrug of You know how it is, eh? but said nothing further on the matter.

The silverwork was exquisite. The cabinet, while it had all the elements of the First Empire Period, had very strong ones of Art Nouveau.

'The action of the drawers is superb,' he said, running his fingers lightly over them. 'When exactly did you first begin the collection?'

Audit silently cursed the Sûreté for its meddling parasites, but there'd been no sense in hiding the cabinet from him, since the other one had found it and they'd be certain to talk.

'In 1930, Inspector. As the Depression came on, good pieces began to appear. Coins that had been kept for years. I bought wisely, always choosing perfection and rarity above all else. Ah, it's like anything else, is it not? Once the collecting bug is acquired, one strives to do the best one can.'

'Four hundred and eighty-seven coins, all of them gold and Roman. That's pretty good for being "best".'

'I planned to donate them to the Louvre on my death – purely for tax purposes, you understand.'

Ah but of course, the Louvre . . . 'Who built the cabinet?'

'I've no idea. There is a mark, but that's of Percier, the designer.'

First Empire then, under Napoleon. The Louvre, the Tuileries . . . so much of the interior designing of those days had been Percier's. 'Might I see it, please?'

'It's on the bottom. We would have to tip the cabinet over, Inspector. Is that really necessary?'

The cabinet was heavy and the mark, a signet brand, was hidden well underneath the thing. 'Percier,' grunted St-Cyr. 'Yes . . . yes, it is as you've said, monsieur. Perfect in every way. Mahogany like this is simply not seen any more. When they did things in those days, they did them right.'

Audit was not impressed.

The *poularde cuite à la vapeur d'un pot-au-feu* was so excellent it momentarily overcame the pangs of worry. A steamed chicken beneath whose tender skin had been inserted thin slices of the *vraie truffe*!

St-Cyr waved an appreciative fork. It would be best to keep Madame Van der Lynn's mind on other things in any case. 'The *pot-au-feu* is first cooked for three hours, madame. Then the prepared chicken is hermetically sealed in its earthenware vessel to steam in the vapours of the boiled beef and vegetables. Served with a cream sauce such as this, it is more than a poor man can bear.'

'Or stomach,' snorted Kohler. 'Give me the cabbage and sausage, with a side order of borsch and a beer!'

'Hermann, please! Madame Van der Lynn is our guest and in need of softly spoken words.'

Kohler hacked off a chunk of the chicken mush. 'No business?' he demanded antagonistically.

'None,' admonished the Sûreté. 'Not until we have finished our repast and found our way back to the manor house for the night.'

He'd say it darkly. 'The coins were only the tip of the iceberg, Louis.'

'Hermann, I know that.'

'Anyone could see it,' offered Madame Van der Lynn. 'A Big One. A *really* big one, isn't that what your friend Pierre Bonny called it?'

'He's not my friend. He never was.'

'Nor mine, Inspector. He helped to murder my husband.'

'Oona, eat your supper. Louis is just being bitchy. He's worried, eh, Louis?'

The Auberge of the Wandering Goose was full of Germans, some in uniform, some not. Fellow travellers and carpet-baggers just passing through the quaint, medieval town of Sarlat. French businessmen, the local priest et cetera. Quite obviously the district Kommandant was a regular also; so, too, its garrison's commander and three striking women – wives of absent soldiers? wondered St-Cyr, thinking momentarily of the horse butcher's wife and the young priest, Father David.

'There are so many aspects to this case, Hermann.'

Had it been said in lieu of an apology? Oona Van der Lynn helped herself to some of Hermann Kohler's chicken. He added a few more vegetables to her plate. 'Let's not go back to Paris,' she said. 'Let's go south and stay there.' A hope.

'Provence,' grumbled St-Cyr. 'A small farm . . .'

Kohler sucked on a tooth. 'Saint-Raphaël, Louis, and a certain villa.'

'Ah yes, Michèle-Louise Prévost, the runaway wife with her perfumer lover, Gerald Kahn.'

'The father of Christabelle Audit – is that not correct?' asked Madame Van der Lynn.

The sky-blue eyes and blonde hair suited the plain silk dress that had been borrowed from a closet in the manor house. Madame Audit would not mind. Indeed, she'd probably not even notice if the dress simply vanished. 'The father, yes, or so we've been told,' acknowledged St-Cyr politely.

'What's that supposed to mean?' asked Kohler.

'That one tells others what one wishes them to hear, Hermann. A "fast" woman, eh? Wild, an artist, a sculptress, a forger, but . . . ah,' he chose a chunk of carrot, 'not a forger of coins because, my old one, those were acquired *after* her death, yet the cabinet was acquired beforehand.'

'She didn't make it, did she?'

'My apologies, my fine Bavarian friend. Please, I have completely spoiled your dinner.'

Kohler shoved his plate aside. 'You know I can't eat because of Giselle, Louis. Give.'

'With pleasure, but first let us sample the cheeses and the pears with cherry brandy, or would you prefer to have them with the chocolate sauce?'

'There are some paintings of hers in a closet, and some pieces of sculpture in the cellar,' confided Madame Van der Lynn. 'I do not think Monsieur Audit could bring himself to throw them away, nor could he dispose of the cabinet.'

'You're not to be trusted to mind your own business,' breathed Kohler, 'but thanks for the help.'

'Madame, if you will permit me the intrusion at this late hour, a few small questions.'

He'd come alone, this one from the Sûreté. 'Will you join me in a *digestif*?'

'But of course. Gladly. Some of the blackberry cordial, I think, or perhaps a little of the choke-cherry? So many, such variety, such beautiful colours . . . One wishes one could try them all.'

'My husband uses everything, Inspector, or hadn't you noticed?'

The girl with the geese. 'A delightful man. A man of the soil, madame. The salt of the earth.'

Touché. He was more likeable, this one, therefore infinitely more dangerous. 'What sort of questions?'

'Oh nothing much. The robbery . . . ' St-Cyr accepted the liqueur she had poured without spilling a drop. 'I believe you were at home here, in the manor house.'

Some three kilometres by road from the château and the night so dark. He hadn't driven but had walked in from the turn-off. 'Yes . . . yes, I was here with my sons, the cook and housekeeper. None of us knew what would happen to France. We all lived in fear. Antoine . . . Antoine was called to Paris. A contract with the Ministry of Defence. The silk, I think.'

As with Hermann, Madame Audit had agreed to see him in the library. It wasn't the main sitting-room where there'd be certain to be a fire, nor the kitchen, but something cold and in between. Ah yes.

'This is lovely.' He indicated the room. 'A Gauron ormolu

clock, a Venetian chandelier, perhaps an early Briati. I'm particularly taken with the plasterwork. Italian, is it? Early eighteenth century?'

'Inspector, what exactly is it that you wish to ask? I can't tell you much. We were all asleep. In the morning, at about eight o'clock, Madame Auger, our housekeeper at the time, came to tell me my husband's study had been broken into.'

'A window?' he asked. Had the housekeeper then been dismissed?

She took a tremulous sip of the cognac she preferred at times like this. Had she realized her mistake? he wondered.

'It's so cold in here,' she said. 'Why don't we go into the sitting-room?'

'But of course. Did the château come completely furnished?' he asked.

'Antoine bought it the way he buys everything. Cheaply.'

Touché to her. 'The window, madame?' They were now in the main hall. Beauvais tapestries hung from the walls, gorgeous things. Another Venetian chandelier, a sumptuous drapery of clear crystal and coloured flowers, hung high overhead.

'A pane of glass in one of the French windows. You'll see it when you go back to the manor house, Inspector. The one right beside the lock. The police said the thief had used a sock to muffle the breakage, but of course they found nothing.'

The main sitting-room was pleasantly furnished in the style of Louis XV. One had only to take it in at a glance to realize its value, even at twenty new francs to the mark.

'The silk embroidery on the chairs is exquisite, madame. My compliments to your good taste.'

'Don't be insulting, Inspector.'

She took a quick sip of the cognac and chose not to sit in any of the chairs but rather to stand and stare at the fire.

He caught her reflection in the gilt-framed mirror that rose to the ceiling above them. 'The coins really were stolen, Inspector. All the drawers of that . . . that cabinet he . . . All the drawers were open and empty.'

'May I sit down?'

'Of course.' She tossed off the cognac. 'Is the choke-cherry not to your taste?' she asked, and he wondered then what she was hiding and why she was so afraid he'd discover it.

'Were any of the coins traceable?'

'At that time? The Defeat . . . Antoine tried of course. He . . . he

243

supplied the proper authorities with a list. The Sûreté were notified. Surely you would have seen the list or heard of the robbery, Inspector? Once again he has . . . '

'What, madame?'

'Supplied them with another list of the contents.'

'When? When did he do so?'

'A few months ago. In September, I think, or was it October? Since there is nothing left, it does not matter.'

The strain was evident, and he wondered at it. 'The cordial is excellent, madame. Please . . . No, I insist. Stay by the fire. You've been most helpful.'

Was he not going to ask how Antoine had first come by the coins? Was he not going to ask why they'd been in the house instead of a bank vault, or why the cabinet had been hauled away to be hidden from view like all the other things of hers that had been kept? Michèle-Louise Prévost!

'Madame, I take it that some years ago coins were put up as surety against a loan which their owner was then not able to repay?'

Caught in the mirror, he was still standing on the carpet behind her, still holding that stupid, stupid glass of that stupid, stupid cordial.

'Yes . . . yes, that is correct. In 1904, a . . . a long time before I . . . before I ever knew him.' Oh damn.

'Did he add to the collection?'

'Whenever he could.'

The dream was bad, the dream was terrible! A trapper, a hunter, a prospector perhaps, was skinning a naked woman. Blood . . . there was blood on the thin, razor-sharp knife. He'd hung her up by the ankles and had pulled the skin down off her buttocks and thighs . . . There was a gaping wound across her throat, blood in her eyes, blood in her nose and hair, her lovely hair. The lights all flashing from the mirrors and from the overhead rider bars. The court jester grinning, grinning . . . 'Faster!' he shouted. 'Faster!' The thing would not stop! Stop! A carousel . . . a pair of violet eyes that were wide with excitement and pleasure, the woman's hands firmly gripping a spiralling brass pole upon which a coal-black charger was mounted . . . mounted . . . mounted . . .

Skinny legs and bony knees and a billowing skirt beneath which were glimpses of white cotton underpants. A wire . . . a wire . . . The child threw out a hand to lean dangerously from the stallion as the carousel came round. Now up in the saddle to stand laughing at everyone, she balancing as the music blared . . . 'Don't! Please don't!' he cried out in alarm, dragging in a breath as he sat up suddenly.

Ah no, another nightmare! Gabrielle again! Gabrielle, but as a child last and a woman first. The flensing-knife had been scraping her peeled skin. A butterfly with a clear, bell-like voice and a shimmering dress.

Gabrielle and twenty-nine hostages. Giselle le Roy also. Ah Mon Dieu, Mon Dieu, where were the coins hidden? Where were Charles Audit and Réjean Tourmel?

St-Cyr flung himself back. The monkey had flitted by on the screen of his imagination carrying its tin cup to the body of what must have been Victor Morande. It had given an excited burst of chattering, had banged the cup against one of the spiralling brass poles and had tried to draw attention to something, but what?

The court jester had grinned and watched. Then the scent of Gabrielle's perfume had come to overwhelm the Sûreté's detective with momentary intrusions of lust.

But then Revenge . . . the sweet bitterness of bitter orange, the pungency of musk and civet, the scent of lemon grass, rosemary and coumarin had come to the clothes of a young girl who had dyed her hair.

A tall and beautiful woman had stood naked by a bath upon which long-legged ibis had been painted, she touching herself with that same perfume. Revenge, but then the woman had become Gabrielle.

She had tried to tell him something. Had it been about the carousel?

At dawn a light dusting of snow was shaken from the backs of ducks that swam or had slept near the wooded shores of the pond from which the walnut mill derived its power.

St-Cyr breathed in deeply. Frost clouded the air. Fog lay everywhere among the blackened trunks of the trees.

The door was opened and then closed. In time the girl, Jeanine, came out of the mill to break the ice in the washbasin by the pump and bathe her face, her throat and underarms beneath the heavy shirt and sweater, then drink.

Unbidden, the musk of her fresh young body mingled with

that of the walnuts and the lingering pungency of the truffles.

The boy soon came along the road with his father, and the girl stood out beside the pump, watching in silence as they approached.

Antoine Audit would be gruff with the girl. He'd have no patience or time for her troubled mind. She'd extend the offer of coffee. He'd say he was too busy and she'd know then that he would have no further use for her.

'That does not mean he is the killer,' muttered St-Cyr to himself. 'Ah Mon Dieu, I wish there was more time.'

He hurried across the little bridge, raising a hand. 'Monsieur, one moment, please. I must ask you to accompany us to Paris today. I think I know where your coins are hidden.'

Audit flung his cigarette away. 'Then find them. I don't want them.'

The boy glanced apprehensively at his father. The girl sought something solid by leaning back against the washstand to place her strong young hands firmly on its ancient boards.

'But surely, monsieur, you want justice?'

Audit tossed his head in anger. 'Justice? What is justice but interference in the affairs of others?'

'Four people have been murdered because of your coins, monsieur. Two others have died while under questioning. The lives of twenty-nine hostages hang in the balance.'

Audit raised the fist of the belligerent. 'Piss off! Who am I to care about them, eh? Jews? Communists? Radicals, eh? Away with you, Inspector. I've too much to do.'

So be it. 'Then come peacefully monsieur, or is it to be the bracelets?'

'On what charge?' he demanded fiercely.

'Why, that of murder, monsieur. Nothing less. If you are innocent, it will be but a small interruption and you can, perhaps, conduct a little business while you are there. If not, then unhappily you can kiss your truffles goodbye and welcome the guillotine.'

'I have friends – '

'And they have others, monsieur, whose duty it is to look into your undeclared wealth.'

A wave of sickness came. It could not be helped, but was it only an act? 'The rue Lauriston . . . ?'

'Orders straight from the avenue Foch.'

'Then I will gladly go with you, because I am innocent.'

9

'Madame Minou, I must ask again, is this the man you knew only as Monsieur Antoine?'

The bosom heaved. 'No . . . no, that is not him, monsieur.'

'But he has *said* he and the girl used that room, madame!' How could she do this to them?

'Absolutely not, Inspector. Absolutely!' she swore, squeezing the cat half to death.

Tough . . . Ah merde, she was tough! In a moment they'd be shouting. 'Madame, is it that you have had yet another visit from the rue Lauriston?'

The Sûreté's left hand was bandaged. The one from the Gestapo had a woman with him. She'd best say something. 'The hat, the clothes, they are not the same. No, Inspector, this one I have never seen before.'

In the Name of Jesus, why was she doing this to them? 'How *dare* you lie to us? This place is shut down as of right now! Enough is enough!'

'My son . . . my son. He . . . he has not come back, monsieur.'

St-Cyr sucked in the breath of caution. 'Why should he have? What's he to do with it, eh? Come, come, madame. Out with it!'

The folds of her throat rippled with indignation. 'Nothing . . . *Nothing*! I'm just a poor woman. I know absolutely nothing!'

'Let me, Louis.'

'Hermann, *please*! Are we to let him go so that he can silence her tongue for ever?'

The woman winced. The soccerball breasts strained at the printed frock and the double layer of knitted cardigans with matching holes and missing buttons.

Audit allowed a small grin of triumph. 'So, my friends, the waters of truth, eh? I did not come here. I did not meet anyone and I, too, know nothing, just as madame has said of herself.'

St-Cyr snatched the key to Number 4–7 from the hook above

the tiny desk. 'Take him up to the room, Hermann. Let him think about it! Leave me alone with this one.'

The cat struggled in vain. Madame Minou gripped it. 'Arfande, stop it! Ah, Mon Dieu!' She gave it a slap.

The claws, caught in the fabric of her dress, dug in and scratched the fleshy thighs. Blood began to seep through the laddered stockings. She tugged the slip and dress down while freeing the cat. 'Monsieur...'

'Madame?' he breathed, and when there was nothing further from her but a concierge's watchfulness, he said, 'Why didn't you tell me your son had made the acquaintance of Antoine Audit?'

'He's gone. My Roland is gone. I've not seen him in years.'

St-Cyr dragged out the dragonfly. 'A simple brooch, madame. A thing that was found clutched in the murdered Corporal Schraum's hand. Roland stole this from the girl's room.'

Vehemently she shook her head. 'No... no, it wasn't like that, Inspector.'

'Then how was it, eh?'

'I know nothing.'

'Don't be so stubborn. Your son could easily have come here on several occasions, madame. He has a key. He stole from your purse. He went into that girl's room and took this, then sold it to the Corporal Schraum or simply gave it to him.'

'When... when could he have done such a thing?'

'After he had first killed Victor Morande.'

She set the cat down on the carpet at her feet. 'Roland is not a bad boy, Inspector, only wrongful in some regards. He...'

Yes, yes, come, come, he willed her.

'Roland worked part-time for this... this Victor Morande, the one who ran the carousel. He helped him out from time to time. Me, I...'

'When we took you there to see the body you thought it might be that of your son.'

'Yes... yes, that is so.' Must she tell him everything? 'Roland was interested in the girl. The Captain Dupuis has said Roland had been watching her, but I...' The foothills of her shoulders lifted. 'I did not believe him.'

'So you went to the carousel and saw it for yourself.'

'Yes... yes. Roland was taking the tickets just as she must have done, but only when the other one...'

'Victor Morande.'

'Had to leave the premises.'

St-Cyr dragged out his pipe but reluctantly decided against it. 'Your son had to have a place to live, madame, and Victor Morande had to come and go a little bit more than you have indicated. From time to time your son lived at the carousel just as Victor Morande did. It was nice and warm with all that lovely coal the Corporal Schraum provided.'

'It's so cold in here these days,' she said, staring emptily past him at the wicket.

'I'm not surprised.'

'What will you do to him?'

'Nothing, if he is innocent. Now when did he make the acquaintance of Antoine Audit?'

'About two months ago. In late October. The Captain Dupuis will tell you more than I, monsieur. My Roland, is he . . . ? He hasn't been seen in some time, monsieur. Me, I had thought . . . a job at last, something solid. A future . . . '

'Bring your shawl and come upstairs. You must identify Antoine Audit to his face. Please, I am sorry but it is necessary.'

'He did not do it, monsieur. He could not have done such a thing.'

'Roland or Antoine Audit?'

'Roland, of course. Oh for sure a mother's love is blind, but disregarding this, I do know my son, monsieur. He wouldn't have killed her. That one liked the girls too much.'

St-Cyr took out his cigarettes and offered one. Lighting it, he waited while she filled her lungs, then watched as she let the smoke trail slowly from her nostrils. 'Last Tuesday, madame, Monsieur Antoine met the girl here in the afternoon at four o'clock. He left the meeting early, after only a few minutes perhaps? The girl seemed quite agitated about it?'

Again her eyes sought some distant place among the rubbish of her cage. 'Yes, she did not change her clothes or wash herself. I have thought the affair over, that Roland . . . '

'Yes, yes,' he urged, reaching for her shawl but letting her have all the time she needed.

'That Roland might have . . . ' She gave the tired shrug of an old woman in defeat. 'Might have spoken to him about the girl.'

'About what Victor Morande and the Corporal Schraum had been up to?' he asked.

'Roland would have demanded money of this Monsieur Antoine. Blackmail, I think.'

249

But never murder. He held the shawl for her and she let him place it over her shoulders as she stood to leave the cage.

'One last thing, madame, before we go upstairs.'

She'd seen it coming all along but now had no way of averting her eyes.

'The night before the Defeat your son came back to steal money from you. Did he know the girl Mila Zavitz who was strangled and raped in the courtyard beside the draper's shop on the Pas-Léon?'

Her eyes had blinked but she'd hold her ground. She'd not admit to anything further.

Pity was unwanted at this time but he felt a wave of it for her anyway. 'Had he been out looting the shops, madame? A few tins of coffee the Germans wouldn't miss? A bolt or two of cloth – things that would become scarce in the years to come? Mila Zavitz went there to seek help from her employer, madame. A young girl who was so afraid of being alone in the city, of being a Jew. She'd become separated from her family. The Nazis were at the gates. It was evening . . . sunset. The shop was closed. They'd all fled. There were two suitcases . . . '

'I know nothing of this. Two suitcases? Roland would not have killed her, monsieur. Not my son. Not even if he had demanded and taken from her that which she had refused to yield.'

'Then let us go upstairs and try to get to the bottom of things before it is too late.'

Lost in thought, Kohler fingered the edge of the pistachio-coloured washstand. The room had been tidied. Attempts at sponging off the blood-spattered sickly green walls had failed. Each finger flick of blood had been rubbed with steel wool as if Madame Minou had had to banish the thought of it from her tormented mind. She'd even dug into the plaster with a knife and now there were shrapnel bursts of pock-marked plaster that could only mean the concierge had been worried sick about her son's involvement.

He'd handcuffed Audit to the painted iron frame at the foot of the bed so as to give himself more freedom and let the bastard sit right next to where the girl's body had lain.

Louis hadn't yet come upstairs. He must still be questioning Madame Minou.

'I threw up my guts,' he said, more to himself than to Madame

Van der Lynn, who, not liking the room, had crowded close and had put a hand on his shoulder for comfort. 'I saw that young girl's throat, her eyes and then her body, and I thought of Giselle.'

'A timid stomach in a Gestapo detective?' snorted Audit. 'Tell me another one!'

'Ignore him, Herr Kohler. Don't let him get to you.'

'I'm not. He killed her, madame. That smug bastard with all his truffles and creams of the walnut, wrapped a wire around that poor kid's throat and strangled her.'

'Slowly – was that how it was done, eh?' snorted Audit. 'If my memory serves me correctly, monsieur, I was never in this room and there are no witnesses.'

'You're forgetting the note he left for her,' whispered Oona.

Kohler nodded. 'Yes. Yes, I've been thinking about that.'

'Are you still in love with Giselle?' she asked, her eyes so very blue and betraying anxiety.

He glanced apprehensively at her, seeing that she needed the truth. 'Look, madame, we never agreed to anything permanent. I said I'd take good care of you and I will.'

'How about a cigarette, eh?' snorted Audit. 'What about my rights, since I've done nothing and could not possibly have killed her?'

'Where the hell is Louis, Oona? Why hasn't he come upstairs?' asked Kohler.

'The rue Lauriston?' she replied sadly.

Kohler cursed their luck. 'Stay here. This one can't get away. I'll be right back.'

'*Hermann*, no!'

But he'd left the room, had left her alone with Antoine Audit just as he'd done with that other one on the Île Saint-Louis. Would the rue Lauriston rush up the stairs? Would they drag her away and demand that she tell them everything? Would they tear her clothes from her and beat her as they had beaten Hermann's Giselle?

It was so cold in here. Freezing! She clasped her shoulders and began to rub them. There was a small mirror on the washstand and she saw the basin reflected in this, saw the open door to the room and the empty corridor – had someone passed by? Had someone looked in to see her standing here?

'What's a good-looking woman like yourself doing with a bastard like Kohler? Hey, listen, madame, it doesn't take a jackass to see those two are has-beens. Why not save yourself and do me a little favour?'

Hermann . . . where was Hermann? Where was Louis? Louis would do all he could for her. Louis would . . .

The hotel seemed to breathe its silence. It was musty and close and yes, the smell of death still lingered in this room in spite of the carbolic that had been used and yes, the rue Lauriston would have kept this place under constant surveillance.

'What sort of favour?' she asked, her eyes fixed on the corridor's reflection in the mirror. There *had* been someone.

'Come closer. Come over here where we can talk.'

'Not on your life! *Never!*' she jumped.

A handsome woman, a woman who was so afraid she could not even look across the room at him. 'Maybe those two won't be coming back, madame. Maybe they've got it all wrong and can't deliver the goods. What then, eh? The rue Lauriston – please, I know that's what you're thinking. Henri Lafont and Pierre Bonny . . . You don't want them to hold you down, do you, madame? Others will then have a go at you.'

'*Bâtard*, you killed that girl!' There was no one standing in the hall. No one had been looking in at them. 'What . . . what is it you want?'

That was better. 'Do yourself a favour and call the Bureau Otto for me, madame. Ask to speak to Captain Brandl personally. Tell him Antoine Audit can deliver.'

The coins? 'Deliver?' she asked, seeing his dark-brown eyes flick over her body as if it would soon be naked and she would be standing here like that girl must have done. A piece of jewellery, a choker of pearls, a butterfly pin, a pair of gold and emerald earrings Christabelle could not possibly have worn.

Audit tugged at the handcuff. Four good yanks and the thing might come loose. 'Yes, *deliver*. A *deal*, madame. Brandl will understand. Do this before it is too late for you. They want the loot, the coins. If we give them the collection, they will let us go.'

Otto Brandl . . . the Bureau Otto . . . 'Is it that you know where the coins are hidden?'

Audit smiled briefly and she knew then that he would kill her if he could.

'Brandl's a personal friend. He *hates* the rue Lauriston, madame, *hates* Henri Lafont and Pierre Bonny because they intrude into business he considers his own. When two sides compete so fiercely, those caught in the middle must choose one or the other. He'll help us. He'll not hurt you. Not Otto.'

Audit dug into a pocket and held out a small notebook. 'The number's under the B,' he said, urging her to take that thing from him. His hands were strong. There was dirt under the cracked nails. He'd grab her. He'd pull her to him. He'd force her to help him or hold her hostage.

Why hadn't Hermann come back? Where was St-Cyr? Where was Madame Minou?

'There is a telephone in the café and *bal musette* on the corner, madame. Here . . . ' Audit half stood up to drag a small change purse from a trouser pocket. 'Go . . . go while there is still time. I'll tell them you've gone to the toilet. Use the tradesmen's exit. It's better. Keep to the wall and then make your way carefully to the courtyard door and out on to the street.'

She had lost everything, the children, her husband, even the job as concierge at the house on the quai Jemmapes, her clothes, her papers – everything.

'I didn't kill her, madame. I, who should have known better, loved her deeply.'

It was a gamble, this last little confession, and when she timidly turned away from the mirror, Audit pushed the notebook out across the bed and then withdrew until he was standing. 'No attempts to grab you, madame. I swear it.'

She snatched up the notebook and the purse and stood there quivering.

'Go,' he said. 'Go now. Everything will be all right if you do exactly as I've said.'

The cellars beneath the hotel were damp and full of rubbish. Two strands of questionable electrical wire ran down into the darkness to wrap themselves about a broken insulator before taking off into the ink. The only lightbulb that Kohler could see had been recently smashed, a bad sign.

He nudged the door open more fully. One of the concierge's felt slippers had become hooked on a nail. Oh-oh.

The rubbish was that of a pack-rat. Broken chairs, broken crockery, tables without one or even two legs. Peeling veneer, cracked chamber-pots and dried-up cans of paint.

It was quite a place, but he'd left Oona upstairs with Antoine Audit and he'd best go back for her. She'd be nervous, she'd be remembering the Île Saint-Louis. She'd be thinking of how Christabelle Audit had died.

Water covered the floor. He could hear his shoes sucking at it with each lousy step. There'd been no sign of Lafont and Bonny, but one could never tell. Louis must be in a jam.

By feeling his way forward, Kohler followed the narrow channel that had been left in the refuse. There were stacks of damp newspapers, each with a brick or piece of iron to hold it down. It wasn't fair of him to have left Oona alone with Audit. Louis would understand the need to go back.

Can't see a thing, he said to himself. Drawing his gun, he found a match and struck it under a thumbnail. At once the cellars opened up with flickering shadows high on the orange-red brickwork of an arched roof above him. He had to stand in awe of it, had to breathe, 'Jesus, a catacomb?'

Madame Minou's other slipper drifted by, the felt strung with slime and hair.

Wine had once been stored here. The cobwebbed racks were piled against the walls. Empty bottles held the mould of age.

Kohler blew out the match and listened. Muttering 'Louis?' he suddenly had the feeling the place was very unhealthy.

A series of tunnels branched to the left and right and continued straight ahead. 'Louis?' he hazarded. *'Louis . . . Louis . . . Louis?'* came the echoes.

'Son of a bitch, don't do this to me! We've got the killer upstairs in that room with Oona, idiot! I know it's him.'

'Him . . . Him . . . Him . . . '

She'd be terrified.

In time he came to another place where wine had once been stored, perhaps in Roman times. It was just beyond a turning and long before the match burned down he heard the muffled curse Louis gave from somewhere in the surrounding darkness.

'Put that thing out and shut up, Hermann! Don't be an idiot yourself! Ah, Mon Dieu . . . '

The sound of the shot boomed and rolled back and forth. Kohler cringed and tried to get out of its way. The slug pinged off the walls, smacked into an empty steel drum and then shattered several forgotten panes of glass.

Madame Minou sucked in a breath. A shrill voice leapt out of the darkness. 'I DID NOT KILL HER, MESSIEURS!'

Louis' urgent entreaty came from somewhere over to the right.

'*Imbecile, I know you didn't! Come out of there at once. Give yourself up.*'

'NO!' A volley of shots ruptured the darkness. The blubbering concierge pleaded with God for salvation.

And then tearfully, 'Messieurs ... Messieurs ... In the Name of Jesus, I'm but a poor woman who is now soaked to the skin! The sewers, messieurs. They have flooded the cellars.'

Ignoring the whimpering, the assailant shouted antagonistically. '*That one upstairs knew Roland, Inspector. Me, I saw them talking. Roland killed her. I swear he did!*'

Kohler began to crawl forward through the flotsam. There was still no light. Louis ... where was Louis?

Again the shrill voice came. '*You attack a veteran, a man who faced death for his country, eh? A captain, my friends. Captains do exist! It's that shit Corbet, that Major next to her who's been talking, eh? Well, my fines, take this and this!*'

The shots cannoned through the caverns and the tunnels, echoing as he shouted, 'ME, I CAN SHOOT BETTER THAN HIM!'

It had to be the Captain Dupuis of the one leg. Again Louis made an attempt. 'Monsieur, *please*! I merely want to talk to you.'

'Questions, eh? More questions. Then *talk*, you parasite! Suck at the blood of an innocent man. Give out a few more of your lousy sous, you cheapskate.'

'Francs ... I gave you one hundred francs.'

'PISS OFF!' Three shots came rapidly. 'DON'T COUNT, MY FINE. I'VE TWO GUNS, OR HADN'T YOU NOTICED? I always have them. That saved my ass at Verdun and I've kept by the rule ever since. One for rats like you and the other one inside the tunic, eh, just in case you stir and need a little more!'

The tunnels must be endless. The water was cold and still ankle-deep. Had he missed a turning?

Kohler doubled back. The stench was pitiful. *Gott im Himmel*, was it safe to strike a match?

'When ... when did you last see Roland Minou talking to the one upstairs, that girl's lover?' hazarded Louis.

'*Lover?*' came the shrill accusation, but from where? 'That bastard? It's men like him who take advantage of sweet young girls like that. I'll show him. I'll put one of these up against that forehead of his. He can laugh all he wants, my fines, but it'll be the last laugh he gives!'

St-Cyr tried to ease his cramped legs. Madame Minou gave a

yelp, then a pitiful entreaty. '*Captain*, you must stop the shooting! Roland did not kill her.'

'You lying old sow. I've seen the way you leered at that little pigeon. A virgin for your son, eh? Well listen good, madame. That bastard son of yours has been in and out of this shit box of a hotel more times than you can count! He met that rapist of young girls in the Bistro Caban. That little shit of a hood told the industrialist exactly where things were at.'

'What things ... what things?' Hermann ... where was Hermann?

'THE GIRL!' shouted Dupuis, reloading the revolver. 'The *virgin*, you bloodsuckers. Roland wanted her cherry, so he put the squeeze on the rapist!'

Four more shots were fired with uncanny ability. 'He'd been following her for months, eh? He knew where she went and what she was up to. One night he even followed her into the villa at Number twenty-three and stole a few things for himself. Now *leave* me alone. *Alone*, I say, or I'll do something crazy. CRAZY! A virgin ... she was a virgin, you idiots!'

The bastard was completely mad. 'Louis ... Louis, where the hell are you?'

'Nowhere,' came a timid voice, quite near now. 'He's got two guns, Hermann. Remember?'

'In the Name of Jesus, messieurs, your company is a great trouble to me!'

'Be quiet, madame. Don't interfere with police officers engaged in their duties. Keep your head down and your heart beating.'

Five minutes passed and then another five, but by then Kohler had finally found them.

'He ... he has gone out by the other way, messieurs. Through the tunnels. He will not come back, not that one.'

'Where ... where do the tunnels end?' asked Kohler.

The woman gasped as she struggled to sit up. 'Beneath the church. That one will go there, to Father Eugène. He will seek sanctuary.'

'With two guns and on crutches?' scoffed Kohler, finding his matches at last.

'Yes ... yes. With two revolvers or pistols. I ... I never can remember which are which.'

But she'd known he'd had them in his room!

Kohler struck a match. 'One has a cylinder like that, madame, the other hasn't.'

She licked her lips in doubt. 'Then he has one of each, monsieur. The pistol *and* the revolver.'

'A nine-millimetre, Louis?'

'Probably, Hermann, but then . . . Ah, my new suit, my new coat! Son of a bitch!'

Another match was called for and then a bundle of them. Madame Minou was still wallowing at their feet. 'He has the wire, messieurs. A coil of it to . . . to tie up the bedsprings. Me, I . . . I have forgotten about this until now.'

The deceitful old sow.

St-Cyr leaned down to help her up. 'Your memory amazes me, madame. We'll be lucky to keep one jump ahead of it. The church, Hermann. We must go there now.'

'I'll get Oona and Audit. They'll have heard the shots, Louis, and thought the worst.'

A gun battle. 'Dupuis must have seen you taking them past his room, Hermann. He panicked and thought we'd come for him. Madame and I saw him hurrying down the stairs, but he was nimble, so nimble. He shot past me and made for the cellars.'

'Wait for me. Let me find out what's happened upstairs.'

The room was empty. The iron bedstead had been removed and now that end of the mattress and springs rested on the floor.

'Oona?' he cried out. 'Louis . . . Louis . . . ' *Gott im Himmel*!

Kohler began to run. There was a Turkish at the far end of the corridor, the handle a piece of porcelain slime. He put a foot up and yanked. Major Corbet, that shit Dupuis had been roundly castigating in the cellars, was squatting. 'Where . . . where the hell did they go?' shouted Kohler.

'Both to the street. The woman first and then, at least some ten minutes later, the giver of unwanted pâtés and liqueurs.' Was nothing private in this place? 'Please do me the honour of closing the door.'

Kohler left him to it. Oona . . . Oona . . . *Bastard* . . . *Bastard*. The door slammed shut only to bounce back but by then he was going down the stairs two at a time.

'Louis . . . Louis, they're gone! I can't believe it.'

St-Cyr squeezed the last of the water from a trouser leg and went calmly up the stairs.

Yes . . . yes, it was quite true. Audit had escaped custody. There was a small notebook in the hall. As he thumbed through it, the telephone number of the Bureau Otto came up and he, too, started to run.

The bedstead was jammed into a crack in the courtyard's outer wall. One loop of iron had been snapped off.

Audit was now a free agent. There was no sign of Oona Van der Lynn.

'The Villa Audit, the Church of Saint Bernard, the *bal musette* on the corner?' offered Hermann.

Since there were no lights, St-Cyr said, 'You to the *bal* and the villa. Me to the church.'

'Take care.'

'You too my old one.'

'That God of yours won't care, Louis. He'll simply laugh at us.'

Which was true. God mocked. God was the High Court Jester on the carousel.

From the zinc to the cluttered tables, the sea of faces measured zero, and in the *bal musette* behind the café, the crowded couples clung to each other as much for warmth as love.

Kohler hunted the dance floor beneath the ball of slivered mirrors. The lights were low, the tobacco smoke thick and reeking of cheap perfume. Older men with young girls; middle-aged wives with husbands or lovers they could no longer trust. Couples turning, turning, going round and round. Where ... where the hell was Oona?

The accordian wept, a disinterested drummer made eyes at the ceiling while the piano player forgot one hand to lift a glass to his lips. There wasn't a German uniform anywhere, not one Nazi or one of their sympathizers. Only himself.

People were beginning to take notice of him. The music was braying Resistance ... Resistance ... The place began to smell of it, to cry out *Hostages* ... You bastards took thirty of them!

He headed for the toilets at a run. Couples were shoved aside, the gaps closing behind him, now opening in front ... Oona ... Oona ...

The corridor was narrow, lit dimly and layered with smoke. Laughing, ox-eyed girls stopped laughing; one old tart in a tight turquoise suit gave up trying to fix a face that could never make it.

'A girl ... a tall woman ... a blonde, for Christ's sake? About forty, with blue eyes – '

'Gestapo?' she asked, giving him an uncertain quiver of wide, painted lips, eye shadow and plucked eyebrows beneath bleached curls that were fast going limp.

Kohler grabbed the woman by the arms and slammed her up against the wall. The compact's mirror shattered, the lipstick tumbled from that fleshy hand. 'GESTAPO!' he roared. 'Now out with it! A Dutch woman in a light-brown overcoat and scarf.'

'With blue eyes?' managed the woman, feeling the urine run freely down her legs. Ah, *merde*! her bladder. The evening was ruined. Ruined! Lie then. Say anything. Say what he wants. 'In the toilets,' she gasped.

He flung her aside and went through the chipped door into the stench. 'Ah Jesus ... Jesus.' Some shrieked, some stood as if struck dumb and unable to move. There were holes in the floor. Turkish again ... girls squatting, girls fixing their garter belts, one caught rinsing rags and glad of it, only to lose all colour at the sight of him. 'A blonde-haired, blue-eyed woman of forty wearing a light-brown overcoat and scarf,' he said.

It was all for nothing – hopeless. Now none of them moved. The girl with the rags discreetly let them fall as the colour flamed back into her cheeks.

'Look, the woman's life is in danger. I ... I only want to help her,' he said.

'Then try the door to the courtyard. Perhaps she went through that one!' said someone acidly.

'Yes ... yes, she did. Me, I have seen such a one, but that was some time ago, monsieur.'

'Was anyone following her? A man, for Christ's sake! Sixty years of age and French.'

The girl with the rags didn't know. The shrug was genuine. 'About half an hour ago?' he asked and heard her say, 'Three-quarters of an hour, I think.'

The courtyard was dark and he didn't like it. The city was too quiet. Louis ... why the hell hadn't they stuck together?

He began to move silently along the narrow pavement. Oona had a little less than an hour before curfew. Would she try for the house overlooking the quai Jemmapes? Would she simply keep walking?

The courtyard door to the villa at Number 23 was off the latch. The street was dark. The shop awnings were folded in and there was nothing ... nothing. Were they saving kerosene tonight? None of the blue pot-lights were in sight.

Distant on the horizon came the steady drone of RAF bombers bound for the Reich. It would all end some day, this carousel of

Paris. If only Louis and he could see it through, if only he could find Oona and tell her that she really did matter to him.

If only he could find Antoine Audit.

St-Cyr ran his eyes over the pews whose emptiness spoke only of vacated penance, piety and sore knees.

The young priest, Father David, was not present. The old priest would stay on his knees in front of the altar all night if necessary, to ward off a confrontation. 'Father, I must talk to you. Please, it's urgent. A Dutch woman's life hangs in the balance, as do those of the remaining hostages.'

Must he be reminded of it? Delacroix brought the rosary to his lips in a gesture so automatic one would have to read impatience into it. 'What is it you want, my son?'

You tough old man, don't you play around with me! 'Captain Dupuis, where is he?'

Shrugging would do no good. Lying . . . Could he lie in the face of God as he'd done so often of late? 'He is in God's sanctuary, Inspector.'

'Then convince him to give himself up.'

The Sûreté was a head taller than himself. 'He's done nothing. You've no right to terrify him like this. He did *not* kill either of those two young girls.'

St-Cyr drew in an exasperated breath. 'He shot at us.'

The stance toughened. 'But not with intent to kill.'

'There is no other kind of shooting when one is on the run, Father. Now, please, where is he?'

Would God forgive his indiscretions? Father David lying in sin with Marie Ouellette, the . . . 'I . . . I have given him my word, Inspector. He is here in God's house and neither you nor that Gestapo friend of – '

'Hermann is not my friend, Father. He is my partner. All of our lives are in danger.'

'Friend . . . partner . . . it is all the same, is it not? My resolve is firm. I have nothing more to say. Now if you will excuse me, I will finish my prayers.'

A depth of sadness came that could not be shoved aside. 'No, Father, your time for prayers is over. Since you force my hand, I must tell you that I believe one of the guns the Captain Dupuis illegally possesses killed the Corporal Schraum.'

'Not the girls?'

'Come, come, Father. You know very well they were both strangled and then raped.'

'Not raped beforehand?'

Again the sadness intruded. 'No, my friend, not raped beforehand.'

The old priest crossed himself. 'He . . . he is with Father David and Madame Ouellette. He is not in God's house, because I could no longer let him enter it.'

Kohler stood in the courtyard of the Villa Audit looking up at the starless sky. The bombers were now directly over the city and the air-raid sirens were wailing eerily through the darkness. Though far too high to hit, some stupid sons of bitches manning an anti-aircraft battery over in Saint-Ouen opened up with all they had. That sparked others and soon the searchlights were coning the skies and the sound of gunfire was coming in from all directions.

As abruptly as it had started, the firing ceased. The sound of the planes soon began to dwindle. One by one the searchlights went out, though they wouldn't have mattered here.

He took two deep breaths and then another before pulling off his soaking shoes and socks.

Padding across the courtyard, he went up the low stone steps and along to the front door. The lock was off and he wasn't surprised, but damn Louis for suggesting they split up!

He eased the door open. No lights . . . The sitting-room was pitch-dark and musty. Stuff everywhere, a *chaise* . . . yes, yes, he had it now . . . cushions on the floor . . .

Michèle-Louise Prévost had been a woman who had known her own mind and who had ached for the freedom to express it. An artist, a forger, a copier of the works of others. But what was that? A scraping in the cellars . . . ? Audit?

The hall was cluttered with things the woman had done. Tablets in clay . . . scenes of bison and deer from the caves of Périgord. The earthy sensuality of the young wife of a stuffy shoe salesman and of the successful younger brother, the hunter of truffles and manufacturer of pâtés and silks.

The cellars weren't deep and there was no water in them, only the dampness of stone flagging in winter. There were several storerooms, now mostly empty, rooms for coal that couldn't be purchased, though there were a half-dozen bags.

Antoine Audit, the handcuffs having been cut away, was working by candlelight. The stone was heavy and he'd almost got it out from the wall. His coat and jacket had been set aside. There was no sign of a gun or knife, no sign of Oona. Just a chisel and hammer.

The kitchen table in the horse bucher's flat above the shop was littered with dirty dishes and the leavings of three pale-green bottles of red wine. The baby had a cold.

St-Cyr watched grimly as Madame Ouellette tried to calm the infuriated child by nervously suckling it at yet another of the swollen breasts. The fourth go at that one, or was it the fifth? Her milk had turned and she hadn't liked having to bare her breasts in front of the Captain Dupuis. Ah yes.

Yet were it not for the two handguns pointed at him, one could almost have thought it a domestic scene of utter commonness. The two priests merely in attendance to discuss a coming baptism.

They were getting nowhere and Hermann ... Hermann was out there some place without backup. 'Please, I will ask you one more time, Captain. The guns, eh? Turn yourself in. It's of no use. I know what happened.'

'*You don't!*' shrilled Dupuis, cocking the Lebel. Tears poured down his cheeks. 'I *didn't* kill them! I would *never* have killed them. I *will* kill you! I WILL!'

St-Cyr cautiously reached for his cigarettes, which had been tossed on the table some time ago. 'Look, I know you didn't kill either of those two young girls. I'm here about the Corporal Schraum.'

'*You're lying!*' The Luger came up, the hammer was clawed back ... No ... no ...

'Alphonse, *don't*! The Inspector does know everything. Please, I beg it of you. Listen to your priest and friend.'

Doubt clouded the reddened eyes. Uncertain still, Dupuis bit the end of his tongue.

'To me,' urged Father Eugène. 'Just the Luger, Alphonse. Come, come. Allow me to do the correct thing, eh? It's a small enough request, since you will still have your revolver.'

The old priest's hand made its way through the clutter. One of the wine bottles teetered. Father David leapt to steady it. The Luger swung his way ...

The bottle was righted. The child threw up. A choking fit followed. Ah, Mon Dieu, never had he been a party to a situation like this!

The gnarled hand of the old priest closed about the barrel of the Luger, which was still pointed at St-Cyr, still gripped by the Captain Dupuis.

Father Eugène looked steadily at the Captain, a test of wills. 'Alphonse, you must trust me. I borrowed this gun from you – you know I did. We spoke of it in the confessional just after the Defeat. You told me you had broken the new laws and had kept your guns and I remembered this. You trusted me and I kept silent, but then I had need of one of them.'

'I didn't kill them, Father. I swear I didn't! They were . . . She was . . . she was just lying on the floor not moving, not saying anything, Father. Naked! He'd . . . he'd . . .'

'The gun, Alphonse. I must have the gun. The Inspector knows everything.'

'Will you kill him?' asked Dupuis, meaning the detective.

Father David's hand closed over both of theirs and the Luger. 'Father, I'm the one who has sinned. I . . . I shot the Corporal Schraum.'

The young priest's sky-blue eyes were moist. 'He was abusing my Marie, Inspector. I couldn't have it happen any longer. Night after night the Corporal would come and she would have to do whatever he wanted or he'd have had me arrested.'

'So you killed him?'

'Yes. Father Eugène had borrowed the Luger. He was planning to get both of the guns away from Captain Dupuis because . . . because he was afraid Alphonse might . . . might do something he shouldn't.'

The confessional and the sins of a tortured mind. Thoughts of a young girl taking off her clothes in the room next door while some bourgeois bastard watched her do it.

'The boy talks nonsense, Inspector. It was I who killed the Corporal,' said the old priest.

Dupuis ducked his red-rimmed eyes lest he steal another glance at the woman's naked breasts, her throat, her lovely throat.

Father Eugène said, 'David, *please*! I beg you. Let me do what is right. It is God's will.'

'Did Schraum know Roland Minou?' asked St-Cyr.

'Yes . . . yes, of course he did,' replied the old priest, testy at the interruption.

'How do you suppose Schraum acquired the dragonfly that was clenched in his fist?'

'Dragonflies . . . He talks of insects at a time like this!' shrilled Captain Dupuis.

The woman wiped her breasts with a filthy dishcloth. 'Roland gave it to him, Inspector. About two months ago. The Corporal showed it to me, but he kept it as . . . as a souvenir, he said.'

Thank God for saneness in the midst of chaos. 'Did he say where Roland had acquired it? Please, madame, this is important.'

She glanced uncertainly at Father David. 'Roland had been following the girl, even when she went into the Villa Audit. He stole the dragonfly from there. The Corporal Schraum only laughed about it and then . . . and then he forced me to . . . to . . .'

'*Marie, don't tell him*! Please! It's . . . it's not necessary.'

Distracted, the young priest looked beseechingly at her. Father Eugène's grip tightened on the barrel of the Luger. Dupuis' grip tightened on the butt, the trigger . . .

The child threw up and threatened to turn blue. The Luger was plucked away by the Sûreté and pointed at Dupuis.

'Now look, Captain. Enough is enough. If we can deliver the killer of Corporal Schraum to the Kommandant of Greater Paris and demonstrate that he was not involved with the Resistance, we might – I say might – just be able to save the hostages. As for the others . . .'

'They are in God's hands, is that what you mean?' asked the old priest wisely.

'You know it is, Father.'

'Then what is it you wish of us?'

Could he trust them, could he *not* take them into custody? 'Look, I have unfinished business. Be at the carousel in the parc des Buttes-Chaumont at seven-thirty in the morning. All of you, Father Eugène. That one too, with his revolver. We may need it.'

Dupuis understood the look he gave him. The old priest hesitated. The young priest didn't know what to do.

St-Cyr placed the Luger into Father Eugène's hand and wrapped the old priest's fingers about it. 'Shoot well, if needed, eh? Break your vows, but break them for the good of others.'

Hermann . . . where was Hermann?

The flame of the candle fluttered. Antoine Audit had yet to lift the heavy stone from the cellar wall.

A chill came. Involuntarily Kohler shivered as the hackles began to rise. Brandl . . . Had Audit managed to call the Bureau? Had Offenheimer and Brandl met up with Oona?

'So okay, my fine, that's enough. The gun's loaded. Don't move.'

Audit didn't. 'Where's St-Cyr?'

'Keeping an eye out. What's in the wall, eh? The coins?'

Could Kohler be bribed? Why hadn't Brandl come? The door had been left unlocked. Had Kohler put the lock back on?

'If you'd lend a hand, Inspector, we could both . . . I assure you, there's far more than the coins.'

'Emeralds?' asked Kohler.

'Yes, emeralds and Mayan gold. Exquisite things. Turquoise, too, and river diamonds. My brother smuggled them into France, but was too afraid to try to sell them. Christabelle showed me a pair of the earrings. It was one of her ways of getting me to co-operate. I did not think Charles would use my hiding-place. It was empty. He . . .'

Kohler drew in a breath. The air was too cold, too damp. Was that whisky he smelled? Scotch whisky?

It was odd how the mind played tricks. Emeralds . . . Mayan gold and diamonds . . . 'You stole the coins from yourself and hid them behind that stone. A month before the Defeat you robbed yourself so as to have a little something laid by in case all else failed. Périgord wouldn't have been any good as a hiding-place – far too many truffle-hunters, eh? You needed Paris because, my friend, you could see where things were heading.'

There'd be no help with the stone. He'd have to force Kohler to come closer. 'I reported the theft, Inspector. I myself came to Paris to advise the Sûreté of the loss.'

Pharand would have seen the original list and so would Boemelburg. Word would have got around. 'Were you or were you not in Paris on the night before the Defeat?'

'I was not. What is more, I can prove it.'

Emeralds and diamonds, gold and more gold . . . 'Lift the stone away. Let's see what's behind it. Maybe the two of us can make a deal.'

The candle flame stirred. His hackles rose higher. Something cold and hard pressed against the back of his neck. Son of a bitch, where was Louis now?

St-Cyr touched the courtyard door and felt it give. He'd come round the corner from the rue Saint-Luc, heading for the foot of the rue Polonceau, and had just stepped into the Pas-Léon when he'd heard something. These old neighbourhoods, the darkness, the imminence of the curfew . . . The courtyard beside the draper's shop. The scene of that other murder. Mila Zavitz.

Roland Minou? he asked. Was it possible that Roland had ducked in here?

Hermann . . . where was Hermann? There had been the sound of screeching tyres heard faintly above that of the shrieking child in Madame Marie Ouellette's arms, but he'd had no time even to consider it.

And now? he asked. Had Otto Brandl been in that car? Had Henri Lafont and Pierre Bonny?

The hinges creaked. He cursed the war, the Occupation and the shortages of lubricating oil and grease. Even goosefat was in tragic absence.

Whoever it was now held the breath and kept very still. The walls were dark, the shuttered windows only a little less so, the slot of winter's sky above the roofs but a whisper of infinity.

Roland Minou . . . was he lurking in some corner of this place?

St-Cyr breathed in softly. The cold and the dampness accentuated the pungency of mouldering plasterwork and window sashes that needed more than paint. But was there something else?

He drew the Lebel and cocked it. One corner of the courtyard proved vacant to all but disused trash cans. No one could afford to throw anything out these days; everything was used up or recycled. The Occupation was good for some things, eh? Rats were in retreat. There was no more of that pissing about with arrogant dustmen who turned up their noses at a bit of honest labour for which they'd been handsomely paid. Pensions, full pensions they still gave them.

Whoever it was had moved.

When he heard a breath being taken in and held, the musk of fear came strongly, and through it a faint bath-soapy odour that was sweet and of woman.

'Madame Van der Lynn, it is me, Jean-Louis. Where is Hermann?'

She threw herself into his arms and he could not stop her shaking. 'I was being followed. I know I was!'

Roland . . . Roland Minou? he wondered.

'Four cars. Two from this end of the rue Polonceau and . . . and two from the other.'

Son of a bitch!

The candle flame flickered. The truffle-hunter's wary gaze had momentarily been fixed on each of the visitors but Audit was far too intelligent to let it linger on either of them.

His hands held high, he forced a grin. Kohler waited. The one behind him shifted his weight. The other one just stood to the left doing nothing. Bergmanns? he wondered. Schmeissers?

'The pistol,' breathed the one behind him.

'Look, Louis is out there some place. I wouldn't want him to get the wrong idea. He might think you're Réjean Tourmel or Charles Audit.'

'The pistol, Herr Kohler.'

'Hey, come on. It's brand-new. I've only just checked it out. *Gott im Himmel*, the paperwork. Stores aren't the same any more.'

Kohler was just fucking about. 'You won't be needing another. You can forget about the paperwork.'

'It's all up to you, my Hermann.'

'Otto . . .' Antoine Audit began to lower his aching arms.

'Don't!' breathed Kohler. 'Just relax. They mean business.'

The grin faded. The hands climbed back up. 'Otto . . . the . . . the coins, they are not here.'

'Nor the emeralds or the diamonds?' snorted Kohler. 'What'd he do, Otto? Call the Bureau for help? Who was it took the message, eh? Offenheimer? Was he the one?'

Brandl stood at the foot of the stairs. Had that been a car screeching its brakes in the street outside? Company so soon? 'As a matter of fact, Hermann, the Captain was the first to take the call, but then I myself talked to Antoine.'

'Idiot! Offenheimer's been working for the rue Lauriston. Lafont and Bonny have been putting the squeeze on him.' Kohler still held his pistol. If only Brandl would lay into Offenheimer. If only . . .

The cellar was too confined. Audit would be killed, himself . . . The candle was not that far. A sudden gust, the toss of something?

The Schmeisser nudged him. 'Don't even think of it, Herr Kohler. Just drop the gun.'

In the Name of Jesus was there nothing that could be done?

Offenheimer would have tipped off the rue Lauriston. Lafont would go berserk! 'Louis knows where the coins are hidden. The Frog's got it all figured out, Otto, but being a Frog, the bastard's kept it to himself.'

The front door slammed. Steps rushed along the hall above them . . . Brandl snuffed out the candle. 'So, we wait, yes, and see what happens.'

A burst of firing shattered the silence of the cellar, ripping boards and smashing things. 'Henri . . . Henri, in the Name of Jesus, slow down!' shouted Pierre Bonny. 'It is *Brandl*, Henri. Otto Brandl!'

'CARBONE . . . It's that Corsican son of a whore's basket! That dog's offal! I'll kill the swine! I'll kill him!'

'Henri, Henri, wait! He's not here,' shouted Bonny desperately. '*Brandl*, Henri . . . the Bureau Otto.'

Another burst of firing tore into the walls, the floorboards above them, and armfuls of wine bottles. Kohler found his pistol on the floor and started to worm his way across the flagstones. If only he could reach the stairs. If only Louis would come by.

Son of a bitch, the place had gone to silence! The stench of cordite was everywhere. Littered shell casings lay about in the pitch-darkness. One of them stirred and fell suddenly from a step. It rolled away.

'*I want the coins!*' shrieked Lafont, his falsetto ringing.

Someone anxiously fumbled for a flashlight but was told to leave it be.

Brandl hazarded a few words from behind a pillar. 'The coins aren't here, Henri, but there is enough gold and emeralds for us to share. What do you say?'

'NEVER! *Goering* has ordered the avenue Foch to find the coins and *they* have ordered me to do the job! You are *trespassing* on my turf!'

Another burst of firing sent splinters everywhere. Kohler cringed and pulled himself along.

'Where's Kohler?' hissed someone.

'*Kohler?*' shrilled Lafont, fighting to reload that thing of his. '*St-Cyr! I'll kill that bastard! I'll tear him to pieces!*'

Kohler made a break for the stairs. He pitched into someone, fell, got up, tripped on the steps, heard shots . . . more shots! . . . and threw himself out of the cellar and into the hall. 'Louis . . . Louis, where the hell are you?' he yelled.

The street was blocked by opposing pairs of cars, one behind the other, engines idling. Headlamps lit up everything. There'd barely be room to pass. The Citroën would have to lose its fenders. Would the doors be taken?

'Get down, madame! Lie on the floor,' shouted St-Cyr.

More firing came from the villa. Men poured out of the car behind Lafont's Bentley. Others spilled from Otto Brandl's backup. Would there be a fusillade, no chance to get away? Ah *Mon Dieu, Mon Dieu*, glass was so expensive these days, windscreens almost irreplaceable.

Someone in bare feet bolted through the open doorway to the courtyard only to leap back from the light. St-Cyr leaned on the horn and trod on the accelerator. These old cobblestones . . . the narrow kerbs and pavements, the lampposts . . . awnings that were folded back but had their side bars low on the walls . . .

Kohler flew through the doorway of the courtyard. Ducking wildly, he shot across the street between the cars.

The brakes were slammed on. The door was flung open. The fenders went. A drainpipe fell. Bursts of firing took out the rear windscreens and then the one in front of them. 'The tyres . . . they have hit the tyres!' shrieked St-Cyr.

Banging and throwing sparks, they just made it around the corner and into the rue Saint-Luc. 'Enough! Enough! Abandon the car! Head for the Church of Saint Bernard, Hermann. Father Eugène will just have to give us a hand.'

They beat it. They went to ground and bathed their faces in the baptismal font.

The church was cold, and like the Hotel of the Silent Life, it had cellars that became tunnels which turned into vaulted rooms where wine had once been stored.

Madame Minou was surprised to see them, but they could not stay long.

Kohler drained his shoes and put them on. At 2 a.m. the Villa Audit was now quiet. Only faint traces of perfume remained to mingle with the stench of cordite.

'The perfume is Mirage,' said St-Cyr sadly. 'Nicole de Rainvelle has been in to have a look.'

'Lafont and Bonny won't touch Gabrielle, Louis. They wouldn't dare.'

'They will and they probably have by now, Hermann. In any

case, we must pry Giselle le Roy away from them and try to save the hostages.'

'There's a telephone in the *bal musette* on the corner. Why not call the Club Mirage and warn her? She might still be singing.'

'That would only let them know where we are. The lines are constantly monitored, eh? No, we will simply have to tough it out. Two things remain to be done before we can lay our hands on those blasted coins.'

'Find Roland Minou and find Charles Audit and Réjean Tourmel.'

'The latter two first, for I'm beginning to believe I know where Madame Minou's son must be.'

'In Hell?'

'Or Heaven.'

'I'll see that the car's repaired, Louis. No problem.'

'Good. So, a small journey for me, Hermann. Let's agree we meet at the carousel in . . . ' he glanced at his watch '. . . in about three hours.'

'You're sure you don't want me to come along?'

'Positive. Madame Van der Lynn will need constant attention.'

'You talk as if Giselle was ancient history.'

St-Cyr looked at his partner and friend. 'Let us just say that I hope I am wrong. Without the car, our hands are tied. In any case, Father Eugène and Father David have only one bicycle.'

'Enjoy yourself then. Take care.'

'You too.'

The night was cold but fortunately there was no rain. It would soon be Christmas. Christmas 1942, and what?

Father Eugène had not gone to sleep, nor, indeed, would he pass the night in anything but prayer.

The bicycle was wheeled from the vestry lock-up, the loan granted without surprise or comment. Muffled thanks were accepted with but a toss of the hand, dark in the darkness of the night.

As with the animals of the carousel, so with the pedals of the bicycle. As they went round and round, they went up and down. Each moment, each facet of the case appeared before St-Cyr. The streets were empty and if not, if the sound of an approaching car or patrol were heard, sufficient time was allowed for cover.

It was not far in any case from the rue Polonceau and the Church of Saint Bernard to the Café Noir on the avenue de

Laumière and the parc des Buttes-Chaumont. Ah yes, the park. The carousel.

Smoke rose from the chimney pipe in the centre of the marquee. The music had stopped, the thing did not go round and round or up and down. There'd be no more dreams, no more terrifying nightmares. Hermann and he would either solve the case or fail.

'Personally, I do not fancy the latter,' he said, the park silent as the city was silent.

Clément Cueillard would be alseep beside the firebox, cosied up with Joujou the monkey. Morning would come. The music could begin again and with it the turning, turning, always the turning and the going up and down.

The Café Noir opened at 5 a.m. just as the curfew ended. The first stragglers were three labourers in for their breakfasts of ersatz coffee, no milk, saccharin, and no croissants with jam or butter.

A sleepy shopgirl wearing a leather jacket was next, her 'Good morning, Monsieur Philou,' given with a yawn that was reflected in the copper coffee machine. Her slip hung below the back of her dress. The lines on her bare legs marking the seams of non-existent stockings were crooked. Some of the beige wash had rubbed or been scratched off.

There was only one place from which to observe such things unnoticed and that was from the front left corner. When Charles Audit and Réjean Tourmel entered, there was hesitation – the proprietor had been warned not to look their way, but of course such a warning in itself had been enough for them.

'Please do not move, Réjean. I will not hesitate to use the gun, not these days, eh?'

The bracelets came out of the overcoat pocket. 'Easy,' said St-Cyr. 'Now your right wrist, Monsieur Charles. Please, it is necessary.'

They'd have their coffee and he'd have a look at them. 'Now the knives on the floor and carefully, my friends. Now the guns.'

'What makes you think we're carrying?' asked Réjean.

'Nothing, but I wish to be certain.'

He'd allow them a cigarette but sit well back and to the side so as not to receive the table in the face.

'You've come alone. Where's your partner?' asked Charles Audit.

'Outside. We often work this way. Myself to make the arrest – '

'For what?' hissed Réjean. 'For cutting you up?'

'Perhaps, but then . . . ' He'd leave it for the moment. He'd take his time to study them. Charles Audit was as his concierge had said, swarthy, of medium height and strongly built. No shoe salesman and shop owner this. Not any more.

The black beret covered a wide head of bushy grey-white hair, thatches of which protruded over the tops of robust ears. The grey-blue eyes were large and, though filled with watchfulness, full also of sadness. Ah Mon Dieu, such pain. Years and years of it.

The nostrils were large and flared.

'May I?' asked Audit, indicating the long-stemmed pipe that protruded from the breast pocket of his black corduroy jacket. The bristly cheeks were ravaged by creases, the skin around the eyes looked as if he had had to squint whenever the sun was high.

Their coffee came and there was both milk and sugar, and it was freely given. 'I am sorry, my friends. This one', the proprietor indicated the Sûreté, 'threatened to have me arrested if I did not co-operate.'

'Think nothing of it,' said Réjean. 'Cows are always flapping their tongues.'

'Quit seeing flames, Réjean. Hey, listen, eh? We know all about it – everything. By now the *quartier* will be swarming with Gestapo. It's useless to be so stubborn.'

The dark-brown eyes of the Corsican were swift. Tourmel would have another knife, a bit of wire; he'd have already begun to assess not just one way out of things but two or three.

'How's Madame Van der Lynn?' asked Tourmel, giving the Sûreté a grin. They'd flip the table and use their feet. Coffee in the face and fists, the bracelets around that throat of St-Cyr's. *Flames!* They'd show him flames like a cow had never seen before.

Kohler pushed open the door. 'Louis, – *Gott im Himmel*, don't you know where to eat breakfast yet? Chez Rudi's, Louis. It's hands down over a dump like this.'

'Me, I wondered when you'd show up, Hermann.'

'So this is the son of a bitch who took advantage of Madame Van der Lynn, and this . . . by God it is, Louis. Charles Audit himself. The brother. Diamonds and emeralds, my fine, and gold coins.'

'Suck lemons. We know nothing.'

Deep inside the carousel, the faint glow from the firebox threw shadows on the punchboards of the calliope. Clément Cueillard wiped breakfast soup from the strainer of his handlebar moustache. The monkey, huddled on his shoulder, was edgy.

'I have found them when I was raking out the ashes, Inspectors. Such clinkers . . . It's shit, that soft coal. It does not burn well. We're running out.' He gave the two of them the look of one who has lived with unpleasantness in what should have been a place of joy.

A tin pie plate held a sand of cinders. Six molars, two incisors and the shattered lower left jawbone were all equally charred. 'Weren't there any more chips of bone?' asked the Sûreté uneasily.

'A few – smashed to smithereens, Inspector. Did they extract the marrow, eh? That's what Joujou and I want to know, not that marrow isn't nourishing in these times.'

Réjean Tourmel snorted lustily. 'So, my fines, another dead one, eh? Who was it did this one? Myself or Charles?'

'Piss off. I'll deal with you in time,' snarled St-Cyr.

'It's Roland Minou,' quipped Charles Audit. 'Hey, Réjean, you remember that little pimp. A real smart-ass. They should have saved the blood for his mother.'

So much for depths of sadness in the eyes of ex-convicts from Devil's Island. 'Look, you two, *speak* only when you're spoken to and not before then.'

Tourmel tossed his head. 'Nervous, eh, Jean-Louis? What's it to be? The Abwehr, the SS or the rue Lauriston, or are they all after you?'

'Louis, this puts another twist on things,' said Kohler, covering the two of them with his pistol.

'Not really, Hermann. No, it only reinforces what we have already come to believe.'

'The mackerel and Schraum killed Madame Minou's son for wanting too much and interfering when he shouldn't have,' said Kohler grimly. 'Morande then cut up the body and disposed of it in the firebox.'

Joujou flitted nervously off Cueillard's shoulder, knocking over the coffee in its tin mug.

As the puddle grew, Cueillard sadly shook his head. 'That was the last of the real stuff, Joujou. It's the end for us then, is it, Inspectors? Back to the beat for me, eh? What's to happen to my carousel?'

'Who's he?' snorted the previous owner.

Charles Audit stood to Hermann's left, Réjean to the right, the two ex-convicts linked by bracelets, yes, and by fraud, murder and revenge. 'He is the man you should have hired to run your carousel, my friend. But since Réjean had a score to settle with Victor Morande, and since Morande was an outsider among the criminal milieu and a small-time hood the Germans would ignore, Victor had to be chosen for the job.'

'Go on, we're waiting,' breathed Charles Audit.

St-Cyr shrugged. 'Since you ask it, my friend, then I will tell you. You could not entrust the carousel to just anyone, eh? Réjean agreed to help and you made a deal so that he became the new owner.'

'There was nothing illegal in that.'

'Ah no, of course not, except for the lack of registration and licensing. But no one cared, the Germans were far too busy. You waited. You bided your time. The desire for revenge only grew with your brother's continuing successes, the scheme developing as an orchid does for that one brief moment when the flower will open to accept the bee.'

The monkey, flitting back and forth on its bit of chain, eyed its former master with guilt, suspicion and outright anxiety.

'What scheme?' asked Audit.

'Don't say anything more, Charles. Let St-Cyr pull all the teeth he wants.'

Réjean had been tough, so tough. One should adopt a tired attitude with these two. 'A scheme of revenge, my old ones. Revenge so deep and sinister, I myself find it hard to accept, but then, after more than thirty years of crime, very little surprises me.'

Kohler sucked in a breath. Louis had used the familiar 'my old ones'. He'd got to know them better and damned if he hadn't let them know it!

'Clément,' said St-Cyr, 'could I ask you to stand by this morning to operate the controls if necessary? Let us show these two a real artiste, eh?'

Cueillard was too smart to be margarined, but knew what was wanted.

'The turtle and the pig, Inspector. The rabbit and the panda, *and* the black stallion in the fourth row, that one most of all.'

The monkey stared viciously at its former master, who stared emptily back at it.

'Louis, what the hell's Cueillard on about? Black stallions, pigs, turtles?'

'My nightmares, Hermann. The ups and downs. I only hope they don't come true.'

'You've heard it then,' sighed Kohler. Moving swiftly, he shoved Charles Audit and Réjean Tourmel out on to the platform and handcuffed them to one of the brass standards.

The throb of engines grew – a race! '*Lafont*, Louis, and *Brandl*!'

'The first of many perhaps,' snorted Réjean.

'At least let us help you,' urged Charles Audit. 'With the four of us, you might stand a chance. They are no friends of ours.'

Headlamps flung their lights over the darkened carousel and, as a sliver of illumination pierced the inner darkness, it touched the monkey's cup.

'Louis, go left. Let them come to me.'

'Hermann, *no*! Cueillard, my friend, be ready at the moment's notice, eh? The roundel lights, the music, the works.'

No sound betrayed the detectives' sudden disappearance. One moment they were there beside him, the next they were gone. 'Joujou . . . ' began Cueillard, nervously wetting his throat. 'Joujou, we must stay at the controls as ordered.'

A woman screamed in terror, the shrieks lifting the hair and causing the monkey to tug at its chain.

One by one, each pair of headlamps went out, and where once the stallions' eyes had been bright and flashing in the dusky light, now there was not even the silhouette of the animals poised suspended in their charge.

Kohler crept among them anyway. The rain came down, thrumming on the canvas roof, reminding him that this whole affair had begun with rain. Paris in winter. The merry-go-round of it. They'd be over by the entrance now. Would Lafont have the Schmeisser with him?

'Hey, Louis, don't play games, eh?' shouted Bonny. 'Just give up the coins and we'll let the girls go.'

A muffled answer came from off to Kohler's left. 'Pierre, you were never one to be trusted. Why should we do so now?'

'Brandl's here.'

'Did he bring the Captain Offenheimer?' asked Louis.

'Hey, what is this, eh? You hold no cards, my friend. *Nothing*!' shouted Bonny.

'Me, I know who did the killings and I know where the coins are hidden.'

'THEN GIVE THEM TO HIM!' shrieked Gabrielle Arcuri. 'Jean-Louis, please, I beg it of you. This bitch has a straight razor. She is going to *slash* my face!'

Nicole de Rainvelle. Ah Mon Dieu . . .

A burst of firing cut the air, sending shrieks and cries from the prisoners.

Droplets immediately began to fall from the holes in the roof. The smell of cordite mingled with the dampness as St-Cyr got cautiously up from behind one of the gondola cars. 'Hermann . . . Hermann, it is – '

'LOUIS, GET DOWN!'

The Schmeisser fired, the splinters flew. Charles Audit cried out in anger, 'YOU BASTARDS . . . *BASTARDS* . . . MY CAROUSEL! My carousel . . . '

Again the place went to silence. Not a thing moved but the patient droplets of rain. St-Cyr could hear them as they hit the turtle's head. Hermann would hear them too.

Out of the silence came the quavering voice of Otto Brandl. 'I have the Van der Lynn woman, Hermann, and the concierge from the Hotel of the Silent Life. You should not have left them at the Villa Audit!'

'YOU HOLD NO CARDS!' shrilled Lafont, firing rapidly – three bursts . . . three. More rain, more shrieks! The tortured wailing of Madame Minou, and then:

'Jean-Louis . . . Jean-Louis, please tell them,' pleaded Gabrielle Arcuri. 'I think I love you, Jean-Louis. I will die gladly, but . . . but there are others. The hostages also.'

'Inspector, don't!' shouted Réjean Tourmel. 'Lafont will only kill you.'

'Yourselves included,' snapped Pierre Bonny.

More silence, but this was broken by the weeping of Hermann's little pigeon.

Lafont, Bonny and their hostages would be off to the left of the entrance; Brandl and the other two well off to the right.

The falsetto voice of Henri Lafont rang out. 'Your guns, Louis. Hurry, hurry, eh? Toss them out and raise the hands. Up! Up! or me, I will chew this place to pieces!'

'Don't do it, Inspector,' shouted Charles Audit. 'Without the gold and the emeralds that one has nothing.'

'But we have four murders, monsieur,' began St-Cyr. 'Surely their solution is worth more than all your hidden wealth?'

Again there was a pause, and then: 'Clément, my friend, are you still at the controls?' hazarded St-Cyr.

Terrified, the monkey raced to freedom, dragging its chain and banging its cup.

'*Clément Cueillard*! I have asked you to do your duty!' shouted St-Cyr tremulously.

From deep inside the workings came the voice of bitterness. 'Is it that you think I am dead also, eh? You *shits*, messieurs. You call yourselves detectives! Are you *not* paid to protect the innocent?'

Ah merde! 'Just start it up,' sighed St-Cyr. 'Let us not have the general strike at a time like this. The lights, eh? and the action.' *Mon Dieu*, Paris . . . Paris these days!

'*For your sake*, I hope that one has not shot everything to pieces, Inspector!' came the cry.

A tragedy, eh? Ah *Nom de Jésus-Christ!*

The thing began to turn, slowly at first and then with gathering momentum. Punctured, the calliope could offer but reedy wheezings of 'The Blue Danube'. The roundel lights came on, broken here and there, and in that moment St-Cyr stepped from behind the cage, blinking as he took it all in.

Hermann's little pigeon had been flung to the earthen floor. Nicole de Rainvelle held a straight razor to Gabrielle's cheek . . .

'Hermann, don't move!' he hissed. 'Please, my old one. I beg it of you. Nothing, eh? Not even a breath. Just leave things in my hands.'

Reluctantly Kohler moved away from Otto Brandl. Madame Van der Lynn ran a trembling hand through her hair; Madame Minou could not find the will to lift her eyes.

There was no sign of Captain Offenheimer and in that moment St-Cyr and Kohler knew Brandl had silenced him for ever.

Kohler tossed his pistol into the gathering mud and went to wrap his overcoat about Giselle le Roy and to brush a tender hand across her battered cheeks.

'Now yours, Jean-Louis,' said Lafont, motioning with the Schmeisser.

The carousel went round and round, oblivious to all that was happening. St-Cyr hesitated. Pierre Bonny lifted his pistol to point it at Gabrielle Arcuri's chest.

Nicole de Rainvelle flicked her lovely eyes over the Sûreté's gumshoe and waited tensely for the one movement that would allow her to slash the *chanteuse*'s beautiful face to pieces.

The Lebel skidded into the mud. 'You *fools!*' seethed Charles Audit. 'Must my brother have everything?'

'Your brother, ah yes,' said St-Cyr. 'Where is he?'

'With me,' confessed Otto Brandl, warily enjoying the moment. 'So you see, Henri, I still hold more cards than you.'

'Then have him brought inside,' said St-Cyr, ignoring the Schmeisser. He shouted for the carousel to be stopped, and the animals in their terrified race began at once to coast slowly into submission, going up and down. The turtle, the panda, the black stallion in the fourth row, ah yes.

He strode firmly over to Pierre Bonny and pushed the gun away from Gabrielle, but found that her lovely eyes would not leave him. 'Please, it will be okay, eh? This bunch, they are nothing, Gabrielle. Some day France will be free of them. Then you and I – '

'Will be dead.'

Must she say it so accusingly? Turning his back on them, he went over to the carousel to set matches, pipe and tobacco pouch on the very edge nearest the cage. 'So, my friends, what really went on in that room at the Hotel of the Silent Life?'

Antoine Audit was thrust forward by two of Brandl's men and left to stand alone under the lights.

'You, monsieur, could answer for me, eh? The granddaughter of your brother Charles, a virgin until after the moment of her death.'

'A virgin . . . ?' snorted Lafont, swinging the Schmeisser in an arc.

'Ah yes. Oh for sure there were the trappings of a liaison, and she did take off her clothes on several occasions but . . . '

'But we did not have sexual congress,' said Antoine Audit. 'Christabelle refused me, Charles. Always she refused.'

'You *bastard*! You killed her! Me, I will – '

'*Silence!* Speak only when told to.'

Kohler was impressed. Never had he seen Louis quite like this. In spite of everything, the Frog commanded respect. Even from gangsters.

Louis lit the pipe but did not take his eyes from Antoine Audit. 'She reminded you of Michèle-Louis Prévost, monsieur.'

'That proves nothing. *Nothing!* All . . . all right, she . . . she was the reincarnation of Michèle-Louise, so what?'

'You had seen her naked in the drawing studios.'

'Yes . . . yes, I had seen her that way enough times to wet the appetite. Is that a crime?'

'*Viper! Cannibal*! You stole her from me just as you *stole* Michèle-Louise!'

'Charles . . . Charles, for the love of Jesus, don't say anything.'

'Réjean, she's gone. Gone! My little bird. He . . . That one, my *brother*!'

'Your brother wanted everything, Monsieur Charles. He took Michèle-Louise, took the few gold coins you had started collecting, took the shop, the villa and left you on the broken rocks of the Île du Diable for fifteen years.'

'She deceived you, Charles!' shouted Antoine Audit. 'Ah, yes, my brother, Michèle-Louise came willingly into my arms.'

'Revenge,' said St-Cyr quietly. 'It was all a matter of revenge, eh, Monsieur Charles? Christabelle was only too well aware of the hatred you and your brother bore each other. Doubtless she adored and trusted you implicitly, and though very brave, made a very foolish mistake.'

'The coins were forgeries!' seethed Lafont. '*Nom de Jésus-Christ*, Pierre, let's *finish* the bastards and get it over with!'

'And end up in disgrace? Is that what you wish the avenue Foch to think, Monsieur Henri?'

'Then get on with it,' snarled Pierre Bonny.

Otto Brandl had kept himself watchful and a little isolated from the others.

'It was all a set-up, Louis,' breathed Hermann. 'The girl was a partner to it with Charles and Réjean. On their okay, she held out the offer of her body to Antoine Audit while behind his back she was arranging the sale of forgeries her grandmother had made years and years ago from the original coins in Charles Audit's collection.'

'Ah, yes, Hermann. First Christabelle shows Corporal Schraum a real coin, one that her grandfather has provided – Roman and perfect. Schraum is not unintelligent. Though he asks to see her papers, he knows enough not to arrest her.'

'The coins would simply have vanished,' said Hermann, taking three small steps no one else noticed.

St-Cyr continued. 'Early in September, the girl agrees to part with this one coin and it travels down the pipeline to Stralsund and the uncle of Corporal Schraum.

'Who judges it in excellent condition and forwards it on to the Reichsmarschall Goering, Louis.'

'Goering then orders the uncle to tell Schraum to proceed carefully.'

'Four hundred and eighty-seven coins!' shrilled Henri Lafont. 'Where are they?'

Louis was quick with a silencing hand. 'They meet again, but now Schraum and Victor Morande *and* Rolande Minou know exactly who she is, where she lives and who she meets in that room. The successful industrialist, eh, Monsieur Antoine? Your wealth and the tantalizing possibilities of hidden valuables.'

'And so do the rue Lauriston and the Bureau Otto,' breathed Kohler. A few more steps, just a few ... 'And a fledgling cell of Resistance hotheads.'

St-Cyr gave his pipe a sudden lift. 'So, the fix is in. The thirty coins are produced – a representative sample that the girl and her co-conspirators know to be false. The sum of 31,250 old francs changes hands, but retribution will be swift once the truth is out. Antoine Audit will be blamed as the perpetrator of the fraud.'

'Revenge?' snorted Pierre Bonny.

'But of course. Please do not forget that on the Defeat of France the coins had been reported stolen. They had been hidden in the cellars of the Villa Audit by your brother, is that not right, Monsieur Charles? But you stole them back and took them away in two suitcases.'

'Two suitcases? What is this?' demanded Henri Lafont.

'In a moment, please. Antoine Audit, realizing what was planned, confronted the girl on that Tuesday afternoon at four o'clock. You demanded the return of the coins, eh, Monsieur Antoine? In great distress, Christabelle agreed to meet you on Thursday evening at the regular time.'

'But by then Victor Morande had been murdered,' said Hermann. 'The girl was then strangled on that Thursday evening and raped, and Corporal Schraum shot to death in the street but a short time later.'

'The coins, I want the coins,' said Henri Lafont.

'Then I will take the emeralds,' said Otto Brandl.

It was the *chanteuse* who anxiously said, 'Jean-Louis, please tell them where they are.'

Again St-Cyr was forced to look into her eyes and then into those of Hermann's little pigeon.

'The hostages, Jean-Louis. Remember?' beseeched the *chanteuse*. 'For France, *mon amour*. For France.'

Ah Mon Dieu, she was so very tragic in beauty.

'Two suitcases, Louis,' prompted Hermann.

'Yes, yes, my old one. Heavy because in addition to the gold coins they contained the iron dies Michèle-Louise Prévost had made some time prior to the year 1905. Also the copies she had cast of some of the original coins. Is that not correct, Monsieur Charles?'

It was.

St-Cyr held up a hand to silence the gangsters. 'It is uncertain in my mind, Monsieur Charles, if at this time you had fully worked out what you intended to do to your brother. I rather doubt this, but the germ of the idea must have taken root.'

'Two suitcases, two and a half years ago? Who gives a damn?' snarled Lafont.

'I DO! As does my partner.'

'There was another killing, Louis. That of Mila Zavitz.'

'Yes, yes, Hermann. The Wehrmacht were to be blamed for that, but . . . ' he paused, 'it was not done by them, was it Monsieur Charles?'

Everyone looked at the ex-convict whose wrists were still handcuffed to those of his friend and to the brass upright upon which an ostrich rode.

'I know nothing of that killing. *Nothing*! Ask Father Eugène.'

'The old priest.' St-Cyr glanced at his watch. Hermann had moved again and was now much, much closer to the entrance.

'Father, it is good of you to have come so promptly.'

Pierre Bonny jerked his head round. Lafont swung the Schmeisser as Hermann leapt to snatch the Lebel from the Captain Dupuis of the one leg and the crutches.

'DROP IT!' screamed Lafont.

Ah *merde*!

The gun skidded into the mud. The razor was held against Gabrielle's cheek. No one dared to move.

'My son, what is this?' asked Father Eugène looking quickly round while still holding the Luger that had killed Corporal Schraum.

'The suitcases, Father. They contained a fabulous collection of Roman gold coins, a bag or two of forged ones, and some iron dies.'

Suddenly lost to them all, Father Eugène studied the gun in his hand, then looked up and across to the carousel.

'Father, gold is gold, and lies are lies,' said St-Cyr. 'On the evening of the Defeat you saw Monsieur Charles leave the suitcases in the courtyard beside the draper's shop on the Pas-Léon. You did not say where he was headed or why he had left them there.'

'Suitcases . . . suitcases,' seethed Henri Lafont.

'*Silence*, you punk! Please do *not* interrupt two officers of the law in their duty.'

The old priest was shaken, but not so much by the outburst. 'Charles went into the church. When . . . when I caught up with him, he asked me to hide the suitcases temporarily for him.'

'Which you did?' asked St-Cyr.

'He was a man much wronged by life and I could not turn my back on him.'

'That is fair enough, Father, but was there not the exchange of a little something to tide you and the church over difficult times?'

'A parish priest's life is not easy, Inspector. Many burdens must be carried.'

'Yes . . . yes, but the murder of that other girl, Father? Mila Zavitz,' urged Louis.

It was as if there were only the two of them and that God of Louis' had suspended the animals of the carousel in final judgement.

'Mademoiselle Jeanne had passed Captain Dupuis in the street, Father. She had noticed there was blood on his shirt,' prompted St-Cyr.

'Yes . . . yes. She had been to confession and had started for home only to return to tell me of the murder. By then Monsieur Charles was waiting for me in the sacristy with the suitcases.'

'No, Father. The suitcases were still in that courtyard but had been broken open. You had seen at a glance what had happened: the girl Mila Zavitz had come upon a thief and had been killed. You lived in fear of discovery, isn't that so? Monsieur Charles was a man so changed by life he could kill to protect what was rightfully his. He had a friend, a gangster, Réjean Tourmel.'

St-Cyr stabbed the air with his pipestem. 'You saw what those suitcases contained, Father, and you panicked, but . . . ' he paused. 'But Charles Audit could not have killed Mila Zavitz because, Father, you had followed him into the church.'

'He . . . he could have left the sacristy unobserved.'

'No, Father, because if he *had* killed her, Charles Audit would not have left the suitcases behind, nor would he have stuck around a moment longer.'

'The girl had been strangled. Roland – '

A keening wail startled everyone. 'My son ... Ah no, Father. Not my Roland!' cried Madame Minou.

'Hermann, get Madame Van der Lynn to calm that woman! *Roland*, Father? He was hiding in that draper's shop and you *knew* this, but did not think he had realized you'd seen him.'

Ah damn the Sûretée! 'Yes ... yes, that is correct and here are my thirty pieces of silver.'

Thirty of the gold coins – real ones taken from the suitcases by the priest. Otto Brandl took a step forward. St-Cyr looked up from them and into the old priest's eyes, ignoring the Nazi. 'No, Father, that is not enough. The girl was Jewish, so she would not have come to you for help, not to an anti-Semite. The girl had been raped.'

Was there nothing one could do? Would God forgive? 'Alphonse, I cannot keep your secret any longer.'

Stung by the accusation, Captain Dupuis pushed his crutches aside and tried to reach the guns on the floor. 'You call yourself a man of God, Father!' he shrilled.

He was very nimble and when the bullet from the old priest's gun smashed into his skull, he flung wild eyes up at the crowd and then collapsed.

'May God forgive me,' gasped Father Eugène.

St-Cyr snatched the Luger from him and in two quick steps jammed it into Henri Lafont's stomach, but looked at Bonny. 'Please do not do anything, Pierre. My patience, it has evaporated.'

'Then who killed Schraum?' asked Lafont, breathing fiercely with barely controlled fury.

'The Schmeisser first and then the razor. Hurry, hurry ... in the dust or the mud, but far enough from us. Hermann, would you see to disarming the others, please? Yes, yes, my friends, the fewer the guns, the better.'

Again they waited, again they stood around just as the animals did.

Kohler crouched over the body of Captain Dupuis. A rapist of the dead, first the girl Mila Zavitz and then Christabelle Audit, their corpses still warm.

The Gestapo looked up sadly at the old priest. 'Father, you killed the Corporal. Please don't deny it. The General von Schaumburg will only release the hostages if you confess.'

Hermann would have made a priest himself, such was the anguish of his look.

'Roland Minou knew all about the coins in those suitcases, Louis, though he must have kept it to himself, since he had killed Mila Zavitz. He followed Christabelle even into the Villa Audit. He gave the dragonfly to Schraum, but soon got too greedy for his own good.'

St-Cyr sought out the industrialist. 'Roland went to you, Monsieur Antoine. A little deal on the side, eh? He told you what you had begun to suspect yourself. Revenge, my friend. A game of revenge.'

'So who killed Victor Morande, Inspector?' asked Nicole de Rainvelle wickedly. 'The rue Lauriston or the Bureau Otto?'

'Or Monsieur Antoine Audit?'

The truffle-hunter collapsed. He didn't cry out as some would, or try to escape, but merely sat down heavily on the edge of the carousel.

St-Cyr stood over him. 'You tried to make it look like a gangland slaying, monsieur – something your brother's friend might do. But Réjean is not so foolish as to bother with such decorations. He and your brother Charles had no reason to kill Morande or Corporal Schraum. Indeed, they had every reason to let them live.'

'The note was left on purpose by Antoine Audit, Louis, as an alibi.'

'Ah, Hermann, I wish that were so. At first I, too, thought the same. A warning – "Christabelle, leave the hotel immediately. Do not go up to the room." But you see, Antoine Audit could *not* have killed her. Others would quite possibly kill him, the Resistance most particularly, but then, too, the rue Lauriston or the Bureau Otto. He wanted the return of the coins, Hermann. He *needed* them. Her safety, in that last hour, became of paramount importance to him because without the coins, he was as good as dead, so too his family and everything he possessed.'

St-Cyr tapped out the pipe and put it safely away in a pocket. 'Your game was revenge, Monsieur Charles, the destruction and ruin of the brother who had robbed you of so much including, and I stress this, the granddaughter for whom you had saved the emeralds and diamonds, the gold bullion and more recently, the gold coins.'

Again Otto Brandl took a step nearer. Again he was ignored by the Sûreté. 'She reminded you so much of Michèle-Louise Prévost, Monsieur Charles. You were very jealous and possessive of her, but she was an artist's model. Her removing her clothes in front of your brother was a small sacrifice if, in the end, it would give you the revenge you so desired.'

He'd let them all have a moment. He'd let the truth take its course. 'There was an elastic band, Monsieur Charles, around the canary you had mounted for your granddaughter. I have asked myself why she would have put it there. Was it to remind her of something? Your love, your friendship – how much she owed you for all you'd done for her? She was used to stroking that little bird, perhaps remembering how things used to be here at the carousel . . .'

'She twisted it like a harlot!' seethed Charles Audit, tugging at the handcuffs. 'He made her – '

'Your brother could not stand to gaze at her nakedness any more, knowing she was conspiring against him, Monsieur Charles. When did Antoine tell you exactly what had been going on in that room?'

'On that Thursday. I . . . I received a note from him at the flat. It said he'd be meeting Christabelle again that night at nine, but of course I already knew this. He . . . he told me Christabelle would be only too willing to go down on her knees between his filthy legs because she had done it often enough before.'

'Ah yes. The elastic band is used by prostitutes to increase ecstasy during the male orgasm, yet she was a virgin until after the moment of her death.'

'I did not rape her. I would never have done that.'

'Of course not, but you did kill her, Monsieur Charles. You could not bear to have your brother take Christabelle away from you, or bear to have her act like Michèle-Louise.'

'Yes . . . yes, I did it. She did not wish to undress in front of me, but didn't resist when I ordered her to. The wire, Réjean. I . . . I had to use the wire. She coughed. She struggled . . . My little one could not believe that I would . . .'

St-Cyr tossed a hand. 'So, it's finished. Please allow Clément Cueillard, who has the skill and patience for such a task, to open those animals in which the coins et cetera are hidden.'

'Do you want a demonstration first, Inspector?'

A last run of the thing, even though it was now so badly damaged. 'Those animals which rise a little more heavily or have a slight hesitation, those are the ones you want.'

'So, Jean-Louis, there are only the two of us and we meet, as we did that last time, at the end of a case.'

The iridescent sky-blue sheath with its vertical rows of tiny seed pearls fitted her body like a glove.

'Look, you're a very understanding man, Jean-Louis, but I greatly fear you are absolutely hopeless at love. Why won't you come and stay at my place? Separate rooms, separate beds. The Nazis can't touch you now. You gave them the coins and the emeralds – emeralds like I've never seen before – and river diamonds, ancient gold. A split between the Wehrmacht and the SS, the Bureau Otto and the rue Lauriston, a show of mutual co-operation for the Führer.'

'It was wise of you to have suggested it.'

'Wise, too, I think, to have told you how best to hide things by leaving them right out in the open.'

'But disguised.' Ah Mon Dieu, she was so beautiful. 'Why me, why not . . . ? You could have anyone, Gabrielle.'

'Hey, listen. Do you think I want a Nazi lover? Me, who has lost a husband to them? No.' She tossed her head and reached for her cigarette case. 'I want a man who understands that a woman must decide things for herself. I have decided on you.'

In the Name of Jesus, decisions, must there always be decisions? 'Christmas, then, and a few days with your son.'

'*Merci*. We . . . we will be expecting you.'

'Good!' He got up to leave. She stood blocking his way. 'Hermann's living with two women, Jean-Louis. One to wash his socks and the other to . . .'

'It won't work. It can't. Not for a detective.'

'It's too dangerous for me, is that it?'

'You know it is. At any moment my German masters can turn on me. Hermann . . . he's not had an easy time of it.'

'Will you have to choose between him and France some day?'

'He'll have to choose between me and the Third Reich. I could never shoot him, not after what the two of us have been through.'

'What about the hostages?' she asked.

'Rerouted to the South, to Périgord. It was the best we could do under the circumstances. Hermann fixed it using two of Antoine Audit's trucks. I got the baker Georges and his girlfriend to go along with them.'

'So, it's only the two of us and it won't work.'

'You're much taller than me.'

'Another excuse?'

'There are eight hundred German servicemen out there and any one of them would give an arm or a leg for what you have just offered but me . . .'

'Yes, yes, I know, Iean-Louis. War is dangerous and so is being a detective when no one really wants one, but we need you to help us in the Resistance cell I've formed, so there is an end to it, and I have laid my life in your hands.'

'You're a very determined woman.'

'One doesn't get anywhere without determination.'

Her arms went about him, her lips . . . the feel of her. Ah Mon Dieu, Mon Dieu . . . the coal-black stallion, the shower of emeralds and gold coins . . .

Paris . . . Paris under the Occupation. A carousel . . .

'Louis . . . Louis, I hate to break things up, but the Chief wants to see us right away.'

'Another murder?' Ah no . . .

'Provence. Some little place in the hills. He thinks it still might be a good idea if we got out of town for a while.'